Once again she
ing too close, fa
what felt like a void of time, of space. She knew she should say good-night and move away, but she was frozen in place, unable to speak, unable to move. His close proximity to her made her feel trapped, unable to escape even if she'd wanted to.

Her heart thundered as he took a step closer to her. "I've wanted to do this since the moment I saw you."

Before she could draw a breath or prepare in any way for what she knew was about to happen, his mouth covered hers in a fiery kiss that was directly at odds with the dispassionate man she'd thought him to be.

He tasted of sweetened tea and hot desire, and she opened her mouth to him as his arms wrapped around her and pulled her close.

A little voice inside her head told her this shouldn't be happening, but it was happening and it was wonderful.

SCENE OF THE CRIME: RETURN TO BACHELOR MOON

BY

CARLA CASSIDY

First published in Great Britain 2013
by Mills & Boon, an imprint of Harlequin (UK) Limited,
Eton House, 18-24 Paradise Road, Richmond, Surrey TW9 1SR

ISBN: 978 0 263 90382 9

46-1113

Harlequin (UK) policy is to use papers that are natural, renewable and recyclable products and made from wood grown in sustainable forests. The logging and manufacturing processes conform to the legal environmental regulations of the country of origin.

Printed and bound in Spain
by Blackprint CPI, Barcelona

Carla Cassidy is an award-winning author who has written more than fifty novels for Mills & Boon. In 1995, she won Best Silhouette Romance from *RT Book Reviews* for *Anything for Danny*. In 1998, she also won a Career Achievement Award for Best Innovative Series from *RT Book Reviews*.

Carla believes the only thing better than curling up with a good book to read is sitting down at the computer with a good story to write. She's looking forward to writing many more books and bringing hours of pleasure to readers.

Chapter One

"Tell me again what we're doing checking out the whereabouts of an ex-FBI agent from the Kansas City field office?" FBI agent Andrew Barkin asked from the backseat of the car.

FBI special agent Gabriel Blankenship slowed the car as they approached the city limits of the small town of Bachelor Moon, Louisiana. "We're doing this as a professional courtesy, because the Kansas City office asked us to."

"A little over two years ago Sam Connelly was a respected FBI profiler before he came out here for a two-week vacation and fell in love with Daniella Butler, who owns the Bachelor Moon Bed-and-Breakfast," Jackson Revannaugh drawled from the passenger seat. "Apparently true love won out over career climbing. Sam quit the agency, moved here and he and Daniella got married."

"Sam not only became a husband but also stepfather to Daniella's daughter, Macy. And this morning we received a call from the manager of the bed-and-breakfast that all three of them are missing," Gabriel said.

"Unusual that we'd be sent out, since it hasn't even been twenty-four hours," Jackson observed.

"According to the manager, they've been missing since last night." Gabriel kept his gaze focused on the road ahead, knowing that the bed-and-breakfast was ten miles outside of the small town.

His gut feeling was that this was all a wild goose chase, some sort of misunderstanding between the manager and the family she worked for. It was an hour and a half drive from their field office in Baton Rouge, and they hadn't been dispatched to leave until past three that afternoon.

Hopefully they could get this sorted out and he would be in his own bed, back in his comfortable ranch house in Baton Rouge, before midnight.

He'd been surprised when Director Jason Miller had assigned two men to travel with him to check out this supposed disappearance, yet he had been grateful for the company of the men, who were not only good agents adept at processing crime scenes and sniffing out bad guys but were friends, as well.

"There." Andrew pointed ahead to a sign that indicated to turn right for the Bachelor Moon Bed-and-Breakfast.

Gabriel made the turn, squinting against the bright hot sun. He drove on for three more miles and then turned again, following another sign leading into a lane that took them to their destination.

"Nice," Jackson said as a huge two-story house with a sweeping veranda surrounded by large trees came into view. On one side of the B and B, a big pond glittered in the overhead sun, and on the other side, a giant carriage house looked inviting with large pots of multicolored flowers along its perimeter.

The employees must park in another area, and there must be no guests, Gabriel thought, for the parking lot in front of the house was empty. He pulled the car to a halt and shut off the engine. At the same time, the front door opened and a woman stepped out on the porch.

With the sun sparkling off her short, curly blond hair, creating a halo effect, she looked like a slender angel. Her long bare legs exposed by a pair of white shorts and her shoulders by a pink tank top, she looked like a very hot angel.

"Sweet," Jackson muttered from the backseat.

"On the job, not on the prowl," Gabriel reminded his fellow agent, who had a reputation around the office as a ladies' man. Still, he was shocked by the quick, visceral warmth that swept through him at the sight of her. Her eyes had to be blue, he thought.

She started down the steps as if unable to wait for them to join her on the porch. As she drew closer, the men exited the vehicle.

Two things occurred at the same time: Gabriel flashed his official identification and noted that her eyes weren't blue, as he'd expected, but rather an electric green. She was more than pretty with her slender face, wide eyes, straight nose and generous mouth, but at the moment all of her features were radiating an emotion somewhere between panic and unadulterated fear.

"Thank God you're here," she said after Gabriel had introduced himself and his two men. "I'm Marlena Meyers, the manager here, and I'm the one who sounded the alarm this morning. I called the sheriff first, but he was afraid to get involved in what might be federal business, so he said I should contact the FBI. I found Sam's contact list in his bedroom and called his former director with the Kansas City field office."

"And Assistant Director Forbes contacted our field office in Baton Rouge and here we are," Gabriel replied. Despite the fact that the sun was slowly sinking in the west, the mid-July heat and humidity made it difficult to breathe. "Can we go inside?"

"Oh, of course." She whirled on the heels of her white sandals to lead them back to the house. Gabriel couldn't help but notice the shapeliness of her butt in the tight shorts as she walked ahead of him—and that irritated him.

It had been a long time since a woman had attracted his attention in any way, and the last thing he needed was to be distracted by this blonde bombshell. He just wanted to get inside, figure things out and get back home as soon as possible.

She led them into a great room, obviously a place decorated for guests to hang out. Besides a couple of couches and chairs, there was a flat-screen television and a bookcase full of paperbacks and puzzles.

She paused in the center of the room, and her gaze shot from Andrew to Jackson and then finally landed on Gabriel. "They're gone." Her voice was a tortured whisper as her eyes became shiny with unshed tears. "When I got up this morning, I knew that something was horribly wrong."

"And how did you know that?" Gabriel asked.

Her eyes darkened, and she twisted her ringless hands together. "You need to see the kitchen." Once again she turned and walked out of the room. The three men exchanged curious glances and followed.

"This is the guest dining room," she said as they entered a room with a table big enough to seat a dozen. A sideboard held an industrial-size coffee brewer, but no scent of coffee lingered in the air.

She paused at the door on the opposite side of the room, her eyes still shiny. "There," she said and pointed into the room. It was obvious she had no intention of going inside.

As Gabriel swept past her, he caught a whiff of her scent, a clean floral fragrance he found instantly appealing, but the allure of her perfume immediately died as he walked into the kitchen and saw the table before him.

The small round wooden table on the far side of the roomy kitchen held the remnants of what appeared to be an evening snack. Three glasses of milk sat next to three small plates with cookies. Milk was missing from all of the glasses, and there was one cookie on one plate and two each on the other plates. A single chair was overturned on its back on the floor, as if the person seated in it had jumped up so quickly that it had flipped over.

"The back door looks like it's unlocked," Jackson said.

None of the three men had taken more than two steps into the room. "Has anyone been inside here besides you?"

She shook her head, her blond curls dancing with the movement. "No. We don't have any guests right now, and I've made sure the other help have stayed out of the kitchen all day."

Gabriel frowned. "Before we do anything more here, I'd like to see their bedrooms."

"They live in the two-bedroom suite upstairs."

"Are they the type of people to take an impromptu trip somewhere?" Gabriel asked as they all followed her up the wide staircase.

"Not at all. If they had planned anything, they would have let me know, and they would have never taken off in the middle of the night." Her voice was laced with a simmering frantic worry. "Something bad happened last night. I just know it. Now they're gone, and nobody has seen or heard from them all day."

Gabriel had known the moment he had stepped into the kitchen that he wasn't going to make it into his own bed tonight. Although his gut told him they'd just looked at a crime scene, he didn't have enough information to fully embrace that as a certainty.

Upstairs there were guest rooms on either side of the hall. Gabriel paused at each doorway to look inside. The first was decorated in blue and white and held two double beds, a dresser, a small table and chairs next to the window.

The second held a king-size bed and was a study in lavender and lace, with the same type of furniture again. There appeared to be nothing amiss in either of the rooms.

"The guest rooms have their own baths, and there are three more rooms in the carriage house," she said, flipping on lights, even though night wouldn't encroach for a couple of hours yet.

"Where does this go?" Gabriel asked, referring to a closed door in the hallway.

"It leads to an old servant's staircase that goes down to the basement and outside. Nobody uses it anymore, and the door is kept locked."

Gabriel nodded, knowing before the night was over that the door would be unlocked and the basement thoroughly checked.

"These are Sam, Daniella and Macy's rooms." The door was already open, and Marlena paused in the hallway and gestured the men in.

The initial space was a large bedroom/sitting area. The king-size bed was neatly made with a black-and-white spread. At the foot of the bed was a settee in front of a wall-mounted flat-screen television. A set of bookshelves held games and books, and it was easy for Gabriel to recognize that this was the family getaway from a houseful of paying guests.

The bathroom was also neat and clean, with no indication that anyone had been there during the day. The smaller bedroom was an explosion of pink with a single bed covered with stuffed animals and dolls.

Gabriel returned to the main room and opened the closet doors as Jackson and Andrew checked the bathroom and Macy's bedroom more carefully.

Gabriel noted a set of suitcases were shoved to the left of the closet, and there didn't appear to be any clothing missing from hangers. He moved to the dresser, where two phones resided side by side. He couldn't imagine the Connellys leaving without taking their cells with them. He picked up the phones and noticed that both were turned off, probably shut down for the night before their owners had gone to bed.

He then pulled out the top drawer of the dresser, dismayed to find Sam's wallet and his gun. A check in the wallet let Gabriel know that his driver's license, credit cards and bank card were all intact.

Gabriel's heart stepped up its rhythm as he tried to imagine any reason a man would take off with his family without his wallet. And an FBI agent would never leave for any extended time without his gun. It just wouldn't happen.

He turned to see Marlena still standing in the hallway. "You'd better set us up with rooms for a night or two. It looks like we're going to be here a while. And don't allow anyone into the kitchen. Right now that appears to be a crime scene."

One hand shot to her mouth in obvious horror. "You have to find them."

Gabriel nodded. "That's the plan, and the first thing I need to do is ask you some questions." Marlena Meyers might be pretty, and she appeared genuinely distraught, but he had to figure out if she was truly scared for the people who had been her bosses or a good actress who was somehow responsible for whatever had happened in that kitchen the night before.

OF THE THREE FBI agents, Gabriel Blankenship intimidated Marlena the most. Since the moment he'd met her, his blue eyes had remained dark and flat, his lips seemingly unable to curve into any semblance of a smile.

Within minutes it was established that agents Barkin and Revannaugh would share the blue room and Gabriel would take the lavender room. While the other two men went out to their car to bring in duffel bags and crime-scene kits, Gabriel gestured her into a chair in the common room downstairs and then pulled up one of the other chairs close enough so that their knees practically touched.

Marlena wanted to scream at him that he was wasting precious time, that he and his men should be out checking the woods, beating the bushes, knocking on doors in an attempt to find the missing family.... Her surrogate family.

From the pocket of the white shirt that stretched across impossibly broad shoulders, he pulled out a pen and a small pad. He was definitely a hunk, his black slacks fitting perfectly to his slender waist and long legs. He also wore a shoulder holster and gun that would constantly remind her he wasn't a guest here but rather a man on a mission.

His black hair had just enough curl to entice a woman to run her fingers through it, but those eyes of his would stop any impulse a woman might have to touch him in any way.

Cold and with a glint of keen intelligence, his ice-blue eyes appeared to be those of a man who had seen too much, who trusted nobody and held not a hint of any kind of invitation.

"How long have you worked here as a manager?" he asked.

"For the past seventeen months or so. Before that I was living in Chicago, although I'm originally from Bachelor Moon. Daniella and I were best friends all through high school. I left here around the time she married Johnny Butler, and when I returned, I found out Johnny had been murdered and she had fallen in love with Sam." She knew she was rambling, giving him far more information than he'd asked for, but it was nerves. Whenever she was nervous and frightened, she talked too much.

"I was maid of honor at Sam and Daniella's wedding, and for almost the past two years, the two of them and little Macy have been my family." New tears burned at her eyes but she quickly blinked them away. "They took me and Cory in when we had nothing and no place else to go. They embraced us, and my friendship with Daniella picked up where it had left off."

He stared at her mouth, and she wondered if he was somehow judging the words that fell out of it. Did he believe she'd had something to do with the family's disappearance? Did he think she was lying to cover up some sort of heinous crime?

He turned his attention to the pad in his hand, made a couple of notes and then gazed up at her again. "Cory?"

"My brother. He just turned twenty, and he works as the gardener's assistant here. My mother abandoned us when we were young, and my father… Well, he did the best he could, but I basically raised Cory. When I was twenty my father died, and I petitioned the courts to get custody of Cory, and he's been with me ever since." Again she realized she was talking too much and firmly chastised herself just to answer his questions as simply, as succinctly as possible.

"And where does Cory stay?"

"He has a small apartment built onto the back of the carriage house, but he'd never do anything to hurt Sam or Daniella, and he thinks of Macy as a little sister. He loves them as much as I do."

"Who else works here?"

How she wished he'd just give her a hint of a smile, a tiny indication that he understood the panic that seared through her soul, that the fabric of her fragile world had come undone and she felt utterly lost.

She frowned and focused on his question. "The housekeeper is Pamela Winters. She lives in an apartment in town and only works two or three days a week, depending on the guest load. Then there's John Jeffries. He's the gardener and lives in a cottage down by the pond. John's the only person who works here full-time besides me and Cory."

"What about other part-time workers?"

She was aware of agents Barkin and Revannaugh returning to the kitchen, where she knew they'd be looking for further evidence to substantiate the possibility of foul play.

"Daniella does most of the cooking for the guests, but she occasionally has Marion Wells come in to take over the job for her. When we're really busy, Valerie King comes in to help with the cleaning. But none of these people would have any reason to do anything bad to Sam and Daniella. We all love them, and Macy is the smartest, cutest little girl on the face of the earth."

A sob caught in her throat and she quickly choked it down. "You shouldn't be wasting your time sitting here and questioning me. You should be out there someplace looking for them," she said passionately.

His blue eyes stared at her dispassionately, and she decided at that moment that she didn't particularly like Special Agent Gabriel Blankenship. "I assume you live here on the premises. Where is your room?"

"Just off the kitchen." She caught her lower lip to keep it from trembling.

He raised a dark eyebrow. "And when was the last time you heard or saw the family?"

"Last night around eight. They went upstairs and I went into my rooms."

"I'd like to see your rooms." He stood and looked at her expectantly.

She felt as if he viewed her as a suspect, and she didn't like the feeling. She stood, her feet leaden as she thought about going through the kitchen to get to her rooms, the kitchen where she knew something bad had happened to people she loved.

She was acutely aware of him following behind her as she passed through the kitchen, where the two agents were fingerprinting the back door. They nodded to her as she went to the door that led to the suite of small rooms she had called home for almost two years. There was a sitting room, a bathroom and two small bedrooms, one where she slept, and one that she and Daniella had turned into a storage room.

The sitting room was relatively plain—a sofa, a rocking chair and a television. There were no knickknacks or trinkets to mark the space as hers. She'd traveled light through life, with her brother the only thing of importance to her.

Gabriel stepped into the room, and it instantly

seemed to shrink in size. She became aware of his scent, a faint but pleasant woodsy cologne.

His blue eyes narrowed and a frown furrowed his brow as he took in the immediate surroundings. He glanced into the storage room and then stood in her bedroom doorway, his back a broad mountain in front of her.

Thank goodness there were no silk panties sneaking over the top of an open drawer, no lacy bra hanging from a doorknob. Marlena was definitely grateful at the moment that she was a neat freak.

He whirled around to gaze at her speculatively. "You were asleep right here, and you didn't hear anything in the kitchen that caused you concern last night?" His deep voice was rife with disbelief.

"I get up at the crack of dawn, work hard during the day and I sleep hard at night. I've always been a deep, heavy sleeper, and unless somebody screamed, I probably wouldn't have awakened." She raised her chin a notch.

"So you don't think anyone screamed."

She hesitated a moment and then shook her head. "I can't be positive, but I'm relatively sure that a scream would have pulled me from my sleep."

He held her gaze, and she fought the impulse to squirm. It was as if his piercing blue eyes attempted to crawl inside her head, look into her soul, and she realized at that moment that she was his number-one suspect in whatever had happened to the family she loved.

Chapter Two

Gabriel woke at dawn, smothered in lavender sheets and a bedspread, pulled from an erotic dream involving himself and his number-one suspect.

Not a good way to start a new day, he thought as he got out of bed and padded into the adjoining bathroom. Minutes later he stood beneath a needle-hot shower spray, trying to burn out the memory of his unusually hot dream.

Marlena Meyer's long silky legs had been entangled with his as they'd kissed and caressed each other. Her green eyes had glowed with a hunger that had made him want to satisfy her. Thankfully he had awakened at that moment.

It had been a short night of sleep. He'd insisted Marlena get her brother and John, the gardener, last night and get them to the house to be interviewed.

The interviews had lasted for several hours, and after a search of the basement and all other areas of the house, it had been around three o'clock in the morning when Gabriel had finally crawled into bed.

Andrew and Jackson had finished processing the kitchen. They'd found hundreds of fingerprints, probably mostly those of the family and the staff. Interestingly enough, the door and frame had apparently been wiped clean, as not a single print had been found there.

There was no question in his mind that the family had not gone willingly with whomever had walked through that back door. The real question was why had they been taken, and how had somebody managed to corral three people and take them away without Marlena in the next room hearing anything?

Other than the overturned chair, there were no signs of a struggle, no indication that anything violent had occurred in the kitchen.

Thank God he and his men had packed bags to be gone for a couple of days, for he had a feeling this wasn't going to be an easy one to solve.

Although his gut told him the Connelly family was either in deep trouble or already dead; the evidence didn't automatically point to a crime taking place. All they had at the moment was circumstantial evidence that something had happened to the family.

He needed to check the financial records, both the personal ones for the Connellys and those of the bed-and-breakfast. Although unusual, the Connelly family wouldn't be the first one to just up and walk away from their current life, leaving behind not only hundreds of questions but loved ones without any sense of closure.

The one thing that bothered Gabriel about this scenario was that he couldn't imagine a former FBI agent walking away without his gun.

Gabriel stepped out of the shower, dried off and dressed in a fresh pair of slacks and another white shirt, and by that time he thought he smelled the faint scent of coffee drifting upstairs.

He checked his watch. It was just after six. Apparently Marlena had been telling him the truth when she'd told him she was up at the crack of dawn.

As he walked down the stairs toward the dining room, his thoughts were scattered on all the things that needed to be done in order to further investigate the disappearance. He carried his laptop, deciding that he'd work from the dining room rather than upstairs in the lavender room.

They had released the kitchen back to Marlena late last night, after they were sure that it had been checked from top to bottom for evidence. Photos had been taken, along with measurements and drawings, notes and impressions.

The coffee smell came from the dining room, and he spied the full pot on the sideboard, along with cups and saucers and all the accoutrements that anyone might need to doctor up a cup of java.

He placed his laptop on the table that had been set with plates and silverware for three and then bypassed the room and entered the kitchen, where Marlena stood with her back to him at the window. Apparently she didn't hear him, and for a moment he said nothing to draw her attention as memories of his inappropriate dream drifted through his brain.

Again today she was dressed in a pair of shorts, denim ones that hugged her pert, shapely butt and showcased the length of her long legs.... Legs that he'd dreamed had been wrapped around his. An apple-green T-shirt topped the shorts, and he knew the color would make her eyes pop.

She turned suddenly, and a startled gasp escaped her. "I didn't know you were there."

"I just got here," he replied.

"I've got biscuits in the oven and gravy ready to make." She took several steps away from the window, and her gaze fell on the table. "I want to thank your agents for cleaning up in here."

"The plates and glasses were bagged and tagged. All they cleaned up was the mess they'd made in fingerprinting."

"Still, I appreciate it." Her eyes were dark, as if in genuine pain as her gaze remained focused on the table. She finally glanced back at him. "There's coffee in the dining room, and you just let me know when you want breakfast, or if you want something besides biscuits and gravy, and I'll be glad to serve you in there."

He nodded. "Biscuits and gravy sounds good, and after we eat, I'd like you to take me on a tour of the grounds."

Her eyes widened in surprise, but she nodded her assent. "I'll have breakfast ready in about fifteen minutes." She turned toward the stove as if to dismiss him.

He hesitated a moment and then returned to the dining room, where he helped himself to a cup of coffee and opened his laptop to begin work.

He hadn't seen a personal laptop in their suite. The only computer had been in the small office off the great room that was obviously used for the business.

Heavy footsteps let him know Jackson approached. Jackson was a slender man, but he walked as if he weighed ten thousand pounds. Gabriel offered the dark-haired agent a tight smile as he entered the dining room.

"Ah, coffee… The drink of gods," Jackson said as he headed for the sideboard.

He poured himself a cup and then joined Gabriel at the table. "So, looks like a potential abduction to me."

"That's what I'm thinking," Gabriel replied. "I've already let Director Miller know how things stand here. I'm in the process of getting a financial picture for both their personal life and this business. After breakfast I'm walking the grounds with Marlena, and I want you and Andrew to search for a personal computer or laptop, plus get into the one in the office, and see if there's been any unusual activity that might yield clues as to what happened here."

Jackson nodded and Gabriel continued. "I also plan on bringing in the part-time helpers sometime this afternoon to interview them, and later I'd like you and Andrew to head into town and start asking questions."

"Breakfast first, and then work," Andrew said as he ambled into the room and headed toward the coffee.

"Of course, breakfast first," Jackson said with a grin. It was office intrigue about what Andrew loved most: his job, his girlfriend or food. There was a rumor that he'd once eaten his weight in meat and desserts at a local buffet in Baton Rouge.

Andrew joined them at the table, and for the next few minutes the men spoke about the interviews they'd conducted the night before with the gardener, John Jeffries, and Marlena's brother, Cory.

John Jeffries was thirty years old, originally from New Orleans, and his alibi for the night of the disappearance was that Cory had been at his cabin and the two of them had been watching horror films and had fallen asleep. According to both Cory and John, they'd slept through the night, John on the sofa and Cory in a recliner, and had both awakened around seven the next morning.

They all stopped talking when Marlena walked in carrying a huge basket of biscuits, a small tray of butter and a variety of jellies. "I'll be right back with the gravy," she said, looking at none of them as she set the basket and tray in the center of the table between where the three sat.

"And what are our thoughts of the lovely manager?" Jackson asked in a low voice.

"The verdict is still out," Gabriel replied. What he'd like to know is if her hair was as soft, if her lips were as hot as they'd been in his dream. He frowned, shoving away these unwanted thoughts. "As far as I'm concerned right now, she's at the top of our suspect list. If nothing else, she's a person of interest who might know something that will solve this disappearance."

He slammed his mouth shut as she returned to the room, carrying a large bowl and ladle of sausage-scented gravy.

"Mmm, smells good," Andrew said, having already opened a couple of the biscuits on his plate.

For the first time Marlena smiled, and the sight of it shot unwanted warmth through Gabriel's stomach.

"I hope it tastes as good as it smells," she replied, and then once again left them alone.

What was wrong with him? Why was this woman already under his skin? Gabriel grabbed one of the warm biscuits and tore it open, irritated by the unfamiliar feelings Marlena Meyers evoked in him.

Although Gabriel had enjoyed sex with a number of women over the years, it hadn't been that often, and it had always been just sex, with the understanding that he wasn't a *forever* kind of man. There was no place for love in his life, never had been, never would be.

Still, something about Marlena Meyers made him think of hot sex, of tangling his hands in her impish blond curls, of feeling the spill of her naked breasts in his hands. It had been a very long time since any woman had affected him this way.

Get a grip, he told himself irritably. She was at the very least a tool to use to gain information on a potential crime, and at the most, potentially responsible for the disappearance of the Connelly family. Not a woman to fantasize about, not a woman to get close to in any way.

All he wanted from her was answers, and to that end, once the meal was over and he knew he'd given her enough time to clean up the kitchen, he went in search of her to accompany him for a walk around the grounds.

It had been too late last night to fully view the surrounding area, and it was possible that some clue or bit of evidence might be found outside.

If the family were being held alive someplace on the property, then before dusk fell, Gabriel would find them. If the family was dead and their bodies were still on the property, then they'd be found as well, before the end of the night.

It was just after eight-thirty when he and Marlena

left by the front door, the heat and humidity already like a slap in the face as they walked outside.

"I thought it was humid in Baton Rouge, but this makes Baton Rouge feel positively arid," he said as they stepped off the porch.

"That's why July and August are our slowest months of the year. We only had two couples booked for the next few weeks, and I emailed them this morning to cancel their visit."

"Hopefully we can tie things up here before the next couple of weeks," Gabriel replied. He pointed toward a shed near a dock that extended out over the pond. "What's that?"

"It's a bait shack. You don't think..." Her voice trailed off as if her thought was too horrible to say out loud.

"I need to check it out," he said grimly.

"I'll wait here." Her voice trembled as he left her side and walked onto the planks at the front of the dock. The bait shop was an oversize shed, and the door was closed.

From outside the wooden structure, he could hear the faint hum of something electric, probably a refrigerator and tanks to hold live bait. He pulled from his pocket a thin latex glove and then reached out for the doorknob, his heart taking on an unsteady rhythm.

Were Sam and Daniella and little seven-year-old Macy dead, their bodies shoved inside this small building? Although Gabriel had worked difficult cases in the past, it never got any easier to work a case where a small child was involved.

He grabbed the doorknob, drew in a deep breath

and then opened it. A whoosh of relief escaped him as he saw exactly what he'd hoped to see: a refrigerator, several wells holding minnows, a screened-in box full of live crickets and no bodies.

He looked back at Marlena and shook his head. Even from this distance, he could see the relief that washed over her pretty face. He met her on a graveled path that led near the edge of the water.

"Does the pond have big fish?" he asked as they fell in step together.

"Some of the guests have pulled out real beauties," she replied. "Mostly catfish and bass and the ever-present bottom-feeding carp."

"Do you fish?"

"No way. This is as close as I ever get to the pond or any body of water bigger than a bathtub." Her eyes darkened with a hint of fear. "I never learned how to swim."

He absorbed this information as he did every minute detail about her and his surroundings. "What other buildings are on the property?" he asked, focusing back on the reason they were taking this walk.

"Just a big gardening shed, John's place and the carriage house," she replied.

"We'll check out the gardening shed, and then I want you to let me into the carriage house. It was too late last night to search there by the time we processed the kitchen and interviewed you, your brother and John, but we need to check the place and make sure nothing is out of order there."

"Okay," she replied, her voice filled with anxiety.

They walked in silence for a few minutes, following

the path that edged the side of the pond. "You think I'm guilty of something, don't you?" she said, finally breaking the tense silence between them.

She was definitely guilty of stirring an unexpected, unwanted fire of desire inside him. He was aware that she was waiting for his answer. He shrugged. The truth was that, at this moment, he had no definitive answer for her as to whether he believed her guilty of having something to do with the Connellys' disappearance or not.

A WEARY EXHAUSTION battled with the pound of a headache as Marlena cut up fruit to make a salad for the evening meal. After she and Gabriel had walked the grounds earlier that day, Gabriel had spent the rest of the morning on his laptop, while Jackson had worked at the bed-and-breakfast computer in the tiny office just off the common room. Andrew had gone into town to ask questions and make arrangements for Marion Wells, Valerie King and Pamela Winters to come to the house to be interviewed.

Around noon Marlena had placed a platter of ham and cheese sandwiches, along with a big bowl of potato salad, on the table. She had stacked the plates and silverware, allowing the men to eat whenever they were ready rather than calling them to a sit-down meal.

All the rules had changed. From the moment she'd awakened and found the family gone, the neat and orderly world inside the bed-and-breakfast had been shattered.

Marlena was on the verge of shattering every time she thought of the missing people she loved. Daniella had been like a sister, and in the past two years, Sam had become like a favorite brother-in-law. Seven-year-old Macy was the icing on the cake in the family Marlena had temporarily claimed as her own.

Marlena had spent most of the afternoon either in her room or in the kitchen preparing dinner. She'd decided to serve the men a hearty meal of smothered pork chops, mashed potatoes and corn. The fruit salad would be perfect to finish off as dessert. She knew that Gabriel had spent the afternoon interviewing Marion Wells, Valerie King and Pamela Winters, but she suspected those women knew no more than she did about what had happened.

The back door creaked open and she jumped, nearly slicing her finger. She relaxed as she saw her brother step into the kitchen. Lately, most of the time she wanted to take him by the shoulders and shake some adult sense into him, but at the moment, the sight of him was a welcome one, and her heart filled with love.

"Hey, sis. How's it going?"

"It's going," she replied.

He slumped into one of the chairs at the table. "This is all so weird."

"Scary weird," she agreed, and then couldn't help herself. "I thought you were going to get a haircut last week."

He raked a hand through his shaggy blond hair. "I didn't get around to it yet, and don't start nagging."

She grinned ruefully. "I don't have the heart or the energy at the moment to nag you. How about a glass of chocolate milk? You know chocolate milk solves everything."

A hint of a smile curved his lips, and she knew he was thinking of all the bad times they'd gone through in the past. Chocolate milk had always been her panacea. "That sounds good," he agreed.

She made the milk with chocolate syrup, stirred it until it was foamy and then set a glass for Cory and a glass for herself on the table.

"Thanks." He took a drink and then looked at her. "I saw you walking with that detective this morning. Is he giving you a hard time?"

"Gabriel Blankenship. And, no, he isn't giving me a hard time, but he's doing his job. By the end of our walk this morning, my head was spinning from all the questions he'd asked."

"Questions like what? Surely he doesn't think you had anything to do with this."

She took a sip from her glass. As always, the sight of Cory caused love to well up inside her. He had the face of a choirboy, open and earnest, with blue-green eyes that radiated a soulful innocence.

"I don't know what exactly he thinks about me, but he asked me the questions I would expect under the circumstances. Did Sam and Daniella have any enemies? Had either of them been threatened recently? Had their moods changed in the past few days? Of course, my answer was no to all of them."

"How did this happen? Do you think whoever took them will come back to take us?" His eyes simmered more blue than green.

"Oh, Cory, I don't think so. I don't think any of us are in danger." But she wasn't sure if she believed the reassuring words or not.

Without knowing who had taken the Connelly family and why, without knowing exactly what had happened in the kitchen the night they disappeared, there was no way to know if there was still danger lurking about or not.

"Are you eating with the others in the dining room tonight?" she asked. Cory often sat with the guests for dinner.

"Nah. John and I are heading into town for pizza."

"It's nice that you and John get along so well." She finished her milk, placed the glass in the sink and then returned to slicing up the last of the fruit.

"He's cool. He's kind of like a father, always telling me how to do things and teaching me stuff. We caught two rattlesnakes today, cut off their heads and threw them into the woods."

Marlena's heart filled with sorrow for her brother, who had lost his mother and father far too soon. Although Marlena had done everything in her power to fill Cory's needs and see to his care, she knew she hadn't been a substitute for a masculine presence in his life.

"As far as I'm concerned, the only good snake is a dead snake," she replied. "I'm glad you have John. Every boy needs a male role model in his life, but don't forget our future game plan."

"Yeah, yeah, I remember." He finished his milk and stood. "I'd better get out of here. We have some work to do outside before we head into town for dinner." He walked over to her and kissed her on the temple. "You sure you're okay?" he asked in a surprising role reversal.

"I'm hanging in there," she replied, a surge of pride fluttering in her heart as she realized the child she'd raised was showing all the signs of becoming a man.

By the time she placed dinner on the table, the house was empty except for herself and the three agents. She served them and then returned to the kitchen, where she ate her dinner at the table where Sam, Daniella and Macy had been interrupted in a nighttime snack.

Their absence was a physical pain in her heart, and she knew it would be there until she got some answers. Hopefully Gabriel and his men had come up with something during the day's investigation.... A clue, a potential motive, something that would find the family alive and well.

After the men had eaten and she'd cleared their dishes and cleaned the kitchen, she retired to her private rooms, figuring the best thing she could do was stay out of the way of anything the FBI agents were doing to investigate.

It was after eight when a knock fell on her door. She got up from the rocking chair and opened the door to see Gabriel.

"May I come in?" he asked.

Surprised, she opened the door farther and motioned him to the sofa, then sank back in the old wooden rocking chair that squeaked faintly with every rock. "Did you find out anything today?" she asked, trying to ignore the pleasant woodsy scent that had followed him into the room.

"Several things, but nothing concrete to provide a trail to follow." As usual, his handsome features appeared set in stone, and there was no warmth, no welcome at all in the depths of his eyes. “I stopped in to tell you that it isn’t necessary for you to cook for us. We aren’t paying guests here, so we aren’t your responsibility.”

“I really don’t mind, and besides, it keeps me busy. I’ll go crazy with nothing to do around here,” she protested.

He leaned against the sofa back, seeming to shrink the size of the piece of furniture—and the entire room—with his presence. “Pamela Winters is not a fan of yours.”

Marlena couldn’t help the short burst of laughter that escaped her at his understatement. “Pamela Winters hates my guts.”

“Why is that?”

Marlena rocked several times, the squeak of the chair the only noise in the room as she thought of the dark-haired woman who worked as the head housekeeper.

Marlena finally stopped her movement and focused on the man asking the questions. “I think Pamela thought she was going to become the manager once Daniella decided to give up some of the reins of the daily running of the place. Unfortunately, when I arrived here, penniless and with no place else to go, Daniella not only took me under her wing, but she instantly appointed me manager. I don’t blame Pamela for feeling betrayed, but somehow her anger has been pointed at me. We’re civil with each other, but she’s made it clear she doesn’t want to be my friend.”

“She thinks maybe you had something to do with

the disappearances because you might be named a beneficiary in Sam's and Daniella's wills."

Marlena gasped, and then laughed again. "That's ridiculous." Her laughter died, and she began to rock back and forth with a sense of both outrage and fear. "First of all, I refuse to believe that they're dead, and I'll repeat again, I had absolutely nothing to do with their disappearance. Second, they would have never made me a beneficiary. Daniella knew this was just a stopping place for me and Cory, that it was temporary until we gathered our resources to get on with our lives, and that we were planning on leaving soon."

"Get on with your lives? What does that mean?"

She was aware of the piercing quality of his eyes and the simmer of some indefinable energy between them. "My goal was never to be a manager of a bed-and-breakfast. Cory and I are planning to eventually move to a bigger city where I can get a teaching degree, and he can get some sort of technical training. I want the house and the dog, the husband and the children. Daniella and Sam knew that this job was just temporary for me, that I had different dreams than staying here in Bachelor Moon. Are you married?"

"No, and have no intention of joining the ranks of the married set. I like living alone. I wouldn't do marriage well, so there's no point in trying it." He stood suddenly. "I'll let you get back to whatever you were doing before I came in."

She got out of the rocking chair and followed him to the door. "Actually, I'm thinking of taking a little walk. I could use some fresh air."

"Then I'll just say good night." Gabriel gave her a

curt nod and left, heading back through the kitchen and dining room toward the stairs to his room.

Marlena left her room and stepped through the kitchen door that led outside. She breathed deeply of the humid, floral-scented air. Darkness had fallen, but a full moon shone overhead, easily lighting the path that led around the pond.

Her head ached with all the questions, the fears, the utter horror of the past twenty-four hours. What had happened to Sam and Daniella and Macy? It was as if an alien spaceship had shot down a beam that had instantly drawn them up and out of the house, leaving no identifying clues behind.

She couldn't imagine who might want to hurt the Connellys. They were respected, warm and giving to both their guests and the community of Bachelor Moon. Daniella served on a half dozen charity committees, and Sam was the man people called on when they were in trouble or needed something done. Macy was everyone's delight with her sassy attitude and sweet, loving heart.

As she neared the area where the walkway came closest to the pond, a chorus of bullfrogs sang a deep-throated tune and a faint splash indicated that the fish were jumping.

It was a beautiful night, and yet all was wrong with the world. Tears burned at her eyes as she thought of the people she loved, people who were missing without any apparent reason.

The path she followed stopped abruptly at the far end of the pond. A trail led off to John's little cabin but a sign indicated that guests weren't allowed on the narrow path.

She turned and started back the way she had come. Her thoughts shifted to the man in charge of the case: Gabriel Blankenship.

She was both drawn to and repelled by him at the same time. His intensity nearly stole her breath away. Something about him made her pulse pound a little harder, her heart race a little faster. She recognized it as some sort of strange attraction, but he was certainly the last man she'd want any kind of relationship with.

He was here to do a job, and when the job was done, he would be gone. He'd just told her that he wasn't the marrying type, and marriage was definitely on her wish list. She'd thought that was where she was headed with Gary Holzman when she'd lived in Chicago, but that dream had exploded and she'd wound up here with nothing but a beat-up car spewing fumes, a suitcase full of clothes and Cory.

She'd just about reached the part of the walkway that was closest to the pond's edge when the sound of rustling in the brush behind her stopped the bull-frog's song.

She had no chance to turn, no time to process that danger was coming before she was shoved from behind with enough force that she flew forward and was weightless for an instant—airborne—and then she plunged into the pond.

Headfirst she went down…down, with no idea how to get up.

Chapter Three

Although it was relatively early, after the short night before, Gabriel had told both Jackson and Andrew to head to bed and get a good night's sleep, as he intended to do himself. He was certain the next day would be a long one, and he wanted them all to start out rested.

He stripped down to a pair of boxers and then opened the window, despite the air-conditioning that kept the room cool and pleasant. Since the age of seven, Gabriel had always kept his bedroom window open, never knowing when he might need to make a hasty escape from a raging drunken father.

Certainly more than once throughout his childhood, he'd used the window to flee the wrath of George Blankenship. Like Marlena's, Gabriel's mother had abandoned him and his father when Gabriel had been seven. She'd left him in the hands of a brutal man who'd either beaten him half to death for unclear reasons or ignored him until Gabriel was old enough to exit and never look back.

He'd lived on the streets, worked a hundred different jobs, and waffled between a life of crime and a life of investigating crimes. He'd finally managed to make his way through college with a criminal justice degree and a minor in psychology, and that's when the FBI had brought him in as a profiler.

He loved his job and he was good at it, but this particular case already had him frustrated by the lack of leads. The bank records had shown no red flags either in the personal or business finances. The email accounts showed no threats or unusual activity. So far he and his team hadn't spoken to anybody who didn't admire or like the family.

Granted, they were still in the beginning stages of the investigation, but he knew that, in many disappearances, within the first couple of hours, the taken were killed.

What he didn't know yet was who had been the intended target. Was it Sam, and his wife and stepdaughter were merely collateral damage? Was there something in Daniella's past that might have brought this on?

He turned off the light in his room and got beneath the lavender top sheet, his mind whirling a million miles an hour. There had to have been more than one person involved; otherwise how was it possible for a single individual to neutralize three people and get them out of their home? And Marlena had heard nothing, which meant either she was lying or whoever had come in and taken the three people had done so relatively silently. How was that possible with a seven-year-old little girl in the mix?

The sound of a splash came from outside the window—a loud splash. Must be a fish the size of a minitorpedo, he thought. A thrashing noise followed, and then a faint cry.

Definitely a female cry. Marlena had told him she was going out to get some fresh air. Who had made that splash? Had it been a fish, or her?

Gabriel bolted up from the bed and flew out of his room. He stumbled down the stairs two at a time, his heart surging with adrenaline as he remembered she couldn't swim.

As he flew through the lower level of the house and into the kitchen, he noted that Marlena's door to her rooms was open, as was the back door.

He burst out into the hot night air and again heard a splashing and a frantic cry from the pond. By the time he reached a vantage point where he could see the water, the moon glittered down on the smooth surface.

He frowned. Had he only imagined the cries? Had he fallen asleep in bed and not realized it, dreaming that Marlena, who couldn't swim, was somewhere in the pond?

As he stared at the water, it bubbled and rippled and then Marlena's pale face broke the surface. Panic etched her features as she managed a single cry before sinking beneath the surface once again.

He raced to a place where he could dive from the short wooden dock into the pond. He hit the water, grateful that it was as warm as a bath, and swam quickly to the place where he had seen Marlena go down.

Diving underwater and opening his eyes, he realized the murky water made it impossible for him to see anything. So he used his hands and legs to search for her, hoping he wasn't already too late.

How long had she been in the water? He surfaced,

drew a deep breath and then went under a second time, his heart pounding frantically.

He swam all around the area where he'd last seen her, his arms outstretched before him. Where was she? Had she already succumbed to the water?

Sharp relief soared through him as he managed to snag an arm. The relief was short-lived as she grabbed hold and frantically wrapped around him like a leech, sinking them both deeper into the water.

Her arms clung around his neck, and in her panic he knew that, if he didn't break her hold on him in some way, they would both drown.

He fought with her, fought for both of their lives and finally managed to wrangle her around the neck and pull her up. They broke the surface of the water, gasping for air, and she immediately tried to crawl onto him to escape a watery grave.

"Marlena." He spewed her name along with a mouthful of water. "You need to calm down. I've got you. Just relax and let me get us to shore."

Still she clung to him, attempting to climb his body with hers as her eyes glowed the iridescent green of a wild animal in the moonlight.

"Marlena!" He managed to dog paddle and grab her by the shoulders, thankful that he was a strong swimmer and a much bigger man.

"Relax, I've got you." He spoke the words slowly and breathed a sigh of relief as he managed to roll her over onto her back. With his arm under her chin, he kept her face well above the water and moved her toward the shore.

Once there, they collapsed side by side on their

backs in the dewy grass, drawing in deep gasps of air. By the time he caught his breath, he realized she was crying and shivering, obviously chilled despite the warmth of the night air that surrounded them.

He got to his feet and pulled her up. "Come on. Let's get you inside and dry."

She continued to weep and shiver as he slung an arm around her shoulder and led her inside. He walked her through the back door to her private quarters and into her bathroom. Spying a stack of towels neatly folded in an open cabinet, he grabbed one for himself and then turned to where she stood as if shell-shocked.

"Marlena, get out of those wet clothes, and then we'll talk," he said. He grabbed a second towel and forced it into her hands and tried not to notice that the wet blouse clung to her like a second skin, emphasizing her breasts and taut nipples.

He turned and left the bathroom, grateful that his boxers were navy and not white. He dried off, wrapped the towel around his waist and sat on the edge of the sofa, waiting for her to emerge from the bathroom.

He needed to find out how a woman who told him she couldn't swim, who obviously had a healthy respect for the water, had wound up in it, nearly drowning.

Had she somehow slipped and fallen into the water? Misstepped in the darkness and wound up sliding down into the pond? There was no question in his mind that if his window hadn't been open, if he hadn't heard the splash and her faint cry, she would have drowned.

After several long minutes, she came out of the bathroom clad in a long pink robe and using a towel to work the last of the dampness from her hair.

Gabriel was shocked by his visceral reaction to her. She looked stunning, and he was grateful for the heavy drape of the towel over his lap, for his body had reacted automatically to the sight of her.

Thank goodness the drama hadn't drawn anyone else's attention. If one of his partners were to walk in right now, the situation definitely looked compromising, as if he and Marlena had taken a tumble into her bed and then showered off afterward.

She walked to the rocking chair and sank down. Dropping the towel she'd used on her hair onto the floor next to her, she looked at Gabriel. Her eyes began to fill with tears. "I would have died if you hadn't been there. You all would have found me floating in the pond in the morning."

The tears that had shimmered and threatened on her long eyelashes fulfilled their promise, and she hid her face in her hands as she rocked back and forth and cried in earnest.

Obviously it had been a traumatic experience for her, Gabriel thought and wondered if he should just leave her alone to deal with the aftermath.

She looked like a woman who needed to be held, who needed to be assured that everything was okay, but he remained firmly seated on the sofa, unwilling to be that man for her.

He told himself it was simple curiosity and nothing else that kept him here in her room after the drama was over. He wanted to know how she'd wound up in the pond.

Finally her tears ebbed, and with a final swipe of her cheeks, she dropped her hands to her lap. "How did you know? How did you know I was in the pond and needed help?"

"I had my bedroom window cracked open and heard a splash and then a faint cry."

"Thank God you heard me." She shivered as if, despite her long robe, there was a core of icy coldness inside her that prevented her from getting warm. "I don't think I could have made it another minute if you hadn't appeared when you did."

"What happened? How did you wind up in the pond?" Gabriel asked, and was suddenly aware of his own bare chest and legs as her gaze swept the length of him, and then quickly moved up to meet and hold his stare.

"I was walking on the path, trying to clear my head. I reached the end and was on my way back when somebody came out of the brush and pushed me hard enough to throw me into the pond." She shivered, more violently this time, as if the full implication of what had just happened to her had been suddenly realized.

Gabriel sat up straighter on the sofa, a thrum of adrenaline rushing through him. "Somebody pushed you? Are you sure it wasn't some sort of animal or something? Did you see who did it?"

"Do I think a crazed raccoon or a big bear suddenly rushed out and pushed me?" She shook her head, as if his question was ridiculous. "It was definitely an animal of the human kind. I felt his hands on my back, and, no, I have no idea who it was. It all happened so fast."

Her eyes darkened and enlarged. "Somebody tried

to kill me, Gabriel. Somebody shoved me off the path and into the water and knew that I would drown."

Gabriel's heart sank. Was she right? Had this been a potential murder attempt, or had it been some sort of weird mistake? Was this somehow tied to the mysterious disappearance of the Connelly family, or was it something completely unrelated?

Time would hopefully answer all those questions. He withheld a deep sigh as he knew this merely complicated what was already a complicated enough situation.

WATER, WATER EVERYWHERE and not a breath to take. Marlena shot up in bed, gasping for the air she hadn't been able to draw in the nightmare she'd just suffered.

A glance at her bedside clock let her know she'd overslept by half an hour, having forgotten to set her alarm the night before.

Gabriel had stayed in her room until she'd finally calmed down. He'd asked several questions about her brush with a watery death, trying to jog her mind into remembering any sound, any scent she might have sensed from the person who had pushed her off the walkway. But she remembered nothing—only the shock and horror of hitting the water and sinking.

What she did remember this morning was how utterly hot Gabriel had looked wrapped in a towel. His broad chest had been sprinkled with just enough black hair to be interesting, and his taut abs had been more than amazing to look at.

But what was really important here was that somebody had tried to kill her last night…or had he?

There was no question that something had bumped

or pushed her into the pond, but had it simply been a figment of her imagination or some sort of mistake, and whoever was responsible had run away, afraid of what he'd accidentally done?

Maybe it had been one of the drifters who occasionally showed up at the bed-and-breakfast looking for a free handout of money or food. Or maybe a local fisherman who had planned to secretly fish in the private pond and had been startled by her presence.

She finally got out of bed, and after a quick shower, refused to dwell on the horror of the night before. In the light of day, she decided that it was probably just some weird circumstance, and she'd been the victim of a sort of hit-and-run accident.

She couldn't imagine anyone wanting to intentionally harm her, but she also didn't plan on taking any more nightly walks alone.

When she left her rooms, she smelled fresh coffee. She entered the dining room to find Andrew seated at the table, a cup of coffee and a plate of leftover biscuits from the morning before in front of him.

"Hope you don't mind that I helped myself," he said.

"Not at all," she replied as she poured herself a cup of coffee and joined him at the table. "Sorry I overslept."

"Not a problem," he replied easily.

She and Andrew had only been talking for a few minutes when Gabriel and Jackson joined them. "Can I get you something to eat?" she asked, half rising from her chair.

Gabriel motioned her down. "Sit and enjoy your coffee. We're heading into town this morning to have a talk with Sheriff Thompson. When I spoke to him yesterday on the phone, I told him I wanted to get the lay of the land here before contacting him face-to-face."

"Jim's a decent man, and maybe he knows something I don't know about Sam and Daniella," she replied.

"Maybe, although he hasn't shared anything useful with us yet. I got the feeling when I spoke to him yesterday that he's still hoping this is a voluntary disappearance and not a crime," Gabriel said.

Marlena shook her head. "There's no way Sam and Daniella would let the people who love them worry about them for this length of time." A new rivulet of fear swept through her for her friends. The only way they wouldn't contact anyone was if they couldn't.

"We have their cell phones in our possession and will be checking any calls that come in, and also looking at those they received before they went missing. Are you going to be okay today with us gone?" Gabriel asked as the other two agents headed for the front door.

She frowned. Last night felt like a nightmare, and even in the light of day a shiver tried to take possession of her, but she shrugged it off. "I should be fine. I'll lock the house and just let in the people I know and trust."

"Have you thought further about anyone who might want to cause you harm?"

He'd asked the same question the night before. "I can't imagine," she said, giving him the same answer. "Maybe I just freaked out a drifter who was hanging around and he accidentally shoved me as he ran away." It sounded lame, but it was the only rational explanation she'd managed to come up with. "Whatever happened, I'm sure it was an accident and whoever was responsible was afraid of getting into trouble."

"Why don't I give you my cell phone number, so if anything comes up, you can call, and we can get right back here?" he suggested.

She smiled at him gratefully. "Thanks. Just let me get a piece of paper to write it down." She hurried into the kitchen, grabbed a notepad then returned to the dining room and wrote down the cell number he gave her.

"We should be back by dinnertime," he said as she walked with him to the door. His gaze held hers for a long moment. "Don't hesitate to call if you need me... us."

As she watched him head to the car where the other two agents awaited him, she decided that maybe Gabriel Blankenship wasn't so bad after all.

She locked the door behind him. Despite what had happened the night before, she felt no real danger directed specifically at her. Still, better to be safe than sorry.

She was back in the kitchen when Cory knocked on the door, eyeing her quizzically through the glass pane. She hurried over and unlocked it to allow him and John to enter.

"Why the locked door?" Cory asked as he sat at the table in the kitchen. John sat next to him. Most mornings the two of them showed up for breakfast, but it was usually Daniella who did the cooking and serving.

"I had a little unexpected encounter with the pond last night." She explained what had happened, and both men looked at her in stunned surprise.

"Thank God one of those agents managed to get to you," Cory exclaimed.

"I didn't know you couldn't swim," John added. "Do you have any idea who might have pushed you?"

"Not a clue," she replied, not wanting to think about how close she'd come to death. "I imagine you two are looking for something to eat. Why don't I whip up a quick batch of pancakes?"

"Sounds good to me," John replied.

As she got out the ingredients to make the pancakes, the three of them talked about the pizza place where the guys had gone the night before, the weeding that needed to be done and the continuing mystery of the Connellys' disappearance.

Marlena liked John. The dark-haired man had an easygoing temperament and had bonded instantly with the younger Cory and kept him busy working by his side on the grounds.

After the two had finished their breakfast, they left by the back door, and Marlena relocked it after them. For the remainder of the morning, she busied herself upstairs, making beds and freshening the rooms where the agents were sleeping.

She immediately knew that Gabriel had slept in the lavender room. As she plumped his pillows and straightened the spread, she smelled his cologne and was surprised by the tiny ray of heat that fired up inside her.

There was no question that she was physically drawn to him, and there was also no question that she had no intention of following through on that attraction. The most important thing right now was that he stay focused on finding Sam, Daniella and Macy.

When she'd finished upstairs, she returned to the kitchen to start a large roast cooking for dinner that evening. An hour or so before mealtime, she'd add in potatoes and carrots.

During the slow months of July and August, Pamela was scheduled to clean two days a week, Mondays and Wednesdays. Since it was Saturday, Marlena would take care of the daily duties to keep the place in shape. Even though Daniella was gone and there were no guests, Daniella would want the routine of maintaining the bed-and-breakfast to continue.

Marlena sank down at the kitchen table with a cup of coffee, her heart crying out for answers. Where were the Connellys? Nobody would ever make her believe that they'd just walked away without a word to anyone.

Daniella was living her dream, loving a man she'd never expected to find, working in this business that had been her desire since she'd been in high school and raising her daughter in the cocoon of family love. No way would Daniella willingly leave her life behind.

Marlena nearly jumped out of her chair as a loud rap sounded on the front door. Her nerves were on edge. Even though there were no guests scheduled, that didn't mean someone couldn't show up.

She relaxed as she approached the front door and saw Thomas Brady on the other side, his pleasant features radiating concern for her. She unlocked the door, and he instantly pulled her into his big arms.

"I just heard about the Connellys," he said as he continued to hold her. "I was working out of town for the past couple of days and got back home only an hour ago."

She was grateful when he finally released her and sat on the sofa in the great room. "How are you doing? Is there something I can do to help? I heard you've got a couple of FBI agents staying here. Do they have a theory on what happened?"

Marlena waited until he'd run out of breath to begin to answer his questions. "I'm doing as well as I can, although I'm terribly afraid for the family. There are three FBI agents staying here, and, no, they don't have a clue yet as to what happened and who might be responsible."

"I don't like the idea of you being here by yourself, especially with nobody knowing what happened to Sam, Daniella and Macy," Thomas said. He leaned forward, his brown eyes earnest. "You should move in with me. You would be safe under my roof."

"You know I'm not going to do that," she said softly. "Besides, I just told you there were FBI agents staying here. I also have Cory, so I'm definitely not by myself. Now tell me about the job you just finished."

Thomas was a local carpenter who not only did renovation work but also specialized in spectacular decks and patios. His skills often got him work in the larger cities in the state.

As he told her about his latest job in New Orleans, she listened absently. She had known for some time that Thomas had a thing for her. They'd even gone out on a couple of casual dates.

Sam and Daniella hadn't thought the carpenter was good enough for Marlena, but they didn't have to worry because Marlena knew her future wasn't with Thomas. She just couldn't seem to make Thomas understand that.

She enjoyed his company as a friend and thought he was a nice man, but she had no romantic feelings toward him at all. She'd told him that a hundred different ways over the past month or so, but he was still a frequent visitor and a man who obviously didn't take no easily. He seemed to think that, if she just spent enough time with him, he could change her mind about their relationship.

He couldn't. She'd rather be alone than be in a relationship without real passion, without true mutual love. Been there, done that, and the results had nearly destroyed her.

As he rambled on, Marlena realized it was the first time that he sat in the house with her. Normally Sam made it uncomfortable for the man to be anywhere but on the porch when he came to visit Marlena.

Thomas was a big man, with wide shoulders and thighs the size of tree trunks. Physical labor had given him the muscles of a bodybuilder, but he had always been gentle and soft-spoken when around her.

He had to have known that Sam and Daniella didn't approve of him. They hadn't hidden the fact that they thought he was all wrong for her.

Her heart began a slightly faster unsteady beat as she stared at the man on the sofa. Was he so obsessed with her that he had removed the people who disapproved of him? Left her alone in the house and frightened, hoping he could step in and be her support, the man she turned to in her need?

Ridiculous, a tiny voice whispered inside her. *You're looking for a bad guy in a friend who has never shown any violent tendencies, a man who has never pushed you to accept any unwanted advances.*

Still, she was grateful an hour later when he finally left with the promise to check in with her soon.

Maybe it was time she moved up her schedule for leaving Bachelor Moon.

And maybe it wasn't such a bad idea to mention Thomas's name to Gabriel.

Chapter Four

Sheriff Jim Thompson was a font of information about the history of Sam and Daniella's relationship, which had formed when Sam had come to the bed-and-breakfast for a vacation.

During that two-week stay, it had become apparent that Daniella was in danger—the first indication the murder of Samantha Walker, the daughter of Mayor Brian Walker.

It had later been determined that the bed-and-breakfast gardener, Frank Mathis, had been obsessed with Daniella and little Macy. He'd killed Samantha Walker as a gift to Daniella, because Samantha had planned on opening a bed-and-breakfast that would directly compete with Daniella's business.

Armed with this little bit of history, the three agents were now on their way to see Brian Walker. "Maybe the old man blamed Daniella for his daughter's murder and exacted some kind of revenge against the family," Jackson said as Gabriel drove down the tree-lined street that would take him to the ex-mayor's house.

"More than two years is a long time to let rage fester," Gabriel replied. "If he does have something to do with the Connellys' disappearance, then there had to have been some sort of trigger."

"A week ago was Samantha Walker's birthday," Andrew said from the backseat where he had a laptop open, checking facts.

"That could definitely be a trigger," Gabriel replied.

"There...on the left," Jackson said, pointing to the house where Brian Walker had lived for the past two years. Gabriel pulled into the driveway of the small, ill-kept house.

Weeds had long ago choked out any semblance of yard and an air of desolation hung upon the faded forest-green ranch house. Gabriel turned off the car engine and the three agents got out.

The heat was nearly overwhelming, pressing against Gabriel's chest and making it difficult to draw a deep breath. He unfastened the safety snap over his gun and knew the two agents behind him had done the same thing. They had no idea what they might be walking into. Brian Walker could be a dangerous man.

Gabriel knocked on the door, his emotions cold as he went into the survival mode that had kept him alive through many heinous cases.

It helped that he knew Jackson and Andrew had his back. He'd worked with them long enough to know they could handle almost any situation that might fly their way.

Gabriel knocked again and heard a faint cry from inside. "I'm coming. Hold your damned horses."

Gabriel drew his gun from his holster, not liking the man's tone nor his delay in opening the door.

When the door finally opened, a man in a dirty

white T-shirt and a baggy pair of black slacks stared at Gabriel and then the gun he held in his hand.

"It would be a great blessing in my life if you'd just shoot me, but I would like to know why you're doing it before you pull the trigger," he said.

Gabriel holstered his gun and instead pulled out his identification. "May we come in and have a chat with you, Mr. Walker?"

"Why not? I haven't broken any laws. Drinking too much, being slovenly and wishing yourself dead isn't a crime if it's done in the sanctity of your own home." He opened the door wider to allow them inside.

The blinds were partially pulled as if to ward off any sunshine and cheerfulness. The living room reeked of alcohol, stale cigarette smoke and old food. Gabriel's initial assessment was that Brian Walker was a man on a mission: to wish himself dead.

"Mind if my partners take a look around the house?" Gabriel asked as Brian eased into a recliner where he'd created a nest of trash around him.

"Help yourself." Brian waved airily and picked up a glass with contents that looked like scotch. "I don't suppose I could interest you in a drink."

"Thanks, but no." Gabriel lowered himself to the sofa.

"I bet I know what you're thinking," Brian said, and then took a deep swallow of his drink.

"And what's that?"

"How hard the mighty fall." Brian took another drink and then set the glass on the nearby end table. "A little over two years ago I was happily married, mayor of this little town and encouraging my beautiful, divorced daughter to follow whatever dream she had in her busy, ditzy head."

"And then Samantha was murdered," Gabriel added, his gut already telling him that this sad, broken man had nothing to do with the disappearance of the Connelly family.

Brian nodded. "And within that moment of insanity in Frank Mathis's violence, he ripped apart my entire world. A month later my wife had left me, I had resigned my position as mayor and had crawled into the bottom of a bottle and a hole that I have no desire to ever crawl out of."

"You've heard that the Connelly family is missing?" Gabriel asked.

"I heard, but if you're here because you think I had something to do with it, then you're wasting your time. I never held Daniella responsible for what happened to Samantha. Daniella was just another victim of Frank Mathis's craziness. The only difference between her and Samantha is that Daniella was lucky enough to survive his insanity."

By that time Andrew and Jackson had returned to the living room, indicating with shakes of their heads that they'd found nothing to link Brian to the Connelly family disappearance.

Minutes later the three agents were back in their car and headed out to check on another man, who Sheriff Thompson had mentioned might have reason to harm Sam Connelly.

"You can't help but feel bad for Brian Walker," Andrew said from the backseat. "Poor guy lost everything he loved—his job, his wife and his daughter."

That's why it is easier not to love, Gabriel thought. Better to keep people at bay, better to not expect kindness or love from anyone else, because when it went bad, it went so terribly bad. Certainly Gabriel had learned, at the absence of his mother's knee and at the end of his father's fist, that some people weren't meant to be loved.

"I think we can pretty much rule Brian out as a suspect," Jackson said. "I'm not sure his alcohol-addled brain could summon the cunning and savvy that our attacker had to possess in order to control the kidnapping of three people all at the same time."

"I definitely agree," Gabriel replied. "Let's see if Ryan Sherman shows a little more potential."

"Ryan Sherman, thirty-four years old," Andrew said from the backseat, once again on the laptop utilizing FBI access to the most information possible about a person.

"He spent two years in prison on an assault-and-battery charge. He's been out of the joint for the past three years and works as a mechanic at Glen's Garage," Andrew continued.

"From what Thompson told us, he and Sam have had several run-ins. Seems Ryan has a real bad attitude when it comes to the law and took a special dislike to former agent Connelly," Jackson said.

As the two of them talked about Ryan Sherman and the case, Gabriel's mind drifted to Marlena and the night before. Would she have managed to make it to shore had he not heard her scream? Somehow he doubted it. Had she been shoved off the path, or merely stumbled and imagined being pushed?

They certainly did not need another element to the mystery they'd already been handed. And the *very* last thing he needed was to think about how soft and vulnerable Marlena had looked in her robe with her damp curls framing her lovely face.

He didn't want to think about how her body had looked with her wet clothes plastered against her. In truth, he didn't want to think about her at all.

Thankfully, they arrived at Glen's Garage. As Gabriel parked on the side of the building, they were met by a man in coveralls who introduced himself as the owner, Glen Grable. "What can I do for you folks this afternoon?" he asked with an affable smile.

Gabriel flashed his identification. "We'd like to speak to Ryan Sherman."

Glen's smile transformed into a frown. "He in trouble again? Damn him. I told him, the next time I had to bail him out of jail, he was finished working here."

"We're not here to arrest him, but we do need to talk to him," Jackson said.

"Is this about the Connellys?" Glen's eyes darkened.

Gabriel took a step toward the older man. "Why would you ask? Do you know something about the Connellys?"

Glen shook his head. "Just heard that they were missing. That's all everyone in town has been talking about."

"Do you know where Ryan was on Thursday night?" Gabriel asked.

"He worked here until seven. After that I have no idea. I don't keep track of my mechanics when they're off duty. I'll go get him for you. I'd rather you talk to him out here than inside my shop where I got customers."

As they waited in the midafternoon heat, Jackson pulled a handkerchief from his back pocket and mopped his forehead. "Jeez, it's hot. It would be nice to wrap this up quickly and get back home."

Gabriel frowned. "The only way we're going to wrap this up quickly is if the family suddenly reappears alive and well, and at this point, I don't see that happening."

"I have a bad feeling about this whole thing," Andrew said softly. "I think the next time we see that family, it's going to be in a shallow grave someplace."

Andrew's words sent a somber pall over the three of them. But Gabriel knew the stats. He also knew how difficult it would be to hide three people and keep them silent and alive for any length of time.

He tensed as he watched a big, bald, tattooed man approach them. It was obvious by the sneer on his face that he wasn't happy to meet them. He was dressed in grimy coveralls and held a red grease-stained rag in his hands.

"Glen told me there were a couple of Feds out here. Just what this town needs, more Feds."

"We've heard through the grapevine that you and Sam Connelly didn't play nice together," Gabriel said.

"That sanctimonious bastard thought he was better than everyone else in town," Ryan said, and it didn't miss Gabriel's attention that he'd spoken of Sam in the past tense. "He had plans to run for sheriff after Thompson retires. I didn't want him as the new sheriff, and I let him know how I felt about it every time we ran into each other."

Ryan's brown eyes narrowed, and the snarl returned to his upper lip. "I heard he and his family are missing, and I'm sure you're here talking to me because I'm an ex-con and must be guilty of something, right? Ex-cons are always guilty of something."

"Where were you on Thursday night?" Gabriel asked, refusing to let the man's attitude get under his skin.

"I was here working."

"According to Glen, you got off work at seven."

Ryan's scowl deepened as a sheen of sweat glistened on his bald head. "I left here and went to my girlfriend's place. I spent the night there. And now if you're finished harassing me, I've got work to do."

"Your girlfriend? What's her name?" Gabriel asked.

Ryan released an irritated snort through flared nostrils. "Tammy Payne. She lives in the Bachelor Moon apartment complex. I got my own place there, too, but most nights we're together. She'll tell you I was with her all night and had nothing to do with whatever happened to the Connellys." Without waiting for a reply, Ryan stalked off back to the garage.

"What do you want to bet that Tammy tells us whatever Ryan tells her to?" Jackson asked as they headed back to their car.

"No question. But I *would* bet that Tammy Payne is either a prostitute or a stripper, because I get the feeling that's the kind of woman who'd take on a loser like Ryan. At least that's been my experience with hotheaded ex-cons, although I know there are exceptions."

Within minutes they were back in the car, the air conditioner blowing welcomed cool air as they headed to the Bachelor Moon Apartments.

"It's frustrating that Ryan Sherman is our first real person of interest in this case," Andrew said.

"Unless you count the lovely Marlena," Jackson added.

"I don't think she had anything to do with this," Gabriel said.

"Is that your professional opinion or a personal one?" Jackson asked with a raise of a dark eyebrow.

Gabriel hesitated before replying, wanting to make sure his crazy physical attraction to her had no part in his reply. "It's both," he finally said.

He hadn't mentioned Marlena's dip in the pond the night before, but he did so now, explaining to the two men how he had dragged her out of the pond.

"Do you really think somebody pushed her?" Jackson asked.

"I don't know what to believe, but she certainly believes it. What I can't figure out is if the incident is somehow tied to the disappearance of the Connellys or not. I have to ask myself if somebody wants the people associated with the bed-and-breakfast out of the way," Gabriel said.

"Out of the way of what?" Andrew asked.

Gabriel flashed him a tight smile in the rearview mirror. "I have questions, but nobody said I have any answers."

"Who is the beneficiary of the place if anything happens to Sam and Daniella?" Jackson asked.

"We need to check that out. I would assume that

initially it would have gone to Macy, with an executor or representative in place until she reaches of age. But with her missing as well, I'm not sure what would happen. I don't even know if they have a will in place."

Gabriel made a mental note to check for that particular information.

By that time they had arrived at the Bachelor Moon Apartments, and they all exited the car to check out Ryan Sherman's alibi with his girlfriend.

Tammy Payne looked like she'd been ridden hard and put away wet. Lanky blond hair fell into her face as she opened the door to allow them inside. She gestured them toward the threadbare sofa and then curled her painfully thin frame into a chair facing them, but that didn't mean she sat still.

"Ryan called a little while ago to tell me to expect you," she said, first pulling on the ends of her hair and then picking at a scab on her chin. She dropped her hand to her lap but continued to fidget in junkie fashion.

"I can tell you that Ryan was here with me all night on Thursday. In fact, he's here most nights, although he has an apartment of his own."

"Is it possible he was here for a while and then maybe left while you were sleeping?" Jackson asked.

She flashed a quick smile, displaying a missing front tooth. "I don't do a lot of sleeping. So, no, that wouldn't be possible. I'll be perfectly honest. I've got a little problem with meth and Ryan is trying to help me stay on the straight and narrow." She giggled like a young girl, although she had to be in her mid-thirties. "He tells me I'm a full-time job for him."

"Have you thought about rehab?" Andrew asked.

"Been three times, and it didn't take. Ryan is the best rehab I've ever had."

The men questioned her for several minutes longer but got no more information out of her that would absolutely confirm Ryan's alibi.

"I don't think Ryan is fixing her problem, either," Jackson muttered as they left Tammy's apartment.

"No, she was definitely tweaking, but aside from that, she's crazy and dependent enough on him to provide him with an alibi for any day or time he'd need one," Gabriel said as he tightened his hands on the steering wheel.

It was dinnertime, and he headed back toward the bed-and-breakfast feeling as if their entire day had been wasted.

"I say we put Ryan Sherman on a persons of interest list," Jackson said.

"And tomorrow you can check around town and see if anyone can specify the last interaction Ryan might have had with Sam." Gabriel turned down the lane that led to the bed-and-breakfast.

"I'm just hoping Marlena has something great for dinner. I'm starving," Andrew exclaimed.

Both Jackson and Gabriel laughed. "What else is new?" Jackson replied.

As Gabriel walked up the stairs to the porch, a fist of tension knotted in his stomach as he thought of seeing Marlena.

"Hmm, something smells good," Andrew said as they entered the house.

Marlena appeared in the doorway to the dining room

and Gabriel was shocked by how the mere sight of her shot pleasure through him.

"Pot roast," she said. "And it's ready whenever you men want to eat."

"Now," Andrew said. "We're definitely ready now. They forced me to eat a sandwich from a convenience store for lunch."

Marlena laughed. "Oh, my gosh, that's a fate worse than death."

The sound of her laughter stirred a well of warmth inside Gabriel's stomach. She was a vision in pink, clad in a sundress that exposed slightly freckled slender shoulders and long bare legs.

"Give us fifteen minutes," he said and instantly turned to go upstairs. He'd scarcely gotten in the door and already felt as if he needed to distance himself from her.

Something must have been in that pond water he'd swallowed last night when he'd pulled her from its depths, for he'd had trouble keeping her out of his head all day long.

He dropped his laptop on the bed, went directly into the bathroom and sluiced cool water on his face. He had to remember that he didn't know Marlena, except that she had a slamming-hot body and the face of an angel.

But he had to stay focused on the fact that she might have something to do with what had happened to the family. He didn't know if she'd somehow manufactured a fall into the pond to complicate what was already a difficult case with few leads.

Finally, he wasn't sure that he believed that anyone could have slept through whatever had happened on the night the Connelly family disappeared. That overturned chair indicated that they hadn't left the kitchen in utter silence.

Minutes later he joined his partners at the dining room table, where Marlena served them pot roast and vegetables, hot rolls and a salad. He was grateful that she didn't sit with them, but instead she disappeared back into the kitchen.

After dinner, Gabriel returned to his room and powered up his laptop, intending to do some background checks on all the players they'd encountered so far.

He felt as if they were no closer to having any answers than they'd been when they'd first arrived two days ago. He hated having to check in with his director and letting him know they were still clueless as to what had happened to the three people who had seemingly led a happy life here.

He gathered information and took notes, and as always, lost track of place and time as he worked. He was a man who'd always been most comfortable at work, hunting criminals and delving into the darkness of sick minds.

Maybe it was because his childhood had been a dark and frightening place, so hunting killers and cuddling up to violence felt familiar to him.

He finally closed his computer and stretched his arms overhead to work out the kinks in his shoulders. He was shocked to look at the clock and realize it was almost one in the morning.

What time had Sam, Daniella and Macy decided to have milk and cookies in the kitchen on Thursday night? He knew it had been after eight in the evening, but surely it would have been earlier than this considering Macy was only seven.

And Marlena had heard nothing.

He should go to bed. It was late, and his mind was going into strange territory. He eyed the bed, knowing that morning was going to come far too early for him.

Still, instead of heading for bed, he quietly opened his bedroom door. From the room next door he could hear the chorus of snores coming from Jackson and Andrew's room.

He crept down the stairs, the house silent around him. *It's a crazy idea,* he thought. Yet there was really only one way to prove just how soundly Marlena slept, and even though he felt a little foolish, he realized this was something he had to do for himself. He had to know.

The kitchen was lit with a small night-light plugged into an outlet next to the stove, giving him enough illumination to see that Marlena's door was closed, as he assumed it had been on the night the Connelly family had disappeared.

What he was about to do could in no way be considered an official experiment where results could be used in any way, except for as an answer to a question in his own mind. It was strictly curiosity that drove him.

He pulled out a chair from the table and pushed it so that it toppled to the floor. Then he went to the back door, unlocked it and opened it and then slammed it shut and locked it. Either noise should have awakened the woman sleeping in the next rooms, but minutes passed and she didn't fly out of her bedroom to see what was happening.

Maybe she was awake and afraid to come out of her rooms, he thought. He walked over to her door and tried the knob, surprised when it turned easily beneath his hand.

He opened the door to the darkness of her sitting room, although he saw the faint glow of another night-light coming from her bedroom.

Was she playing possum? Had she heard the noise in the kitchen and recognized what he was doing? Had she heard the sound of Sam's family being kidnapped and been too afraid to rush to help?

With quiet stealth he moved through her sitting room and stood in her bedroom doorway. She was on her side, curled up beneath the sheet. The sound of her deep, even breathing let him know she was truly asleep, that the noise he had created in the kitchen hadn't awakened her.

He should turn and leave, but instead found himself inching forward, closer to the bed. His fingers itched with the desire just to stroke softly down the side of her face, to tangle in her soft-looking curls.

As he reached the side of her bed, he wondered whether, if he pressed his lips to hers, she would awaken, like a princess responding to the kiss of her prince.

He stumbled, the ridiculous thought startling him. He backed out of her bedroom and from her apartment area. Closing the door softly behind him, he uprighted the chair he'd cast to the floor and hurried up the stairs to his bedroom.

Shutting his door, he slumped down on the bed and shook his head to dispel all thoughts of Marlena. But the action didn't work. She'd been wearing a pastel-pink nightgown, and the fragrant scent of her had filled the air. Her features had been soft and dreamy in sleep.

Why was he thinking of her as a princess and he the prince who would kiss her? He sure as hell wasn't a prince. He knew what he was—a cold man who expected no kindness, a dysfunctional man who had no desire to attempt to love anyone.

He was an FBI agent on a job and Marlena was nothing to him but a bit of fluffy distraction. If she wasn't part of this case, he'd take her to bed, satisfy the lust that ate at him and then be rid of her.

He had a family to find, a mystery to solve, and no matter the depth of his physical attraction to Marlena, he had no intention of following through on it. He just had to keep his distance from her. If he needed more information from her about the family or anything else, he'd let Jackson take over the interviewing process.

Gabriel couldn't afford to delude himself into thinking he was anyone's hero, anyone's prince. He knew the truth about himself: he had no heart and very little soul, and he'd do well to remember that.

Chapter Five

Marlena sat on the front porch, nursing a glass of iced tea and watching John and Cory work in the distance in the yard. She had spent part of the day making beds and dusting. Pamela would be in the next day to change the bedding and dust and vacuum the entire house.

Marlena hadn't made dinner tonight. She'd gotten a call from Gabriel earlier telling her the men wouldn't be home until late this evening and would eat out.

She hoped to talk to him about Thomas Brady when Gabriel returned, even though there was no possible way she could believe the affable carpenter could have anything to do with whatever had happened to the Connellys.

She'd wanted to talk to Gabriel yesterday, but he'd made himself scarce after dinner and had stayed in his room for the remainder of the night.

She took a sip of her tea and thought about the woman who would be here in the morning to clean. Pamela was usually cool and unfriendly, speaking to Marlena only when necessary and barely hiding her resentment. Marlena had learned to basically ignore the dark-haired woman and her nasty attitude.

She knew that Pamela and Daniella had been close,

especially before Marlena had arrived back in town. She also knew that Pamela saw her as an interloper who had stepped into the position of manager that Pamela had assumed would eventually be hers.

Marlena had tried to be amiable with Pamela in the first couple months after Marlena had arrived here, but when her friendly overtures had been met with disdain, she'd given up.

She now waved to Cory as he looked toward the porch, and he waved back. Her heart swelled with love for her brother. Oh, there were days she wanted to knock him in the head, but he was basically a good kid at heart.

Where was little Macy with her diva attitude and silly antics? Where were Sam and Daniella? Marlena's heart ached with their absence with an all-encompassing fear for them.

Sunset had just begun to splash gorgeous colors across the sky when Gabriel pulled up and parked. She could tell by the body language of all three men that it had been a frustrating day for them.

Jackson and Andrew nodded to her and went inside, but as Gabriel followed she halted him by calling his name. "Could I talk to you for a minute?" she asked and gestured to the wicker chair close to hers.

He frowned as if he found her request unpleasant, but sank into the chair with a weary sigh. "What's going on?" he asked.

"I thought of somebody else you might want to check out," she said.

He sat up straighter in the chair, the tired lines on his face seeming to magically disappear. "Who?"

Marlena hesitated a moment, wondering if she was creating problems for a man who'd done absolutely nothing wrong. "His name is Thomas Brady."

"And what exactly does he have to do with the bed-and-breakfast or Sam and Daniella?"

"Actually not much. It's more that he has something to do with me."

Gabriel's eyes darkened. "What do you mean?"

"Why don't I get you some lemonade, and then I'll explain." As he nodded his assent, she jumped out of her chair and hurried inside. She poured him a tall glass of the cold liquid and told herself that she was doing the right thing by mentioning Thomas. The last thing she wanted was to be responsible for not giving them information that might prove valuable.

When she returned to the porch, she handed him the drink and then returned to her chair, aware of him watching her intently as the purple shadows of twilight began to fall.

"Thomas Brady is a local carpenter who has made it clear that he wants to have a romantic relationship with me. We went out a couple of times, but for me the relationship has never been anything but a friendship. But Thomas has been persistent, and he believes we belong together."

In the deepening shadows Gabriel's features looked sharper, a little bit dangerous. "So what could your relationship with Thomas have to do with the Connellys' disappearance?"

Marlena paused to take a sip of her lemonade. She set the glass on the wicker table between them and released a sigh. "Sam and Daniella don't like Thomas, and they've made their feelings toward him fairly clear. They don't think he's good enough for me. They don't want to see us together as a couple. They've always been cool to Thomas when he's come here to visit with me."

She frowned and looked out to where John and Cory were loading up their gardening tools into a wheelbarrow. "Thomas stopped by yesterday, and we visited for a little while. He was more at ease than he'd ever been, with Sam and Daniella not around." She shrugged. "He suggested it would be safer for me if I moved in with him. I just thought you should maybe check him out. He was supposedly out of town working on a deck in New Orleans when the family disappeared."

"I will check him out," Gabriel replied. He took a drink of his lemonade and leaned back in the chair, looking nothing if not exhausted.

"Bad day?" she asked sympathetically.

"Bad case," he replied. He looked out to where John and Cory headed to the gardening shed. They stopped suddenly, and John grabbed a hoe and began to smack the ground.

"What's he doing?" Gabriel asked.

"Must have stumbled across another snake. We have a nest of rattlesnakes and way too many cottonmouths on the grounds, and John is our official snake killer. Cory would rather try to catch them. He loves snakes and reptiles, but John has a healthy fear of them and always cuts off their heads."

They both watched as John picked up on the hoe what was obviously now a dead snake and tossed it into the wheelbarrow.

"I hate snakes," Gabriel admitted. "I'd rather face a perp with a gun than stumble on a snake."

She released a small laugh. "I'd rather not face either of those situations."

"Your brother seems like a good kid."

"He's a pretty normal kid. And by that I mean one day I want to kiss him to death and the next day I want to wring his neck," she admitted and was rewarded with a brief smile from Gabriel. "What about you? What kind of a kid were you when you were around Cory's age?"

"Tough. I was basically living on the streets, working at a fast-food joint to get by."

"Where were your parents?" she asked.

His features took on a dark and dangerous mask. "My mother took off for parts unknown when I was seven, leaving me in the custody of the meanest bastard in the state of Mississippi—my father. I lived in constant fear of him from the time my mother left until I left home at sixteen."

He paused and took another sip of his lemonade. "That's why I had my window open the other night, because from the time I was a little kid, I had to have an escape route from my old man." He was silent for a moment and then jerked, as if pulling his thoughts back to the present.

"After I left home, for the next couple of years I did whatever I needed to do to survive on my own."

"So how did you wind up as an FBI agent?" What she wanted to say was that she was sorry for what he'd gone through with his father, that her heart ached for the little boy he had been, but she knew he'd hate her for going there.

"A street cop got friendly with me and encouraged me to finish school, get into college, and that's when the FBI tapped me on the shoulder. And here I am, working on the right side of the law."

"Funny, we have similar backgrounds. I think I mentioned before that my mother took off when Cory was young. The truth of the matter is she discovered she loved drugs more than she loved her husband and her kids. Cory was about four when my father told her she had to leave. She came around a couple more times after that looking for money, and when my father refused to give her any, she finally disappeared for good."

She picked up her glass and finished the last of her lemonade. "One of the final times she came to the house, I remember she hugged me and told me how much she loved me and then asked me for my allowance. I was so mad at her that I told her I never wanted to see her again, and I didn't. My dad tried to hold it together, but when Cory was thirteen, he died of a heart attack."

Her whole body ached as she remembered those moments when her mother had held her close, stroking her hair and telling her how much she loved her. She had so wanted to believe, had needed to believe that her mother had changed and their family would be put back together. When her mother had asked for Marlena's allowance money, it had irrevocably broken any mother-daughter bond that might have survived.

"I guess we both got tough breaks," he said. His features were no longer visible in the darkness that had finally claimed the area.

For a few minutes they sat in silence, and Marlena wondered what he was thinking. What scars had been left behind by his mother's absence and father's brutality? By life itself?

"You think they're dead, don't you?" she asked. It had been a question that had tormented her since the morning she'd awakened to find Sam, Daniella and Macy gone; a question she'd been afraid to ask until this very moment.

"It's possible that they're still alive. We can always hope for the best," he answered after a long hesitation.

She was grateful that it was dark enough that she couldn't see his features, for she heard the lie in his voice but was glad she didn't have to see it in his eyes.

Minutes later, after he'd gone inside, Marlena remained in the chair, watching the fireflies begin to take over the area. Tears blurred her vision as she remembered Macy chasing the flashing bugs and her squeals of delight when she managed to capture one in a jar.

How Marlena wished Macy was out there now, chasing fireflies, her laughter filling the air. How she wished Daniella and Sam were sitting on the porch with her, enjoying the last of the evening before bedtime.

As the sound of bullfrogs rose in the air, a shiver swept up her spine as she thought of her plunge into the pond. She no longer knew if she'd really been pushed or had stumbled and fallen off the path and into the lake. It all felt like a bad dream now, unclear and fuzzy.

But the night air suddenly felt fraught with danger, and she quickly jumped up from her chair and went inside, even knowing that for Sam and Daniella and little Macy, the house hadn't been a safe haven.

SUNDAY EVENING GABRIEL told his two agents to take the next day off. Their Sunday had been a long one, and he felt as if they all needed a little downtime to clear their heads.

On Monday morning, Gabriel was still in bed when Jackson and Andrew knocked on his door and asked if he wanted to go with them for breakfast at a café in town. He declined, but as he went downstairs to the dining room and heard Marlena humming from the kitchen, he was sorry he hadn't gone with his two partners.

As he poured himself a cup of coffee from the pot in the dining room, he realized he liked the sound of her humming. It was an unfamiliar but pleasant feminine noise he'd never enjoyed before.

He followed it into the kitchen and paused and watched as she stirred a big pot of what smelled like rich spaghetti sauce. He noticed that her bottom wiggled with each stir of the big spoon.

"I checked out your boyfriend last night," he said.

She whirled around, obviously startled by his presence. "You scared me." She placed the spoon in the spoon rest. "And he's not my boyfriend." She grabbed a cup of coffee that was on the nearby counter, then sat at the table and motioned for him to join her.

He hesitated. He could smell her scent, clean from a morning shower, sprayed with the fresh floral fragrance that had imprinted itself into his head. Her scent, combined with the tomato-and-herb odor of the sauce, somehow brought to his mind what home might smell like.

Stop it, he mentally commanded himself. He sat at the table and tried to staunch the alien thoughts that drifted through his mind.

She sat across from him and looked at him expectantly. "So what did you find out about Thomas, and how on earth did you do it so quickly?"

"Ah, the wonder of the internet and the magic of the FBI's powers." He paused to take a drink of his coffee and then continued. "Thomas Brady, thirty-seven years old. Never married, no criminal background—the man appears on paper to be squeaky clean."

"That's good to know."

"I still need to have a face-to-face meeting with him and check out his alibi. Just because somebody has managed to keep a clean record doesn't necessarily mean he's not a bad guy."

Marlena frowned, the dainty line dancing in the center of her forehead doing nothing to detract from her beauty. "I can't imagine Thomas being so upset that he would do something terrible to the family." She got up from her chair. "You want some breakfast? I've got bacon already cooked, and it would take me just a minute to fry up a couple of eggs."

"Okay, if it isn't too much trouble," he replied. Maybe he would find her less distracting if she was doing something instead of sitting across from him and gazing at him with her amazing eyes.

"Sam and Daniella never talked about having a will?" he asked as she moved across the room to the refrigerator.

"Never. It wasn't something we would have talked about." She carried the egg carton to the counter next to the stove. "Scrambled, over easy or hard cooked?" she asked.

"Scrambled is fine. Pamela seemed to think that if Sam and Daniella had a will, then Macy would be a beneficiary and so would you."

Marlena laughed and turned to face him. "I told you before, there's no way I would be in any will. Daniella would never do that. This bed-and-breakfast was her dream from the time she was a teenager, but she knew it was never mine." She turned back around to the counter and placed two slices of bread in the toaster, then moved an iron skillet over a heating burner.

"Daniella knew that my plan in the next couple of months was to move to either Baton Rouge or New Orleans. She and Sam paid me a good wage, and I've managed to squirrel away most of it so I can go to college and get my teaching degree. I've even made Cory put half of his paycheck each week into a savings account so that when we get to the city, he can enroll in a trade school. Daniella would have never left me this place because she knew I wouldn't want it."

She looked at him again with a wry smile. "I guess that removes me as a suspect with a financial motive."

"You've pretty much been taken off my suspect list anyway," he replied.

"Thanks. I appreciate your clarity."

He was surprised by the small burst of laughter that escaped him. "That's about the only clarity I've had about this case so far."

She turned back around, and as she tended to his

breakfast, they fell into silence. He sipped his coffee and stared out the window where a flower bed exploded with a variety of colorful blooms.

"John came up clean, too," he said as she set his plate before him and then rejoined him at the table. "What do you know about him?"

She shrugged, her bare, faintly freckled shoulders enchanting him. "I know he's from New Orleans but used to work for some big hotel in Shreveport, and was looking for a change of pace and a smaller town. When he saw the ad that Sam had run in the paper, he applied for the job and then came here for a visit."

"Apparently Sam liked what he saw in the young man," Gabriel said as he picked up a slice of his toast.

"I like what I see in John. He's been like a big brother to Cory, and he seems to know everything there is to know about plants and trees and flowers. I think he has a degree in horticulture. He came here with a glowing recommendation from his former job." She frowned. "Surely he isn't on your suspect list. Sam and John got along great, and he was considered part of the family."

Gabriel fell silent as he ate his breakfast, his thoughts going over what little they knew about the disappearance. He had no idea specifically what time the family had vanished. They had now been missing over three days, and his hope to find them alive was shrinking.

"Our suspect list stinks, we have no real leads to follow and we're no closer to figuring out what happened to the family than we were when we first arrived," he said with disgust. He shoved his empty plate aside and reached for his coffee cup.

Marlena got up and went for his plate, but before she grabbed it, she laid her hand over the back of his. His heart stopped as she gazed at him, her smaller hand warm over his.

He fought an impulse to snatch his hand away, unaccustomed to anyone touching him for any reason. She offered him a smile of encouragement. "You're going to figure this out, Gabriel. I just know you and your men are going to get to the bottom of things." She gave his hand a quick squeeze and then released it, leaving him feeling oddly bereft.

As she moved to the sink with his plate, he once again stared out the window, his thoughts jumbled with both the crime and her. She topped up their coffee and then sat across from him.

"Tell me about the people on your suspect list," she said.

"To be honest, we don't even have a real suspect list at the moment. All we have is a person of interest list."

"Then tell me about your persons of interest."

He leaned back in the chair. "Your boyfriend, until I can check his alibi." He'd deliberately called Thomas that to get her reaction.

His reward was the flash of aggravation in her delicious green eyes. "He is not my boyfriend." She must have seen a spark of something in his eyes, for she suddenly grinned. "Ah, the big dark FBI agent does have a sense of humor after all."

"I have my moments," he said easily. "In any case,

for now Thomas Brady is on my list, along with Ryan Sherman."

"I'd forgotten about Ryan," she said. "He's a thug, a creep, and he hated Sam with a passion. Of course, he hates anyone who has anything to do with law enforcement."

"The problem is that Ryan has an alibi. He was supposedly with his girlfriend the night of the disappearance. The other issue is, if somebody took the family and is keeping them alive, then they have to have a place for them. There's no way Ryan would be keeping hostages in his dinky apartment. Jackson spent some time Saturday morning at City Hall checking to see if Ryan owns any other property in the area, but we came up with nada."

"His parents own some property out in the boondocks. I think Ryan does mechanic work on the side in an old shed out there."

"You have an address?" Gabriel asked.

"No, but I can give you directions."

He held up his finger and then pulled his cell phone from his pocket. He called Jackson and explained the situation to him, and then put Marlena on the phone to give him the directions.

"Check it out and get back to me," he said to Jackson when Marlena handed his phone back to him.

"We're on it," Jackson replied, and then the two men disconnected. Gabriel pocketed his cell phone, but was surprised to realize he wasn't in a hurry to leave the kitchen or Marlena.

He told himself it was because she might hold some nugget of information that could advance the case, such as the fact that Ryan's parents owned a place where perhaps people could be stashed. Who knew what other little tidbits she had that she didn't even realize might be helpful for finding anyone who posed a threat to the family.

He told himself he was here at the table with her because he still believed she was part of the key to solving the mystery of whatever happened to the Connellys.

He assured himself it had nothing to do with the sunshine in her curls, the graceful motion she displayed when she got out of her chair to stir the sauce and then return to the table or the warmth of her smile when she gazed at him.

"We know they weren't taken for ransom because we haven't received any kind of a money demand for their safe return," he said, trying to focus on business and not the pleasure of her company.

"Who would pay any kind of ransom? Neither Sam nor Daniella had family, and although this place holds its own, they aren't exactly millionaires," she replied.

"I keep thinking there had to be more than one perp. Otherwise how could a single person control three people at the same time, one of them a seasoned FBI agent?"

"Simple," she replied. "It was love that kept them easily controlled."

He looked at her curiously, wondering if she was being silly, but her eyes held a glow of knowing, of certainty that told him she was being serious.

"Love?" Disbelief laced his tone.

"All it would take would be a single person getting through the back door and putting a gun to Sam's head. Daniella and Macy would instantly become compliant to whatever he told them to do. It would be the same thing if somebody threatened Daniella or Macy. It would only take a threat to any one of them to effectively neutralize the others because of their enormous love for one another."

"I've never experienced that kind of love for or from anyone," he said.

She gazed at him for several long moments, her eyes holding a wealth of emotion. "That's the saddest thing I've ever heard."

He felt the need to escape, run from the faint pity in her eyes, the cozy atmosphere of the kitchen and the feeling that somehow he was missing an integral piece of what made up a human being.... He was missing a heart.

Chapter Six

For the next several days Marlena scarcely saw the three agents who were living in the house. They ate a quick breakfast each morning and then took off for town to sniff out whatever they could about the disappearance.

There had been nothing on Ryan Sherman's parents' acreage to indicate that the Connellys had ever been there. Even though they had considered Brian Walker, the ex-mayor, as a nonplayer, they'd checked his finances to make sure he hadn't made a big withdrawal that would indicate the possibility of a kidnapping or killing for hire.

Marlena learned bits and pieces about the investigation as she served them their meals each evening. Since that long-ago morning in the kitchen, Gabriel hadn't sought her out for any conversations, and instead he had distanced himself from her.

She told herself it didn't matter, that he meant nothing to her. Besides, they were obviously two people with very different ideas about love.

Marlena wanted—needed—to believe that eventually she would be deeply in love with somebody who loved her back. She wanted the husband and the house, a couple of kids and a dog. Love had already kicked her hard in the butt while she'd been living in Chicago, but that hadn't turned her off the idea of everlasting love; it had only made her yearn for it more.

But love hadn't saved Sam and Daniella and Macy. Somebody had possibly manipulated their love for each other to do harm. And with each day that passed, she couldn't imagine who that person might be.

Thomas's alibi still hung in the balance as far as Gabriel, Andrew and Jackson were concerned. Although records showed that Thomas had checked into a motel in New Orleans for a week prior to the disappearance, and he had worked on a deck for a family residence, there were increments of time missing when Thomas couldn't tell the FBI exactly where he'd been or what he'd been doing.

Considering the approximate time of night that the disappearance had occurred, it was possible he would have had enough leeway to drive back to Bachelor Moon, do something with the family and then be at his motel again for the breakfast buffet the next morning.

She could feel the frustration of the agents each night when they settled in the dining room for the evening meal, a frustration that let her know they were no closer to solving the mystery.

How long could they remain here trying to solve a crime that had no clues? With no trails to follow? When would this become a cold case with no answers, and when did somebody decide for sure that it had changed from an open investigation to a hunt for bodies?

It had been a week ago tonight that the Connellys had disappeared, leaving behind empty glasses of milk and uneaten cookies. Marlena knew from the FBI inquiries that their bank accounts hadn't been touched, their ATMs and credit cards hadn't been accessed. The family was just…gone.

And how long did she and Cory stay here? Wondering, hoping that Sam and Daniella and Macy would magically walk through the front door and declare that it had all been a joke, a spur-of-the-moment vacation?

As she fixed the evening meal of roasted chicken and vegetables, she listened for the front door, knowing that if the agents stayed true to their schedule of the past few days, they should be walking in any minute.

It was crazy how much she'd missed the quiet moments of conversation with Gabriel. He not only drew her on a physical level, but since she'd seen a glimpse into his past, he drew her on an emotional level, too. But she knew that was dangerous to her own mental health.

He was a man who didn't believe in love, and she was a woman who desperately believed and wanted that in her life. He obviously had no desire for home and hearth, and the desire for such a thing was integral to who she was as a woman.

She'd just pulled the chicken and veggies out of the oven when she heard the front door open. Setting the large pan of food on a cooling rack, she left the kitchen and went through the great room to see all three men wearing the wearied expressions of another fruitless day.

"Dinner is ready whenever you all want to eat," she said. Although she spoke to all three, her gaze lingered on Gabriel. His eyes held the darkness of frustration, and the lines of his face indicated not just a physical weariness but a soul-deep weariness, as well.

What she wanted to do was walk to him and pull him into her arms. What she wanted to do was caress the tired lines that creased across his forehead, to do something that would ease some of the torment he obviously felt.

"Give us fifteen minutes to wash up, and then we'll be down," Andrew said, already heading up the stairs.

As the other men followed him, Marlena turned and went back into the kitchen. The table in the dining room was already set, so she placed the two chickens on a big serving plate and the veggies in a large dish, and carried them to the table with her first two trips. She'd also made a cherry Jell-O salad and hot, yeasty rolls.

With the entire meal on the table, she returned to the kitchen and poured herself a glass of iced tea, then sat at the kitchen table and stared out the window.

They were all in a state of limbo, waiting for people who might never return, afraid to leave without answers. She'd planned to head to one of the bigger cities with Cory in the next couple of months, but wondered if maybe she needed to move up their plans to go.

Pamela would be thrilled to take over the daily running of the bed-and-breakfast in Daniella's absence, and Marlena knew the woman was competent enough to make sure it was all done to Daniella's high standards.

No will had been found in any of the paperwork Sam kept in the office. So what would happen to this place if Daniella and Sam never returned?

Long after dinner was over and she'd cleaned up the kitchen, she carried a glass of iced tea out to one of the wicker rockers on the porch. Cory had stopped in earlier to let her know that he and John were going to the movies to see the latest action-adventure release that was playing.

As always, Marlena thanked the stars for John's friendship with her brother. Cory would have gone stark raving mad here if not for John's company.

She rocked the wicker chair and sipped her tea as she watched the sun dip lower in the sky. "No place are the sunsets prettier than in Louisiana," Gabriel said as he stepped out on the porch, a glass of tea in his hand.

She sat up straighter, surprised by his appearance as he eased into the chair next to hers. Instantly she was overwhelmed by the scent of minty soap, shaving cream and that now-familiar woodsy cologne, letting her know he'd recently taken a shower.

"I think the sunsets here in Bachelor Moon are pretty spectacular, because they don't have to fight with city skylines or bright lights," she replied.

"Dinner was delicious."

She smiled at him. "Thanks. I don't claim to be a professional chef, but thank goodness Daniella has some great cookbooks and all I have to do is follow directions."

He placed his tea on the table between them and then rubbed the center of his forehead, as if to ease his pain. "Headache?" she asked sympathetically.

He nodded and dropped his hand to his lap. "I woke up with it this morning, and it's been relentless."

"Want some aspirin or something?"

"No, thanks. I know it's just a bad case of stress." He released a deep sigh. "This has been the case from hell. We've spent the past week spinning our wheels and getting little information for our efforts. I even checked to make sure Frank Mathis is still in prison."

"He is, isn't he?"

"He's safe behind bars and completely out of the picture for whatever happened here a week ago."

"It feels like they've been gone forever," Marlena said, her throat closing up as she felt the imminence of tears. "I can't imagine them not being in my life in one way or another."

"I wish I could promise you a happy ending," he said softly. "But to be perfectly honest, I don't have a clue how this all might end. I think this may be one of the most frustrating cases I've ever worked."

"I just wish I could be of more help, but I've gone over and over it in my mind, and I can't think of anyone who would have the capacity or the desire to kidnap Sam, Daniella and Macy." Her voice cracked slightly with emotion and she reached for her tea as if a swallow would wash away the pain in her heart.

She took a drink and then cleared her throat. "What happens if you don't find out the answers? How long will your director allow you to work a case where there are no clues, no leads to follow?"

"I don't know. Right now he's given us no indication he wants us pulled off the case." He sat up a little taller in the chair. "The one thing I've learned while doing this work is that you never know when a clue will drop in your lap, when something will occur or some information will be learned that forms a lead.

We've only had a week, and in the world of criminal investigations that's just a minute."

As the sun began to fully dip below the horizon and the shadows of night crept in, Marlena stood, taking her tea glass with her. "Since the night of my impromptu swim, I'm no longer comfortable sitting out here when it gets dark."

"Do you still think somebody intentionally shoved you in the pond?" He grabbed his glass and also rose from his chair.

She frowned thoughtfully. "I'm not sure right now what I think about that night. It's possible that I was so freaked out by the family's disappearance that I imagined I was pushed when I actually just stepped the wrong way."

"You haven't felt threatened by anyone or anything since then?" he asked.

She realized they stood too close to each other, that his eyes, normally midnight blue and so hard to read, appeared softer in the glow of twilight.

"No, nothing." She turned quickly and went into the house. He followed behind her, and as she placed her glass in the kitchen sink, he did the same.

They were close together, facing each other in what felt like a void of time, of space. She knew she should say good-night and move away, but she was frozen in place, unable to speak, unable to move. His close proximity to her made her feel trapped, forbidden to escape even if she'd wanted to.

Her heart thundered as he took a step closer to her. "I've been fighting the need to do this since I first saw you on the front porch a week ago." His voice was a mere whisper as he raised a hand and drew it softly through her curls.

He nodded as if satisfied. "I knew it would be soft as silk." He dropped his hand from her hair and instead ran his thumb across her bottom lip. "I've also wanted to do this since the moment I saw you."

Before she could draw a breath or prepare in any way for what she knew was about to happen, his mouth covered hers in a fiery kiss that was directly at odds with the dispassionate man she'd thought him to be.

He tasted of sweetened tea and hot desire, and she opened her mouth to him as his arms wrapped around her and pulled her close.

A little voice inside her head told her this shouldn't be happening, but it was happening, and it was wonderful. His body was solid against hers, and she instantly knew he was aroused.

Their tongues battled together as if desperate to explore and know each other, as if both of them knew this explosion of simmering lust that had existed between them would never happen again, culminating in this, their first and last kiss.

It was he who broke the kiss, dropping his arms from around her and jumping back as if she were on fire.

His ragged breathing matched her own as he stared at her. "I just had to know," he said. "And now I do, and that won't happen again." Without waiting for her response, he turned and left the kitchen.

GABRIEL SAT IN the Rusty Nail Tavern just off Main Street in Bachelor Moon, nursing a beer alone at the end of the counter. Most of the people who shared the space with him knew that he was one of the FBI agents who'd come to town to investigate the Connellys' disappearance, and he knew that most of them didn't like the fact that he'd invaded their space.

He wasn't a native. He wasn't one of them. Nobody approached him, and that was just fine with him. He was doing what he did best—watching people, eavesdropping on conversations, perfectly satisfied being alone.

It had been two nights since he'd kissed Marlena and he was still trying to get the taste of her out of his mouth. He took a drink of his beer as if that would do the trick, and his gaze constantly moved over the Saturday-night crowd.

Was the perp in the room right now? Silently crowing over how easily he'd managed to fool the agents who had been sent here to investigate? Gabriel tightened his hand around the neck of his beer bottle. Within days it would be two full weeks since the Connelly family had last been seen, and they were no closer to having any answers.

This case was driving him crazy. *She* was driving him crazy. That kiss had been one of the biggest mistakes he'd ever made in his life, for now it was emblazoned on his brain, and he couldn't stop thinking about kissing her again.

He took another pull of his beer, wondering if they were ever going to get a break on this case. For the past couple of days, he and Andrew and Jackson had beat feet across the town, checking abandoned storefronts, empty storage units, old barns and sheds, anywhere that a family of three could be stashed away and anyplace bodies could have been disposed.

They'd listened to gossip, to rumors and had chased down a dozen dead ends. With each day that passed, his belief that the Connelly family was alive had slowly died. He believed it was just a matter of time before their bodies were discovered by somebody walking in a field, strolling through a forest or fishing near a swamp.

What he found hard to accept was that it was possible he and his small team of two would leave here and never have any answers, never know who was responsible.

If he looked deep inside himself, he also knew that he found it hard to believe he would leave here without following through on that steamy kiss he'd stolen from Marlena.

He wanted more.

He wanted a lot more from her.

He wanted to slide his mouth down her neck, cup her bare breasts in his hands while she moaned in acquiescence. It had nothing to do with love or romance. It had nothing to do with anything but the raging lust she created inside him.

What made it so difficult to get out of his head was the fact that he thought she felt the same way about him. She'd eagerly accepted his kiss, had pressed herself against him as if she'd been willing to give him more. And he'd wanted to take more.

"Smells like pig in here—a big fat federal pig," a deep voice said from nearby.

Gabriel turned to see Ryan Sherman and his girlfriend, Tammy, seated at a table for two near the bar. Gabriel whirled around on his bar stool and stared at them. He mentally groaned. He was in no mood to deal with a yahoo. Ryan apparently didn't realize he was baiting a pit bull.

Gabriel continued to stare at Ryan, almost begging him to do something stupid so Gabriel could fly into action and get rid of the energy building inside him. But Tammy placed a hand on Ryan's arm and whispered in his ear, and Ryan broke the intense, challenging stare, and instead got up and wandered toward the pool tables on the other side of the room.

Gabriel turned around, finished his beer and checked his watch. Nearly midnight. The crowd had begun to thin out a bit, and he knew if he had one more beer, it would be one too many to drive back to the bed-and-breakfast. It was time to leave.

He hadn't invited Andrew or Jackson to come along with him to the tavern. As much as he liked them, he'd needed a break from them, too. They would be in their room by now, their deep snores mingling to create a discordant form of music.

As he left the bar, the night air wrapped around him, thick and humid and with the tang of ozone that preceded an approaching storm. As he got into the car, he saw in the distance a zigzag of lightning split the darkness of the black, clouded sky.

If he was lucky, he would make it to the bed-and-breakfast before the storm hit. Driving with his window down, breathing in the heavy, thick air, the distant rumble of thunder pealed and he stepped on the gas, eager to get inside before the wind and rain arrived.

He felt as if the storm was inside of him, and he understood the interior tumult mirrored the unstable atmosphere around him. He also knew the genesis of his unhinged emotions.

Marlena.

It had only been nine days since he'd met her, and yet he felt as if he'd wanted her for an entire lifetime, as if he had been born wanting her, and he wouldn't be satisfied until he had her.

It's the beer talking, he tried to tell himself as he pulled up in front of the house and parked the car. He got out of the vehicle and stood, taking several deep breaths of the wildness of the night around him, flinching slightly as a slash of lightning slivered brilliantly in the stormy skies. It was followed within seconds by a loud clap of thunder, letting him know the storm was nearly upon him.

He used the key Marlena had given him to enter through the front door quietly. He relocked it behind him, but before going upstairs, he needed a big glass of water. He'd learned a long time ago that the best chaser for too many beers was water. It helped to keep a morning hangover to a minimum.

He crept through the darkness of the great room and dining room, guided by the small night-light in the kitchen.

Stepping into the kitchen, he froze at the sight of Marlena standing in front of the opened refrigerator door, clad only in a short filmy pink nightgown. As if sensing his presence, she closed the refrigerator, her eyes wide as she looked at him.

Lightning flashed in the room as he took several steps toward her, unable to stop himself even if he'd wanted to. He felt as if the wicked hand of fate was at work, and he was helpless not to follow where it led.

Without saying a word, he approached where she stood with her hand pressed against the fridge. He placed his palms on either side of her on the cool white exterior of the appliance, his arms effectively trapping her in place.

He was wild with want, and couldn't help but notice that her breasts rose and fell in a rapid rhythm that matched the quickened beating of his heart. Her nipples were outlined against the thin material of her nightgown as if to taunt him, as if inviting his touch.

"Are you drunk?" she finally asked, her voice husky and breathless.

"Apparently not drunk enough," he replied, and then took her mouth with his as he pressed against her. If she was smart, she'd smell the wildness on him, run from it… Run from him.

But she apparently wasn't smart, for instead of running away from him, she looped her arms around his neck, pulled him closer and opened her mouth to him.

He was vaguely aware of thunder and lightning and rain beginning to pelt the windows, and then he was conscious of nothing but kissing Marlena.

Her soft floral scent surrounded him, invading his senses to the point that nothing else mattered but her. He would have her tonight. He knew it by the fire in her kiss, by the way her body met his in mindless yearning.

He would have her tonight, and then this desperate wanting of her would finally be satiated, and he'd be done with her haunting his thoughts, invading his dreams.

Chapter Seven

Marlena had known she was in trouble the minute she'd seen him in the kitchen doorway. A primal energy had wafted from him, an energy that fed one inside of her.

She knew what he wanted, and she wanted it, too. From the moment he had kissed her two nights before, she'd known that eventually they would make love. *No, not make love,* she mentally corrected herself. She'd known they would have sex.

She wouldn't delude herself into believing that what they were about to do had anything to do with love. He was a man who couldn't love, but still she somehow knew he could take her to sexual splendor, and at the moment that was enough.

It was the last rational thought she had as Gabriel's lips plied hers with fire, and he ground his hips against hers, letting her know he was already fully aroused.

There had been instant tension between them from the moment they'd first met, and now she recognized that it had been physical desire, a desire nearly impossible to deny even if she had wanted to.

As his lips left hers and blazed a slow trail down her throat, she tangled her fingers through his thick dark hair and whispered his name.

He leaned back and looked at her, as if expecting her to tell him this was enough, that he needed to go to his room now and stop what they both knew was about to happen.

"Come with me to my room," she said, taking any doubt out of the situation.

He stepped back from her, his eyes glowing as another flash of lightning momentarily lit the room. "Are you sure?" His voice was taut with tension.

As a reply she took his hand firmly in hers and led him into her private quarters. He stood in the center of the sitting room as she locked the door, and then he followed her into the bedroom, where a small lamp pooled a glow from the nightstand.

She turned, and before she could say anything or draw a single breath, she was back in his arms, his mouth covering hers in a kiss that seared her to her very core.

They fell onto her bed, their embrace unbroken, his mouth still covering hers. The tumult of the storm was personified in her bedroom, barely restrained, as he fumbled with his buttons to remove his shirt.

She helped him, wanting to feel his naked chest, to run her fingers across his warm, firm muscles. When his shirt was finally undone, he broke the kiss, sat up, shrugged out of the shirt and threw it into the darkness beyond the bed.

She watched hungrily as he stepped from the bed, kicked off his shoes and pulled off his socks then removed his slacks, leaving him clad only in a pair of black boxers. The light from the bedside table loved his skin, emphasizing lean muscle and wiry strength. With eyes that glittered with unbridled need, he returned to the bed and pulled her back into his arms.

His skin was fevered as his legs wound around hers, and she grabbed hold of his broad, bare shoulders. They kissed again, his mouth feeling as if he touched her everywhere.

He broke the kiss and stared at her, the faint light dancing silver shards in the depths of his blue eyes. "You know that tomorrow it will be as if all of this never happened."

She heard the words he didn't say, words to let her know this night meant nothing to him, that it wasn't the beginning or the end of anything. It just was.

She nodded. "I know, and that's okay with me."

It was as if these simple words unleashed the most powerful part of the storm. He grabbed the hem of her nightgown and pulled it up and off her, leaving her clad only in a small pair of matching panties.

"You are so beautiful," he said, his voice deep and husky as his gaze lingered on her bare breasts. He cupped them with his hands and rubbed his thumbs over her nipples until they were taut and aching. "I haven't been able to get you out of my mind."

When he drew one of her nipples into his mouth, a moan of pleasure escaped her. He teased the tip, licking and sucking as she tangled her hands in his hair and pulled him closer, tighter against her.

In all of her twenty-seven years, she'd never known the need she felt at this moment, never experienced the kind of out-of-control passion she felt now for him… for Gabriel.

As he continued to tease and lick her nipples, first

one and then the other, one of his hands slid down the flat of her stomach. Her breath caught as he rubbed his hand over her intimately, the only barrier the silk panties she still wore.

His hand heated the silk, and she arched her hips up to encourage the contact. She was on fire, and he was the only person who could put out her flame.

She reached down and wrapped her hand around his hard length, shielded only by the cotton of his boxers. He released a groan as she squeezed slightly and moved her hand up and down.

He allowed her to continue for only moments, and then rolled away from her and took off his boxers. This time when he kissed her, he started in the center of her breasts and nipped and licked downward.

She stopped breathing in anticipation as his mouth moved along her stomach and then whispered across her panties, warming her with his breath. He removed her panties by inches as she raised her hips to aid him. When his mouth touched her there, she climaxed and cried his name again and again.

As she came back to earth, he hovered between her thighs, his boxers gone, his face taut and beautiful with his need for her.

She grabbed his tight butt and pulled him forward, reveling in his need, welcoming her own. He slid into her with a deep sigh, and then his lips found hers in a kiss of aching tenderness.

He ended the kiss and then began to stroke, slow and deep inside her. Their breaths became pants as his motions became faster, more frantic, and she felt the rise of exquisite pleasure building again inside her.

She clung to him, encouraging the piston of him rubbing against her, into her, until she flew over the edge at the same time he stiffened with his own release.

They remained locked together, their breathing ragged as faint thunder sounded, indicating that the storm had passed. He finally moved off her and stood. He grabbed his boxers from the floor and stepped into them, then grabbed his shirt and pants, as well.

"Just think of this as a dream you had," he said, and then he was gone from the bedroom. A moment later she heard the sound of the door leading to the kitchen open, then close.

She remained in bed, satiated and drowsy and feeling like it had all been some sort of crazy dream. But the scent of him lingered on her sheets, and her body still retained his imprint.

Reluctantly she got out of bed, picked up her panties and nightgown from the floor and went into the bathroom. Minutes later she was back in bed, but sleep was the last thing on her mind.

She'd awakened earlier and felt hungry. She'd been staring at the contents of the refrigerator trying to decide on a late-night snack when he'd appeared, and any appetite she might have had for food had disappeared.

Her head was filled with Gabriel. Although she had told him she'd pretend they'd never had sex, that this night would mean nothing in the light of dawn, she knew she had lied.

Although she had no expectations from him, understood that this night would remain just a single night of hot sex in his mind, she would hold it tight in her heart to be remembered whenever she thought about how fragile life could be, how haunted she'd felt when Sam and Daniella and little Macy had disappeared.

She would retain this memory inside her mind, inside her heart, because being in Gabriel's arms tonight had made her feel safe and loved, even though she knew it had been a false illusion.

She awakened before dawn, and after a shower she headed into the kitchen to start the coffee and think about what the men might want for breakfast.

As she got out the ingredients to make waffles, she consciously shoved thoughts of Gabriel from her head. When the coffee had finished brewing, she poured herself a cup and stood at the kitchen window, watching the sun peek over the horizon.

There was no sign of the storm that had passed in the middle of the night, just like she knew not to expect Gabriel to even acknowledge that anything had happened between them, either.

As she sipped the strong brew, her thoughts turned to the people who were missing from the house. She was losing faith in anyone finding them alive, and that lack of faith horrified her.

Like the men working the case, a deep frustration welled up inside her. Who could have taken the Connellys? Why had they been taken?

And when was it time for her and Cory to leave here? There was a part of her that wanted to flee the pain of being here, where shadows of the missing danced in every corner, yet there was also a part of her that felt anchored here. She felt like a caretaker who had been given the responsibility for maintaining this place until Daniella returned.

With each long day that passed, she had a terrible feeling deep in her heart that Daniella was never coming back. She left the window and sat at the table, the last place the family had been before their disappearance.

She looked up in surprise as Andrew walked into the kitchen carrying a cup of coffee from the pot in the dining room. "You're an early bird this morning," she said.

He grinned and joined her at the table. "I went to bed early last night and slept deep and hard." He took a sip of his coffee, leaned back in the chair and looked out the window. "It's so peaceful here. It's hard to believe that anything bad ever happened."

"It's getting more and more difficult for me to hold on to my faith that they'll be returned safe and sound," she replied, the ache in her heart audible in the softness of her voice.

Andrew gazed at her, his brown eyes soft with sympathy. "I think missing persons cases are the worst. It's like a state of limbo that never ends. Even if they're gone for good, it would be nice if we could find them and give everyone who loved them a sense of closure."

"I'd rather get my closure by you all finding them alive," she said.

He nodded. "That's what we'd all like to happen." He frowned thoughtfully. "But I have to be truthful with you—the statistics are working against us with every day that passes and they aren't found."

"I know," she replied somberly. "I'm making waffles for breakfast this morning," she said, needing a change of topic. "Do you want me to go ahead and whip up some now, or should we wait until your partners are up and around?" she asked.

"Jackson was in the shower when I left the room. Who knows when Gabriel will be up. He went into town late last night for some alone time and a few beers. Thank the Lord he isn't the type to get drunk and do anything stupid," he said with a wry grin. "That man is definitely all work and no play."

Marlena jumped up from the table. "I'll go ahead and get started on the waffles," she said.

Special Agent Gabriel Blankenship was all work and no play, except for last night in a dream that she knew she'd never forget.

GABRIEL WAS IN a foul mood. At the moment he, Andrew and Jackson were headed toward a storage facility where the owner of the property had indicated one of the units was emitting the smell of decomposition.

But that wasn't what had him in a foul mood. It was Marlena. Last night, he'd thought that he'd rid himself of whatever it was about her that had him itching with the need to possess her. He'd thought that by taking her he'd be rid of her, that she'd be completely out of his mind.

The moment he saw her this morning, he knew he'd been wrong. Just watching her serve them waffles had reset what felt like a ticking time bomb inside him.

Although he'd barely acknowledged her presence, somehow he'd noticed that her peach-colored sundress was cinched at her slender waist, her sandals were gold and she smelled like a bouquet of fresh flowers.

He now clenched the steering wheel tight, trying to

erase the night before from his mind. She'd been more than he'd expected, and he had trouble forgetting the taste of her, the feel of her silky flesh against his.

"I sure hope this is a wild goose chase," Jackson said, pulling Gabriel from thoughts of Marlena. "The last thing I want to find is that family rotting away in some storage unit."

"That makes three of us," Andrew said from the backseat. "I feel bad for Marlena. I was having a cup of coffee with her this morning before the two of you got up and we were talking about how these kinds of cases put the people left behind in limbo. As much as I'd hate to find the Connellys dead, at least that would be some closure for the people at the bed-and-breakfast."

"We all know they're probably dead by now," Jackson said matter-of-factly. "It's been almost two weeks since they disappeared. There has been no ransom demand to give reason for belief that anyone wants to keep them alive."

"Yeah, but the problem is we haven't been able to find anyone who might want them dead," Gabriel replied. Although he, too, believed that the family was dead, he wasn't willing to give up all hope just yet.

The vehicle was filled with the stale air of frustration that had ridden with them each time they headed into the small town of Bachelor Moon.

Gabriel had utilized all the tools he had at his disposal to check into Sam's and Daniella's backgrounds, to see if a red flag would pop up, but there was nothing. He'd checked with Sam's director at the Kansas City field office to see if Sam had worked any cases that might have come back to haunt him, but the odds of that were slim considering Sam had been gone from the agency for over two years.

He'd called his own director this morning to check in and to admit that they still had no clues, no trail, no way to advance the investigation. He'd been hoping that they'd be pulled off the case, that he'd be forced to leave Bachelor Moon and the temptation of Marlena Meyers behind, but that hadn't happened.

He'd been instructed to give it more time and continue to seek answers. Gabriel knew he had to forget his preoccupation with Marlena and get back to focusing solely on solving this mystery.

The storage yard was on the west side of the small town, and as Gabriel pulled up to the tiny building that served as the office, he had a bad feeling in his gut.

If they found the family dead in one of these tin-box units, he could only hope that the perp had left behind some kind of evidence that they could use to hunt him down.

If the family had been killed, Gabriel would not only want to find the killer, but he'd also like to know why they were killed. Motives always intrigued him. As far as he was concerned, the intents of criminals were almost as fascinating as the criminals themselves.

The work was what was important to him, and nothing more. Women came and went, and love was a make-believe emotion that sold Valentine's Day cards and flowers but had nothing to do with his world.

The three of them got out of the car and were met by the manager, a tall, thin older man who introduced himself as Burt Buchannan. "I'm normally not here on Sundays, but I decided after church to come in this afternoon and do a little lawn work. I was weed eating around some of the units this morning and noticed the smell." His long nose wrinkled up as if recalling the foul odor. "I figured you all would want to know who rents it, so I looked it up in my records, and for the past four years, it's been rented by a Carl Gifford."

"We appreciate you calling us so quickly," Andrew said. "We'll try not to take up too much of your time."

Burt shrugged. "Got nobody at home waiting for me. My wife passed three years ago."

"Sorry to hear that. Do you know Mr. Gifford?" Gabriel asked.

Burt shook his head. "I've been working here for over ten years. I had to have met him once when he came in to rent the unit, but I have no real memory of it, and I don't think I've seen him since."

"How does he pay his monthly bill?" Jackson asked.

"It's an automatic draft from his bank account, so he never has to come into the office." Burt gestured toward the official entrance to the storage units. "Everyone who rents a unit gets an electronic card that they swipe, and it opens the gate so people can access their units at all times of the day or night."

"Do you have keys to all the units?" Jackson asked.

Burt nodded. "It's part of the rental agreement that I have a duplicate key to all the units, and no other locks are allowed. You wouldn't believe how many people don't pay after the first month or two and leave me with a shed full of crap locked up that has to be taken away." He pulled a ring filled with keys from his pocket.

"Let's take a look at the unit in question," Gabriel said with a hint of impatience. The sun was hot, he was irritable, and he just wanted to know if the family was here or not. He wanted to solve this case and get the heck out of Dodge.

He needed to be back in Baton Rouge, where meals came from the closest fast-food restaurant or from a can, not served by a sexy woman he couldn't get out of his mind. He wanted his own bed, not the one where he could tell she'd plumped his pillow and pulled up his sheets, because the scent of her was everywhere in the room.

He followed the rest of them through a maze of metal buildings with painted numbers on each one and wondered what was hidden behind the doors, trying to stay focused on the here and now.

They stopped in front of unit 2137. "This is it," Burt said. "If you walk around the back, you can really smell it."

The three agents walked to the rear entrance of the unit where half the weeds had been cut down, and the smell instantly hit Gabriel.

"Oh, wow," Andrew said, and took several steps back from the building as his face turned a faint shade of green.

Andrew had the biggest appetite and the weakest stomach of anyone Gabriel had ever worked with. He grinned as Andrew worked to keep down the big lunch he'd eaten.

The smell of decomposition was one you never forgot and would never mistake for anything else. It had a distinctive odor all its own.

"Something is definitely dead in there," Jackson

drawled. "And whatever it is, it's been dead for a while."

"I doubt that. Decomposition would have happened pretty fast in this tin box in this kind of heat," Gabriel replied. It would be tragic if they opened the unit only to discover that the family had been killed just a day or so earlier.

They walked back around to the front where Burt awaited them. "Open it," Gabriel said, mentally preparing himself for the worst.

Burt fumbled with the keys, seeming to take forever to finally find the right one. He bent down and unlocked the padlock, removed it and then pulled up the garage-style door.

A thick cloud of black flies flew out as the afternoon sunshine filled the inside. The smell was nearly overwhelming, and as Jackson and Gabriel moved forward, Andrew and Burt stepped back.

For a moment Gabriel and Jackson remained frozen in place.

"Sweet Jesus," Jackson finally whispered.

Gabriel stared at the three blood-covered canvases on the concrete floor, each covering something big enough to be a body. His heart dropped to the pit of his stomach.

He'd hoped it wouldn't end like this. He didn't realize until this moment how badly he'd wanted to find the Connellys alive, not just for them, not just for himself but for Marlena, as well.

"Go get some gloves and booties," he said to Andrew.

Andrew ran back to the car to retrieve what was

required. Gabriel looked at the rest of the interior of the unit, seeking something that might aid them in an investigation.

They had one thing in their favor. Even if the name Burt had been given by whomever had rented this place was false, they could follow the money back to the source.

"Why would a criminal who's been smart enough not to leave a single clue behind be stupid enough to use an automatic withdrawal from his bank account to pay for this place?" Jackson asked, his thoughts mirroring Gabriel's.

"Maybe he figured nobody would ever know the bodies were here. Maybe he was just stupid enough not to realize that Burt might smell something funny out here."

"Looks like the only thing in here is whatever is under those canvases and that big dolly." Jackson pointed to a red dolly standing in a far corner. It had probably been used to cart the bodies into the storage unit.

By that time Andrew was back. Both Gabriel and Jackson put on the booties and gloves, and then advanced on the first bloody canvas.

Gabriel had seen a lot of horrible things in his years as an FBI agent, and he'd been desensitized up to a point, but as he approached the corner of the first canvas to see what lay beneath, he prayed the first thing he saw wasn't little Macy's face staring sightlessly in death back at him.

He exchanged a glance with Jackson, who he knew

had to be feeling the same emotions that now roiled through him: dread, disappointment and, finally, failure.

He grabbed the canvas, drew a deep breath and then yanked it back. All the air in his lungs whooshed out of him as he stared at what lay beneath.

"What in the hell?" Jackson's voice rang out with anger as the two of them stared at the big dead, decomposing alligator beneath the canvas.

An overwhelming rage welled up inside Gabriel as he stalked over to the other two forms and threw back the canvases to expose two more decaying alligators.

"Call Sheriff Thompson," he said to Burt. "Tell him he's got a situation out here that needs to be resolved. This isn't our problem."

Gabriel stepped out of the unit, pulled off his gloves and booties and stalked toward the car, aware of Jackson and Andrew hurrying after him.

Chapter Eight

That evening Marlena found Gabriel seated on the sofa in the great room, the television turned on, but the volume so low it couldn't be heard.

He was half sprawled on the sofa, fingers rubbing back and forth in the center of his forehead. She'd heard about the alligator event and knew that it had been a particularly difficult day for the three agents.

"Headache?" she asked sympathetically as she walked into the room.

"A killer," he admitted.

"Can I get you something?"

"It's just stress. Eventually it will go away." There was pain in the sound of his deep voice.

"Sometimes a really good massage helps." She moved around the sofa to stand behind him and placed her fingers on his temples. "May I?" she asked.

He dropped his hand to his lap. "Knock yourself out."

She moved her fingers lightly at his temples and then began to massage with more force, working across his forehead and then back and around to the base of his skull. His thick, soft hair felt good beneath her fingers, but her desire was strictly focused on easing his pain.

He began to relax, his shoulders losing their tenseness, his neck moving more freely with her instead of fighting her.

She didn't know how long she had massaged Gabriel's head before Andrew came downstairs. "Hey, I could use one of those," he said.

Gabriel stiffened and sat up straighter. She dropped her hands from his head. "Do you have a headache, too?" she asked.

Andrew cast her one of his easygoing smiles. "Nah. I'll settle for leftover apple pie from dinner."

"In the refrigerator. Feel free to help yourself," she replied as she walked around the sofa and sat on the opposite end from Gabriel.

"Better?" she asked the moment Andrew disappeared from the room.

"Actually, it is a little better. Thank you, but you didn't have to do that." His dark blue eyes gazed at her with weariness.

"You were in pain. I wanted to do whatever I could to ease that pain," she countered.

"Is that because of what happened between us the other night?" His gaze was wary.

"I don't know what you're talking about. I had an amazing dream the other night, and then I woke up." She frowned at him, wondering what was going on in his head. "Gabriel, don't read anything into it. I was just trying to be nice to you."

He stared at the far wall for a long moment and

then looked back at her. "I'm not used to people being nice," he replied.

"Then you've been running around with the wrong kind of people," she observed. Sensing that he wanted to be alone, that further conversation would only make him more wary, she told him good-night and then went into the kitchen to sit with Andrew for a few minutes at the small kitchen table before turning in for the night.

"Tough day," she said.

Andrew dug a fork into an oversize piece of the left-over pie she'd made that day. "The worst. We were sure that those canvases covered the bodies of your friends. None of us wanted to come back here and tell you that we'd found them in that storage unit." He paused to shovel a large bite into his mouth and washed it down with a sip of milk.

"You like him," he said.

"Who?" she asked, although she knew exactly who he was talking about.

"Gabriel. The air practically snaps when the two of you are in the same room." He eyed her sympathetically. "Just a little word of warning. I've been partners with Gabriel for a couple of years now. He's a tough nut to crack, and he doesn't do love. I wouldn't want you to get hurt."

"Trust me, I know exactly what kind of person Gabriel is. You don't have to worry about me," she said, warmed by his attempt to let her know Gabriel wasn't a man looking for a future with any woman. "What about you? Do you have a girlfriend or wife back in Baton Rouge?"

"Girlfriend, soon to be fiancée," he replied, his eyes

lighting as if merely mentioning her caused his heart to soar. "Her name is Suzi, and she's the love of my life. We've been together for two years, and I'm just about ready to put a ring on her."

"That's nice. She's a lucky woman," she replied and then got up from the table. "And thanks for the warning about my own love life, but it was completely unnecessary. I have no illusions about anything, and now I think I'll say good-night. Just put your dishes in the sink when you're finished."

"Good night, Marlena, and thanks for taking such good care of us."

"My pleasure," she replied and then went into her private quarters.

Minutes later, as she got into bed, her thoughts naturally drifted to Gabriel. Despite Andrew's warnings, and what Gabriel had told her himself, she could love him if he'd let her, if she allowed herself to.

But she couldn't, and tomorrow she intended to ask him if it would be okay for her and Cory to move on, to leave Bachelor Moon and the bed-and-breakfast and begin their new lives. She'd already told Cory to prepare to leave, that their time line had been moved up by the Connellys' disappearance.

She wasn't sure what would happen to the bed-and-breakfast if she left. She assumed Pamela would step in to manage the business until something broke with the case.

Marlena awoke early as usual the next morning, and as she sipped her coffee, she made a list of things she'd need to do to transition from this place that had felt like home for the better part of the past two years to a new city, a new location to start over.

Although she knew Cory would hate to leave here, she also knew he'd do well with the move. He was a friendly kid and would make a circle of friends easily, especially once he was enrolled in a trade school.

She had enough money tucked away to pay for a year of college tuition for herself, and she knew that Cory had enough money in savings to pay for trade school. She could get a job waitressing to pay their living expenses, and life would go on.

Without Daniella. Without Macy and Sam. Her heart ached with their absence, but if there was one thing Marlena had learned over the years, it was that she couldn't control fate and could only deal with the consequences of her own actions and whatever fate cast her way.

Fate had taken away Sam and Daniella and their little girl, and after this much time, deep in her heart she didn't believe they were ever returning.

She stopped her list making to fix breakfast for the men, who were quiet and somber. Even Andrew appeared subdued as he ate his usual big breakfast.

Gabriel barely met her gaze, appearing distracted as he ate quickly and then waited on the front porch for the other two to join him.

Once they had left, Cory and John appeared at the back door looking for breakfast, as well. She fed them bacon and eggs, and then watched at the window as they left the house to get to work in the yard.

With breakfast taken care of, and assuming the men wouldn't be home for lunch, she pulled some thick steaks out of the freezer and washed potatoes for baking for dinner that evening.

By that time Pamela had arrived to do the Monday cleaning. Marlena went into her own quarters to stay out of Pamela's way. There she did a little cleaning of her own, pulling out the dusty old suitcase that she'd brought with her to Bachelor Moon from Chicago and opening it in the storage area to eventually begin to pack.

Pamela worked until one o'clock and then left, her chores taking less time since the only guests were the three men. Once she was gone, Marlena was surprised and a bit dismayed when a knock came at the door, and she looked out to see Thomas Brady on the porch.

"I've been thinking about you all week," he said as she let him inside and gestured him toward the sofa in the great room. "How are you holding up?"

"As well as I can." She sat on the far side of the sofa from him, aware that the agents hadn't yet cleared him off their persons of interest list.

"Is there anything I can do? You must be worried sick about Sam and Daniella and little Macy."

"I am worried," she replied.

"You know I'm here for you whenever you need me, Marlena." His gaze was soft and caring. "I just don't know how to help you through this difficult time."

Even though she felt no personal fear of him, she couldn't help but notice again how much at ease he seemed without Sam and Daniella's presence in the house. His arm was flung across the back of the sofa as if he owned it, and he appeared completely relaxed.

"Maybe what you need is a nice dinner out. Surely

you aren't responsible for feeding the FBI agents seven nights a week. How about this Friday you take some time off for yourself and let me take you out and wine and dine you?"

Marlena realized it was past time to put an end to this romance that never was. "Thomas, I've appreciated your friendship over the past year, but my feelings for you are always just going to be as a friend, nothing romantic."

"Ouch." His smile crumbled and his brown eyes darkened. He pulled his arm from the back of the sofa and leaned toward her. "Are you sure with more time the friendship wouldn't develop into something romantic? Because I have to tell you the truth, Marlena. I definitely feel very romantic feelings toward you, and I have since the moment we met."

"I'm sorry," Marlena replied, truly meaning it. She knew all about unrequited love, about the pain of rejection, but she also knew she couldn't allow Thomas to go on pretending that they were in any way involved in a romantic relationship.

"This isn't something that's going to build into a romance with more time," she replied. "Besides, if the FBI allows it, I intend to move away from here in the next week or so. I'm sorry, Thomas, but you deserve to find a wonderful woman who will love you with all her heart. I'm just not her."

"I knew it," he finally replied. "I knew you didn't feel the same for me as I did for you. I feel it when we're together, but I had hoped with more time it would change." He shrugged and stood. "This place won't be the same without you and Cory around, but I guess I'll be leaving you alone now."

He walked toward the door, and when he reached it, he turned back to look at her. "I hope you have a great life, Marlena. Wherever you go, whomever you wind up with, I wish you only happiness."

"And the same for you," she replied.

She remained on the sofa for a few minutes after he'd gone. Life might have been easier if she'd fallen head over heels in love with Thomas. She believed he was a good man, and found it hard to believe that he might have had anything to do with whatever had happened to the Connelly family. Thomas was a hard worker who lived in a nice ranch house that had more than enough room for a wife and a brother-in-law young enough to be considered a stepson.

Cory could have remained here, working with John. She would have been able to maintain the friendships she'd made in Bachelor Moon, and she knew Thomas was a man who would have been satisfied with her being a homemaker and mother.

But instead she found herself precariously close to loving a man who would never love her back, a man she'd already had steamy-hot sex with and a man who would probably never think of her again once they parted ways.

She could only hope that the beginning of finding true happiness and love was just around the corner, that starting fresh with new purpose and drive would bring different things and exciting people into her life.

Nobody could be as exciting as Gabriel, a little voice

whispered in her head. *Nobody will ever match the way he loved your body,* that voice taunted.

"Shut up," she said aloud, and got off the sofa, deciding that maybe she'd cut some fresh flowers for bouquets for the house.

The late afternoon air was hot and humid as she walked down to the gardening shed, and grabbed a wicker basket and cutting shears. She schooled her mind to blankness as she went about the pleasure of picking out the most colorful blooms that would make the prettiest bouquets.

Daniella had loved to keep the house filled with fresh flowers, and John kept the flower beds blooming throughout the heat of the summer.

By the time she had her basket full, it was almost three o'clock. She put the shears back in the shed and then hurried into the house, hoping to get the bouquets made before it was time to start supper preparations.

As she worked on arrangements, not only for the center of the dining room table but also smaller ones for the bedrooms where the men slept, she found her thoughts drifting to Gabriel.

He'd given her just enough of a peek into his childhood to understand how he felt about love and about loving. She got it, and yet she had responded to her own mother's abandonment by wanting love more than ever. She and Gabriel were flip sides of the same coin.

She would guess that they both suffered abandonment issues, but they had responded in diametrically opposite ways. She could only hope that someday in the future he would discover the desire to love and be loved. Maybe someday a very special woman would be able to break through the shield he'd erected to keep himself from any more pain when it came to love.

It hurt her more than she expected to know that she wasn't that woman. It surprised her to realize how badly she wished she could be that woman for him.

Carrying the two smaller arrangements of flowers up the stairs, she decided to place the one with sweet peas in Gabriel's room. The heady scent of the blooms might please him. He wouldn't know that she'd specifically chosen the prettiest of the arrangements for his room.

Once she'd delivered the flowers, she started down the stairs, but paused on the first step as she heard a noise from someplace behind her.

Before she could turn, before she could consciously assess what kind of sound it had been, hands shoved her back. Just like the night at the pond, she had a moment of weightlessness, only this time there wasn't a dark pond to fall into—there were thirteen steps that in the span of an instant she knew she was going to hit.

GABRIEL, ANDREW AND Jackson stood in Sheriff Thompson's small office as he filled them in on the details of the debacle in the storage unit with the dead gators.

Thompson sat back in his leather chair behind his desk and scratched his protruding belly, then leaned forward with a deep frown cutting across his broad forehead.

"Carl Gifford is a stinking slimy swamp rat whom I've suspected of illegally poaching for years. That storage unit and the banking records finally confirmed it." Thompson shook his head and uttered a small laugh.

"Only an idiot would put his illegal goods in a storage unit paid for every month out of his own bank account."

"I'm sure he never expected anyone else to open up the door to that unit. Where is he now?" Gabriel asked, his stomach knotting as he thought of those first moments staring at the bloody canvases.

"He's been in my custody for the past two nights. Got himself drunk and stupid and assaulted one of my deputies, so I locked him up. Apparently the gators were supposed to be sold to another party the night that I threw him behind bars. He'll be in my jail for a while since I've got all I need now to add the additional charge of poaching."

"So the mystery of the alligators has been solved," Jackson said.

"But it moves us no further in our own investigation," Gabriel added in frustration.

"I wish I could be more help to you all, but I just don't have anything else to give you," Thompson said.

"We appreciate you calling us in to let us know about the gators. It was the damnedest thing I've ever seen," Jackson said, and shook his head in disbelief.

"Let's get out of here," Gabriel said. "I think it's time we call it a day." He thanked the sheriff, and then the three of them headed for their car.

It had been another fruitless day of interviews and walking the streets, and Gabriel was ready to get back to the bed-and-breakfast, out of the heat and humidity.

He was tired. It was the bone weariness of failure, a weight he wasn't accustomed to carrying. He was supposed to be leading this team investigation, and he'd never felt more helpless.

He was out of ideas and out of energy. At the moment the only place he could lead his team was back to the B and B where they would talk over the facts they didn't have, eat without appetites—except for maybe Andrew—and dream about the family they couldn't find.

They rode home in silence, the kind of silence that filled the interior of the car like a pool of stagnant water. Gabriel breathed a deep sigh as he pulled in front of the house. It was early, just before four in the afternoon, but as far as he was concerned, their day was done.

Gabriel was the first one through the door, and he froze at the sight of Marlena sprawled face down on the floor at the foot of the stairs.

Although his heart remained stopped, he raced to her side, relieved to see that she was conscious, but scared to death as he crouched down next to her.

"I fell," she said, and tears began to course from her eyes.

"From where?" he asked as Jackson and Andrew joined him by her side.

"From the top stair."

"Call for an ambulance," Gabriel said urgently. His heart banged painfully against his ribs. Who knew how many bones she might have broken? What kind of internal damage she must be suffering?

"No, I think I'm okay. I've just been afraid to move without anyone here in case I'm not all right." Despite her words, her voice was filled with a pain that rattled through his bones.

"Make the call," Gabriel said.

"Really, I don't think anything is broken." Her green eyes held a wealth of emotion as she gazed at Gabriel. "Just help me sit up and I'll be fine." With a deep moan, she rolled over from her stomach to her back.

Gabriel held up a hand to halt the call Jackson had been about to make, and then he took Marlena's hands in his and pulled her to a sitting position.

"Anything feel broken? Can you move your legs?" Her face was bleached of color, and she winced with the movement. Gabriel didn't release her hands as his heart pounded a million beats a minute. The tightness in his chest eased a little as she managed to move both of her legs.

"I don't think anything is broken. Just help me up off the floor," she said, her gaze never leaving his. It was as if she were tapping into his strength. She didn't realize how little he had. She couldn't know that the sight of her unmoving on the floor had sapped all his energy and had weakened his knees.

He stood and pulled her up. She got to her feet and instantly leaned against his chest, deep sobs escaping her as he ran his hands down the length of her back to assure himself he felt nothing broken.

"I'm taking you to the emergency room," he said as he stared up the staircase that suddenly appeared horrifyingly steep and endless. If she'd fallen from the top, she was lucky she wasn't dead. "You need to be thoroughly checked out by a doctor."

With his decision made, he gently lifted her up in his arms, terrified that he might hurt her more than she already was, yet needing to get her to the hospital as quickly as possible. Andrew opened the front door and then hurried ahead of them to open the passenger side of the car, too.

Gabriel eased her down onto the seat as gently as possible, then went to get behind the wheel. "We'll be back after she's been examined from head to toe." Andrew nodded and stepped away from the car.

Gabriel shot out of the bed-and-breakfast entrance and headed to the small hospital he'd seen in Bachelor Moon. "How long had you been lying there?" he asked, his heart tied in a painful knot as he thought of her on the floor, all alone and hurting.

"Not too long. I never lost consciousness or anything. I tucked and rolled. When I knew I was falling, all I could think about was, if my head hit a stair, I would probably die." She raised her hand to her face and began to quietly weep again.

Gabriel didn't know if it was emotional wounds or physical ones that kept her crying. All he knew was that he needed to get her to the hospital as quickly as possible.

They didn't speak again, and when he pulled in front of the emergency room door, he got out of the car and yelled for assistance. Shock might have allowed her to move, allowed him to pick her up in his arms without her even knowing that she had broken bones or internal injuries. He wasn't about to let her walk in on her own without knowing more about her current condition.

It took only minutes for her to be loaded onto a gurney and whisked away. Gabriel was led to a waiting room where he sank down and worried a shaky hand through his hair.

For just an instant when he'd seen her on the floor,

he'd thought she was dead, and his heart had plummeted with a sharp grief he'd never known before in his life.

And in that instant, he'd recognized that he did care about her. He didn't want to—he had no intention of allowing her any deeper into his heart—but he had to acknowledge that she'd made a little headway where nobody else ever had before.

He jumped as his cell phone rang. He pulled it from his pocket to see Jackson's number. "Hey," he answered.

"We just wanted to let you know that she appeared to be alone in the house when she fell, and we didn't find anything on the stairs that might have made her fall."

"Thanks. I didn't notice what kind of shoes she was wearing. Maybe she just got tripped up in her own feet," Gabriel replied. "We'll know within a couple of hours. She's in with the doctor now, and I imagine they'll want to x-ray every part of her body."

"I hope she's okay. We'll just see you when we see you," Jackson replied.

"One more thing," Gabriel said. "If you see Cory around, you might want to tell him what happened."

"Will do."

Gabriel disconnected and placed his phone in his pocket, then leaned back in his chair and closed his eyes. She could have died. The mere thought increased the beat of his heart.

Thank God she'd been smart. She'd tucked and rolled when most people made the mistake of trying to break their fall and in the process broke bones in their arms or legs, or their necks.

She'd been smart, and she'd been lucky. He just hoped the doctor didn't find something that contradicted that belief. He didn't want her hurt. He didn't want her in pain.

He remembered how she'd massaged his head when he'd had a simple headache, her fingers firm and yet so caring as she'd attempted to work his misery away.

He hadn't been sitting in the waiting room long when Cory came flying in the door, his eyes wild with fear.

"Is she okay?" He started for the door to the examining rooms, but Gabriel stopped him.

"Cory, sit here." He patted the place next to him. "She should be fine. We just need to wait for the doctor to let us know for sure."

Cory sank down, bringing with him the scent of the outdoors, a faint hint of sweat and the unmistakable odor of marijuana.

"Jackson said she fell down the stairs. She could have died." His blue-green eyes looked at Gabriel and filled with a mist of tears. "She's all I've got. If anything happened to her, I don't know what I'd do."

Gabriel clapped the young man on the shoulder. "She's going to be just fine, Cory. She managed to get up, and nothing appeared to be broken."

"But if she hit her head, she could have brain bleeding or something. John told me that's what happened to his mother. She fell down some stairs, and everyone thought she was fine until they found out her brain was bleeding."

"I'm sure the doctor will check Marlena all over," Gabriel assured the young man.

Cory released a deep sigh and dropped his head to his hands, as if silently praying. Gabriel gave him a few minutes of silence.

"Does your sister know you're smoking pot?" Gabriel finally asked softly.

Cory's head shot up and his eyes widened. "What are you talking about?" he replied.

"Come on, Cory. I've been around a long time, and I can smell it on you. Don't try to fool me."

"I just smoke it sometimes," Cory replied defensively. "I got freaked out when I heard about my sister, so I took a few puffs on the way here. Are you going to turn me in to the sheriff?" he asked fearfully.

"No."

"Are you going to narc me out to my sister?"

"I think she has enough on her mind right now, but I'm sure Marlena isn't stupid, either. Smoking dope isn't going to get you anywhere, Cory."

"I know. John has told me the same thing."

"Then you should listen." Gabriel sat back in his seat, deciding enough had been said on the topic. As far as he could tell, Cory was a good kid and hopefully he'd make good choices in his life, but he wasn't Gabriel's problem.

It felt as if they had waited for hours. The two men took turns pacing up and down the length of the waiting room. The longer it took, the more worried Gabriel became. Should he have called for an ambulance? Had he hurt her by moving her? By lifting her up and carrying her?

The memory of the sound of her weeping resonated through him, bringing with it an ache that refused to vanish. He couldn't remember the last time any woman's tears had moved him. Yet hers had.

He didn't want to think about the reason for this anomaly. He didn't want to pull out whatever emotions he felt for Marlena and examine them. He told himself he'd be as worried, as frightened for any person who'd been a caretaker for him and his team for almost two weeks.

Both Cory and Gabriel jumped out of their chairs as a white-coated doctor approached them. "I'm Dr. Frank Sheldon, and Marlena is one lucky woman. I found no broken bones, no head injury and no reason to keep her here. She's free to go as soon as she gets dressed."

Gabriel wasn't sure who released the biggest sigh of relief, him or Marlena's brother.

"I need to warn you that she's badly bruised, and I expect by tomorrow she's going to feel pain in places she didn't know she had body parts. What she needs most is bed rest for a couple of days. I've written her a prescription for pain medication, and it can be filled here at the hospital pharmacy. She should go home, take a couple of pills and go directly to bed," Dr. Sheldon said.

"We'll take good care of her," Gabriel replied.

The object of their conversation came through the swinging doors that led to the emergency units, shuffling like an old woman even as a forced smile curved her lips.

"Cory, why don't you sit here with her while I get her prescription filled?" Gabriel suggested. There was no way he wanted her walking any farther than she needed to.

"Works for me," Marlena said as she eased down on the waiting room sofa with an agony-filled sigh. Cory immediately sat next to her, and as Gabriel took the prescription from her and left to hunt down the pharmacy, Marlena was assuring Cory that she'd be fine.

Gabriel followed the signs that led him to the pharmacy, and within minutes he had the pill bottle in hand and was hurrying back to where he was surprised to find Marlena sitting alone.

"What happened to Cory?"

"I sent him home." She stood, the simple action obviously painful as she winced. "There was no point in him hanging around here. There's nothing he can do to help me."

"Should I get a wheelchair to take you out?" he asked with concern.

"No, I'll be fine. Let's just get out of here." She took baby steps toward the exit, and Gabriel walked at her side, a hand under her elbow, afraid that she might fall at any moment.

He didn't breathe a sigh of relief until she was back in the passenger seat, her seat belt around her waist. "You're going straight to bed," he said once he was behind the wheel.

"But I had steaks laid out to cook for dinner," she protested weakly.

"Andrew will know what to do with the steaks. You are to go home, take a couple of these pills and not worry about anything else. The doctor said you need a couple of days of bed rest, and that's what's going to happen."

She nodded as if too sore, too weak to argue. "I sent Cory on home so that I could talk to you in private before we get back to the bed-and-breakfast."

He tensed, wondering if she was going to bring up the night they'd shared, a night that had haunted him ever since—but a night he refused to dwell on.

"Talk in private about what?" he asked. He glanced over and met her gaze. In the depths of her wide green eyes, he saw something more than pain.

He saw fear.

"I didn't accidentally fall down those stairs. I was on the top step when I thought I heard something behind me, and that's when I was pushed."

Chapter Nine

Marlena awakened to pain. Her shoulders hurt, her hips ached and her ribs screamed in harmony. Even her eyelids protested, and for several long minutes she remained unmoving in her bed, trying to decide if she wanted to open her eyes and face a new day or not.

She'd been awake late despite taking two of the pain pills. After telling Gabriel she'd been pushed down the stairs, he'd given her the pills, waited for her to change into her nightgown then tucked her into bed and left her quarters.

Although she'd been groggy and half out of it, he'd checked back in with her a bit later to let her know that the door that led to the old servant stairs had been unlocked and the door that led out of the basement had been open, as if somebody had exited in a hurry.

It was an easy guess that whoever had pushed her had crept through the basement door, up the stairs and then waited for the opportunity to shove her.

It had been attempted murder, and now there was no doubt in her mind that the night by the pond she had been shoved into the water, as well. Two attempts on her life.

This thought was enough for her to finally open her

eyes and ease up to a half-prone position against her pillows. Her heart beat an uneven rhythm. Who would want her dead? Why would somebody be after her? She had nothing. She hadn't had any problems with anyone. Was this somehow tied to the disappearance of Sam, Daniella and Macy? But how? And why?

Just thinking about all of it made her head ache. She smelled coffee and the lingering scent of bacon and glanced at her bedside clock, shocked to see that it was after eight. She couldn't remember the last time she'd slept so late.

She sat up straighter as Gabriel appeared in her doorway carrying one of the TV trays that were kept for guest use in the great room.

"Good morning," he said.

"Right now it's not feeling so good," she replied.

He flashed her a grin, and the warmth of that quick gesture seemed to magically ease some of the aches and pains inside her. "I thought you might like some coffee and a little breakfast. You're supposed to take your pain pills on a full stomach."

He placed the tray next to her bed and then sat in the chair nearby. "Eat," he commanded.

With effort, she moved to a full sitting position, and the first thing she reached for was the cup of coffee. She took a sip and eyed him over the rim. "You didn't have to do this for me."

"I can't take credit for the bacon and eggs. That was Andrew's talent. But I did make the toast and fix your coffee on the tray to present to you."

"And a fine presentation it is," she replied. She picked up a piece of the toast and took a bite, then chased it with another swallow of coffee while he continued to gaze at her. "I don't suppose you found footsteps or fingerprints in the basement or on the door upstairs that would help you catch a bad guy."

He frowned. "Of course not. That would make it all too easy."

She frowned and realized that even her forehead hurt. "Do you think this is all somehow tied to whatever happened to Sam and Daniella?"

He hesitated a moment and then sighed. "I don't know, Marlena. Eat first, and then I've got some questions to ask you. But eat now—there's nothing worse than cold eggs."

Dutifully, she picked up her fork but only ate about half of the food on her plate and then proclaimed herself finished.

"Now take your pills."

"Not yet," she replied. "They make me really groggy, and you said you had some questions for me."

"Let me take the tray out of here first." He placed her coffee cup on the end table next to the bed and then carried the tray away. When he returned, he sat on the edge of her bed.

She was unaware that her nightgown had slipped from her shoulder until she saw him gaze there and curse beneath his breath. Her shoulder was badly bruised and in a variety of shades of deep purple.

"I'm sorry, Marlena."

She was surprised by the wealth of emotion in his voice, emotion she hadn't believed him capable of feeling.

"I'm so damned sorry."

"It's not your fault," she protested and reached out to cover one of his hands with hers.

He turned his hand over and grabbed hers. "I just feel so damned helpless. We have a missing family, and now somebody has tried to hurt you not once but twice, and I can't get a handle on any of it."

"The good thing is that both attempts on my life have been unsuccessful," she said.

He squeezed her hand. "And I'm going to do everything in my power to make sure there isn't a third. Last night the three of us decided the best way to approach everything that's happened is that Andrew and Jackson are going to continue to look for leads concerning the disappearance of the Connellys, and I'm going to focus on the threats against you." He released her hand and sat back.

She immediately missed the warmth, the security of his hand around hers. "So how do you do that?"

"I need to learn more about you, about where you came from. If you can't think of anyone from Bachelor Moon who might want to hurt you, then maybe somebody followed you from your past. Tell me about your recent life before returning here."

She hated to tell him. She hated to admit how stupid she'd been during the time she'd been in Chicago, especially the past two years there. But she knew she had to be truthful with him, even though she didn't believe she'd brought any danger with her by moving here.

"The first few years we were there, it was all about survival. I was a twenty-one-year-old with a fourteen-year-old in tow. We rented a small apartment, I got a job as a waitress at a fairly nice restaurant and Cory went to school. When I was working, I had a neighbor lady who watched Cory for me, even though he insisted he was old enough to watch himself. I knew he was an at-risk kid, with no father figure and just me to depend on."

"Must have been tough."

She winced as she shifted positions. "At times it was. And then I met Gary Holzman. He was an insurance salesman who came into the restaurant frequently, and we struck up a friendship. He was a nice man, a widower with two little daughters, and it wasn't long before we were dating."

"Were you in love with him?"

Marlena wondered why it mattered to him. "I was lonely, and unlike you, I was looking for love and family and a sense of security. When he asked me and Cory to move in with him, and I knew I could stay home and take care of his little girls, be there for Cory plus be a homemaker, I jumped at the chance. I cared about Gary and I enjoyed his company, but looking back on it now, no, I wasn't in love with him. I was in love with the idea of being part of a family."

She reached for her coffee cup, took another drink then continued. "I was definitely in love with the notion of being in love. I loved Gary's little girls and thought Gary would be a good role model for Cory. So for the next two years we lived together as a couple. I cooked and cleaned and cared for his children. I just assumed that eventually he'd propose to me, and we'd get married and live satisfactorily ever after."

"But he didn't."

A small, bitter laugh escaped her. "No, he didn't.

Instead he came home from work one night and out of the blue told me he thought the relationship aspect of his life was too complicated, that it was easier for him to just hire a housekeeper to keep the house and watch the girls, and he'd appreciate it if Cory and I would be gone by morning."

Marlena leaned her head back against the pillow, overwhelmed with emotion as she thought of that moment in time. She'd expected a ring, and instead she had gotten the boot. She wasn't sorry that she had never been married to Gary, but she'd been sorry that he'd wakened her to the fact that she'd just been settling with him, and in any case he certainly wasn't in love with her.

"That's when Cory and I wound up here. I was broke, numbed by the sudden change of our circumstances and unsure where else to turn."

"Is it possible that this Gary person may want to harm you?" Gabriel asked, his eyes dark and unreadable.

Marlena laughed again, and then winced and grabbed her ribs. Gabriel leaned forward and reached for her pill bottle. He shook out two and held them toward her. "Go on, you need them."

She took them with the last sip of her coffee and then continued talking. "I haven't heard a word from Gary since we left Chicago. He didn't want me with him when I left. I can't imagine why he'd want to hurt me after all this time. Or anyone from my life in Chicago following me here and wanting to hurt me after two years."

"Tell me about your day yesterday, from start to finish."

"After you all left, I cleaned up the kitchen, did my usual chores and took the steaks out of the freezer for dinner." She frowned, trying to remember even as a headache began to bang across her temples. "I made breakfast for Cory and John, and then they went back outside to work. Pamela came and cleaned for a couple of hours and then left."

"What else? What were you doing upstairs?" he asked gently.

"Flowers. I picked flowers." Already she could feel the edge easing off her pain, the whisper of drowsiness sweeping over her. "I wanted to put flowers in your rooms. I'd picked some beautiful ones for your room."

"I noticed them this morning. They're lovely," he replied. "It was a nice thing to do."

"I like to do nice things for you. I don't think people have been kind enough to you in your life." She felt the warmth that crept over her cheeks and hoped that later she could blame her frankness on the medication. "Anyway, I'd just put the flowers in the rooms and was about to come downstairs when somebody pushed me."

"And as far as you know, there was nobody else in the house."

"Nobody," she agreed. Tired. She was suddenly so tired, but then she remembered her conversation with Thomas. "Wait… Thomas was here."

"Thomas Brady?" Gabriel sat forward in his chair.

"He was here before I picked the flowers." She fought against the drowsiness, realizing what she had to tell him was important. "He came to ask me out to dinner, and I told him we didn't have any future together, that I'd never be in love with him in a romantic way."

Gabriel rose from his chair. "And how did he take it?" His voice was deceptively calm.

"He seemed to take it very well." She tried to keep her heavy-lidded eyes open. "He said he understood that you couldn't make somebody love you if she didn't, that he'd sensed I wasn't feeling the same about him as he was about me. Surely you don't think he..." Her voice trailed off as she couldn't fight the effect of the pills any longer.

As she closed her eyes, she thought she felt the press of Gabriel's lips against her forehead, but it had to be a dream because he would never do anything like that in reality.

"ANDREW, YOU STAY here and keep an eye on Marlena. Jackson, you come with me." Gabriel had a head full of steam as he left Marlena's quarters and entered the dining room where the two other agents were seated.

He hadn't realized the sunshine Marlena had brought into his life until he saw her now, bruised and broken, and what he wanted more than anything was to find the person responsible and beat the hell out of him or her, make whoever it was feel the same kind of pain Marlena was feeling right now.

The sight of her slender shoulder and dainty freckles hiding beneath vivid, violent purple bruises made him want to tear somebody's head off.

"Where are we going?" Jackson asked once they were in the car.

"To Thomas Brady's house. I want to find out where he was yesterday afternoon when Marlena was shoved down the stairs."

Jackson shot him a look of interest. "You think he's responsible?"

"It's possible," Gabriel replied. "Apparently he was here yesterday, and Marlena told him there would never be a romance between them. She said he took it well, but he might just be a good actor, and was angry enough to sneak back here and try to hurt her." Gabriel tightened his hands on the steering wheel. "If he did this to her, then I'll kill him."

"Whoa, partner. It sounds like you're taking this more than a little personally," Jackson said.

Gabriel felt his partner's speculative gaze on him and slowly eased the pressure his fingers had had on the steering wheel. "She's a nice woman, and she's obviously a target for some reason. I just want to get to the bottom of it, that's all."

Gabriel thought about the silky softness of her skin when he'd kissed her, skin that was now mottled and bruised, causing her enormous pain.

"Maybe I am a little personally involved," he finally admitted. "First somebody tried to drown her in the pond, and now this happens. She needs a champion."

"And you've decided you're that man?"

"Yeah, I guess I have," he replied. It didn't mean anything, he told himself. It had nothing to do with any kind of an emotional connection between them. It was his job. Besides, she'd said she wanted to do nice things for him.

Damn, but that single statement had punched him in

the gut. There had been no kindness in his childhood, and there certainly hadn't been any when he'd been out on the streets alone. Even when he'd joined the FBI, he'd found camaraderie among his fellow agents, but he hadn't known softness until now...until Marlena.

While he didn't intend to get drawn into it, he at least wanted her to be okay to go on with the life she'd planned in the big city, with a husband who adored her, and babies to hold and love.

When she'd talked briefly about her life with Gary Holzman in Chicago, he'd heard the yearning in her voice, the desire for the fairy-tale ending.

What amazed him was that, despite her painful experience with her mother, and then again with Gary, her desire for love hadn't waned. She didn't seem to fear being hurt again but rather was open to loving without restraint.

He might hunt down killers and put himself in dangerous situations, but he could admit to himself that between the two of them, she was the one with real courage.

"Even if Thomas did get angry and pushed her down the stairs, that doesn't explain Marlena's unexpected dunk in the pond," Jackson said, pulling Gabriel from his thoughts.

"No, it doesn't." Gabriel frowned. "But maybe he'd already sensed that she didn't want to date him. Maybe he's a psychopath who goes around trying to kill women he dates. Hell, I don't know what to make of it all." He slammed his palm against the steering wheel.

"I think maybe now would be a good time to take a few deep breaths," Jackson said. "Either that, or I'm going to have to slap you, because you're having some sort of a hysterical breakdown."

Gabriel drew in a long draw of oxygen and then grinned at the man in the seat next to him. "Thanks for warning me before you tried to slap me."

"You're welcome." Jackson returned his grin.

By the time they pulled up in front of Thomas's attractive two-story house, Gabriel had calmed down a bit. Jackson had reminded him that before yesterday, Thomas shouldn't have had a motive for attempting to hurt Marlena, which put the near drowning in question.

It was easy to speculate that whoever had pushed her in the pond was the same person who had shoved her down the stairs. The M.O. was the same…and it would appear somebody wanted Marlena dead, but they also wanted it to look like an accident.

"Are we getting out, or are we just going to sit in the car and meditate?" Jackson asked drily.

Gabriel shut off the engine. "We're getting out. I was gathering my thoughts."

"I'm glad one of us has some thoughts left to gather."

The two got out of the car and approached the house. They'd been here before to ask Thomas questions about the Connelly family.

While they had learned that he had, indeed, been in New Orleans during the time the family had been taken and they had in their possession copies of the receipts of his motel-room bill, Thomas was an independent contractor, so there were no copies of work hours, no coworkers to question about his schedule.

He'd never fallen off their list of persons of interest because of how close New Orleans was.

Be honest with yourself, Gabriel thought as they headed toward the front door. *He's still a person of interest on a short list of two.* Thomas Brady and the hotheaded Ryan Sherman, with his shaky alibi provided by his dopehead girlfriend, were the only two names on the list.

Gabriel knocked on the door with a firm fist. Brady's work truck was in the driveway, so Gabriel assumed the man was at home.

The door opened as Gabriel was about to knock again. Thomas Brady looked at the two FBI agents in confusion. "I thought I was done with you all. I gave you everything I had from my trip to New Orleans."

"We're here about another matter. Mind if we come in?" Gabriel kept his voice calm. In fact, he attempted to be pleasant but knew he hadn't quite made it when Thomas's brown eyes narrowed suspiciously.

"I can't imagine any other matter we'd have to discuss," he replied, not indicating any desire to allow them into his home.

"How about Marlena?"

"What about her?" There was no missing the slight softness that filled Thomas's voice or the sudden uncertainty that darkened his eyes as he looked first at Jackson and then back at Gabriel.

"She was shoved down the staircase in the bed-and-breakfast yesterday after you left," Gabriel said.

Thomas's features twisted in what appeared to be obvious shock. He reached out and grabbed Gabriel's arm, his big thick fingers squeezing tightly. "Oh, my God, is she all right?"

Gabriel pulled his arm out of Thomas's grasp. "She's pretty banged up, but she's okay."

Thomas opened his door to allow them inside and out of the heat. "You can't believe that I had anything to do with that? I love Marlena." He gestured the two agents to an overstuffed sofa and fell into a chair as if his legs would no longer hold him. "She's really okay?"

"She'll be fine," Jackson said as he and Gabriel sat down.

"We understand you had an unpleasant conversation with her yesterday," Gabriel said, his gaze focused solely on Thomas's face and body language.

Thomas leaned back in the chair and shook his head. "It wasn't unpleasant, and it wasn't completely unexpected. I've never hidden my feelings for Marlena. I think she's a wonderful, beautiful woman. And I'd hoped that we could have a future together, but I also recognized that she wasn't at the same place I was, that she didn't love me like I love her. Yesterday she just confirmed to me what I already knew in my heart, that there was never going to be an *us* with me and Marlena."

"Did that make you angry?" Jackson asked.

"No, it made me very sad," Thomas replied without hesitation. He leaned forward, his features radiating with intense emotion. "I would never lift a finger to harm Marlena, whether she loved me or not. Even though she told me she'd never love me in a romantic way, I still love her and would never want to hurt her in any way."

"Where did you go yesterday after you left the bed-and-breakfast?" Gabriel asked.

"I went to the café and had a late lunch. You can check—I talked to half a dozen people while I was there, and I left the café with Chuck Gomez, who wanted an estimate for building a deck. I was at his place until after five."

"And if we check with Chuck, he'll tell us the same thing?" Jackson said.

"Of course he will, because it's the truth."

Gabriel believed him. As much as he wanted to, he didn't think that Thomas was responsible for Marlena's heart-stopping ride down the staircase.

Jackson rose from the sofa, as if knowing they were done here. The next step would be checking out the alibi Thomas had given them.

"I don't suppose it would be a good idea for me to see her," Thomas said as the two agents headed for the front door.

"No, I don't think that's a good idea," Gabriel replied. He wasn't sure if he didn't want Thomas around Marlena because he thought Thomas might be guilty of something or because he knew Thomas loved Marlena. He was surprised to find a tiny knot of jealousy residing deep inside his heart, one that flared bigger at the thought of Thomas and Marlena together.

"Any ideas?" he asked Jackson when they were back in the car together.

"I don't know. Maybe we should check out Pamela Winters again. I know it sounds crazy, but both attempts on Marlena feel feminine, if you know what I mean."

"I know exactly what you mean," Gabriel agreed, although he hadn't consciously thought about it until now. "I do know that it's fairly obvious that whoever is trying to hurt her is also trying to make it look accidental." He started the car so he could run the air conditioner to cool off the interior.

"But what would Pamela hope to gain now? The family is missing, and Marlena has already made it clear that she intends to leave town in the very near future." Gabriel frowned. "It doesn't make sense."

"Sometimes things just don't make sense. We both know that Pamela hates Marlena. Maybe Pamela doesn't trust that Marlena will really leave. Maybe Pamela believes that if the family is found safe and sound, then Daniella will talk Marlena into staying on as manager."

As the air conditioner began to blow cool air from the vents, Gabriel backed out of Thomas Brady's driveway. "Maybe we should check out Pamela's alibi for yesterday after she cleaned the bed-and-breakfast."

The last thing Gabriel wanted was to leave any stone unturned. Both attacks on Marlena had been attempted murder. Whether the threat against her was connected to the family disappearance wasn't clear.

All he knew was that when he thought of the bruising on Marlena's body, how lucky she was to be alive, he wanted—no, needed—somebody to pay for her pain.

Chapter Ten

Marlena awakened from her drug-induced sleep just after two in the afternoon, surprised to see Andrew sitting on the chair near her bed.

"Where's Gabriel?" she asked.

"He and Jackson left a while ago to talk to Thomas. Hey, are you hungry? I could whip us up a little afternoon snack." He rose from the chair.

She swallowed a smile. She had a feeling Andrew had been just waiting for any excuse to have a snack. "Actually, I am a little bit hungry," she replied, surprised to discover it was true. Although her body still ached from her fall down the stairs, her appetite apparently hadn't been affected.

Andrew reappeared minutes later with a platter of several kinds of cheese, some sliced salami and a variety of fruit cut into bite-size pieces. "I'll be right back with iced tea." He set the platter on the nightstand and then left her room again.

A few moments later he'd pulled his chair up closer and they were munching from the platter. "Those pain pills really knock you out," he said, and then popped a square of apple into his mouth.

"I've always had a low tolerance for any kind of pain medication."

"Cory came by to see you, but I sent him away with the assurance that you were resting comfortably."

"I'm sure he'll stop by later this evening." She tried to keep her mind off Gabriel. She didn't want to think about how gentle he'd been with her, the deep worry that had cut lines into his face and the anger that had darkened his eyes as she'd told him about Thomas.

"He won't kill Thomas, will he?" she asked half-seriously.

Andrew grinned. "Only if he has to, although if he finds out Thomas is the person who tried to kill you, then all bets are off."

"I just can't imagine Thomas being responsible for any of this. But I can't imagine *anyone* who would be responsible for these kinds of horrible things."

"That's because you're a nice woman. Nice people are always the ones who are totally blindsided by evil." He reached for a piece of salami. "I've seen a lot of crazy in my career as an agent. Nothing really surprises me anymore."

As they continued to consume the platter of food, they talked about Andrew's soon-to-be fiancée, some of the past cases the three-man team had worked on, and Jackson and Gabriel.

"Jackson is the proverbial Southern gentleman with the soul of a riverboat gambler," Andrew said with a laugh. "He's charming, has a reputation as a bit of a ladies' man and is sharp as a pin. Gabriel is the dark angel of our team. He's solitary, a lone wolf and has a heart that's made of coal."

"Is that another warning of some sort?" she asked.

Andrew shrugged. "Jackson and I both can't help but notice that there seems to be an…energy…between the two of you. Gabriel seems more invested in this case than in others. I don't know—maybe we're seeing something that isn't there, but I just wouldn't want to see you get hurt."

"I appreciate the concern, but I know exactly who Gabriel is and what he's not capable of giving." Besides, it was too late for her not to be hurt by him.

She wasn't sure when exactly in the span of nearly two weeks she'd given him her heart, but she recognized now that he owned it. She was in love with him.

IT WAS LATE in the day when Gabriel came into her room, looking as tired and defeated as she'd ever seen him. He sat in the chair that had been pulled up by her bed and released a deep sigh.

"I'm assuming because you're here you didn't kill Thomas," she said, trying to alleviate some of the darkness in his eyes.

She succeeded. A smile lifted one corner of his mouth as he shook his head. "Nah. I managed to get through the entire day without killing anyone."

"Then that's a good day, right?" She reached out and grabbed his hand, unable to stop her need to connect with him.

He appeared surprised, but then wrapped his fingers around hers. "I would have at least liked to get somebody under arrest. That would have been a great day."

He stared down at their entwined fingers. "You put

it all out there, don't you? Despite your childhood and what happened in Chicago, you just go for it."

"It? You mean human connection? Love?"

He gave a curt nod.

"You know the old saying, 'I'd rather love and lose than never love at all'? That's what I believe. I believe you might have to kiss a lot of frogs, but eventually you find the prince who will love you as you need to be loved, who you'll love with all your heart and soul."

He started to pull his hand from hers, but she held tight. "It's okay. I know you don't believe the same thing I do. Although we share similar experiences of being abandoned by the women who should have loved us more than anyone or anything else on earth, we came out on the other side with very different views of love and relationships."

"Did you take a psychology lesson while I was gone this afternoon?" he asked drily.

She laughed, and then winced as her ribs protested. "Actually, I've had very little to do today besides sleep and think. You just happened to be what I thought about."

This time he managed to pull his hand away. "You shouldn't do that. You shouldn't waste time thinking about me."

"You might be a big bad FBI agent, but you don't get to dictate who I think about," she replied. She wasn't sure why, but she was feeling reckless. Maybe it was because she'd felt the brush of death on her neck one too many times.

"You should be thinking about why somebody pushed you into the pond, why somebody shoved you down the stairs." His voice was more forceful than the situation warranted.

"I know, and I've tried. But I can't come up with a name for you to make it all easier." She released a small sigh. "I've lost three people I love, and twice now somebody has tried to kill me, and I have no clue what's going on or who is responsible for any of it."

At that moment Cory appeared in the doorway, holding two tall glasses of chocolate milk. "Uh…want me to come back later?" he asked hesitantly.

"No, it's okay. I'm done here for now." Gabriel jumped up out of the chair as if he couldn't escape her fast enough. "I'll be in to check on you later," he said, and then with a nod to Cory he left the room.

"Chocolate milk always makes you feel better," Cory said as he sat in the chair Gabriel had vacated. He set one of the glasses on the nightstand and took a sip from his glass, then eyed her critically. "Do you feel as bad as you look?"

She smiled as she reached for the treat he'd prepared for them. "I'm stiff and sore, but at least I'm alive."

"Who is doing this, Marlena? Who and why?" Cory's eyes darkened. "I can't believe this has all happened to you."

"I wish somebody had some answers for me." She took a sip of her chocolate milk. "Mmm, you got it just right."

Cory grinned. "Yeah, one part milk and thirty parts chocolate. I know how you like it."

Marlena took another sip and then set the glass back on the nightstand. "I think tomorrow I'm going to talk to Gabriel and see if you and I are allowed to leave here. Who knows when or if Daniella, Sam and Macy will come back, and we can't just live in limbo until we have answers to what happened to them."

Cory frowned. "I'm going to miss hanging out with John when we leave."

"I know, but you'll make new friends. Besides, there's no reason why you couldn't drive back here on weekends occasionally to visit him."

Cory nodded and downed the last of his milk in several gulps. "Have you decided where we're heading?"

"Probably New Orleans." Her first choice had been Baton Rouge but she had changed her mind, knowing that's where Gabriel lived. She didn't want to run into him at a grocery store or see him on the streets. When she left here, she had to put him firmly out of her life forever.

"So when are we heading out?"

"Maybe by the end of next week."

"That soon?" Cory looked dismayed.

Marlena nodded her head. "It's time, Cory. We never planned to stay here forever, and it's time for us to move on. You need to get into a trade school, and I need to get started in some college classes. We can't do either of those things staying here."

"I know." He gestured toward her glass. "Finish your milk, and I'll take the glasses back into the kitchen."

She dutifully did as he asked. "We're going to be fine, Cory," she said as she handed him the empty glass.

He smiled at her. "We're the two musketeers, right? We've always been fine." He leaned down and pecked her on the forehead. "I'll check in on you in the morning. You rest like the doctor told you to."

"Don't worry. I have no desire to jump out of bed and do anything," she replied.

It was long after dinner when Marlena turned on her side and faced the window, where she could see the night shadows begin to take over the day.

Andrew had brought her a dinner tray earlier, but she'd only picked at the food. The chocolate milk that Cory had brought her earlier in the afternoon had filled her up.

It was time to take two more of the pain meds she'd been prescribed, but she wasn't ready to sleep yet and knew the pills would knock her out fairly quickly.

The truth of the matter was she had hoped Gabriel would stop in to tell her good-night, but as the darkness outside the window grew deeper and it got later and later, she realized he didn't intend to see her.

And why would he? she mentally scoffed. He didn't owe her a good-night or a sickroom visit or anything else. He was working his job, not babysitting her.

She sat up and shook out two of the pills, and then washed them down with a sip of water from a glass on her nightstand.

As she waited for the pills to take effect, her mind flew in a thousand directions. She knew initially it would be hard to leave here and start all over again, but it was what she'd always planned for, and now it was time to set those plans into motion.

Gabriel really was just a dream, not a man who had any place in her life. She'd be foolish to expect him to be anything else to her. He was an FBI agent sent here to solve a crime, not a man looking for a love interest.

Finally, her mind drifted back to those moments when she'd been in the pond, terrified that she would meet her death there, unable to save herself if Gabriel hadn't rushed to her rescue. Now she knew it had been an intentional shove, that somebody had wanted her to drown in the pond. She couldn't write it off as some sort of weird accident. It had definitely been attempted murder.

Drowsy now, she thought of that single second when she'd felt the hands on her back, hands that had shoved her at the top of the stairs. Who had done such a terrible thing? Who had wanted her dead?

Despite the sleepiness now nearly overwhelming her, a sliver of fear raced up her spine. Would there be another attempt? Was it possible that the third time would be a charm?

GABRIEL PACED THE length of the great room. Jackson was sprawled on the sofa watching television and Andrew was in the kitchen looking for a snack.

Gabriel had consciously chosen not to go in and tell Marlena good-night…because he'd wanted to, because he'd wanted her face to be the last thing he saw before he went to bed.

He felt like she was messing with his head, talking to him about love and such nonsense. For the first time since he'd been a young boy he felt vulnerable, and he didn't like it. He didn't like it at all.

He'd checked in with his director again late today and had the unpleasant duty of reporting that there was nothing to report in the disappearance of the former FBI agent and his family.

He had been instructed to remain in Bachelor Moon with his team until further notice. So here Gabriel was with no leads, nothing to do and nothing to think about except the woman who haunted him far too frequently.

At ten o'clock, both Jackson and Andrew headed upstairs to bed, and Gabriel sat at the dining room table with all the reports and copies of interviews they had generated while in Bachelor Moon.

Somehow, some way, they had to be missing something, an important piece of the puzzle that had been overlooked or thrown out as insignificant.

He was not only checking what they had in relation to the family disappearance but also to the attacks on Marlena, even though in his gut he didn't believe the two were connected.

He leaned back in the chair and blew a sigh of frustration. They only had three persons of interest at this point, Thomas Brady, Ryan Sherman and Pamela Winters, and there was no way that Pamela had any motive to harm the family—but she did have a motive to harm Marlena.

Marlena. He looked toward the kitchen and then checked his watch. It was almost eleven o'clock. She'd be asleep now. Maybe it was a good idea for him just to peek his head into her room and make sure she was okay.

Almost without conscious will, he rose to his feet and padded through the kitchen and to the door to her quarters. He told himself it was just his job to check on her, that it had nothing to do with any desire to see her, to watch her while she slept.

Whatever the reason, he knew he wouldn't sleep himself until he'd checked on her. Softly opening her door, he saw the small glow of the night-light in her room that led him unerringly to the side of her bed.

The faint light just reached her face, bathing her sleeping features in pale illumination. Who could ever want to hurt such a good, beautiful woman? Why would anyone want to douse her flame of life, of gentleness and caring?

He crept back out of the room, satisfied that he'd done his job. He'd seen that she was safe. He returned to the dining room, closed his laptop and shut the manila file of his materials on the table, then headed upstairs to bed.

Even as he slid beneath the lavender sheets, his mind whirled with elements of the crimes. What were they missing? Who had they overlooked? The only place they hadn't searched was John's little cottage because they'd had no legal reason to enter his home.

Was it possible the gardener was hiding something there? First thing in the morning, Gabriel intended to check it out. If John had nothing to hide, then he should allow the men inside to look around.

The other thing Gabriel had realized was that a little over two years ago, Daniella had been in the middle of a crime they knew little about other than what the sheriff and Marlena had told them. He needed to get the files from that particular crime and see if there were any clues in there that might yield some answers. He knew that Frank Mathis had been arrested for the murder of one woman and the kidnapping of Daniella and Macy, but was it possible Frank had had a partner?

That was his last thought before he fell asleep.

THE NEXT MORNING Gabriel, Jackson and Andrew stood on John's doorstep at seven-thirty. Gabriel knew that by eight the young man was usually someplace out on the property working, and he'd wanted to catch him before he left.

John opened the door, obviously surprised to see the three agents. "Hey, what's up?" he asked.

"You mind if we come in?" Gabriel asked.

"Sure." John opened the door to allow them inside the small cottage.

Gabriel's first impression was one of surprise at the tidiness of the living room. Although the sofa and recliner were worn and the wooden end tables had seen better days, there was nothing out of place, and the air smelled faintly of orange furniture polish.

"What's going on?" John asked as he gestured for them to sit. His eyes widened slightly. "Has something else happened to Marlena?"

"No, she's fine," Gabriel replied. None of them had taken John up on the offer of sitting. "Look, I'll be straight with you, John. This is one of the places we haven't checked to see if you have the Connellys shoved in a closet or locked in a room. So do you mind if we look around?"

John eyed him somberly. "I'd never do anything to hurt Sam and his family. There's not much to see, but you're welcome to search." He sank down on the sofa as the three men moved through the rest of the two-bedroom cottage.

The smallest room was obviously a guest room, with a single bed and a dresser and no closet space. The bathroom had a stand-up shower, no tub and a sink and stool.

It was easy to tell which room John used. Not only did it contain a double bed, but on the nightstand was a horticulture book, and a small bookshelf held more books about flowers, bushes and landscaping.

The three men returned to the living room to find John still seated on the sofa. "I didn't expect to find anything here, but I had to check," Gabriel said.

"I get it," John replied. "No stone unturned and all that. Don't worry, I'm not offended." He stood. "Is there anything else?"

"No, we're finished here," Gabriel said.

"Then I'll head out with you. Most days I have to haul Cory out of bed to get him on the grounds." John smiled and shook his head. "Kids."

"You know he's smoking pot," Gabriel said as they all started up the trail that led to the walkway around the pond.

"I know he dabbles a bit," John admitted. "I've been giving him hell about it. I think he's found some guys in town who party."

"Maybe it's a good thing Marlena is planning a move," Jackson said.

John shrugged. "If he wants to party, he'll find the party people wherever they move. But Cory has a good head on his shoulders. I think, once he gets into school, he'll buckle down to real life."

"For Marlena's sake, I hope you're right," Andrew said. "She definitely loves her brother."

They came to the place where they parted ways, John heading to Cory's small apartment around the back of the carriage house and Jackson, Andrew and Gabriel heading toward the car. It was going to be another long day of seeking clues to two crimes that had occurred at the cursed Bachelor Moon Bed-and-Breakfast.

Chapter Eleven

It had been two weeks and two days since the Connellys had gone missing, and five days since Marlena had been pushed down the stairs. The agents had spent the past couple of days doing what they'd been doing since their arrival—beating the bushes, walking the streets and coming up with nothing.

Gabriel had managed to keep his distance from Marlena, stepping into her room only when they arrived home after another disappointing day to keep her up-to-date. Her bruises had begun to change from the original violent purple to an ugly yellow, and he knew she was spending more time out of bed while they were gone during the daytime.

As usual, when he pulled into the parking lot just after six, a pall of frustration covered the three men in the car like a heavy old coat. Even Andrew's easy smile had been usurped by a weariness of expression they all felt.

They were men used to action, to finding answers to the most difficult questions, and yet they'd spent the past two weeks spinning in place like hamsters on wheels going nowhere.

Gabriel was surprised when they walked through

the front door and the scent of cooking filled the air. Since Marlena's crash down the stairs, dinner duty had fallen on Andrew's shoulders, but apparently Marlena was up and at work.

As the door closed behind them, she appeared in the dining room doorway. Gabriel tried not to notice how his heart gave a little jump at the sight of her.

"Should you be out of bed?" Jackson asked with concern.

She smiled. "If I spend another minute in that bed, you're all going to have to lock me in a padded room because I'll go out of my mind."

Gabriel didn't want to be captured by the warmth of her smile. He didn't want to feel a rush of heat as his gaze lingered first on her face and then swept the length of her.

She wore a white-and-green-striped T-shirt that hid the last of the bruises on her torso, along with jeans, which hid those that had marred her hips and thighs.

"I've got hamburgers just about ready, so dinner can be served within the next ten minutes or so," she said.

"Sounds good," Andrew said. Together he and Jackson headed upstairs while Gabriel followed her as she turned and went back into the kitchen.

"Are you sure you feel well enough to be out of bed?" he asked as she removed a large pot of baked beans from the oven and set it on the stovetop.

"I'm still a little stiff and sore, but it's past time for me to be up and around." She didn't look at him as she removed the hamburger patties from the skillet and set them on a plate already filled with burgers. "I think I needed to get up and work out the last of the kinks."

She sidestepped him to open the refrigerator and pull out ketchup and mustard bottles, then set them on the counter. "I'm assuming there's nothing new to report."

She finally looked at him, her green eyes pleasant yet distant.

"Nothing." He held out a thick file folder that he'd carried in with him. "I finally decided to go back to when Daniella was kidnapped and look at everything Sheriff Thompson had on file about that crime."

"Surely you can't think what's happening now is tied to that. The man responsible for Daniella and Macy's kidnapping is behind bars."

"I know." He heard the frustration in his own voice. "We've gone over everything with a fine-tooth comb. We've interviewed and reinterviewed most all the people in Bachelor Moon and we've come up empty-handed." He dropped the fat file on the nearby table. "This is my last gasp, my reaching for straws in an effort to gain some answers."

"I hope you find something." She pulled a platter of sliced tomatoes from the refrigerator and then faced him again. "I've been meaning to ask you when Cory and I can leave here. We can't just wait around forever for something to happen. We have to get on with our lives."

"You're still part of an ongoing crime," he replied. He hated the distance he felt emanating from her even as he recognized he'd been the one who'd put it there.

She tilted her head slightly, her eyes confused. "So what does that mean? Can we leave or not? I would think if somebody is trying to kill me here, then probably the best thing I could do is leave."

"But what if the person follows you? Then you'll be vulnerable." Gabriel had no idea if he spoke from his head or his heart; he only knew he didn't want her alone in some big city without closure as to what was happening here in Bachelor Moon.

"Then is that a no? We can't leave yet?"

"Give us one more week," he finally relented, and knew it was more than a professional request. He didn't want to see her go. He didn't want to be here without seeing her smiling face, basking in the warmth of spirit that wafted from her.

"One week," she agreed. "Now you better go get washed up while I get the food on the table."

He left the kitchen with a sense of something lost, something that might have been precious if he'd allowed it. But he couldn't allow it. It would be foolhardy for him to pretend that he could be the man for her, that he was capable of giving her what she wanted, what she desperately needed in her life.

He didn't want her to go, and yet he needed to get her away from him. As he washed up and headed back down the stairs, he was determined to continue maintaining the almost painful distance he'd created between them.

Dinner was a silent affair. The three agents had run out of things to say to each other and so they ate without conversation. Gabriel was about halfway through the meal when he realized Marlena was humming in the kitchen. It was an old standard song about love, and her pitch was perfect.

The sound wrapped a chord of desire around Gabriel's heart and stole away the last of his appetite. He could imagine himself next to her in bed after they'd made love, her soft humming lulling him to sleep. The pleasure of the vision pulled a visceral response from him, one that he'd never felt before.

With a murmured excuse, he left the table and went upstairs to his room, needing to be alone, the way he had always been.

He sat on the bed, cursing the fact that he'd left the file on Daniella and Macy's kidnapping on the kitchen table. He could have holed up here for the rest of the night if he had the file.

Instead he stretched out on the bed and stared up at the ceiling, his thoughts so scattered he couldn't focus on any one thing.

Somehow during the past two weeks, he'd realized at his very core he was a lonely man, afraid to reach out to others, having grown comfortable in his isolation. It didn't feel as comfortable as it used to.

Marlena had banged against the armor of his heart over and over again, denting it to unrecognizable properties. He couldn't let her pierce through the steel that had been forged so many years before.

He didn't know how long he'd been on the bed when a soft knock fell on his door and Jackson peeked his head in. "You okay?"

Gabriel sat up on the bed. "Sure, I'm fine. Why?"

"You scooted out of the dining room pretty fast." Jackson eased down in the chair next to the bed. "She's gotten to you, hasn't she?"

Gabriel didn't even try to pretend to play stupid.

"Maybe a little," he admitted. "But it's not going anywhere."

"Why not? It's obvious she's into you and you're into her. Why not take a chance, Gabriel? Aren't you tired of being alone at the end of each day?"

Gabriel raised an eyebrow. "I could say the same thing about you. You're a good-looking guy. Why aren't you married?"

"Thanks for noticing that I am rather hot," Jackson replied with an easy, facetious grin. The grin lingered only a moment and then fell away. "The problem with you is that you don't love. The problem with me is that I love all women. I haven't found the single woman I want to share my bed with every night and wake up with every morning yet. But I know eventually I will. I think you've already found yours, but you refuse to acknowledge it even to yourself."

"Jackson, I appreciate your concern for my personal life, but I figure within a couple of weeks, we'll be out of here. Marlena had her own life planned and I'll go back to mine. It's best that way. She deserves more than I could ever give her."

"You sell yourself too short, Gabriel," Jackson said as he rose from the chair.

"I'm fine with my life, but I do appreciate your concern." Gabriel got up from the bed.

Jackson cast him his legendary lazy smile. "Hey, that's what partners are for. Are you coming back downstairs?"

"Actually, I think I'll take a little walk before it gets dark. Maybe some fresh air will help clear my head."

He followed Jackson down the stairs and as he sat down on the sofa, Gabriel walked out the front door.

The air certainly wasn't fresh but rather the usual hot and humid blanket that had been unrelenting for the past two weeks. At least out here he couldn't hear the sound of her melodic humming as she cleaned up the kitchen, and he couldn't smell the scent of her that made an aching need throb inside his veins.

He didn't want to take a chance with her. He didn't want to be another man who let her down, another man who broke her heart. He cared about her enough not to be that man.

He waved to Cory and John, who appeared to be storing their shears, hoes and landscaping equipment in the shed. Sam and Daniella must have been special people, because everyone who worked for them continued to keep the place in pristine order.

Gabriel didn't believe they were coming back. In his heart, in the depth of his soul, he'd already realized they had to be dead.

What happened to the bed-and-breakfast after he and his team left wasn't his problem. Eventually it would be in the hands of lawyers and probate courts to decide what to do with the business and with the property.

Marlena and Cory would also be long gone by then, living a new life in a new city. He was certain that she would meet the man she'd dreamed about, a man who would not only be her best friend but also her lover, her husband. He wanted that for her, and yet he couldn't halt the pain that pierced his heart.

He paused at the end of the walkway and stared into

the murky, dark pond water, the sun at an angle where he couldn't see his own reflection.

He wasn't sure how long he stood there lost in thoughts when he gazed again at the water, this time not only seeing his own reflection but that of Marlena standing just behind him. He jumped in surprise and turned to face her.

"I'm sorry. I didn't mean to startle you," she said. She held out a tall glass of lemonade. "I just thought you might find this refreshing."

He frowned even as he took the drink from her. "You've got to stop doing things like this." He started up the walkway toward the porch, aware of her following close behind him.

"Doing things like what?" she asked, looking genuinely puzzled.

He didn't reply until he sat in one of the chairs on the porch and set the drink on the table beside him. She sat next to him.

"Doing things like what?" she repeated.

"Nice things. Thoughtful things. And I wish you wouldn't hum when you worked in the kitchen."

She stared at him as if he'd lost his mind, and perhaps he had. "My humming bothers you?"

"Yeah, it does. It sounds nice, but it's irritating." He knew he was being a jerk, and yet he couldn't help it.

"Does my sitting out here next to you bother you?" she asked, her eyes narrowed slightly as if in thought.

He looked out at the pond again, unable to watch her features when he replied. "Yeah, actually, it does."

"Then I'll just head back inside." She jumped out

of the chair and disappeared into the house before he could form the words to stop her.

He turned and stared at the glass of lemonade she'd brought him. Damn her for making him want her, and damn him for wanting her. He didn't just want to taste her lips again, feel her naked body moving against his own. He wanted her thoughts, her dreams. He wanted to be her best friend and her lover. More than anything, he wanted to be strong enough to reach out for love, but the truth was that when it came to matters of the heart, he was nothing but a coward.

MARLENA STOMPED BACK inside and sank down at the kitchen table, her feelings stinging from his words. Her humming bothered him? Tomorrow night when she fixed dinner, she'd sing at the top of her lungs, and the next time she made him a glass of lemonade, she'd pour it over his handsome head.

She finally decided to take her hurt feelings and go to her own rooms. She would watch a little television and then get a long night of rest. Although her bruises were starting to fade, she still felt as if she'd been run over by a truck. She'd stopped taking the pain pills during the day, but took a couple at night to help her sleep.

Maybe tonight the pills would not only ease the ache of her muscles but also banish the pain in her heart. Loving Gabriel wasn't hard. Realizing he didn't have the capacity to love her back was devastating.

She settled onto the sofa in her private sitting room and tuned the television to one of the few sitcoms she thought was funny. But tonight no laughter escaped her lips. In fact, she found herself drifting off in thought rather than watching television.

One week.

She only had to see his handsome face, to smell his familiar scent and to be around him for one more week, and then she and Cory would be free to leave here.

The sadness that she would pack in her suitcase would make a heavy load if it had true weight. She would carry with her the ache of absence for the loss of Sam and Daniella and Macy. And she would take with her a heart filled with love for a man incapable of loving her back.

Her love for Gabriel had been formed by a hundred different elements. While their lust for each other had certainly been undeniable, over the past two weeks she'd also fallen in love with his dry sense of humor and the soft vulnerability he certainly didn't realize occasionally shone from his eyes.

It was impossible to dissect why she loved Gabriel. She just did. It was as simple and as complicated as that. She was about to go to bed when she heard a soft knock at her door.

"Come in," she said.

Gabriel stepped into her room. "Mind if I have a seat if I plan on offering up an apology?"

She wanted to be angry with him, but he truly looked contrite, and she just couldn't summon any emotion except the love that threatened to bubble out of her.

"Sounds like a fair trade," she replied and made room for him on the sofa.

He sank down as if he weighed a thousand pounds. "I'm sorry. I acted like a jerk earlier."

"Yes, you did," she agreed easily. "You're lucky I'm not a woman who holds a grudge. And tomorrow morning when I make your breakfast, I promise you I'm not going to hum. I'm going to sing at the top of my lungs just because it will aggravate you."

"Your humming doesn't aggravate me. This case has aggravated me, and you were a handy scapegoat." He raked a hand through his thick hair and leaned back. "As if Sam's family's disappearance isn't enough, we still haven't figured out why anyone would want to hurt you."

"Maybe because they heard me humming?" she said in an effort to bring a smile to his face.

It worked. His sensual lips curved upward and he released a small laugh. "You aren't going to let me off the hook, are you?"

"You're off the hook. I just wanted to see your smile." Her love for him pressed hard against her chest and teased on the tip of her tongue with the need to be released, with the intense desire to be spoken aloud. "I care about you, Gabriel."

His smile fell away, and instead a deep frown cut across his forehead.

"It upsets you that I care about you."

"That's your problem, not mine," he scoffed.

"I know, but you can't do anything about how I feel about you. You can't stop me from caring about you, from wanting to comfort you when you're sad, from sharing your laughter when you're happy. You can't stop me from falling in love with you, Gabriel, and I am in love with you."

His shoulders stiffened defensively. "Those pain pills you've been taking have definitely addled your mind." It was obvious he was uncomfortable with the conversation. He twisted on the sofa as if to gain more distance from her, as if afraid she might decide to reach out and touch him in some way.

"It's okay, Gabriel. You don't have to do anything about it. You don't even have to care. I just want you to know that you are loved, that you're worth something and that somebody cares about you and wants you to find happiness."

For the first time since she'd met him, he appeared speechless and more than a little bit stunned. "Why are you telling me this?" he finally asked.

"I don't know. I just felt like I needed you to know. Maybe it's because I've been reminded in the past weeks how fragile life is and I wanted you to know how I felt about you if something happens and I don't get a chance to tell you. Consider it a gift from me to you."

"Nothing is going to happen to you," he said firmly.

"I hope not, but there are no guarantees, and you have to admit you don't have a clue who might have tried to hurt me."

"After talking to Thomas, we went by Pamela Winter's place to speak with her." It was an obvious attempt for him to guide the conversation away from personal things and back to the reason he was here at the bed-and-breakfast. "Her alibi for the time that you were pushed down the stairs is that she was at home alone.

She received no phone calls, nobody saw her, so there's no way for us to know if she's telling the truth or not."

"I don't understand. What would Pamela hope to gain by killing me now? Daniella is gone, and in one week, Cory and I are heading out of here."

Gabriel shrugged. "We figured maybe Pamela doesn't believe you're really going to leave."

"I don't know. Considering that Daniella is missing, it just doesn't make sense to me that Pamela would do something like this."

"I can't figure any of this out, but I know you're wrong about me." He stood. "My own mother decided I wasn't worth loving, and nobody has made me feel any different about myself since then."

Her heart ached as she heard the empty hollowness in his voice. "I could," she said softly. "I do."

"Hey, sis." Cory's voice came from nearby. He appeared in the doorway holding two glasses of chocolate milk. He stopped short as he saw Gabriel. "Oh, is this a bad time?"

"No, I was just leaving." Gabriel shot out of the room as if he'd just been looking for a reason to make a hasty retreat.

As he left, he took her heart. She'd laid it all out on the line, had spoken the words of love that had burned inside her, and he'd refused to either accept or return that love to her.

What shocked her was that she'd believed she was prepared for exactly the response she'd gotten from him. She hadn't been prepared for the sweeping heartache that filled her as she watched him leave.

Chapter Twelve

She loved him.

Gabriel had left her sitting area and had immediately gone upstairs to his own room, where he'd paced the small confines and tried to erase her words of love from his mind.

Somehow her actually saying it out loud had shocked him, but if he looked deep in his heart, he'd already known she was falling in love with him. He'd seen it in her eyes when she gazed at him, had felt it in the most simple of touches.

He'd warned her in a dozen ways not to love him, that he was incapable of returning that emotion, but it obviously hadn't made any difference to her.

One week, he told himself. In a week she'd be gone. She and Cory would leave here the way they had arrived: in her beat-up old car, with a suitcase full of clothes. The only difference was she'd leave with enough money to start a new life.

She would not leave with him, and he refused to return her gift of love back to her. It was her problem, not his, and she would just have to fall out of love with him.

Once he felt as if he had his wayward emotions under control, he went back downstairs to retrieve the information about Daniella and Macy's kidnapping. He knew it was a long shot that he'd find anything in that paperwork to help with the current situation, but he had to do something, and at least it might take his mind off Marlena.

It was just after nine when he took off his gun and holster and sat at the dining room table with the folder in front of him. Marlena's door was closed, indicating that Cory had left and she was probably in bed.

Andrew had gone upstairs a few minutes earlier, and Jackson was planted on the sofa in the common room watching the end of an old movie.

Other than the distant sound of the television drifting through the air, the house was silent. For several long moments he sat with his eyes closed, playing and replaying every second he'd spent with Marlena.

For the first time in his life he'd felt softness, he'd experienced kindness and, yes, he'd felt the nudge of love attempting to take possession of his heart.

With an irritated sigh, he opened his eyes and stared at the thick folder on the table in front of him. *First things first,* he thought, deciding to make a small pot of coffee before delving into the elements of a case that had occurred over two years before.

The coffee was dripping into the carafe when Jackson stepped into the kitchen. "I'm heading off to bed, unless you want me to help you go through that material."

"Nah. I'll be fine by myself." Gabriel stepped closer to the coffeepot that had finished making the four cups that should see him through the rest of the night. "I'll catch you in the morning."

Jackson nodded. "Good night, Gabriel."

Gabriel poured his coffee and returned to the dining room table. This time the silence of the house was complete around him. He took a sip of coffee and opened the file.

Within minutes he had disappeared into the crime that had occurred so long ago, a crime that had brought two people to love but not before danger had struck.

As Gabriel read, he scribbled away in his own notebook, noting the people who had been players in Daniella's drama and listing who of those players was still around.

He paused occasionally to sip his coffee and stare out the nearby window, fighting thoughts of Marlena and her words of love for him.

Was it truly possible that he could be loved, that he wasn't a throwaway child who had become a tossed-away man? Had he so embraced the fact that his mother hadn't wanted him, that his father had needed to beat him, that he'd never let go of that baggage? That he'd become what they'd indicated him to be? Not worth caring about, not worth loving? So then, why could Marlena believe herself in love with him?

At thirty-four years old, he was far too old to change his ways now. He was alone and had always been alone. Besides, Marlena was in a state of transition and grief. Her friends had been missing for over two weeks, and her own life had been threatened twice. With all that emotion inside her, she was probably grasping onto something solid, and he just happened to be there.

Feeling a little better, being able to rationalize away Marlena's words of love, he got another cup of coffee, and then left the dining room and headed to the bathroom just off the common area.

Once there he sluiced cool water over his face in an effort to fight the drowsiness that had begun to overtake him as he'd pored over the notes, lists of evidence and interviews.

He leaned back against the door, wondering how it was possible that three trained, professional FBI agents couldn't get a grasp on what had happened here.

They had worked many cases together and separately in the past, and they'd always closed the case, found the bad guy and seen him or her thrown in jail.

But this case had them all stymied, spinning around like Keystone Kops, hoping to bump into a bad guy. He splashed water on his face once again, dried off and then left the bathroom.

He walked back through the common room and returned to the dining room table, where he focused on the crime of Daniella and Macy's kidnapping.

Frank Mathis had obviously been psychotic. He'd not only killed Daniella's first husband, Johnny, but he'd believed Daniella and Macy were destined to be his own family.

He'd managed to get in through the window of the rooms Marlena now called home, then had dragged Daniella and Macy outside and carried them away.

As the investigation had continued, Frank hadn't even been on the list of suspects until Sam had run out of potentials and had begun to look at the gardener more closely.

Sam, along with Sheriff Thompson, had finally decided to follow Frank home, and on that night they'd discovered that what had been an old storm shelter in the ground near Frank's cottage had been transformed into a bunkerlike apartment where Daniella and Macy had been locked away.

Gabriel sat up straighter in the chair. A bunker? Hidden someplace near the cottage? He hadn't heard anything about it until now.

He doubted that John, the current gardener, even knew it was there. He stared out the window to the darkness beyond. Did Marlena know about the bunker? Had its existence simply slipped her mind?

Was it possible that the Connelly family could be that close? Held for some reason on their own property in a secret bunker under the ground?

Adrenaline shot through him as his gaze searched outside the window where the darkness was profound. How could he find a secret bunker at night when he didn't know precisely where it was?

And why hadn't Sheriff Thompson mentioned the place where Daniella and Macy had been confined? Did the man have one foot so far out the door into retirement that he'd missed an important element to share with the agents who had taken over the latest crime?

Again he glanced at Marlena's door. Was it possible she was still awake? That she might be able to pinpoint for him the entrance to the underground bunker?

There was only one way to find out. He knocked softly on the door that led into her private quarters, unsurprised when he didn't hear an answering response.

He grabbed hold of the knob and breathed a sigh of relief as it turned in his hand. He opened it and followed the faint glow of the night-light that shone from her bedroom.

It was just a little after eleven. Maybe she wasn't so deeply asleep that he could wake her enough to find out what she knew.

Surely Daniella would have talked about her time in captivity. She might have taken Marlena to the place near the cottage where Frank Mathis had held her and Macy against their wills.

Silently he crept toward her bedroom door. If he couldn't get the answers he needed from her now, then he'd get the good sheriff and some of his men out here with lights to find the cellar door apparently built into the earth.

He took a step into Marlena's room and instantly froze in horrified shock. Marlena was in the bed, but she wasn't alone. In the pale illumination from the night-light, he could see the slithering of snakes at all four corners of the bed. They were not just any snakes, but cottonmouths—poisonous, deadly snakes.

Two things instantly pierced through his shock. First, Marlena lay on her back, not moving. He couldn't even be sure if she was breathing. Second, his gun. He needed his gun.

As he took a step backward, the snakes coiled and vibrated their tails as their mouths gaped open to display a startling whiteness.

Afraid of moving too fast and agitating them further, with agonizing slowness he backed out of the room and then raced toward the dining room where he'd left his gun on the table.

She'd looked dead. Had the cottonmouth snakes already bitten her enough times to deliver sufficient venom to stop her heart? His hand shook as he grabbed his gun, and then he crept silently back to her bedroom doorway.

The snakes stirred with ominous intent. It was like a picture from a nightmare, the snakes guarding the innocent princess…or determined to keep her as their own.

The only sounds in the room were the snakes' hissing and the thunder of his heartbeat. His hand slickened with nervous sweat as he tightened his grip on the gun, trying to decide if he could shoot one without the other three striking at her, if he could kill one without the bullet winging her at the same time.

A fear he'd never known backed up in his throat, making him feel nauseous as he tried to make a decision, any decision that would do no more harm to Marlena than had already been done.

His aversion to snakes disappeared as his only thought was to get them away from her. She had yet to move, making him worry he was already too late.

He stared at the snake closest to where he stood. Could he grab it by the tail and pull it off the bed without stirring up the others? He had to do something. If Marlena had been bitten, then she needed emergency care as soon as possible.

Despite his own healthy fear and repugnance of snakes, he knew he couldn't stand by any longer. With a deep breath, he grabbed the tail of the nearest snake and whirled around to smash it against the nearby wall. He turned quickly and shot the snake at the top of the bed closest to Marlena.

As he popped off two more shots to kill the others, he was vaguely aware of the rumble of footsteps. The air smelled of cordite and snake guts, and one more lingering odor.

As Jackson raced into the room and flipped on the overhead light, he gasped in stunned surprise.

"What the hell?" Andrew said from behind him.

"Call the sheriff and call for an ambulance," Gabriel cried as he dropped his gun and then rushed to Marlena's side. The deafening gunshots hadn't awakened her. She hadn't moved during the entire drama, and that terrified him.

"Marlena." He touched her face and still she didn't stir, although he was grateful to realize that she was breathing—but that didn't mean she wasn't in grave danger.

He had no idea if the snakes had been beneath her covers, if there were bite marks he couldn't see, but he was also afraid to move her, afraid that doing so would make her heart pump faster, make the venom flow more freely through her veins.

"Sheriff Thompson and an ambulance are on the way," Andrew said from the doorway.

"Marlena, open your eyes." Gabriel fell to his knees at the side of the bed, his gaze focused solely on the woman there and how dead she already looked. "Marlena, for God's sake, wake up." Anguish squeezed his heart so hard he could scarcely breathe.

Jackson placed a hand on his shoulder. "Gabriel,

get up. She's not going to wake up." Gabriel shot him a frantic glance.

"She's not sleeping. She's unconscious."

Gabriel stumbled to his feet and fought against a burning pain in his eyes, the squeezing vise of his heart. How had this happened? She'd told him she loved him—she couldn't die now.

"I came in…and she was there on the bed, with four snakes next to her…. I shot three of them…." His voice trailed off, and then he continued, "They didn't end up in here accidentally."

Within minutes the ambulance arrived, and two stocky paramedics moved Marlena from the bed to a stretcher. They were focused on their victim, professional in their demeanor. Neither of them mentioned the dead snake parts and guts that littered the room.

As they wheeled Marlena to the awaiting ambulance, Gabriel ran after them. At the same time, Sheriff Thompson arrived and got out of his car. Obviously the call had pulled him out of bed. His shirt was half-buttoned, and his thin gray hair stood on end. "What's going on?" he asked.

"Talk to Jackson and Andrew," Gabriel said as he started to climb into the back of the ambulance, only to be stopped by one of the paramedics.

"Nobody can ride back here. Regulations and all that," he said. He slammed the back door and the ambulance backed up to leave.

Gabriel fumbled in his pocket, grateful that he still had the car keys. Ignoring the sheriff, he raced for his car. He had to be with her. He had to see if she made it to the hospital alive.

GABRIEL SAT IN the hospital waiting room alone, after explaining to the doctor that it was possible Marlena had suffered numerous cottonmouth bites.

He'd been thankful that she'd still been breathing when they'd taken her back to the examining room. And as he waited to see that she would survive this night, new emotions warred inside him.

Seated in an uncomfortable yellow plastic chair, he recognized that he loved her, that he would always care about what happened to her. That didn't mean he intended to walk side by side with her for the rest of her life, but it did mean he was capable of loving and being loved, and that was an epiphany he'd have to explore another time.

The second emotion that built up inside him was rage of overwhelming proportions. Somebody had wanted those snakes to bite her, to deposit their venom inside her and kill her.

Somebody had wanted her dead, and he believed he now knew who that somebody was. The only reason he wasn't going after the person now was because he had to know if Marlena lived. He had to know if he was going to beat the hell out of somebody for a murder or an attempted-murder rap.

And he wanted to beat the hell out of somebody. He wanted to cause pain to the person who had been behind the attacks on Marlena. He needed to know why, and he needed to know if that person was also responsible for the Connellys' probable deaths, too.

If he was doing his job correctly, he would have called Jackson and Andrew to capture the culprit. He would have called Sheriff Thompson to make an arrest. But he didn't want this done correctly. Selfishly, it needed to be him who faced the perpetrator.

He jumped out of his chair as Dr. Sheldon approached him. "Is she going to be okay?" Gabriel asked before the doctor could say a word.

"We checked every inch of her body and couldn't find a single snake bite," he said.

The air blew out of his lungs with relief, but it lasted only a second as he stared at the doctor. "Then why isn't she awake?"

"She's definitely unconscious. I've taken some blood and we're running tests, but it's my belief that she's been drugged."

Gabriel's blood ran cold even though he'd suspected as much. Drugged and left alone in a bed with vipers—the only reason for that was a murder attempt. Those snakes hadn't crawled in through the back door.

"Needless to say, she'll be staying here for the night. We'll monitor her, and hopefully by tomorrow afternoon she'll have metabolized whatever she was given and will be awake." The doctor frowned, as if he wasn't sure she'd ever awaken.

"I'll be back later tonight or first thing in the morning," Gabriel said, not wanting to hear anything bad the doctor might have to say. He simply couldn't handle the idea of Marlena never waking up. "You make sure you take good care of her."

"We're going to take very good care of her," the doctor assured him.

With a curt nod, Gabriel turned on his heels and headed for the exit, his rage building. He couldn't wait to get back to the bed-and-breakfast. He was certain that he knew who was responsible for the attacks on Marlena. He just couldn't figure out why.

Before this night was over he'd have his answers, and before the sun rose, the culprit would be behind bars. Of that he was determined.

Chapter Thirteen

Gabriel walked into the bed-and-breakfast to find Jackson, Andrew and Sheriff Thompson sitting in the common room. All three men stood at his appearance. "Is she going to be all right?" Andrew asked worriedly.

"The doctor couldn't find any snake bites on her, so she should be fine, although he believes she was drugged." He looked at the sheriff. "I suggest you get some men out here and process that bedroom. It's definitely a crime scene."

He was vaguely irritated that he had to tell the man to do his job, that Thompson wouldn't already have called out men to begin his own investigation into Marlena's near-death experience.

"I didn't know if this was something you all wanted to handle or you wanted my men to handle," Thompson replied.

"We're here to investigate the disappearance of a family. These attacks on Marlena fall under your jurisdiction," Jackson replied.

Maybe legally, but there was no way Gabriel intended to allow the lazy, mostly retired sheriff to do what needed to be done for Marlena.

"John and Cory aren't here?" he said, stating the obvious.

"We figured they either haven't heard the commotion or are out somewhere together in town," Jackson replied.

Gabriel nodded and then turned his attention back to Sheriff Thompson. "The first thing you might want to collect is the glass on her nightstand. If she was drugged, I imagine you'll find trace evidence of it in that glass," Gabriel said. "And I've got to get my gun. I dropped it after I killed those snakes."

He didn't wait for a reply but went back into Marlena's bedroom. The sight of the dead snakes fed the rage that filled him. He grabbed his gun from the floor near the bed and then walked into the kitchen to grab a flashlight he'd seen beneath the sink. Armed, he went into the dining room table to pull on his holster.

He was about to go hunting.

As he stepped back into the common room, Jackson looked pointedly at his gun in the holster. "What have you got in mind?"

"I want you and Andrew to oversee the evidence gathering in the bedroom. I'm going for a walk."

Jackson's eyes narrowed. "You need your gun to go for a walk?"

Gabriel shot him a cold, bloodless smile. "You never know when you might need to shoot a snake." He slid out the door and into the darkness of the night.

Thankfully the moon was a bright half sphere, spilling down enough illumination that he didn't need to use the flashlight. The first place he went was to Cory's small apartment, although he knew if the young man had been there, he would have heard the gunshots and come running.

He knocked three times before confirming that Cory wasn't inside, which meant he was probably down at the cottage with John, the great snake hunter.

As he walked the pathway around the pond, Gabriel knew he'd gone rogue, that he should have his partners out here by his side. But this was personal, and he wanted to finish it for Marlena's sake, for his own sake.

As he walked past the area of the pond where he'd dragged Marlena to the shore, he balled his hands into fists. As he thought of her lying on the floor at the foot of the stairs after having been pushed, he wanted to slam his fists into somebody's face.

He knew he had to push past the rage and instead reach for the cold professionalism that had always gotten him through difficult cases.

No emotion, just get the job done. No thoughts of Marlena, or Sam and Daniella and little Macy, just get the job done. It was a mantra that calmed him as he reached the end of the walkway where the path veered into the woods that would eventually lead to John's cottage.

Here he needed his flashlight, and he cupped the beam with his hand to allow him to maneuver with a minimal amount of light. What if Marlena wasn't just unconscious, but rather was in some kind of overdose coma? His heart beat the rhythm of an agony he'd never known before.

He shoved these thoughts away, needing to focus on the here and now and nothing else. He'd just reached the bottom of the path. John's cottage was on his left, and he took several steps toward it but then paused as he saw a flash of light just to his right.

He turned off his flashlight, and in the moonlight that filtered down through the trees, he saw two figures magically appear as if spewed out of the earth.

The bunker. His heart pounded so loud he was surprised John and Cory couldn't hear it. They were laughing about something, but their laughter halted as Gabriel stepped into the moonlight, his gun in hand.

"What's going on, boys?" The question shot out of him like a bullet.

The two froze, and then suddenly John took off in the direction of the cottage and Cory ran up the walkway that Gabriel had just come down.

With a muttered curse, Gabriel holstered his gun and took off after Marlena's brother. He wasn't about to shoot him in the back, but he definitely wanted to get him into custody.

Cory was fast, but Gabriel was driven by the sheer adrenaline of a desire for justice, the need for answers. He chased Cory around the pond and finally managed to tackle him in the lawn at the side of the parking lot.

"Leave me alone," Cory cried as he managed to escape Gabriel's hold. They both got to their feet as Jackson, Andrew and Sheriff Thompson came out on the porch.

"Why did you do it, Cory? Why are you trying to kill your sister?"

Cory looked around wildly and then back at Gabriel. "I don't know what you're talking about."

"I smelled you, Cory. I can smell you now, and it's the same odor I noticed when I first walked into your sister's room and saw those snakes on her bed. It was the scent of pot lingering in the air."

"You're crazy," Cory replied, his boyish features twisted in anger in the moonlight.

"No, but I think you might be crazy for trying to kill your own sister, for trying to hurt a woman who has nothing but kindness and love in her heart."

Cory's eyes narrowed, and his features became almost feral. "She doesn't love me. She's just had to put up with me. Eventually she'll leave me like my mother did. She'll find a man or get a good job. She wants to drag me to some other town and make me get on with my life so she doesn't have to take care of me anymore."

It was as if a dam had broken. "I hate her. I wish she was dead. I don't love her. All she's ever done is make my mom go away and nag me all the time. I'll never love anyone except myself, and she was screwing up what I wanted for my own life. Well, screw her."

"I'd say you've managed to screw up your own life," Gabriel replied. He took a step closer to Cory. "Thompson, toss me your handcuffs."

The cuffs landed in the grass near Gabriel, and as he bent to pick them up, Cory stepped forward and delivered an uppercut to Gabriel's jaw that nearly threw him to his back.

Gabriel had been containing himself, trying to go easy on Cory for Marlena's sake, but with that single punch to his jaw, Cory had changed all the rules.

Gabriel grabbed the cuffs and then tackled Cory once again. He planted his fist in Cory's nose, hearing a satisfying crunch. As Cory screamed, Gabriel flipped him over on his belly and cuffed him behind his back.

Gabriel pulled him up off the ground.

"You broke my nose," Cory cried.

"You want to be a big tough murderer, suck it up, big guy," Gabriel returned. He looked up at the porch, where none of the three men had moved from their positions.

"Thompson, come and get this trash and take him to your jail. I'll be in touch with you later." He motioned for Jackson and Andrew to follow him, and then Gabriel turned and hurried back around the pond.

"Where are we going?" Andrew asked.

"To a secret underground bunker where I hope we'll find the Connelly family alive." Gabriel's jaw ached, and his heart hurt for Marlena. If and when she awakened, she'd discover that it had been her own brother who had tried to kill her.

"An underground bunker?"

"Yeah. While I was reading through the old file on Daniella and Macy's kidnapping, I found out they were kept in an underground bunker someplace here. I came to check it out and just happened to see Cory and John coming up from it."

"Where's John now?" Jackson asked as they started down the path toward the cottage.

"He ran the opposite way of Cory, and my first goal was to get Cory under arrest. I don't know what part John played in what's happened, but he shouldn't be too hard to find even if he runs all the way to a different state," Gabriel replied.

They veered off to the narrow trail that led to the

cottage, and when they reached the end of it, the bunker door was still open, emitting a faint glow of light.

"Wow," Andrew exclaimed. "Who would have thought?"

Gabriel's heart began a new bang of anxiety…and of hope. "I just want to find the family safe and secure, and this definitely seems like a likely place to keep them."

"Let's just hope they're all okay," Jackson said softly.

The door led to a set of earthen stairs that went down to another door. The one at the bottom was secured with a padlock. "Stay here," Gabriel told the other men as he drew his gun.

He went down the stairs and placed his ear against the wooden door, praying that he might hear one of the Connelly family members crying out for help, anything that would indicate there were people alive on the other side of the door.

He heard nothing. He moved to one side of the small tunnel and aimed his gun at the padlock, hoping to hell that the bullet didn't ricochet back to kill him.

He shot off the lock, grateful to find himself still standing after the flash and bang that nearly deafened him. The lock hung in pieces, and as he waited for them to cool off, Jackson and Andrew moved to stand just behind him.

"I hope we open this door to find Sam and Daniella and Macy being held inside," Jackson said.

Gabriel nodded. He wanted that. At least when he got a chance—not *if* he got a chance—to talk to Marlena, it would be nice to have news of the Connelly family being okay to counter the utter heartbreak he knew she'd feel at her brother's betrayal.

He pulled off the last of the pieces of the lock and grabbed hold of the doorknob. Drawing a deep breath, he opened it, gun ready, and stepped inside.

Disappointment shuddered through him as he stared at what the bunker contained. Pot plants, rows and rows of marijuana plants, thriving beneath a ceiling full of brilliant grow lights.

"So Cory didn't want to leave here and get on with any life other than growing and selling weed," Andrew said, his voice filled with disgust.

"I'll let you all deal with this and hunt down John. I'm heading back to the hospital to check on Marlena." Now that Marlena's attacker had been arrested, and with no other place to look for the Connelly family, Gabriel's need to be at Marlena's side reared up in full force.

Half an hour later, Gabriel eased down in a chair next to Marlena's hospital bed. It seemed like a million hours ago that she had told him she loved him, that she'd offered up her love as a gift for him to carry with him wherever he went.

He stared at her still, lifeless face in the illumination from a light over the bed, and his heart ached for her. Upon Gabriel's arrival a few moments ago, he was told by the doctor that he felt certain she was going to be just fine, and it was only a matter of how long it would take her to slough off the effects of the drug she'd been given.

She was going to be fine. She'd wake up and wonder what had happened, and then he'd have to tell her about Cory. He'd watch her beautiful eyes fill with disbelief, then horror and then a sadness that would take his breath away.

He didn't want to tell her about Cory, but he refused to allow anyone else to break the news to her. She would need comfort, and he wanted to be the man who gave it to her. He was the only man he felt could give her what she needed.

He leaned his head back and closed his eyes. They'd managed to solve half of the crime. Marlena would no longer be in danger, but they'd still failed to find the Connelly family.

There would be nothing holding her to the bed-and-breakfast anymore. As soon as she was on her feet, she would leave alone to discover what life might hold for her, and he would remain here until his director pulled them off the case or sent them on another one.

The moment she drove away from the bed-and-breakfast, their lives would diverge, and he would do nothing to stop that from happening. He realized he cared about her deeply, and maybe it was possible that she did truly love him, but that only made it more important that he let her go.

He'd never learned to give or accept love, and Marlena deserved far more than he'd ever be capable of giving her. That must have been his last thought before drifting off to sleep, for when he opened his eyes the next time, the sun was shining bright, and he knew it was midmorning.

Marlena still slept, and so he slipped into the bathroom to clean up as best as he could. He washed his face, used a finger to brush his teeth and then raked his hands through his hair, trying to restore some sense of order.

When he stepped out of the bathroom, she remained in the same position in bed, but her eyes were open, and she looked at him in confusion. "Gabriel, I'm in the hospital."

"Yes, you are." He returned to his chair next to her.

She sat up, a hand raised to her head as if she were dizzy. "What happened?"

"First things first. How are you feeling?" he asked.

"A little groggy and a lot confused," she replied.

He leaned forward, hating what he was going to do to her, hating Cory even more for what he'd done to his sister. "What's the last thing you remember from last night?" he asked.

She dropped her hand from her head and frowned thoughtfully. "I remember talking to you." Her cheeks flared a becoming pink. "And then Cory came in. He brought me a glass of chocolate milk." Her frown deepened. "And I don't remember anything after that. What happened, and how did I get here?"

He reached out and drew one of her hands in his as her eyes grew wary. "You were drugged."

She stared at him as if he'd spoken gibberish. "Drugged? When? By whom?"

He held her gaze and squeezed her hand, and he saw the realization darken her eyes.

"No," she whispered as she tried to pull her hand from his.

He tightened his grip on her hand, not allowing her to draw away from him.

"There must be some mistake." Her voice was faint, and a tremble had begun in her.

"Cory drugged you, Marlena. He drugged you, and then he put cottonmouths in your bed."

She gasped, and tears shimmered on the length of her lashes.

"I came into your room to ask you a question, but you were unconscious, and the snakes were in bed with you."

Even though she shook her head no, he didn't stop, wasn't even sure he could stop if he wanted to. He needed to get it all out, one hard cut and then bandage it up as best he could.

"It was Cory who pushed you into the pond that night. It was Cory who shoved you down the stairs, and last night he drugged you and hoped that venomous snakes would kill you."

The tears that had barely clung to her eyelashes released, streaking down her cheeks. But he knew she believed him, knew he would have no reason to lie to her.

"Why?" she finally asked. "Why would he hate me so much?" She pulled her hand away, and this time he released hers as she began to cry in earnest. She hid her face with her hands, deep sobs wrenching through her.

Her pain was a visceral ache inside him, and his need to hold her, to comfort her, was too big for him to contain. For the first time in his life he felt the need to be close to another human being. He wanted a physical contact that had nothing to do with intimacy and everything to do with the desire to soothe.

Before it was even a thought in his head, he got out of his chair and got into the bed with her. She turned and sank into him as he wrapped her in his arms and held tight until the storm inside her had calmed.

Even after she'd stopped crying, he continued to hold her. Somewhere in the back of his mind he knew that, like the night they'd made love, a moment like this would never happen between them again.

"All I ever did was love him." The words were warm against his neck as she cuddled against him.

"I guess sometimes that isn't enough," Gabriel replied, and stroked her hair. "There is a core of rage inside him that I think might be tied to your mother's abandonment. He believes he doesn't need anyone."

He finally released her and returned to the chair. "He and John apparently had a plan for their future that they didn't want you to screw up by taking Cory away."

"A plan?" Even with her eyes reddened from her tears, she looked beautiful as the sunlight from the windows caught and sparkled on her blond curls.

"Did you know about the bunker where Daniella and Macy were held when Frank kidnapped them?" he asked.

"Daniella mentioned something about it, but nothing specific."

"I found it last night, and it's now filled with marijuana plants and grow lights. I can only assume that Cory and John have been in the business of selling dope for a while now."

Marlena closed her eyes and shook her head. When she looked at him again, her eyes were filled with a wealth of sadness but also a weary acceptance.

"I want to see him," she said.

"He's in jail, along with John." Jackson had texted

him at some point while Gabriel had slept to let him know that John had been pulled over in his car heading out of Bachelor Moon and was now residing in a cell next to his business partner.

"What's going to happen to him?" Her voice trembled from the depth of her emotions.

"He's facing a lot of charges. It will be a while before he even goes to trial, but I expect he'll do time in prison." He didn't try to soften it. He knew Marlena was strong and wouldn't want anything but the truth.

She sat up taller. "When can I get out of here?"

"The doctor has to release you. Are you ready to leave?"

"I feel sick to my stomach, my heart aches and my whole world has been turned upside down, but other than that I feel fine."

"Once the doctor releases you, then I'll take you to the jail to talk to Cory if that's what you feel you want to do," he offered.

She gazed at him for a long moment. "Actually, I'd rather go to the jail alone. You've done enough for me, Gabriel. You found out who was trying to hurt me, and you've removed the threat. You need to get back to your team and proceed with your investigation into the disappearance."

She looked down at her hands in her lap. "I appreciate everything you've done. You've saved my life twice, and I think if I feel up to it tomorrow, I'll pack up and be on my way. There's absolutely nothing left for me here."

It was a goodbye. Gabriel felt it in his heart, the sharp ache of absence that was about to begin. Wasn't that what he wanted? A sharp, clean break? A return to what had been his normal for so many years?

"Are you sure you don't want me with you when you go to see Cory?" he asked as he got up from the chair.

Her amazingly beautiful green eyes held his gaze. "Thanks, but I'll be fine alone." There was a new strength in her voice, a glint of steel in her eyes. She had spoken of her love of him, and he knew that now she was letting him go.

"How do you plan to get back to the bed-and-breakfast?" he asked.

"Don't worry. I'll figure it out," she assured him.

Gabriel took several steps toward the door. "Then I guess I'll see you back at the house."

"Just expect me when you see me," she replied.

He nodded and then left her room. He stood out in the hospital corridor and realized there was a part of him that wanted something more.

Then he shook his head, as if to dislodge the alien desire, and headed for the exit.

Chapter Fourteen

Marlena left the jail near dusk. It had taken forever to convince the doctor that she was fine and ready to be released. He'd insisted that she remain until after lunch, and then she'd realized she had nothing to wear home. She'd apparently been brought into the hospital in a nightgown, and nobody had thought to bring her any clothes.

A kind nurse had offered to loan her a spare set of scrubs, and so she'd finally left the hospital clad in a lavender short-sleeved scrub top, matching bottoms and a pair of flip-flops that had been in the lost and found.

It wouldn't have mattered if she'd been dressed in diamonds and pearls; nothing would have made her conversation with Cory any less difficult.

As she'd faced the young man she'd raised and loved, it had been like speaking to a stranger. He didn't even pretend to have any feelings for her other than hatred. He'd accused her of being the one who had driven their mother away, the one who had ruined his life. He'd told her over and over again that he would never love anyone, especially not her. He had nothing but hatred for her.

She'd left the sheriff's office around five and had sat on a bench just outside the building, trying to process everything that had happened, what had gone so terribly wrong.

She'd tried to be a mother to Cory. She'd sacrificed over and over again for him, not because she'd needed to but because she'd wanted to do whatever she could to keep him safe, healthy and happy.

Something was broken inside of him. She realized that now. Something had broken a long time ago that could never be repaired. She couldn't love him enough to fix him.

Twilight had begun to fall when Sheriff Thompson walked out of the building, obviously surprised to see her seated on the bench. He sank down beside her, his face wreathed with lines of age and weariness. "It's tough."

"It is," she replied. "I'm planning on leaving town tomorrow. Is that a problem with you?"

"Shouldn't be, although I'd appreciate an address for wherever you wind up, in case we need you when this all comes to trial."

She nodded, not wanting to think about a trial where she would have to stand and face Cory in a court of law.

"Cory confessed to trying to kill you, and both he and John have confessed to the pot field in the bunker, but both of them are adamant that they had nothing to do with the Connellys' disappearance," he said.

"Do you believe them?"

Thompson released a deep sigh. "I tend to believe them, but it's hard not to consider the possibility that Sam found out about the bunker, so John and Cory did what they had to do in order to save their illegal business."

"I might believe that if it wasn't for Macy. No matter how much Cory hated me, I can't imagine him doing anything to harm that little girl."

"And John maintains he had no idea what Cory was doing to you, that he's never committed a violent act against anyone in his entire life." Sheriff Thompson shrugged. "I suppose time will tell what really happened to the Connellys. Are you waiting for somebody to pick you up?"

"Actually, I'm not sure how I'm getting back to the bed-and-breakfast. I sent Gabriel home before I got out of the hospital."

"I'll take you home." He stood and hitched up his pants over his protruding belly.

"Thanks, I'll take you up on that." Together they headed for his patrol car parked in front of the office.

They drove for several minutes in silence. Finally it was the sheriff who spoke. "I should have retired after Daniella and Macy were kidnapped the first time. I've tried to help the Feds in any way I can, but I forgot about the bunker. Hell, the door was so well hidden Sam and I would have never discovered it if he hadn't followed Frank and found it. I never thought anyone would ever find it again. That was a huge mistake on my part." There was a wealth of regret in his voice.

"Don't blame yourself. There were things going on here that none of us saw."

Silence filled the car again for the remainder of the ride. As they drove into the parking area of the bed-and-breakfast, Marlena was surprised to see Gabriel sitting on the front porch, the shades of sunset painting him in orange and pink.

She thanked the sheriff for the ride, and as she got out of the car, Gabriel stood. As she came closer, she realized he'd been waiting for her. Two glasses of lemonade sat on the table, their ice cubes nearly melted. He must have been waiting for a while.

Sheriff Thompson waved to him and then pulled out of the drive as Marlena climbed up the porch steps and sank into a chair next to the one he had vacated.

He sat back down, and for a few minutes they remained there, watching the sun ease lower in the sky. "There's lemonade here if you're thirsty," he finally said.

"Thanks." She picked up the glass nearest her and leaned back in the chair. Numb. She felt a numbness sweeping over her. She hadn't fully processed what Gabriel had told her in the hospital about Cory until she'd come face-to-face with her brother behind bars.

She almost blessed the numbness that kept a wealth of sadness at bay. Tomorrow she would leave here without her brother. All the plans she'd made for him, for his future would never occur.

Funny, she'd never felt truly alone because she'd had Cory to care for, to love. And now there was nothing...nobody. For the first time in her entire life she was truly alone.

"Where did you get the clothes?" He frowned. "I didn't even think to bring you anything when I rushed back to the hospital last night."

"A nice nurse let me borrow these. I'll return them to her tomorrow on my way out of town."

"So you're still planning on taking off tomorrow?"

"There's nothing to keep me here." She took a sip of her lemonade and placed the glass back on the table. "How did it go at the jail?"

She continued to stare at the sinking sun, not wanting to look at him, for a large part of her heart would remain here with him. "Awful. I always believed he was a good, well-adjusted kid. Oh, I knew he occasionally smoked pot. He thought I was too stupid to smell it on him, but I did. I just didn't see the darkness inside him, how much he hated me, how much he was afraid to love for fear of being let down again."

She stood, not wanting to spend another minute out here, where she could feel his concern for her wafting from him, where his scent rode the soft evening breeze.

She refused to sit out here and allow her love for him to lighten the darkness Cory had placed in her heart, to let Gabriel offer her support without love, caring without commitment.

"I have a lot of things I need to get done now so that I can take off tomorrow. I won't be cooking tonight, so you all are on your own."

"We'll be just fine," he assured her.

She picked up her glass and paused at the door, stupidly waiting for him to tell her not to leave, to get up and take her in his arms, to tell her he'd discovered he was in love with her.

"Maybe you and Cory have it right," she finally said dispiritedly.

"What do you mean?"

A wariness bounced into his eyes, and she knew he

probably didn't like to be compared to a person like her brother.

She shrugged. "Maybe it isn't good to love people because somehow, someway, they always let you down." She didn't wait for his response but hurried into the house.

She set her glass in the kitchen sink and then went into her private rooms, locking the door behind her. She sank down on the sofa and eyed the doorway to her bedroom.

Snakes. Cory had drugged her and then had put snakes in her bed. He'd tried to drown her in the pond and he'd pushed her down the stairs, all in efforts to kill her.

She hadn't realized that his hatred of her had begun when their mother had left and Marlena had taken over caring for him. He'd resented her, resented everything she'd done for him. She'd loved him, and he'd hated her.

It was definitely time for her to move on with her life, and this time she'd focus on working her way through school, getting her teaching degree and building a life for herself.

Alone.

Without love.

Because she wasn't sure she believed in love anymore. It was something that had brought her far more pain than it ever had pleasure. It had been a teenage girl's fantasy, and now she was a woman. It was time to put away foolish dreams.

"WHAT ARE YOU doing sitting out here in the dark?" Jackson asked as he stepped out on the front porch where Gabriel had remained long after Marlena had gone inside.

"Just sitting," he replied, glad that his voice didn't sound odd around the huge lump lodged in the back of his throat.

"Want to talk about it?" Jackson sat down next to him.

"Not really." Gabriel's stomach had been tied in knots since Marlena had left the porch.

"Andrew rustled up some soup and sandwiches for dinner. It's on the table."

"Thanks, but I'm not hungry. In fact, I think I'm going to head into town and have a couple of beers." It was the last thing on his mind, but he felt the need to escape, to run, and now with his decision made, he got up from the chair and pulled the car keys from his pocket.

"Are you going to be late?"

"No, Mom. I shouldn't be too late," Gabriel said sarcastically.

"Hope it helps," Jackson said as he got up from the chair. As he went inside, Gabriel headed for the car, his thoughts and emotions in turmoil.

He intentionally tried to keep his mind blank as he headed to the Rusty Nail Tavern in town, but thoughts skittered like wind-tossed leaves inside his head, with no direction or focus.

They still had no clues as to what had happened to the Connelly family. When he'd learned of the existence of that bunker, he'd wished that they would be in there safe and sound.

No clues, no direction in which to take the investigation and now no Marlena. He tightened his hands on the steering wheel. He didn't want to think about her. Tomorrow she would be on her way, and he and his team would remain at the bed-and-breakfast until they were told to leave.

He pulled into the parking lot of the tavern, grateful it was early enough that there wasn't much of a crowd. Once inside he found a stool at the end of the counter and ordered a beer.

As he nursed the drink, he thought about everything that had happened. Cory had been a shock. He couldn't imagine the depth of masked anger that had built up to a point where he'd tried to kill Marlena not once but three times.

What bothered Gabriel more than anything was that, while Cory was screaming to him that he hated Marlena, that he would never love anyone but himself, Gabriel had seen a tiny piece of himself in the young man.

Like Cory, Gabriel had internalized his mother's abandonment to mean that love had no place in his life. Like Marlena's troubled brother, Gabriel had chosen to turn his back on love, to live his life alone without loving or being loved.

But Marlena loves you, a little voice whispered inside him. She'd dug in, seen the good inside his soul and fallen in love with him.

What he found far more disturbing than anything that had occurred over the past couple of days was her parting words before she'd gone into the house.

Somehow this entire experience had made her believe that she was wrong about love, that her belief in love was stupid. And that broke Gabriel's heart.

He felt as if somehow he and the circumstances had destroyed something beautiful inside her, and that sent a searing pain through him.

By the time he'd finished his second beer, he realized coming here was a mistake. There was no amount of beer in the world that would set things right.

It was time for him to wrap his mind back around the Connelly case and nothing else. He'd come to Bachelor Moon to find a missing family, not to fall in love, and it was time he got back to doing what he did best.

He left the tavern feeling no more settled than he had when he'd arrived. It was just after nine when he returned to the bed-and-breakfast, and Jackson and Andrew were seated on one of the sofas in the common room in front of the television.

"Back in one piece," Andrew said as Gabriel sprawled in a nearby chair.

"Yeah, I had a couple of beers and decided it was time to come home." He forced a grin at Jackson. "I didn't want to stay out so late that I got grounded."

Jackson returned his smile and then sobered. "So where do we go from here on the Connelly case?"

"I don't know," Gabriel admitted with frustration. He glanced toward the kitchen area. "Has Marlena been out of her rooms?"

"No. When I was making dinner, I heard her moving around. I assumed she was packing things up to take off tomorrow," Andrew replied.

Gabriel stood. "I think I'll head on to bed. We'll sit down in the morning and figure out our plan of attack on this case."

As he climbed the stairs to the lavender bedroom,

he thought of how beautiful Marlena had looked in the lavender scrubs. Even after a night of being drugged, without makeup and beaten up by life, she'd looked stunning.

She'd looked like a woman he'd want to see every morning, like a woman he'd want to hold every night before falling asleep. He shucked his clothes and got into bed, willing himself to sleep so he wouldn't have to think anymore.

He awoke at dawn, and after a long, hot shower he headed down the stairs, where the scent of coffee indicated that Marlena was up.

He poured a cup of the fresh brew and sat at the dining room table. He could hear her moving around in the kitchen, apparently preparing to fix breakfast. Other than the soft rattle of dishes, there was no other sound.

No soft, sweet humming to start the day. Apparently that had even been stolen from her by the events that had happened. *You stole it from her,* a little voice screamed inside his head. *You stole her music, her joy of life...you and Cory.*

Within minutes he was joined at the table by Jackson and Andrew, and the talk turned to the Connelly case and what their possible next steps might be.

Marlena entered the room, carrying with her a platter of waffles and another of sausage patties. Gabriel barely noticed the food. Instead he drank in her loveliness. But as he looked closer, he noted that her eyes were dark, sad and haunting.

"I'll be right back with the syrup," she said and left the room. She returned only a moment later with a large jug and set it in the center of the table.

"This will be the last meal that I'll fix. After I clean up the breakfast dishes, I'll be on my way."

"Where are you headed?" Andrew asked, his plate already filled with the food she'd delivered.

"I'm thinking New Orleans."

Gabriel couldn't help but notice that her gaze had refused to meet his.

"You'll like New Orleans," Jackson said. "It's my favorite place to party in the entire state."

She smiled at him, and Gabriel found himself jealous that her smile wasn't directed at him. "I'm not looking for a party. I'm just looking for a life."

"I wish you all the happiness in the world," Andrew said around a mouthful of waffles.

She smiled at him fondly. "And I wish you and your almost fiancée happiness, and I hope you never have to eat a convenience-store sandwich again."

She returned to the kitchen, and Gabriel felt the emptiness inside him. He had to cast her out of his head. He grabbed two waffles and smothered them with syrup, as if the food on his plate could fill the emptiness in his heart.

He ate without enthusiasm, not tasting anything, and afterward he went upstairs to his room to retrieve his laptop. He lingered in his room, not wanting to hang around downstairs while she cleaned up the dishes.

When he finally returned to the dining room, she'd disappeared into her quarters, and Jackson and Andrew awaited him at the dining room table to discuss their investigation.

Just as Marlena walked out of the room with two suitcases in her hands, Jackson's phone rang. He held up a hand to halt any conversation and listened to whoever was on the other end of the phone. "Yes, sir. Yes, I've got it. I'll tell the others."

He disconnected and placed his phone on the table. "That was Director Miller. We're being pulled out of here."

"Why?" It was Marlena who spoke. "Sam and Daniella and Macy are still missing." She dropped her suitcases to the floor.

"What's going on?" Andrew asked.

Jackson frowned. "You two are being sent back to the office in Baton Rouge and I'm heading to the Kansas City office to work a new case. An FBI profiler and her sheriff husband have vanished into thin air from a small town called Mystic Lake."

"So this may be bigger than the Connelly family," Andrew replied.

Jackson nodded. "I'm going to see if what they're dealing with there is what we have here."

"I called Pamela last night and told her I was leaving today, so she could move in here or whatever." Marlena's eyes held a new sadness. "If you all aren't going to be here, then I can't imagine what's going to happen to this place."

She leaned down and picked up her suitcases, then looked at Jackson. "Find out what's going on, Jackson. You might be the only one with access to some of the clues that will lead back to Sam, Daniella and Macy."

He nodded. "I'm going to do my best. I guess we need to head upstairs and pack." Together he and Andrew headed for the stairs, leaving Gabriel and Marlena alone.

He'd noticed as he'd come down from upstairs that she'd already parked her car in the lot out front. He reached out and took one of her suitcases from her. "Come on. I'll walk you out."

HER FOOTSTEPS FELT heavy, even though she knew she should be happy to be finally moving on. She'd hoped that when she left Bachelor Moon, Cory would be in her passenger seat and that Sam, Daniella and Macy would be standing on the porch to wave goodbye.

As devastating as Cory's betrayal had been, her stupidity over loving Gabriel was almost as hard to deal with. He'd warned her, and she hadn't heeded his warnings. He'd told her to pretend that their night together had only been a dream, but it was the one piece of reality she wanted to take with her.

They reached her car, and she opened the trunk. She put her suitcase in and then moved aside so he could do the same with the one he carried.

Instead of placing it in the trunk, he dropped it to the ground. "We need to talk," he said.

"There's nothing left to say. Two bad guys are in jail, three people are still missing and you're going back to Baton Rouge while I'm heading to New Orleans." She didn't want to talk any more with him. It hurt too much. Even standing here in the midmorning sunshine and looking at him created a deep ache inside her.

"I can't let you leave here disillusioned and no longer believing in love," he said, his eyes a dark, troubled blue.

"I think I've told you before that, even though you're

a big bad FBI agent, you don't get to tell me how to think or what to feel."

"But it's important to me that you believe in love." He took a step closer to her, too close.

Why was he torturing her? Why didn't he just throw the suitcase into the trunk and let her go? Why on earth did he suddenly want to talk about love?

"I don't know why what I believe is important to you now," she replied.

He took yet another step toward her, bringing with him that scent that had always made her feel safe and secure. She wanted to run away from him. She also wanted to run into his arms. Instead she stood frozen in place until he moved so close to her that she could feel his body heat.

"It's important to me that you believe in love, because you've made me believe in it. You've made me believe I'm worthy of being loved, of taking a chance and giving a special woman my heart."

A lump rose in the back of her throat and tears began to burn behind her eyes. "Then I hope you find that special woman." She was grateful her voice didn't crack, that she didn't dissolve into tears. She should be happy that she'd been able to do that for him, that he would go into his future with an open heart.

"I've already found her," he said softly. He raised a hand to touch one of her curls, and then swept his hand down the side of her face in a caress.

Her heart stopped beating and then began to bang rapidly at his words. He dropped his hand from her face and instead streaked a hand through his own hair.

Stepping from one foot to the other, he looked decidedly uncomfortable.

"I'm not very good at this," he confessed, as if she didn't know him well enough to figure that out, but she had no intention of making it easier on him, despite the fact that her heart was on the verge of soaring.

"You're going to have to do a lot better than that," she replied. "Right now you're just a dream that I was supposed to forget."

"Marlena, without you I'm a man only half-alive." His eyes were the blue of truth. "I'm in love with you. I fought against it. I didn't want it." He looked down at the ground and then back at her. "I was definitely afraid to give my heart to anyone. I saw a little part of myself in Cory, and it scared the hell out of me."

"You could never do what Cory did," she replied, the thought of her brother churning up her heartbreak where he was concerned.

"True, but I was well on my way to being a lonely, bitter man, and then I came here and met you. You made me believe in love, and I don't want you to go to New Orleans. I want you to come with me to Baton Rouge. I love you, and I don't want to spend a single day without you in my life."

"Are you going to keep talking or are you going to kiss me?" she finally said.

His eyes turned the deep blue that always made her heart soar. He pulled her into his arms and lowered his mouth to hers. His kiss spoke all the words he might not have said and more. It tasted of love, of desire and of a sweet commitment she'd never expected to find.

As somebody cleared his voice, Gabriel broke the

kiss. Andrew and Jackson stood nearby, their duffel bags in their hands, obviously ready to leave Bachelor Moon behind and get on with new assignments.

"What's up?" Jackson asked.

Gabriel didn't break his gaze with Marlena. "Is it a yes?"

"Is this a dream that I have to forget later?"

His gaze softened. "No, this is a reality I want to live for the rest of my life. You and me together—that's the reality I want."

"Oh, Gabriel, I want that, too."

He finally stopped staring at her to look at his partners. He reached into his pocket, pulled out the car keys and threw them to Jackson. "You two go ahead. Marlena and I will head out in her car in a few minutes."

"Looks like something good came out of our time here," Andrew said, looking first at Gabriel and then at Marlena, his face wearing a broad smile. "In fact, it looks like something great happened."

Gabriel reached for Marlena's hand, and she came willingly to his side. "I found a new partner, and I think it's going to be one of those forever partnerships."

"I know it will be," she replied with conviction and squeezed his hand. Some of her joy tempered as she gazed at Jackson. "I hope you find something in your investigation in Mystic Lake that will lead to answers about the Connellys."

"That's the plan," he replied. "And now we're heading out. Marlena, I expect I'll be seeing a lot of you when I get back from this new assignment."

"And thanks for everything you did for us to make our time here as pleasant as possible," Andrew added.

She smiled at Andrew. "Go home and put a ring on Suzi's finger. Life is too short to waste a minute."

A moment later she and Gabriel watched as the car with the two agents pulled out of sight. She turned back to the man she loved. "Are you sure this isn't a wonderful dream?"

"I'm sure." He pulled her back into his arms. "You are the woman I want by my side until the day I die. I want to hear you humming in our kitchen. I want to see that beautiful smile every morning. I want your love surrounding me, as I intend to surround you with all the love I kept bottled up inside me for so many years."

Once again his lips claimed hers, taking her breath away. She was leaving Bachelor Moon with the heartbreak of her brother's betrayal, with unanswered questions about the missing people she loved, but she'd also leave with the man she knew would fulfill her dream of love forever.

He might have needed a special woman to awaken his capacity to love, but he was the special man she'd wanted, the man who would be her best friend, her lover and eventually her husband.

She would embark on her new life not alone but with Gabriel, the man she knew would make all her dreams of love and family come true.

* * * * *

He had a hollow feeling in his stomach.

The urge to run hit him, but he stood immobilized as he listened to heels clicking on the floor in the main office area. On reflex, he catalogued the weapons within range: his gun at his hip, his backup firearm in the ankle holster, the knife in his pocket.

Then the door swung open and a pair of familiar eyes, fringed with thick lashes, scanned the break room before they zeroed in on him.

Oh, heck. She was definitely *his* Lilly Tanner.

Yet she was nothing like the girl he remembered.

"Good morning, gentlemen." Her voice was a sexy purr, enough to make a man sit up and pay attention.

SPY IN THE SADDLE

BY

DANA MARTON

First published in Great Britain 2013
by Mills & Boon, an imprint of Harlequin (UK) Limited,
Eton House, 18-24 Paradise Road, Richmond, Surrey TW9 1SR

ISBN: 978 0 263 90382 9

46-1113

Harlequin (UK) policy is to use papers that are natural, renewable and recyclable products and made from wood grown in sustainable forests. The logging and manufacturing processes conform to the legal environmental regulations of the country of origin.

Printed and bound in Spain
by Blackprint CPI, Barcelona

Dana Marton is the author of more than a dozen fast-paced, action-adventure, romance-suspense novels and a winner of a Daphne du Maurier Award of Excellence. She loves writing books of international intrigue, filled with dangerous plots that try her tough-as-nails heroes and the special women they fall in love with. Her books have been published in seven languages in eleven countries around the world. When not writing or reading, she loves to browse antiques shops and enjoys working in her sizable flower garden, where she searches for "bad" bugs with the skills of a superspy and vanquishes them with the agility of a commando soldier. Every day in her garden is a thriller. To find more information on her books, please visit www.danamarton.com. She loves to hear from her readers and can be reached via email at danamarton@danamarton.com.

This book is dedicated to my amazing Facebook fans and my fabulous editor, Allison Lyons.

Chapter One

As Shep Lewis, undercover commando, strode into his team's office trailer on the Texas-Mexico border with his morning coffee, his bad mood followed him. To do anything right, a person had to give his all—and he did, to each and every op. But it didn't seem to make a difference with his current mission.

He adjusted his Bluetooth as Keith Gunn, one of his teammates—currently on border patrol—talked on the other end. They all took turns monitoring a hundred-mile stretch along the Rio Grande, in pairs.

"Do you think they'll really send in the National Guard to seal the border?"

"They won't," Shep said between his teeth. "It would just delay the problem." For some reason, the powers that be didn't see that the National Guard was a terrible solution, which frustrated him to hell and back.

His six-man team had credible intelligence that terrorists with their weapons of mass destruction would be smuggled across somewhere around here, on October first—five short days away. His team's primary mission was to prevent that. Switching out players for the last five minutes of the game was a terrible strategy.

They had the exact date of the planned border breach. If they could somehow discover the exact location, they could lie in wait and grab those damned terrorists as they crossed the river. The bastards would never know what hit them.

The National Guard coming in to seal the border could not be hidden, however. Which meant the terrorists would move their crossing to a different place at a different time and might slip through undetected. The sad fact was, even the National Guard didn't have the kind of manpower to keep every single mile of the entire U.S. border permanently sealed.

"The op has to be small enough to keep undercover to succeed," he said, even if Keith knew that as well as he did.

"Except, we don't have the exact location for their crossing."

"We will." But he silently swore. They were running out of time, and the stakes couldn't have been higher—national security and the lives of thousands.

There could be no more mistakes, no distractions. They had five days to stop the biggest terrorist attack on U.S. soil since 9/11. Failure wasn't an option.

Keith cleared his throat. "The FBI's guy will be here today."

"Don't remind me." Frustration punched through Shep. Everybody seemed to have a sudden urge to meddle. "Where are you?"

"Coming in. Ryder's cutting the shift short. He wanted to talk to the whole team at the office."

"More good news?"

"He didn't say. We'll be there in ten."

They ended the call as Shep strode through the empty office that held their desks and equipment, passed by the interrogation room to the left, then team leader Ryder

McKay's office. Ryder had been on border patrol this morning with Keith.

Voices filtered out from the break room in the back, so Shep kept going that way.

"She burned down his house, stole his car and got him fired from his job." Jamie Cassidy's voice reached him through the partially closed door.

Okay, that sounded disturbingly familiar. Shep's fingers tightened on the foam cup in his hand as he paused midstep, on the verge of entering. His mood slipped another notch as old memories rushed him. He shook them off. *No distractions.*

"She broke his heart," Jamie added.

All right, that's enough. Shep shoved the door open, maybe harder than he'd intended.

He stepped into the room just as Ray Armstrong said in a mocking tone, "Must have been some love affair." He glanced over and grinned. "Hey, Shep."

Shep shot a cold glare at the three men, all hardened commando soldiers: Jamie, Ray and Moses Mann.

The latter two had the good sense to look embarrassed at being caught gossiping like a bunch of teenage girls. Jamie just grinned and reached back to the fridge behind him for an energy drink.

The fridge and wall-to-wall cabinets filled up the back of the break room, a microwave and coffee machine glinting in the corner. In front of the men, high-resolution satellite printouts covered the table.

This close to D-day, they didn't take real breaks anymore. They worked around the clock, would do whatever it took to succeed.

Yesterday's half-eaten pizza, which they were apparently resurrecting as breakfast, sat to the side. Jamie pushed it farther out of the way as he lifted the drink to his mouth with one hand while he finished marking something on one of the printouts with a highlighter.

"So—" He looked at Shep when he was finished, too cheerful by half. "Want to tell us about her?"

Shep stepped closer, in a way that might or might not be interpreted as threatening. They'd all been frustrated to the limit lately, and a good fight would let off a lot of pressure. "I liked you better when you were a morose bastard."

Ray leaned back in his chair. "He's mellowed a lot since hooking up with the deputy sheriff." He turned to Jamie. "She's definitely changing you, man."

And not to his advantage, Shep wanted to add, but that wasn't entirely true, so he didn't say it.

Jamie didn't seem concerned about the perceived mellowing. A soft look came over his face as he capped his highlighter. "Love changes everything."

"Really?" Shep narrowed his gaze at them. "Four of the roughest, toughest commandos in the country and we're going to sit around talking about love? What the hell? Are we still part of the top secret Special Designation Defense Unit, or is this now the Wrecked by Cupid Team? Have changes been made while I've been out?"

He believed in true love. He'd seen it work; his parents had had it. But he also knew that—like anything else important—it only worked if you gave it your all. People like him, and the other guys on his team, could never do that.

He wasn't the type to do things halfway, anyway. He either charged full steam ahead or wouldn't even start. Love just wasn't in the cards for him.

"Romance is the kind of—" he began, trying to be the voice of reason.

But Mo gave a warning cough.

He would. He was another recent, unfortunate casualty.

He looked Shep straight in the eye. "Love is nothing to be ashamed of."

Shep wished the best for him and Jamie, but in his heart of hearts, he had doubts about their long-term chances. Yet what right did he have to be discouraging? He laughed it off. "It's sad to see battle-hardened soldiers turn sappy." He shook his head, looking to Ray for support, a good laugh or some further needling in Jamie's direction.

But, in a stunning display of betrayal, Ray turned against him. "So what's this about your psycho girlfriend?" he asked between two bites of cold pizza, sitting a head taller than anyone else in the room.

If Mo was built like a tank, Ray was built like a marauding Viking—his true ancestry. Jamie, between them, was the lean and lithe street fighter.

They didn't intimidate Shep one bit. "We're not talking about me."

A roundhouse kick to Jamie, then vault on Ray, knock him—chair and everything—into Mo. That would put an end to all the smirking.

Except that Ryder, the team leader, had forbidden fighting in the office after an unfortunate incident when they'd first set up headquarters here. As it turned out, even though the reinforced trailer was bulletproof, the office furniture, in fact, was not indestructible.

So Shep threw Jamie only a glare instead of a punch that would have been way more satisfying. "She was a kid, all right? I wasn't her boyfriend. I was her parole officer. End of story."

"He never pressed charges," Jamie told Mo under his

breath in a meaningful tone, obviously in the mood to make trouble this morning.

Shep threw his empty coffee cup at him. "Didn't anybody ever teach you to mind your own business?"

Jamie easily ducked the foam missile. "How about you tell us about her and then it'll all be out in the open? It'd be good to know what we're dealing with here."

When they built ski resorts in hell and handed out free lift passes.

"Any reason we're discussing Lilly Tanner this morning?" Saying her name only made him flinch a little. His eyes didn't even twitch anymore when he thought of her.

Ray suddenly busied himself with the printouts on the table. Jamie had a look of anticipatory glee on his face.

A cold feeling spread in Shep's stomach. "How did her name come up?"

He'd made the mistake of mentioning her to Jamie when they'd been on patrol together a while back. He hadn't expected that she would become the topic of break-room discussion. Jamie wouldn't have brought her up for gossip's sake. But then why?

"She's the consultant the FBI is sending in," Mo said with some sympathy. He might have been built like a tank, but he did have a good heart.

Shep stared, his mind going numb. Individually, all of Mo's words made sense. But having them together in a sentence defied comprehension. "Has to be a different Lilly Tanner."

The one he'd known over a decade ago had been a hellcat. He'd always figured she would end up a criminal mastermind or an out-of-control rock star—she had the brains and deviousness for the first, the voice and the looks for the second.

Jamie tapped the highlighter on the table and grinned. "She's the one. I checked when I heard the name."

He didn't like the new, cheerful Jamie. He was used to the pre-love morose Jamie who could curdle milk with just a look. As a good undercover commando should.

The only thing he liked less at the moment was the thought of Lilly Tanner reappearing in his life. The possibility caused a funny feeling in his chest. "They'll have to send someone else."

"Unlikely." Ray grimaced. "We've been read the riot act."

"Sorry about that." Jamie had the decency to look apologetic at least. "My bad."

He'd crossed the border and taken out someone he'd thought to be the Coyote, the crime boss who set up the transfer of terrorists into the U.S. Except the man Jamie had shot had been a plant. The Coyote had gotten away, and the Mexican government was having a fit over a U.S. commando entering their sovereign territory.

Hell, none of the team blamed Jamie. But now the FBI was sending in their own man...*woman.*

Shep closed his eyes for a pained second.

His team would either stop those terrorists from entering the country with their chemical weapons or die trying. The last thing they needed was the FBI meddling and putting roadblocks in their way at the eleventh hour.

Ray shrugged. "D.C. city girl coming to the big bad borderlands. Give her a few days and she'll be running back to her office, crying."

Shep swallowed the groan pushing up his throat. The

Lilly Tanner he'd known didn't run crying to anyone. He was about to tell them that, but gravel crunched outside as a car pulled up, then another.

"Ryder and Keith are coming in early," he told the others. Maybe Jamie was wrong. Their leader would have the correct information.

Keith, the youngest on the team, came through the door first, tired and rumpled after a long night on the border. He did the best with people they caught sneaking over. One of his grandfathers was Mexican. He had the look and spoke the language like a native. People told him things they wouldn't have told the rest of the team.

He looked around and apparently picked up on the tension in the air because he raised a black eyebrow. "What's wrong?"

Shep couldn't bring himself to answer. He sank into the nearest chair and reached for a slice of cardboard pizza, then stared at it for a second. He wasn't even hungry.

"The FBI agent who's coming… She's a woman," Mo said. "She's—"

Ryder pushed in. "I was just talking to the Colonel, too. Lilly Tanner. Isn't it great?"

Shep's jaw tightened. "How do *you* know about Lilly?" He shot a dark look at Jamie. Couldn't he keep his mouth shut?

But Jamie shrugged with wide-eyed innocence.

"She's Mitch Mendoza's sister," Ryder said.

A moment of confused silence passed as the men looked at each other, processing the unexpected information.

Jamie spoke first. "The one he's been looking for?"

His sister was married to Mendoza, so this was family business for him. "I thought her name was Cindy."

"Got changed at one point along the way. You can ask her all about it when she gets here."

Mo clapped Jamie on the back. "Hey, that makes her your sister-in-law, doesn't it?"

A stunned smile spread on Jamie's face as he nodded. "Kind of. Yeah."

Ryder headed to the back for coffee. "Mitch found her just recently. Different name and everything, but it's definitely his sister. They had the DNA test done to confirm it."

Shep rubbed his temple where a headache pulsed to life suddenly.

Mitch Mendoza, another member of the SDDU, Special Designation Defense Unit, the large team that Shep's smaller group belonged to, came from a family destroyed by drugs. He'd been a teenager when his father had sold his little sister for coke. Mitch had been looking for her ever since.

And now he'd found her at last.

Except that through some bizarre turn of events, Mitch's Cindy Mendoza was Shep's Lilly Tanner. Shep swallowed. And she was coming here.

He tried to remember if he had any aspirin in his desk drawer. "They'll have to send someone else."

Jamie lifted an eyebrow, a warning look forming on his face. "She's my family," he said, in case somehow Shep didn't get that.

He did. *Shoot me now.*

"She can't be my Lilly Tanner. There must be a hundred Lilly Tanners out there." He stubbornly clung to denial.

"She's yours." Jamie extinguished that hope with

ruthless efficiency. "I ran a background check on her when I got the name. Right age. Came from the juvie system. Right city."

Shep pushed to his feet.

"Where are you going?" Mo wanted to know.

"Taking a break." He needed an hour at the gym.

He needed a little time to clear his mind so he could focus fully on his work. His thoughts were all over the place, and he had plenty to get done today.

No distractions. He had to erase the picture that filled his mind: the seventeen-year-old bundle of holy terror that had made him quit the juvenile justice system. *Sort of.* Okay, fine, they fired him because of her.

But even as he moved toward the fridge to grab a bottle of water to go, another car pulled up outside. A throaty engine rumbled, sounding nothing like the team's SUVs. A car door slammed.

He had a hollow feeling in his stomach.

The urge to run hit him, but he stood immobilized as he listened to heels clicking on the floor in the main office area. On reflex, he cataloged the weapons within range: his gun at his hip, his backup firearm in the ankle holster, the knife in his pocket.

Then the door swung open and a pair of familiar devil-black eyes, fringed with thick lashes, scanned the break room before they zeroed in on him.

Oh, holy hell. She was definitely *his* Lilly Tanner.

Yet she was nothing like the girl he remembered.

Her full lips stretched into a smile that made Ray stare openmouthed. Shep considered throwing the water bottle at the idiot to snap him out of it. Then he realized that the rest of them were just as bad, staring at her, more than a little dazed. *Great.*

"Good morning, gentlemen." Her voice was a sexy

purr, enough to make a man sit up and pay attention, nothing like the disdainful teenage tone Shep still heard sometimes in his nightmares.

She had stretched up and filled out, and somehow managed to look like a *Playboy* Playmate even in a straight-cut charcoal FBI suit. She wore her wild, dark curls pulled back into a no-nonsense bun, her five-inch heels a somber black, yet everything about her somehow spelled sex, which made Shep feel all wrong and uncomfortable.

She'd been his charge once. He was pretty sure he shouldn't be standing there thinking how she was the hottest thing he'd ever seen.

Good thing he knew too much about her to fall for the new look. Hell, he even knew where her tattoos were—

He caught himself and tried to backpedal out of that thought. Too late. A strange heat flooded him.

She strode straight to him on endless legs, her hips swaying in a mesmerizing way. "Hey, Shep. Long time no see."

Enough roundness was happening in that skirt to make a man's palms itch. And her breasts, too, had come into their own since he'd last seen her. Definitely. His brain was short-circuiting, unable to reconcile his old image of her with the new.

"Are you going to introduce me to your friends?" she asked when she stood close enough for him to catch the light scent of her perfume, her head at a slight tilt, an amused look in her eyes.

He had a hard time recalling his friends.

"Ray Armstrong." Ray came around the table and took her hand, held it longer than necessary.

Keith deftly pushed Ray out of the way. "Keith Gunn."

She shook his hand, too, then Mo's and Ryder's as they came up to introduce themselves. Then she turned to Jamie. "You must be Jamie Cassidy, then."

Jamie stood with a bigger smile than Shep ever remembered seeing on him, and walked over to her, then enveloped her in a hug that made Ray and Keith look decidedly unhappy.

"We're family," he said when he pulled back. "I'm glad they found you. Now maybe Mitch will learn to relax a little." He grinned. "What are the chances?"

She stood a little stiffly, as if not entirely sure of the hearty welcome. But she said, "From what I've seen of him, very little."

Jamie grinned, then shot a *watch yourself* look at Shep, who wished he knew where the button was to project him into an alternate universe.

Ryder and Mo looked rather protective of her, too. They both had tremendous respect for Mitch Mendoza. Both would have laid down their lives for him. Or his little sister, from the looks of it. Ray and Keith, all googly-eyed, were obviously in lust with her and didn't care who knew it.

Shep swallowed in disgust. Less than five minutes had passed since she'd walked through the door. The disciplined, battle-hardened team of six of the best commandos in the country stood in shambles.

That was Lilly Tanner.

He drew a slow breath, careful not to inhale too much of her perfume that wreaked havoc with his senses. He was a well-trained undercover operative. He could and would figure out how to stay away from her.

He stepped back, ready to leave the insanity behind, but her voice stopped him.

"While we're all together here, I do have some information to share." She paused, as if to make sure she had everyone's attention but of course she did and then some. "We have confirmed intelligence that on October first, terrorists and their chemical weapons will be smuggled across this section of the border."

"We know that," Shep told her.

She went on. "This team is not large enough to monitor a hundred miles."

Ryder nodded. "But a larger force would be noticed. Then the transfer would just be delayed or moved to another location." They'd been through this many times in the past weeks.

She held up a slim hand. "A small undercover team catching the terrorists would have been the best option," she agreed. "However, orders have been given for the National Guard to seal the area in question. They'll be arriving on the thirtieth. If you can't show results by then, we do need to be ready with plan B."

Ryder's face darkened. "It's been decided and approved?"

She nodded. "This morning."

"How long will they stay?"

"An indeterminate period."

"But an incomplete and temporary deployment?"

"Yes."

Shep watched her. "The terrorists will just wait them out. Or find another spot." Ryder had just said that, but it seemed she hadn't heard him.

She pulled her shoulders even straighter. "There's no guaranteed perfect solution."

Her not meddling in his team's business would have

been perfect, Shep thought as Ryder asked, "And if we *can* pin down the exact transfer location within the next couple of days? In time to set up an ambush."

"Capture is preferable to deterrence. If you obtain an exact location, your team will be allowed to go ahead as planned with the apprehension on the first."

The phone rang out in the office area. Shep, already near the door, went to answer it, needing some space.

Jamie and Mo followed him. They were heading out to the border for their shift, so they went to their desks for their backup weapons and started loading up.

They had the date, but the tangos could change their minds. And catching even a regular smuggler could always turn into gold, if the guy could lead them to the Coyote.

As Shep picked up the phone, the others came out of the break room, too. He turned his back to them to focus on the call.

"Hey, I got those prints for you," Doug at the lab said on the other end. "They belong to one Jimmy Fishburn. Petty criminal." He rattled off the address.

Shep entered it into his cell phone GPS before turning back to the others.

Jamie and Mo were already gone. Ryder was heading into his office with Lilly. He glanced back from the doorway. "Anything important?"

"We got an ID on the fingerprints."

They'd been supposed to catch the Coyote when he came up to the U.S. for a medical procedure two days earlier. Instead, they'd chased and shot a stand-in. The driver had escaped, but they'd gotten his car and prints.

They'd never even laid eyes on the Coyote. The crime boss was pretty good at the game he played. Too bad. Because if they had him, he could give them the exact location for the terrorists' trip across the river. He'd know. He'd set up the transfer.

"You need someone to go with you?" Ryder asked.

Shep shook his head. He wanted to be alone to regain his composure a little, and so he could swear loudly and at length on the way. "According to the lab, he's a small-time crook. I can handle it."

But Lilly flashed him a dazzling smile. "I can meet with Ryder later. I'll go with you. We can catch up on the way."

Just what he'd been hoping for. *Not really.*

If he'd learned one thing in the past couple of years, it was that you always played to your strengths. You figured out what your strengths were, built on them, made them even better and used them. You didn't go into your weak territory. Your weak territory was where bad things happened.

Women were his weak territory. Especially Lilly.

He opened his mouth to protest, then caught another look of warning from Jamie. She was his sister-in-law. Okay, that added another layer of trickiness to all this.

It wasn't as if he couldn't handle her. He could.

So he forced his lips into something he hoped might resemble a cool, unaffected smile. "Can't wait."

LILLY SAT IN the passenger seat of Shep's super-rigged SUV and tried to suck in her stomach while doing her best not to stare at him. Not that the arid Texas countryside provided much distraction. Low brush and yellow grass covered the land they drove over, a handful of farmhouses dotting the landscape here and there.

The cool, confident FBI agent thing back in the office had been a complete sham. Truth was, he made her nervous. Very. Not that he needed to know that.

"This Jimmy is our strongest lead?" She glanced at Shep from the corner of her eye.

Life was so incredibly unfair.

He hadn't changed any in the past decade. Okay, maybe a little. His shoulders seemed even wider, his gaze more somber. He had a new edge to him, as if he'd been to hell and back. But he could still make her heart skip a beat just by breathing.

No, she caught herself. There'd be none of that this time around. She was a grown-up, a self-possessed, independent woman. Or she would act like one, at the very least.

"Yes." He responded to her question. "If it pans out, Jimmy could be a direct lead to the Coyote."

She tugged on her suit top, wishing she knew how to hide the pounds she'd put on since their last meeting—*thank you, office work.* Being a cop had been bad like that, but working for the FBI was worse. A week's worth of fieldwork could easily be followed by a month of debriefings, reports and other documentation, with her going cross-eyed in front of a computer.

His stomach was as flat as the blacktop they drove over, and probably as hard. Not that she'd looked. Much. She lifted her gaze to his face.

"Hot down here," she said, then winced at how inane she sounded.

She had tagged along to catch up, maybe even apologize for her past sins, but suddenly she couldn't remember a thing she'd meant to say. Shep still had a knack for overwhelming her.

He kept his attention on the road. "How long have you been with the FBI?" he asked in that rich, masculine voice of his that had been the center of her teenage obsession with the man.

"Five years. Police force before that."

He turned to her at last, his eyebrows sliding up his forehead. "You were a cop?"

"For a while. After I got my act together. My juvenile record was expunged."

He grunted, sounding a lot less impressed than she'd hoped he would be. As she tried to think of what to say next, he turned off the county road and down a winding lane, which led to a trailer park.

A hundred or so trailers of various sizes sat in disorderly rows, all in faded pastel colors. No people. Nobody would want to sit outside in this heat. Broken-down cars and rusty grills clogged the narrow spaces between trailers, garbage and tumbleweeds blowing in the breeze.

He drove to the back row, checked the address, then backed his SUV into the gravel driveway next to a derelict shed that sat between two homes.

"This one." He nodded toward a pale blue single-wide directly across from them that had its siding peeling in places. A tan recliner with the stuffing hanging out sat by the front steps.

When Shep got out, so did she. She caught movement at last—nothing sinister. Behind the shed, in a half-broken blue kiddie pool, a little boy was giving a graying old dog a bath. The dog didn't look impressed, but still stood obediently and let the kid dump water all over him.

The kid paid them no attention. He should be safe where he was. They weren't expecting trouble, but even if they found some, the little boy was out of sight and out of the way.

Shep looked at her. "What do you think?"

She scanned the blue trailer, mapped all the possible

venues of approach in her head. "Anybody going up the steps could be easily picked off by someone in one of the windows." That would be the most vulnerable part of the exercise. "Do you need backup?"

"I can handle it." He checked his weapon with practiced movements, as if he'd done this a million times before. He probably had. "You keep an eye on the kid. Make sure he stays where he is."

She watched the trailer's windows. If anyone moved behind the closed blinds, she couldn't see them. "Any guess who the big boss is? Any clues to the real identity of the Coyote?"

Shep shrugged. "Our best leads have an unfortunate tendency to die before they can be questioned."

Which was one of the reasons why she had come.

While the six-man team was made up of the best commando soldiers the country had to offer, they'd been trained to fight, and fight they did. The body count was going up. She'd been sent to tone that down a little.

They weren't in the mountains of Afghanistan. Running an op inside the U.S. was a more delicate business. Border security was a touchy issue. International relations were at stake. They needed to catch the terrorists without starting a war.

Well, they weren't going to lose any leads on her watch. She glanced at the boy still busy splashing in the water, then something else drew her attention. A souped-up Mustang roared down the street.

The dog barked, then jumped out of the pool to chase the car. And the little boy chased after. "Jack! Come back!"

Something about the car set off Lilly's instincts, but there was no time to react, no time to stop what was happening.

Brakes squealing, the car slowed in front of Jimmy's trailer, and the next second the trailer's windows exploded in a hail of bullets.

"Get down!" Shep shouted over the gunfire and dived after the kid.

She'd never seen a superspy lunge like that, straight through the air, covering an unlikely distance in a split second as she took cover behind the SUV. She was on the wrong side to help, but at the right angle to get a look at the license plate, at least.

Shep went down, protecting the boy, rolling back into the cover of the shed with him as the dog ran off. The Mustang was pulling away already.

Her heart raced as she jumped up. "Shep!"

Was he hit?

Chapter Two

She couldn't see him. "Shep!"

Then he popped back into sight and shot at the Mustang, blew out a window as the car picked up speed, roaring away.

Lilly rushed forward and aimed at one of the back tires, barely seeing anything from the dust cloud the car was kicking up. She missed.

"You stay right here," she heard Shep call out, probably to the kid, then he was next to her.

"Call in the plate. Call the office." He rushed forward, up the shot-up trailer's steps. "Law enforcement," he called out when he reached the top. "Don't shoot. Are you okay in there, Jimmy?" He kicked in the already damaged door and disappeared inside.

She moved after him, glancing back as the dog returned and ran into the gap between the shed and the trailer next to it, back to the boy. One step forward and she could see the kid, his arms tight around the dog's neck as the animal licked his dirty face. Didn't look as if either of them had gotten hurt.

She pointed at him. "You stay there. Don't move. Okay?"

Neighbors peeped from their homes.

She scanned them and evaluated them for possible

trouble even as she held up her badge. "FBI. Please go back inside."

She clipped the badge onto her jacket so she could dial, gun in one hand, the phone in the other, her blood racing.

The line was picked up and she summarized in a sentence what had happened, reported the license plate, listed the make and model of the car, and asked for assistance. Then she went up the stairs after Shep to help him.

She found him in the back of the trailer, standing in a small bedroom that smelled heavily like pot. Clothes and garbage were thrown everywhere. Their brand-new lead, a scrawny twentysomething she assumed to be Jimmy, lay in the middle of the floor. Frustration tightened her muscles as she took in the bullet holes riddling his body.

Shep crouched next to him, feeling for a pulse with one hand, still holding his gun with the other. He straightened suddenly, swearing under his breath, then speaking out loud what she pretty much knew already. "Dead."

He pushed by her, out of the trailer, and she ran behind him, noting the young mother who now had the little boy wrapped tightly in her arms.

"You," Shep called to a man in his late forties who'd also appeared, probably from a neighboring trailer, while they'd been inside. He wore denim overalls over bare skin and held a hunting rifle.

"This is FBI Agent Lilly Tanner," Shep told him as he hurried to his SUV. "She's deputizing you." He turned when he reached the car. "You sit in this chair—" he pointed to the recliner by the steps "—and don't let anyone go inside until the authorities get here. Do you understand?"

The man looked doubtful for a second, but then he nodded. "Yes, sir."

Shep jumped into his car, and she had to follow if she didn't want to be left behind.

She snapped on her seat belt, keeping the gun out. "What happened to standing still long enough to think and come up with a plan?"

"No time." He turned the key in the ignition.

"I'm not a sheriff. I can't deputize people," she said through her teeth as he gunned the engine. "You just left a crime scene to a civilian. Is this the kind of Wild West law enforcement your team is running here?"

"It's called doing what it takes." He stepped even harder on the gas pedal and shot down the lane at twice the speed she would have recommended, people scampering out of his way.

A grim, focused expression sat on his face, his weapon ready on his lap, rules and regulations the farthest thing from his mind, obviously.

He was a different man from what she remembered. He belonged on the battlefield, not among civilians. She pushed the thought back. She'd barely been here; the determination was too early to make. She'd give him a fair shake. He deserved that much from her.

But she *would* have to make that determination at some point. Her mission here had an extra component his team wasn't aware of. She was to make recommendations whether to keep the SDDU's Texas headquarters in operation or have one of the domestic agencies take over their duties.

The law forbade U.S. military from being deployed inside the borders of the United States. The Special

Designation Defense Unit didn't technically belong to the military—their top secret team reported straight to the Secretary of Homeland Defense—but they were a commando team, no matter how they sliced and diced it.

The few FBI and CIA bigwigs who did have knowledge of the SDDU were more than uncomfortable with them being here. And then there was, of course, the rivalry. The very existence of the SDDU seemed to imply that the bureau and the agency weren't enough to handle the job.

She was supposed to write up an evaluation and recommendation based on her experience here. But her judgment of the small Texas headquarters would have implications for the entire SDDU team. There was some pressure on her to come up with recommendations that would restrict their operations to outside the borders, like the military.

Pressure or not, however, she was determined to keep an open mind. Even if Shep wasn't making that easy for her.

He drove like a maniac. The Mustang was nowhere to be seen. It'd gotten too much of an advantage. Not knowing where it was headed, they would have little chance of catching up.

She cleared her throat. "We would have been better off staying and searching the trailer, I think."

Instead of responding, Shep made a hard left without hesitation when they hit the county road, and without yielding to oncoming traffic.

"How do you know they went this way?" she asked over the blaring horns and squealing tires, her right hand braced on the dashboard, her blood pressure inching up.

"Burned rubber on the road. Wasn't there when we came. They didn't slow to take the turn."

She glanced back but, of course, they'd long passed the spot. *Burned rubber...* She should have picked up on that. Would have, normally. She needed to snap to instead of allowing him to distract her.

He overtook a large semitrailer and nearly ran a car off the road in the process.

She had to brace herself again. "You can kill someone like this." She might have raised her voice a little. "What happened to waiting for backup? Also known as *standard procedure.*"

Back in the day, he'd been a lot more balanced—the sane voice of authority and all that. Rules used to mean a lot to him. He'd had a ton of them. But not anymore, it seemed.

Which he further proved by saying, "We don't run things by the company manual here."

"No kidding."

God help her if the other five were like him. She pushed that depressing possibility aside and put on her business face. The bureau had sent her here to keep this wild-card team in line, and she was the woman to do it.

Shep might have been her parole officer at one point. She might have had a crush on him so bad she hadn't been able to see straight, but a lot of things had changed since then. She was here to do a job.

She opened her mouth to tell him that, but he pointed straight ahead, cutting her off. "There."

The red Mustang was a speck in the distance ahead of them.

He floored the gas and did his best to catch up, scaring innocent motorists half to death in the process as he whipped around them like a race-car driver.

But when he finally reached the red Mustang, it picked up speed. So did he. Was he insane? Nobody could fully control a car at speeds like this.

She meant to read him the riot act, but he cut her off, once again, before she could have gotten the first word out.

"Take over the wheel."

"What? No—" But she had to grab the damn thing when he let go without even looking at her.

Then he took the safety off his gun, rolled down his window, pulled the upper half of his body outside and started shooting at the men in the car in front of them.

Of course, they shot back.

SHEP TRIED TO HIT the back tire, but the Mustang sat low to the ground and he was high up in the SUV, nearly sitting in the window, so the angle wasn't much to work with. He couldn't shoot at the two idiots inside the car, which would have been easier. They needed them alive for interrogation.

"Coming in." He popped back onto his seat and grabbed the wheel from Lilly, who slid back into her own seat to make room for him, shooting him a murderous look, her full lips pressed into a severe line.

He floored the gas and rammed the car in front of them.

The Mustang nearly swerved into oncoming traffic.

Lilly braced herself on the dashboard. "Slow down! You're endangering civilians on the road. Shep!"

"Take over the shooting. It's easier for you to use your right hand." He needed both hands for the ramming.

"This isn't how it's done. Public safety always comes first."

When the hell did she turn all prim and proper? "The public is safe. Unless you're a bad shot."

She said something under her breath he didn't catch.

"Listen—" He rammed the Mustang again. "I don't know how you do things at the FBI, but this is not white-glove law enforcement. You're in the combat-boot section now. If you want to stay here, you're going to have to step up to the plate."

She unsnapped her seat belt, muttering something under her breath, then rolled her window down and leaned out.

He did his best to keep the car steady for her.

She shot at the tire, didn't have any more luck than he'd had, with the Mustang swerving. She leaned out a little farther.

The man in the passenger seat shot back at her.

She didn't even flinch.

Shep could see from the corner of his eye as she lifted her aim. And shot the bastard straight through the wrist.

"Good shot." He flashed her a grin as she pulled back into the cab. But then the smile froze on his face.

Crimson covered her ripped suit sleeve.

His blood ran cold as he watched hers drip. "You're hit."

He slammed on the breaks and did a U-turn, tires squealing, horns beeping around them as he plowed into the opposite lane, back the way they'd come. *Oh, hell.*

She was shooting him the megadeath glare. "What are you doing? Are you insane?"

If he was, he was entitled to it with her showing up in his life after all these years without warning. He straightened the car on the road. "Taking you to the hospital."

"The bullet didn't hit bone. It's not that serious." She held the bloody arm up, bent at the elbow, and looked under her sleeve for a few seconds before she flexed her elbow. She winced and tried her best to hide it, turning her head.

He stepped harder on the gas. *Oh, man.* He'd had her for only an hour and he'd broken her already.

Jamie was going to kill him. Mitch Mendoza, too. Mitch was probably going to torture him first. "Push your seat back. Head down, arm up. I'm going to get you help."

"I'm not bleeding out. Take it easy."

He couldn't. He'd been responsible for her in the past and that somehow stayed with him. Plus she was Mitch's baby sister now.

Dammit, he should have never let her come with him to Jimmy's place.

He glanced into his rearview mirror, but the Mustang had already disappeared. "From now on, you work out of the office."

"I don't think so."

Anger rolled over him. "If you didn't get shot, I would have those idiots by now." She had no idea how distracting she was.

"You could have killed us with your driving," she snapped back. "You could have killed innocent civilians."

He swallowed a growl, hoping to God they would sedate her at the hospital. He wondered who he'd have to talk to to get her knocked out for a week.

He drew a steadying breath and focused. "When we get to the E.R., you need to keep in mind that my team is doing undercover work here. We're consulting for CBP as far as everyone else is concerned."

"I'm not going to the E.R. Seriously." She paused for a moment before she continued, "If you want to, you can take me back to my hotel. I wouldn't mind changing clothes."

"You need a doctor."

"I have a first-aid kit in my room. It'll be faster. I go to the E.R. with a non-life-threatening injury, and we'll be there for the rest of the day."

He chewed that over. She was right. Not that he had to like it.

"Fine. I'll take you back to your hotel. But I'm looking at your arm. Then I'll decide if you have to go to the E.R."

She scowled and, even scowling, managed to look beautiful. "You were always bossy."

She was talking about the bad old days.

"I was supposed to tell you what to do. That was my job." And he'd failed spectacularly. He didn't like to think about that, so he asked, "Where are you staying?"

"Pebble Creek. Prickly Pear Garden Hotel. Right in the middle of town."

He knew the place.

He picked up his phone and called the office, updated Ryder on what had happened at the trailer park. With the license-plate info Lilly had already called in, half the team was already out looking for the Mustang, and so was local law enforcement, so that was good. They'd get them. Shep told Ryder the direction the car had been headed when last seen.

"How are you doing?" he asked Lilly when he hung up. They were reaching Pebble Creek at last and he had to slow a little as there were even more cars on the road here.

The small border town was getting ready for a rodeo.

There were signs all over the place and billboards with images of cowboys and bucking bulls. The rodeo circuit was a big deal around these parts, a lot of outsiders coming in, which wasn't helping their investigation one bit.

"You're not responsible for my well-being," Lilly was saying. "I'm not seventeen anymore."

"Yeah, I noticed that," he said aloud, without meaning to.

A quick laugh escaped her, the sound sneaking inside his chest. Even her laugh was sexy, heaven help him. He turned down Main Street, drove straight to the hotel and pulled into the parking structure.

"Are you okay? Why don't you just sit here for a minute?"

She shot him a dark look. "I'm not going to pass out."

Good. Because he really didn't want to have to carry her up. He didn't think he could handle touching her.

They walked to the elevators together. He kept close watch on her from the corner of his eye. At least they were alone when they got on. Her bloody arm would have brought on some questions, for sure. But they reached her room on the third floor without running into anyone.

She had a suite, small but tidy. She walked straight to the closet and grabbed some clothes. "I'm going to clean up. Make yourself at home," she said before she disappeared behind the bathroom door.

He looked around more carefully. The space, like any hotel room, was dominated by a bed: king-size, plenty of room for two. He cut that thought right off and turned his back to the damn thing. He blew some air from his lungs. He shouldn't be here. He shoved his hands into his pockets and reassured himself with the thought that he was here only in a professional capacity, and this would be the last time.

He scanned the rest of the furniture: a desk and a table with chairs in the small kitchenette. Plenty enough for the week she would be staying.

The sound of running water drew his attention to the bathroom door. He bent his head, rubbed his thumb and index fingers over his eyebrows as he squeezed his eyes shut for a second. He so didn't want to think about the new, grown-up Lilly naked under the hot spray of water.

He did anyway. Maybe he had more self-discipline than the average Joe, but he was still a man.

She kept the shower brief. Long before he could have reined in his rampant imagination, she emerged from the bathroom, wearing soft white slacks and a pale green tank top that emphasized the green of her eyes. A nasty red wound, at least four inches long, marred her lower right arm. It still seeped blood.

She went to the closet again and bent to the bottom. She grabbed a jumbo first-aid kit, then came over to sit on the edge of the bed. "I wouldn't mind if you helped me bandage this up. I'm not good with my left hand."

The bed? With five chairs in the suite, she had to sit *there?*

He almost suggested the kitchen table, but he didn't want her to guess that she affected him in any way.

He stepped up to her, trying not to notice her fresh, soapy scent. "You travel with an emergency kit?"

She'd been a pretty haphazard person back when he'd known her, definitely not the Girl Scout type. More of a "let the chips fall where they may" sort of girl.

She popped the lid open. "I like to be prepared."

Of course, she was an FBI agent now. She'd probably been shot at before, even if he didn't want to think about it. Obviously, she'd lived and learned.

He looked at the brown bottle of peroxide in the middle of the box. "Let's start with the disinfecting."

The bullet ripped along her skin but didn't go through, didn't damage muscle, or not too badly. That was good. She was right—she didn't need the E.R. Although, it might have been better if a nurse was doing this.

He hadn't planned on seeing her in so little clothes that he would have to notice her toned arms. He hadn't planned on getting close enough to her to touch her.

But fine—he was a soldier. He could suck it up for ten minutes. As long as he didn't look at the curve of her breasts, which the tank top very unhelpfully accentuated.

"This won't hurt a bit," he said.

She raised an eyebrow. "That's what they always say."

He slipped into latex gloves and disinfected the wound then dabbed it dry. To her credit, she didn't make a sound. He leaned closer to get a better look at the damage now that dry blood didn't obstruct his view.

She held still. "So?"

"The missing swath of skin is too wide for butterfly bandages, but the gash isn't deep enough to really need stitches."

To her credit, she didn't say *I told you so.*

He put on antiseptic cream then a sterile pad, wrapped her arm in gauze. "It's going to leave a nasty scar."

"Good thing I'm not a photo model."

As she shrugged, his gaze strayed to her naked shoulder, to her soft, tanned skin. Feeling lust at this moment had to be wrong for at least half a dozen reasons. Trouble was, she had him so bamboozled, he couldn't remember any of them.

He cleared his throat. "Good to go."

She flashed a smile. "Thanks."

"Don't mention it." He stepped back.

"And thank you for…before," she added with a tilt of her head, her eyes growing serious. She filled her lungs, a consternated look coming over her face for a second. "I'm sorry if I was a difficult teenager."

Difficult didn't begin to describe her. "You were something."

She smiled again.

He didn't smile back. "And by that, I mean trouble. And it was pretty obvious you'd be even bigger trouble in a couple of years. I was just hoping we wouldn't be running in the same circles by then."

She watched him. "And here I am."

"And here you are." He drew a slow breath, and the flowery scent of her soap hit him all over again.

LILLY WATCHED THE WARY expression on his face.

Being alone in a hotel room with Shepard Lewis had been her teenage dream. To have him here now seemed beyond strange, even if under vastly different circumstances than she'd spent hours daydreaming about back in the day.

She'd written *songs* about him, for heaven's sake.

She pushed all that away.

"You kept insurance on the car I borrowed," she said. Okay, stole. But seeing how they were practically colleagues now, there was no sense splitting hairs.

He shifted where he stood. "Figured you couldn't

afford it. Driving without insurance is illegal. Didn't want you to get into more trouble if you got caught."

"You never reported it stolen. That car saved my life. I lived in it the first year after I ran away."

He nodded.

"How come you're no longer a parole officer?"

His dark eyes focused a little sharper, his jaw jutting out a little, his masculine lips tightening.

Oh, God. "Did you quit because of me?" Had she been that bad?

He backed away from her, to the window, and looked out. He said nothing.

"You did?" She stared.

He did a sexy, one-shouldered shrug. "Technically, I was let go."

She stared some more as she tried to make sense of that.

"Why? You were really good. You were the only decent person I met in the system. If anyone could have made me go straight, it was you. You just got me too late. I was… Look, nobody could've gotten through to me by that point. Why on earth would they let you go?"

He turned back to her, holding her gaze. "There was that letter."

For a long second, she had no idea what he was talking about. Then it clicked. "The email I sent?"

"Work emails are not private."

"But I was thanking you for all your help and apologizing for the car—"

And then it hit her.

Heat flushed her face. The email… *Oh, God.* At the end, in a fit of teenage drama, she'd confessed her undying love. She might have even mentioned that she would be saving her virginity for him.

She'd blocked that memory, apparently, until now. She cringed as she pushed to her feet and busied herself with packing up the first-aid kit. FBI agents didn't blush, she tried to remind herself, too late.

"I'm sorry," she said without looking at him. She couldn't just now.

She had a fair idea what had happened. He'd probably been accused of encouraging her teenage fancy. He hadn't. The opposite, if anything. He'd always tried to treat her as a big brother would, which used to frustrate the living daylights out of her.

"I'm really sorry," she said again, feeling it in the bottom of her soul.

"Don't worry about it. I found my place."

She didn't know what to say. She put away the white box and moved out to her kitchen to put a little distance between them. "Would you like a drink?"

"I better get going." But he stayed where he was and watched her for a long minute. "There was one thing I could never figure out. Why did you set fire to the house?"

The air got stuck in her lungs. "Your house burned down?"

Again, he waited awhile before he spoke. "Could have been an accident." He shook his head, then scratched his eyebrow as he thought. "I had the oil pan over to the side. You knocked a few things over when you drove the car off the metal ramp, come to think of it. Something might have thrown a spark."

She'd burned his house down.

She sank into the nearest chair as the stark truth hit her. "I ruined your life."

He gave a wry smile. "Don't be too hard on yourself."

For the first time in a long time, she had no idea what to say. He was armed. Why hadn't he shot her yet?

She wasn't about to ask him and give him any ideas.

For her, coming here, seeing Shep again meant… tying up some loose ends from her past. He'd been a good memory. She might have even looked forward to showing off to him a little…*look, I've made it,* that kind of thing.

She might have spent some extra time on her hair and makeup this morning. He'd pushed her away years ago. Now part of her wanted him to see what he'd missed and maybe even regret it.

She closed her eyes. What a fool she'd been.

All these years, he must have thought of her only as his worst nightmare.

His phone rang, breaking the silence, and he answered it. She was ridiculously grateful for the chance to gather herself.

He listened before he said, "Okay, I'll be right there."

"What is it?" she asked, still a little dazed by his revelations. "Did they find the Mustang?"

He slipped his phone back into his pocket. "Not yet. It's probably hidden somewhere in a garage right now. It belongs to a Doug Wagner, who doesn't seem to be home at the moment. Keith went out there. He got a list of Wagner's buddies. A neighbor said Wagner likes to hang out with them at The Yellow Armadillo."

"Which is?"

"A seedy bar in Pebble Creek. Known smuggler hangout." He shrugged. "But he wouldn't be out in public right now, after a hit. We're going to run down his friends and see if he's holed up with one of them or, at least, if one of them is holding the Mustang for him."

He held out his phone for her, with a mug shot on the

screen. The man in the picture was average-looking—beady dark eyes, greasy hair, giant chin.

She'd seen only a little of the Mustang's driver, but enough to match him to the photo. She pushed to her feet. "That's him. I'm coming with you."

"No." He said it as if he meant it, in that stern, disapproving tone she knew only too well. "You just got shot. You're probably still tired from flying out here. And now you're injured. Stay and rest. Just take the rest of the day off, all right? Give your body a chance to recover."

She bristled for a moment but then, just this once, she decided to give in to him. A few hours of distance might be just what the both of them needed to put the past behind them. They needed to do that so they could move forward.

"I'm really sorry about before. Do you accept my apology?"

He nodded without having to think about it. "I'm glad it all worked out for you in the end. It's good to see you doing well."

"You, too." It was a relief that she hadn't driven him to alcohol or something. "When I come into the office tomorrow morning, we'll start over. Could we do that?"

"It's a deal." He walked out the door with a brief nod at her, then closed it behind him.

She had to give it to him, he wasn't one to hold a grudge. She wasn't sure she could have been as understanding. She thought for a minute about their past, about where they were now, and tried to put things into perspective. *Think positive.*

She did that, and she also thought of something that would let her show Shep that she'd changed, that she wasn't the same person who'd nearly ruined his life, that she was good at what she did now.

The sudden need to prove herself to him took her by surprise.

When she'd received the assignment, she got a list of the team members and a one-page memo on each. She knew she would have to face Shep and she didn't really think she'd have any problem with it. She'd expected an awkward moment or two, maybe, but then they'd get over it.

Reality, however, turned out to be a lot more complicated.

She looked up the address of The Yellow Armadillo on the internet, then walked to her closet. Just because she'd agreed to stay away from the office for the rest of the day, it didn't mean she was done with investigating. She wasn't here on vacation. She wasn't here just to observe and evaluate the team.

She was here to help them achieve their objective.

She'd come prepared, brought undercover clothes in addition to her FBI suits. She pulled on blue jeans, cowboy boots, left the tank top and combed her hair out, then pushed a cowboy hat over her head. *Ready.* She would hang out at the bar, nurse a beer and get a feel for local activity.

Wagner was the key. The Coyote must have sent him to take out Jimmy, a loose end. Wagner could lead them straight to the Coyote, who could take them straight to the terrorists. They needed Wagner.

Her car was at the office, but The Yellow Armadillo was just a few blocks away. A chance to clear her head was more than welcome. And she could use the walk to get a better feel for Pebble Creek. She took the stairs, adding a little more to the exercise.

Her phone rang. Unknown number.

"Hey, it's Jamie. Shep said you got shot. How are you doing?"

Okay, that was weird. She wasn't used to family checking up on her. "Just a scratch. Not to worry."

"If you need anything—"

"I'm fine." As a rule, she handled her life on her own. She didn't depend on people.

Jamie paused for a second. "Okay. Just wanted to check in."

The day was hot but not unbearable as she hung up and walked out onto the street from the hotel lobby. She turned right after the bank and walked down the side street until she found the bar.

Its sun-faded, chipped sign hung over a reinforced steel door, every inch scuffed, crying for a paint job. The parking lot was half-empty. Still, considering that it was before noon, that didn't seem like bad business. But if the bar turned a profit, the owner sure didn't invest in appearances.

When she stepped inside, the smell of beer and unwashed bodies hit her. At least a dozen people were drinking and talking at the tables. Could be they'd been out on the border, smuggling all night, then came here to grab a drink before they went home to sleep. Their gazes followed her as she cozied up to the bar.

The bartender towered more than a foot over her, drying glasses. *Definitely a bruiser.*

"Howdy." He glanced at the bandage on her arm, but said nothing about it. The bar wasn't the kind of place where people would ask questions about something like that, apparently.

"Hey." She sat by one of the columns that extended from bar to ceiling, holding a dozen ratty ads for local services and whatever. That way, at least one side of her was protected. She scanned the short hallway in the back, could see a turn at the end that probably led to the office, then the back exit.

The bartender looked her over. "What's your pleasure, little lady?" He raised a bushy eyebrow. She didn't belong here and they both knew it.

She thought about a beer before lunch, and her stomach revolted. "Wouldn't mind starting with coffee."

He pushed a bowl of peanuts a few inches closer to her and turned to the coffee corner. He was back with her cup in two minutes, powdered creamer and sugar on the side. "You new in town?"

"Traveling through."

A waitress sailed by and winked at her. "Looking for your next heartache?"

Lilly gave a smile, hoping like anything that she hadn't already found it. "No, definitely not." Letting her teenage crush with Shep reemerge would be beyond stupid. "Nice town, though. Might stay awhile," she added, suddenly inspired by the bottom ad on the post that caught her eye. The bar band was looking for a new singer.

"If I can find a gig." She nodded toward the ad and tried not to think how many years it'd been since she'd been onstage. But hanging out at the bar wouldn't give her half the chance to snoop around as working here a few hours a night would. It'd make her an insider.

"You sing?" the waitress asked as she waited for her orders to be filled. She was in her early forties, a bottle blonde, slim, wearing a white T-shirt with the bar's logo on it and a short black skirt with an apron.

"Ain't much else I can do. I got just the voice the

good Lord gave me." Lilly tried to sound country, as if she might just fit in.

The woman looked doubtful, but she said, "Come back tonight. Brian's the boss. He'll be holding tryouts."

"Thanks—"

"Mazie. And this one here's Shorty." She snorted as she indicated the bartender with her head. He fairly towered over the both of them, busy with the beer tap.

"Lilly. I think I might just try for that gig."

Even if Shep was totally going to kill her for it.

Chapter Three

Night had fallen by the time Shep and Keith made their way into town and pulled up in front of The Yellow Armadillo, after a long and dusty shift on border patrol that netted them nothing whatsoever. Normally, they would have taken a break before going into the office in the morning. But as close as they were to D-day, they'd decided to snoop around the bar a little first.

Lilly's hotel was just up the road. Not that Shep planned on stopping by for a visit. He watched for an empty space in the parking lot. He had to drive around to find a spot.

"Looks like they do good business." Keith scanned the cars, then turned to Shep. "So, did Lilly Tanner really burn down your house and steal your car and all that?"

"Don't want to talk about it."

But Keith kept waiting.

Fine. "It was an accident."

"How does somebody steal a car by accident?"

"The fire was an accident. She needed the car and..." He shrugged. There was really no good way to explain. "She wanted to start over." He'd never really held a grudge. "She was a messed-up kid and with reason. She had rough beginnings."

"True that. Sold for drugs by her own parents. That's harsh. Can you imagine?"

"Not really." He'd grown up in a happy, loving family.

"That's why you never reported the car stolen?"

He parked the car and shut off the engine. "She was just turning eighteen—she would have gone to jail. Being locked up would have broken her. She'd always been special, always stood out. I didn't want to see her broken."

He was glad she'd turned out okay. He would be even gladder when she left again. He stopped for a second and turned to Keith. "And now we're done talking about her. She's only here for a few days. It's not important."

Keith flashed one of his quick grins. "Whatever you say."

The bar sat on a side street a little back from the main drag, among service-type businesses: dry cleaner's, key copying and photocopying, a car mechanic a little farther down. The road back here was narrower and darker, the streetlights smaller and not as fancy as Main Street's, no lone-star flags, no advertising posters on the poles.

Keith got out. "Hope Wagner is here."

Shep followed. "Or the guy who was with him at the shooting. Look for anyone with a damaged wrist."

They'd put out a call to the local hospitals, but none had a patient with a gunshot wound like that. He might have gone to one of the underground clinics that served illegal immigrants. If so, they'd have no way of finding him through the health-care system.

Music filtered out to the street through the front door as they walked up, the smell of stale air and beer hitting them as they stepped inside.

Mostly men filled the bar, very few women. It seemed like the kind of place where farmhands would go to get sloppy drunk at the end of the day. A scrawny cowboy wailed on the stage, a sad song about losing his girl. The clientele paid little attention to him.

Shep and Keith bellied up to the bar and flagged down two beers. They were dressed as rodeo cowboys. With all the cowboy shirts, jeans and cowboy boots surrounding them, they fit right in.

He didn't spot anyone suspicious at first glance, except a bookie in the far corner doing some business, probably taking bets on the rodeo that would start later in the week.

The bartender slid their beers in front of them. "In town to try your luck?"

"We're in it to win it." Keith gave an enthusiastic grin. "Hoping for a break in the weather. No fun trying to train in over hundred-degree heat."

The bartender nodded with sympathy. "Where you boys from?"

"Pennsylvania." Keith puffed his chest out a little.

The man gave a whoop of a laugh. "There ain't no rodeo in Pennsylvania." He shook his head as a pitying look came into his eyes.

"There sure is." Keith grinned. "There are crazy bastards everywhere." He managed to sound proud of it.

An older guy on Keith's other side toasted them with his beer. "Amen to that."

The bartender kept laughing as he walked away.

Shep didn't mind some mocking. Being considered the village idiot was the perfect cover.

He pretended to watch the band and the out-of-tune singer onstage while he continued checking out the customers. He looked for specific faces, not just something suspicious in general. That helped. If Doug Wagner or his partner showed up tonight, they could grab him, take him in and ask him who'd paid them to shoot Jimmy.

None of his buddies had given up his location. And Shep's team couldn't find the Mustang, either.

The sad cowboy onstage finished his song and stood awkwardly for a lackluster applause before lumbering off the stage. The band stayed and another singer came on. This was one was a woman.

And then some.

Next to Shep, Keith gave a soft whistle.

She wore cherry-red cowboy boots, a denim skirt that was so short it was barely legal and a light green tank top that looked familiar.

He leaned forward to see better. Those curves… He didn't want to be thinking what he was thinking. He had to be mistaken.

She stopped in front of the microphone with her hat pulled low over her eyes, her head bent. She hadn't sung a word yet, but already she held the crowd's attention, something the previous performer hadn't managed. Chins were hitting the tables all over. The men ogled her as if they were ready to devour her.

Then she looked up and flashed a dazzling smile that lit up the room. She had a face to match the body, for sure. A couple of men growled with appreciation. Others let out more wolf whistles.

"Hot damn." Even Keith couldn't keep quiet, his voice laden with reverence.

Shep came halfway to his feet then caught himself and dropped back down just before he would have blown his cover. "What in blazing hell is Lilly doing up there?" He hissed the words between his teeth.

But Keith was too dazzled to listen.

SHE LOCKED HER KNEES so they wouldn't shake. It'd been a long time since she'd sung onstage. And she'd never been a country singer. Lilly flashed another smile before she nodded to the three-man band behind her and started into a country ballad, similar to the one the singer before her had chosen.

She was one minute into it when she realized it wasn't going to work for her, not at a place like this. The sweet love song was something women would listen to in the car while driving to school to pick up their kids. The rough-and-tumble men who filled the bar weren't looking for sentimental, no matter how good the chords were.

Brian had been clear that he wanted a performance that hit the ball out of the park. Revenue was weak on band nights now that their lead singer had quit. He wanted some serious dough coming in. He wanted something that would bring people in early and make them stay until the closing bell.

She tried her best, putting all the heart she had into the song. Unfortunately, nobody was listening. A lot of the men were looking at the stage, but they were staring at her legs.

Since the audition was to be decided by applause… If the men kept staring instead of clapping when she finished, she was sunk.

Brian had asked for one song from each singer. She glanced at him as he sat up front, paging through a ledger book. He'd paid very little attention to the auditions so far. He certainly didn't look as if he was ready to offer her the job on the spot. She needed to get his attention and she needed to do it in a hurry. Her ballad was almost over.

Oh, what the hell, since when did she play things

safe? As she sang the last note, she glanced back and winked at the band, then turned to the audience.

"I like country," she said and flashed a smile when a couple of men hooted in agreement, "but I'm a versatile kind of gal, so how about I show you a little bit of something else?"

A drunk shouted a few suggestions of what he'd like her to show him. The rest of the men laughed.

She had the lights in her eyes, so she could only make out the first row, but she knew the bar was packed. Tryouts for a new lead singer brought in some extra people, Mazie had told her just before Lilly came onstage. People liked the idea of getting a vote. Liked to check out fresh meat, too, probably.

Lilly took the ribbing in stride and tossed her cowboy hat into the audience, whipped her long hair and belted out the first line of the chorus to "I Love Rock 'n' Roll" at the top of her lungs.

There was a second of pause. This was the moment where she might get thrown off the stage. But nobody booed and the manager simply watched her.

Then the band picked up the song.

Relief flooded her as she went on singing, excitement filling her little by little, and she danced across the stage as she sang, suddenly feeling like a kid again, without any worldly possessions, just the road and her guitar. She sang her heart out like she used to, the old moves coming right back as she rocked the hell out of the place.

She'd already been thrown back to the past by seeing Shep, and now this finished the job. She felt a decade younger and couldn't say she didn't like it.

"Yee-ha!" someone shouted.

Boots slapped against the wood floor, the applause

deafening when she finished, with a few marriage proposals thrown in, and the men demanding more.

She felt a surge of satisfaction and just plain pleasure. She'd worked so hard to make herself into something more, something serious, that she'd forgotten how good this had felt.

"You have a fun night, now!" she called out to acknowledge the support.

The manager was grinning at her, looking pleased as peaches.

She grinned back then ran backstage, passing the next act going up, another lanky cowboy who stared at her with a troubled look on his face. She set aside the buzz of adrenaline and turned her attention to her true purpose for being here: covert surveillance. She turned off the rock chick and turned on the FBI agent.

For the moment, she was alone backstage. The narrow hallway connected the main bar with the office and the kitchen that prepared a dozen food items—all well salted to keep the drinking at an optimum. Her attention settled on a closed door at the end on her other side. She'd seen that earlier, had wondered where it led. This could be her chance to investigate.

The next contestant started into a song on the stage, sounding unsure. He had a good voice, but it seemed that her performance had thrown him. He didn't seem to be able to find his footing.

Lilly tuned him out as she hurried over to the mystery door and tried the knob. Locked. Since she was pretty sure they were close to the outside wall and there was no upstairs above the bar, if the door hid stairs, they'd be going to a basement.

She had lock picks in her pocket. She reached for them, but footsteps behind her made her spin around.

The music was so loud, she hadn't heard him in time, not until the man was right behind her.

Brian's face was expressionless as he watched her. He said nothing, waiting for her to speak first.

She flashed him her best smile. "Is this the staff bathroom? I think somebody's in there."

"No staff bathroom. We all use the one by the jukebox." He didn't volunteer any information on where this door led.

She could have asked, but didn't want to sound as if she was snooping. "So how did I look on your stage?" she asked instead. "Felt right—" she grinned "—I tell you that. Nice crowd, too. I sure could get used to it."

He measured her up. "We've never done anything but country." He paused. "You know, from anybody else, this might not have gone down as well. But you…" His gaze stalled on her breasts for a second. Then slid to her injury. "What happened to your arm?"

She shrugged. "An argument with my last drummer."

"You fit the harder music, I guess. Maybe it's time for a change here. Let's try it for a few weeks. When can you start?"

"As soon as possible." They needed to find Wagner, and so far the bar was their only lead. "When could I get back on that stage, do you think?"

"We do live music Fridays and Saturdays. So how about tomorrow?" He named a dollar amount per night.

She didn't argue with him. She couldn't risk him changing his mind. It was Thursday. Tomorrow and the day after would give her two full nights to snoop around here.

"I'm in. Thanks. I'll be here tomorrow." She moved to pass by him, but just as she did, she felt his hand patting her bottom.

Really?

Oh, man.

She could have put him on his back with a single move. But right now, going undercover at the Armadillo was more important. So she smiled as she turned and said, "Hey! There'll be none of that."

Brian raised his eyebrows, then shrugged after a second. "As long as you bring in money, it's all good," he said and simply watched as she walked away from him.

Would have been nice if that was the last word on the subject, but she didn't think it would go as easy as that. Still, she'd cross that bridge when she got to it. She was in, and for now that was all that counted.

She grabbed her bag from behind the bar, then headed for the back door. She wanted to get a good feel for the place inside and out. Supposedly it was a known smuggler hangout. Did Brian know? Was Wagner involved? Did anyone smuggle any contraband straight through here? Did anyone here know anything about the terrorists coming through? She had two days to find out.

She pushed the metal door open. Grabbing some fresh air after her performance shouldn't raise any suspicions.

She'd driven around the block before she'd shown up tonight to sing, so she knew the bar backed onto a narrow alley. She expected that she might run into a couple of smokers out there. But she didn't expect to run into Shep.

He was about to come in as she stepped out. He looked pretty steamed about something.

She pulled up short to keep from running into him. "What are you doing here?"

His eyes glinted with fury as he grabbed her by the arm and pulled her aside. The door clicked closed behind her. They were alone in the alley that led to a side street on their left and ended at a brick wall two stores down on their right.

"What are *you* doing here?" He was all decked out in cowboy gear. And looked hot in it, dammit. The shirt perfectly fit his wide shoulders, the jeans pretty nice on his long legs.

While part of her appreciated the view, he didn't look as if he appreciated anything about her at the moment. He looked mad enough to commit violence.

"Why are you here?" He snapped the question at her again.

"I'm going undercover." She kept her voice down even if there wasn't anyone else out there in the ten-or-so-feet-wide space between buildings.

"Like hell." He dragged her away from the door.

She went with him, but only because anybody could come out from the bar at any moment, and she didn't want them to hear the conversation. She didn't want to blow her cover before she had a chance to use it.

He finally stopped next to an empty Dumpster. "Gyrating around the stage like that. In that…skirt." His nostrils flared. "What were you thinking?"

"Listen—" She yanked at the skirt that had ridden up her legs from walking, revealing the winding tattoo on her inner thigh—an old mistake. "The bar is connected to smuggling. Through Doug Wagner, it's also connected to the Coyote. In all likelihood, the Coyote was the one who hired Wagner to take out Jimmy before the law could catch up with him. The Yellow Armadillo is a decent lead. It's worth checking out. Isn't that why you're here?"

Instead of congratulating her on her good work, he looked as if he was grinding his teeth.

She remembered his mad face. It was as if they were back in the past all over again. She'd hoped he would be more…impressed with her this time around. Not that she needed his validation. She glared right back. "What's your problem?"

"You." He spit out the word. "On a stage. Naked."

Oh, for heaven's sake. She was fully clothed. "I've done worse on the road."

His shoulders stiffened. "I don't want to know about it." He drew in a ragged breath. "That shouldn't have happened. You shouldn't have run away. I should have found a way to stop you."

All he ever wanted was to save her somehow, back then and now, apparently. While all she'd ever wanted, at least back then, was for him to see her as a woman. "Nobody could have stopped me. And it wasn't bad. Nobody beat me like at some of the homes. I was my own person. I grew up. I turned out okay."

"Better than most runaways," he grudgingly agreed, then let several minutes pass before he asked, "Is this what you did after you left? Singing?"

"You expected a crime spree?"

A hint of a smile tugged at the corner of his lips. "It crossed my mind."

She shook her head. "Things could have easily gone that way. But for whatever reason, I decided to go in another direction." She allowed a hint of a smile of her own. "Maybe it was your good influence. Believe it or not, your car was the last thing I lifted. I tried odd jobs, but I figured out pretty soon that singing paid the best."

"And then?"

"When I found a steady gig, I finally made enough to rent a room. The landlady was all right. She offered me fifty bucks off the rent as long as I attended GED classes."

Pat had been the closest thing to a mother Lilly had ever known. Never judged her, had never gotten in her face about anything. She'd taken Lilly seriously and treated her like somebody instead of a problem. Shep had done that, but for some reason she hadn't been ready with Shep. Then she was suddenly ready with Pat. Maybe spending some time living in a car had made the difference.

Shep let his hand drop from her arm at last. "And then?"

"One of the GED teachers talked me into taking a few college classes in criminal law. I think to discourage me from getting too cozy with some of the shadier guys at the bar where I was singing. I thought, why not? It was an area where I had some experience." No one knew that better than Shep. She'd gone to him with an impressive juvie record.

He looked skeptical. "College grew on you?"

"You know? It did." She'd liked the challenge of it, the thought of doing something she'd never figured she could be capable of. "I even got a scholarship. And singing brought in enough money to pay the rest of my expenses. I didn't quit the bars until I got hired full-time by the police department. They paid me to do more college. Then I moved to the FBI eventually."

He took a second to take that all in. "Why aren't you married, raising two-point-five kids in the suburbs?"

"Who says I'm not?"

His eyes widened. "Are you?"

She waited a moment before she shook her head. "I'd rather do something I'm good at." And she had time. She wasn't yet thirty.

He frowned. "You can be anything you want to be—"

"And I can achieve anything I set my mind to." She finished his old mantra for him. She'd heard it a few dozen times, or a hundred. "Why aren't *you* doing the family thing?" The brief she had on him said he'd never been married.

"I'd rather do one thing and do it well."

"Live to work?"

He watched her. "You made it up the ranks pretty fast."

She grinned into the darkness. "Turns out I'm good at something other than criminal mischief."

"Yeah, like giving me a headache without half trying," he said, but he no longer sounded mad.

"I'm sorry. About the past. Again. I didn't mean to—" She didn't finish. Rehashing her sins wouldn't work in her favor. "The point is, having someone undercover here would be an asset to the team—"

Movement at the opening of the alley caught her eye. She was facing that way, while Shep faced toward the bar.

The dark shape that had appeared was walking toward them. Then he walked under the bare lightbulb hanging above a rusted back door of some other business, and she recognized him from the mug shot. Doug Wagner, the guy in the red Mustang who'd shot Jimmy.

He eyed them with suspicion as he came closer. There was only one thing a rodeo cowboy and a woman dressed like her would be doing in the back alley, and it wasn't having a serious conversation, she realized in a flash.

Shep had been half leaning against the brick wall. She shifted to push him fully against the wall and nestled her body against his.

"Lilly." He said her name in a strangled whisper. He still hadn't seen Wagner.

She nuzzled his neck. "Just play along for a minute," she whispered into his ear as she ran her hands up his chest. She didn't mean anything by it, but found herself distracted suddenly. *Okay. Nice.* He definitely wasn't lacking in the muscle department.

For a moment, he stood stiffly, then he probably heard the footsteps at last because he caught on and put his hands on her waist. And nuzzled her right back, setting the sensitive skin on her neck tingling.

God, it'd been a long time since a man had made anything of hers tingle. She'd been married to her job for too long, had taken too many back-to-back assignments lately. This felt nice. It made her miss…something she'd never really had.

Of course, he was all her teenage fantasies come true. And then some. The hard planes of his body fit perfectly against hers. He was all sexy, hot male.

"You smell like leather," she whispered to him.

"New boots, new belt."

"Huh." Okay, so her response could have been a shade more intelligent, but…

Shep Lewis had his hands on her!

She'd pictured this happening a few hundred times when she'd been seventeen, but reality was so much better. Thank God she was grown up and had moved on and all that. It would be a disaster if she let that old crush come back, considering Shep was one of the men she was supposed to be observing and reporting on.

His hands tightened on her waist and he pulled her even tighter against him as Wagner passed by them, then went inside.

Her breasts flattened against Shep's hard chest. Heat flashed through her.

But when he said, "Was that Doug Wagner?" his voice held no desire, only anger.

She sobered a little as he set her away from him.

His eyes narrowed. "Why the hell didn't we grab him?"

"Let's see who he talks to first. If Wagner doesn't pan out, there might be another lead here at the bar. As you said, it's a known smuggler hangout. I want to keep my cover. I want to be able to come back tomorrow and Saturday."

"Our goal for coming here was Wagner."

"What if whoever he gets his orders from is here? The higher up we get on the chain of command, the more likely we're to find actionable intel. Wagner might not know the Coyote's true identity. But the guy he reports to could have that."

Shep's expression was that of supreme annoyance, but he pulled out his phone. "I'll call the office. You go in and keep an eye on him."

So she went back inside, aggravated that their close encounter had affected her, while it had done nothing to Shep. Like back in the day—with her mooning after him, and him ignoring her. She was so not ever going back to that. She might have been lonely. He might have looked hotter than ever. But she had her pride, dammit.

She barely walked three steps down the hallway before she spotted Wagner, the sight of him distracting her from Shep. He was hurrying toward that closed door she'd checked out earlier. He had a key. He turned it in the lock and quickly disappeared.

She hurried after him but, of course, he'd locked the door behind him. She tried to listen, but the band was still playing, a woman was singing now, and she couldn't hear anything else. She glanced around and pulled her lock picks from her pocket. Hopefully, Brian wouldn't show up this time. How bad could her luck get?

Not too bad, as it turned out. The manager stayed out of sight. And she had the door unlocked in under thirty seconds.

A semidark staircase led down in front of her. *Bingo.* A basement. That certainly had potential if any nefarious activities were going on around here.

She left the door open a crack so when Shep came inside, he might get a clue as to where she'd disappeared. Then she started down, trying to listen if she could hear anyone talking down there.

Until she went around the turn in the stairs and ran into a three-hundred-pound chunk of bad attitude, wearing sweat shorts, a black muscle shirt and a full gallon of sweat. Pockmarks covered his face, his eyes small and mean.

She smiled at him, and did her best to look harmless and clueless. "Sorry. I was looking for Brian."

Two beefy, hairy arms reached out to grab her. If the dark glare and snarl the man shot her was any indication, he wasn't particularly happy to see her there.

Chapter Four

"Up," the man said.

Lilly didn't argue, but backed away from him as soon as he let her go. "Sorry." She smiled again, even wider. "I'm brand-new. Don't actually start until tomorrow. I got the gig. Can you believe it?"

"Auditions are still going on."

She lifted her shoulder. "I suppose Brian wants to let everyone who showed up at least sing. He seems so nice," she lied cheerfully.

The guy didn't look touched. His hand hovered near his waist.

She was pretty sure he had a gun tucked into his waistband behind his back. She was unarmed and obviously so. Her skimpy clothes couldn't have hidden anything. There was no reason for him to escalate.

But if he did, at least she was higher up on the stairs than he, in a better position, and was trained in hand-to-hand combat. She could take him down if things came to that. But only if she had to. She'd much rather keep her cover.

She kept backing up, looking lost and apologetic.

He didn't go for the gun. Maybe he was buying her act. When they were at the top of the stairs, he waited until she was up and out, then closed the door in her face. She heard the lock turn.

Okay. That could have gone better. But it could have gone worse, too. Bottom line was, she needed to find a way to get back down to that basement so she could figure out what on earth was going on down there.

Shep, who was just coming in through the back door, caught her eye and raised a questioning eyebrow.

She hurried over and filled him in.

"You went down there? Alone?" He said the words between his teeth.

She smiled in case anyone was watching them. They could be seen from the bar. Plenty of people hung around waiting on Shorty for a drink.

"Next time, you tell me." Shep spit out the words. "You're here to observe and advise."

"And assist."

"Dammit, Lilly."

Since she didn't want to argue with him—or be seen with him too much—she simply walked away. She meant to hang out at the bar for a while and talk to Shorty and the waitresses if she got a chance. But Shep came after her. They came out of the hallway into the main area.

"How big is the basement?" he asked right next to her, so only she would hear.

"I didn't get far enough to see."

"I'll try to get down there later."

"They keep the door locked."

"If you managed, so can I."

Of course, because *he* would have to do everything, Mr. Hot Stuff Commando. She couldn't possibly be enough. He was never going to forget what a screwup she'd been. She pressed her lips together and turned away from him, just in time to see Doug Wagner head for the door up front.

He must have come up from the basement and gone around the stage the other way.

Keith was about six yards behind him.

She gave a double take. *Keith?* Were they all here? Lilly scanned the tables but didn't see the rest of the team.

He nodded to Shep, then toward Wagner, who pushed through the front door and was out of sight the next second. Keith followed.

"You stay," Shep told her under his breath. "We need to grab him before he disappears." Then he took off after them.

SHEP STEPPED OUTSIDE just in time to see Wagner walk to a white sedan parked at the end of the street and drive off. Keith was already at the beat-up pickup they used as their undercover car, on his cell phone, probably calling in the development. Shep caught up with him and jumped behind the wheel, then took off after Wagner.

Keith stayed in phone contact with the others. "Suspect heading south. We're two cars behind." He muted the phone before he turned to Shep. "How did it go with Lilly?"

"Fine."

"She's hot. I mean, like—man, did you see the way she moved up there? Those curves…"

Shep gave an annoyed grunt. Not only had he seen them, they'd been pressed against him in the alley, a sensation he wasn't about to forget anytime soon, unfortunately. But just because he couldn't forget the incident, it didn't mean he was going to share his feelings about it.

Keith made some more appreciative noises, keeping the phone on mute. "You sure you're not going to hook up with her?"

"Absolutely not."

"I wouldn't mind asking her out for a drink," the idiot went on. "She's here to work with us. No sense being rude to her."

Shep's fingers tightened on the steering wheel. He hated the idea of *anyone* asking Lilly anywhere. But she was a grown woman, entitled to her own decisions, so he stayed quiet.

Wagner turned off the main road and they followed. He stopped his sedan in front of an apartment building and got out.

The building had four levels, maybe a hundred apartments. Looked like a fairly new place, the siding clean and trim, the windows double paned. Pebble Creek was growing, adding some housing around the edges. The complex was one of a dozen like it that Shep had seen while driving around.

What was Wagner doing here? His official address was a trailer park across town. Who was he visiting? With a little luck, it would be a connection to the Coyote.

The man turned back to the sedan, reached into the back and pulled out a rifle. He left his car running as he walked away from it.

Shep watched as the man hurried into the building. "I don't like it."

"Definitely not a good sign," Keith said, then called in the address to the rest of the team, who were on their way.

Still, it'd be at least twenty minutes before they got here. He had no time to wait for reinforcements. They had to take Wagner into custody before he killed anybody else, or got himself killed.

Shep checked his weapon. "I take the front, you take the back."

They got out and ran toward the building, then separated when they reached the steps. Keith went around to see if there was a back entrance. Shep pushed through the front door, weapon in hand but down at his side, in case he ran into civilians.

The main lobby stood empty—Mexican tile floor, no trash, no graffiti, a decent middle-class kind of place. The far wall held a hundred or so mailboxes. Two pink kid bikes stood in a back corner. Didn't seem like drug-dealer-lair territory.

He could hear footsteps on the floor above him. That would be Wagner most likely. Shep followed, keeping his gun ready. He stole up the stairs silently, hugging the wall.

When knocking sounded from above, a sharp rap on wood, he moved faster. Seemed as if nobody responded, because the knocking continued. Then he could hear some small noise from below. Probably Keith coming in from the back. Was there a back staircase? There should be. A fire escape if nothing else. It'd be nice if they could corner Wagner.

Shep kept moving up. One flight of stairs to go. Just a few more steps. He looked right when he made it up all the way, and saw Wagner raise his rifle as the door he stood in front of inched open.

Shep raised his gun. "Drop your weapon!"

Wagner swung toward him just as the door slammed in his face. He squeezed off a shot at Shep, missed, then started running in the opposite direction down the hallway.

"Drop your weapon!" Shep ran after him.

Wagner squeezed off another shot.

Shep ducked, but he had nothing to duck behind for cover. He kept moving anyway, wishing he had his bulletproof vest. But since they were coming from the bar, dressed as rodeo cowboys, neither Keith nor he had any real protection.

Wagner reached the end of the hallway and turned.

Okay. Shep slowed. *Showdown.*

But instead of surrendering, the man squeezed off another shot, then slammed through the last door to his left.

Shep ran forward to the spot where the man had disappeared. Emergency fire exit. With any luck, Keith would be coming up and they'd have Wagner trapped between them.

He pushed the door open and inched forward carefully, kept his weapon raised in front, in case Wagner was waiting for him. But he saw no one, and judging from boots slapping on the steps above, Wagner was going to the next floor up in hopes of escaping instead of going down.

Shep ran after him. "Stop right there and throw down your weapon!" He needed to catch up to the bastard before an innocent civilian got in the middle of this.

And then someone did.

He heard screams, ran faster. Saw Wagner at last in the next turn. The man was holding his gun at two teenage girls who'd apparently snuck into the staircase for a smoke. They were fifteen, tops, dressed in summer skirts and flip-flops. They were white with fear, their eyes rapidly filling with tears as they whimpered, their half-smoked cigarettes having fallen at their feet.

Wagner's eyes darted back and forth as he tried to

figure out his next step. "You stay back," he demanded from behind the girls.

"Listen—" Shep didn't get to finish.

One of the girls panicked and dashed forward, tumbling down the stairs, throwing herself at him, screaming, nearly knocking him off his feet. Her flailing arms knocked his weapon aside as she tried to get behind him to safety.

"Get down!" Shep pushed her out of the way, doing his best to keep her from hurting herself, dammit.

Wagner used the momentary distraction, shoved the other girl down the steps, too, on top of Shep and tore off running once again.

The girls didn't seem to have any injuries worse than a scraped knee.

Shep called back to them as he ran up the stairs. "Get back into your apartment, lock the door. Call 911 if you need medical help." Then he turned his full attention to the man running from him and gave chase as if he meant it.

Three more floors before he reached the door to the roof. He wasn't even breathing hard. Every man on his team trained every single day. He could go a hell of a lot longer than this little sprint.

Once again, he went through the door carefully, gun first, and prepared to duck from fire, but no bullets came.

Chimney and vent stacks broke up the flat, long roof that radiated back the sun's heat, making the air shimmer above it. He had a flashback, for a second, to his days in the Iraqi desert. He shook that aside and pushed forward. When a shot finally did ring out, he rolled behind a vent stack.

"Cease fire!"

But bullets kept coming, pretty hard and fast. Wagner had to be hiding behind one of the chimneys. Looked as if he'd decided to make his last stand here.

"Cease fire!" Shep rolled over into the cover of a chimney that provided more substantial protection, caught sight of another fire-stairs door on the far end of the building just as Keith ducked through it.

He signaled, pointing at the spot where the shots had come from so far. Keith nodded back and rushed forward, into cover of a vent stack.

Shep waited until he was in place, then rushed Wagner. While Wagner was focused on him, Keith took his shot and sent a bullet through the guy's right shoulder.

Wagner went down screaming.

"Stay down! Hands behind your head!" Shep reached him and kept his gun trained at him. "Stay down! Drop your weapon!"

Down in the parking lot, cars pulled in squealing. Keith glanced over the edge of the roof. "They're here."

Good. The rest of the team could help with cleanup and damage control. Especially since police sirens sounded in the distance. It'd be a full-on party soon. Maybe the girls had called in. Probably other residents had also reported the gunshots. The police would want explanations.

He slapped the cuffs on Wagner, grabbed him by the elbow and pulled him up. The man was crying and yelling about his shoulder. The idiot could dish out violence, but it didn't look as if he could take much when the tables were turned.

"You have the right to remain silent." Keith Mirandized him before Shep had a chance.

Had to be done. The man needed to be put away.

No sense in letting him slip through the cracks due to a technicality.

They took Wagner down, met with Ryder who was rushing up the stairs.

"Anyone else?" he asked. "I had the rest of the team spread out through the building."

Shep shook his head. "Just this one."

Ryder talked into his radio unit. "Shooter in custody. Coming down the south-end fire stairs. Withdraw from building." He ended the connection before he asked, "Any injuries?"

"Just him as far as I know." Shep glanced at the bleeding wound on Wagner's shoulder. "He'll live." But they'd have to take him to the hospital before they could interrogate him. "Local police can go through the building."

Bullets had flown, and they had the ability to go through wood and walls. Somebody could be lying bleeding in one of the apartments for all they knew.

Jamie and Mo walked Wagner downstairs while Ryder haggled with the local cops over who should have the man in custody.

Shep caught Keith's attention and gestured back toward the building with his head as he backed toward the entrance. Keith followed him.

"I want to know who he came to take out," he said once they were inside. He didn't want the local cops to see them and get it into their heads to interfere.

They moved up the stairs together and took up position on either side of the door in question, then pulled their weapons.

Careful, Shep mouthed. Whoever was inside had been face-to-face with an assassin just minutes ago. He might start shooting and ask questions later.

Keith rapped on the door then pulled back into cover. "Customs and Border Protection. Open up."

Footsteps sounded inside. "There's a shooter in the building."

Not anymore, and the man would know that. His apartment was in the front, his windows overlooking the parking lot. He would have heard the cops arriving, would have looked and seen Wagner taken outside in cuffs.

Shep kept his focus on the door. "He's in custody. We need to talk to all the residents."

A long moment passed before the key turned in the lock. Then a small gap appeared, only a sliver of the man's face visible.

Shep put on his most trustworthy look. "We need to come in and check the apartment, make sure there are no other attackers."

"There aren't."

"We have to check for ourselves. Are you armed, sir?"

"What the hell do you think? People are shooting up the damn place."

"Please, put your weapon down and step back from the door."

Seconds ticked by until the guy made up his mind and they heard the metal of his gun click on the tile floor, heard him move back.

Shep pushed in and kicked the weapon to Keith with the back of his boot.

The man was in his mid-fifties, nearly bald with a handlebar mustache. He was tanned, but not weather-beaten like most cowboys and ranch hands who worked outside. His mouth was pressed into an angry line. His right wrist was bandaged, bloodstains on the white gauze.

Shep's gaze flew back up to his face, his eyes narrowing. He hadn't gotten a good look at the trailer park, but this one could definitely be the guy who'd ridden shotgun with Wagner. The one who'd shot Lilly before Lilly shot his hand.

"What's your name?"

"Shane Rosci."

"All right, Shane. I'm going to check your place to be on the safe side. You stay where you are." Shep moved forward, farther into the apartment, while Keith stayed with the man.

The place was a one-bedroom efficiency, clothes on the floor, dirty dishes in the sink. Didn't look as if the half-open closet held any other clothes but his. Seemed as if he lived alone here.

Shep checked for other weapons and drugs, signs of any kind of illegal activity. He went back to the living room when he didn't find anything. Didn't mean the guy wasn't a user or a dealer. He could have flushed everything when he heard the police sirens.

Shep nodded toward the bandages. "What happened to your hand?"

"Burned it cooking."

"How do you know Doug Wagner?"

"Who?" Shane's eyes went a little too wide with supposed innocence.

"The man who came here to shoot you."

He looked away. "I don't know what you're talking about."

Shep shifted his weight, tired of playing games. "Then you don't mind going to the police station in the back of the car with him?"

The man took a step back, outrage flashing across his face. "You can't arrest me. I haven't done anything."

"How about the murder of Jimmy Fishburn yesterday?"

The man paled, sweat forming on his forehead. "I didn't—"

"Are you involved in smuggling?"

"No. I'm an honest citizen. I swear. I work at the electronics store."

"What do you know about the Coyote?"

"Who?"

"Why did Doug Wagner come here today to shoot you?"

The bluster leaked out of the guy, his shoulders going down. "I owe him money."

"For what?"

The man's gaze darted from Shep to Keith then back as a look of misery came across his face. "I want to talk to my lawyer."

Keith stepped up to him. "You can call him from the car. We're taking you in for further questioning. Let's go." He herded the guy out of the apartment as the man loudly protested.

They got down to the parking lot in time to see Ryder drive away with Wagner. Apparently, he'd won the argument with the police. Then the deputy sheriff came into view, and Shep realized why the cops had backed off. As Jamie's girlfriend, Bree had some idea of what their team was doing here. She and Jamie had probably made some kind of a deal.

She came right over. "Everything okay?"

Shep put the man into the pickup. Keith moved over to the other side so the guy couldn't skip out that way.

"We're taking him over to the office." Wagner would

be at the E.R. for a while with his shoulder, which meant they could have the interrogation room for Shane.

Bree raised a slim eyebrow. "I assume at one point I'm going to be updated on what's going on here?"

"That's not my decision. Sorry." If Jamie trusted her, so did he, but he wasn't the one setting the confidentiality level of the op.

She shook her head with a long-suffering look and waved them off.

Unfortunately, as it turned out an hour or so later, Shane had no knowledge of the Coyote. He owed money to Wagner for drugs. When he couldn't pay, Wagner insisted on his help with a job. Wagner had told him they were going to send a "message" to some guy. He'd said nobody would be at the trailer.

Shane had no idea they'd killed someone until he saw it on the morning news. He'd called Wagner in a panic, who then showed up to shoot him.

"I'm innocent here." He was sweating buckets now. "I'm as much a victim as that Jimmy guy was. I swear. I did nothing."

"You shot at me and my partner when we went after you," Shep reminded him. "You hit her, actually."

"You weren't in a cop car. How in hell was I supposed to know who you were? You can't spit around here without hitting a gangbanger. I thought you were maybe the guy whose stupid trailer we hit, all mad about it."

After leaning on him pretty hard for another hour, Shep was tempted to believe him. He called Bree to come pick him up. He'd be charged with Jimmy's murder and whatever could be proven on the drug angle with Wagner.

Once they'd left, Keith and Shep drove back to the

office for their own cars so they could head back to their apartments for some shut-eye before their border shift started.

Their break passed pretty fast. Long before Shep was ready for it, they were on patrol duty. Didn't seem as if they ever really slept lately, just ran from one task to the other.

"Wouldn't have minded being in on the Wagner interrogation," he told Keith over the radio as they drove along the Rio Grande, each in their own SUV.

"They'll lean on him hard." Keith was a couple of miles ahead of him, out of sight.

Yes, they would. His team was the best of the best. Whatever the bastard had, they'd get it out of him. He thought about that as he scanned the area, taking advantage of the moonlight, switching to night-vision goggles when something moved and he needed to see better.

But they saw nothing all night other than deer and a couple of stray armadillos. Plenty of time to think about the op, and plenty of time to think about Lilly, unfortunately.

He hated the idea of her at The Yellow Armadillo, drunk ranch hands drooling all over her. He felt responsible for her. His first instinct was to protect her. Except their relationship now was completely different than when he'd been her parole officer.

In more than one way.

Why in hell did she have to throw herself into his arms in that back alley, dammit? Now he couldn't get the shape of her, the feel of her pressed against him, out of his mind.

She didn't want his protection. Too bad. She would have it anyway.

But other than for the purpose of saving her life, if it

became necessary, he wasn't going to touch her again. Ever. Because it was wrong. And because—

The hell of the thing was, he wasn't sure if he could stop again once he started.

Chapter Five

Since Lilly got the gig, she was invited back onstage to sing the last set.

The audience was pretty rowdy by then, The Yellow Armadillo still packed at close to two in the morning. Brian should be happy. The men certainly looked as if they'd had plenty to drink. The cash register should be close to bursting.

She watched her inebriated audience as she sang, searching for any possible illegal activity. She tried to figure out who the regulars were, and kept an eye on who went out to the back hallway that led to the basement, how long they stayed, if they returned.

She wished she could afford risking another try at that basement door after she sang the last song, but she couldn't. She couldn't get caught twice in the same evening. She got the gig, would have access to the bar again tomorrow. That was sufficient progress for her first day.

She wondered how Shep and Keith had made out with Wagner. Not that either of them had thought to call and let her know.

She finished her last song to enthusiastic applause, gave a smile and a quick bow before running off the stage, ignoring the catcalls. She thanked the band as they came off the stage behind her, bringing some of their instruments and going back for the rest.

She smiled at the keyboard player, Sam. "Can I give you a hand?"

The band was here two nights a week. They must have seen a thing or two. She could do worse than getting friendly with them.

The fiftysomething man grinned at her. "Sure."

"Is it always like this?" she asked as she helped him take apart the keyboard stand.

"On a good night."

"And on a bad?"

"Fistfights. Or some idiot will pull a gun."

She tried to look scandalized. "I hope the cops don't shut us down on a night when I'm singing. I really need the money."

Sam shrugged. "Brian doesn't call the cops. He has people to deal with guys who get out of hand. Shorty's got a mother of a rifle behind the bar."

She'd bet he did. And then there was the meat mountain if Shorty needed backup.

"You guys make a pretty good band." A compliment could go a long way toward establishing goodwill, and maybe a connection.

"You're not bad yourself," he said as he walked out back with his equipment.

The back door stood propped open for the band, letting in some fresh air. One of his buddies had pulled the band's van up to the back door. The alleyway was just wide enough to allow a single vehicle.

She helped them load. It gave her another few minutes to hang out with them. Then they were done and getting into the cab. "Hey, thanks. See you tomorrow night."

"You bet."

The main area of the bar was mostly cleared out by the time she went back in. She sidled up to the bar and asked for some ice water. She was hot and sweaty from jumping around onstage, but she saved icy drinks for when she was done. Anything cold constricted her throat and made singing more difficult.

Shorty put a glass of ice water in front of her. He gave a lopsided smile. "Damn if you didn't make me feel twenty years younger."

She narrowed her eyes as she watched him. "Are you trying to tell me you're over twenty?"

He gave a booming laugh. "You're all right for a drifter, you know that?"

"I prefer to think of myself as a woman of the world."

He snorted.

She drank. "How long have you been working at The Armadillo?"

He shook his head. "Think I might have been born behind this bar. Mama used to waitress here."

"You like working for Brian?" she asked carefully, glancing at the jumble of ads on the column by the bar, pretending that the question wasn't important, just something to say.

Shorty shrugged as he put up the clean glasses. "Boss man's the boss man. They come and go every couple of years."

No big surprise there. Bars and restaurants changed hands frequently.

She grinned. "I'm just glad he likes the way I sing." She made sure she sounded super enthusiastic, as if this was her big break.

The meat mountain she'd encountered in the basement slogged by, nodded at Shorty. "Wagner came back yet?"

"Haven't seen him."

Lilly waited until the man walked away before she asked, "Who is he?" He'd been down in the basement with Wagner. Maybe he was Wagner's connection to the Coyote.

Shorty turned back to his work. "He delivers the booze for Brian," he said over his shoulder.

A name would have been better, something Lilly could have run through the database back at the office. But she didn't ask. Not tonight. Asking too many questions would jeopardize her cover.

She hung around until the very end, observing the dynamics among the staff, noting who was friends with whom, who goofed off, who took their job seriously. Mostly everyone just went about their job. They all looked tired. As hard as she watched, she didn't see anything suspicious.

Yet she felt that she wasn't wrong about the place. Something was going on here, something not quite on the up-and-up. She wished she had more time to get to the bottom of it.

Tomorrow night she would be back to sing a full set. She would get meat mountain's name. And she would find a way to get down into that basement.

Brian emerged from his office and called to Shorty as he strode to the front door. "Don't forget to put up the notice."

Shorty shook out the dishcloth. "I'll do it as soon as I'm done with the glasses."

"Thanks." The manager said good-night to the staff, then left for the night, leaving them to finish the work.

Lilly swallowed the last of her drink and pushed her glass to the dirty pile. "What notice?"

"We'll be closed on the first. Need to have some electric work done. Boss wants to put in a bigger air conditioner, but first we have to upgrade the wiring. There'll be people here working on that. We won't have power most of the day."

"That's tough." She glanced at the air-conditioning system, which looked fine to her and worked okay tonight. "Nobody likes to lose a day's income. Hope the electrician works fast." But her mind was turning the information this way and that, trying to see if it might fit the rest of the puzzle pieces in her head.

The bar would be closed on the first of October. The day when those terrorists were to sneak across the border.

She didn't believe in coincidences.

SHEP DIDN'T CALL Ryder until he got off his shift Friday morning. He'd wanted to give the guys at the office time to work on Wagner.

"Did he talk?"

"Idiots like him, they're only big boys while they have their big guns. Once we had him in interrogation and convinced him of the gravity of his situation, he would have given up his mother for a deal."

"His mother is the Coyote?"

"Funny guy," Ryder groused on the other end, probably rolling his eyes. "Anyway, the order to kill Jimmy came through a man at The Yellow Armadillo. A guy who goes by the name Tank. Know him?"

"I'll find him. What else?"

"Wagner got ten grand for the hit, also through Tank."

"What was he doing at the bar last night?"

"He says he just went for a drink. Maybe he needed to fortify himself before the hit."

Shep chewed on that for a minute before saying, "Lilly will be at the bar tonight."

Ryder grunted on the other end. "I'm not any happier about that than you are. She called to let me know about her undercover stint. Next time she does something like this, she better clear it with me first."

She better not ever do anything like this again.

"She said the bar will be closed on the first. Supposedly they're upgrading their wiring," Ryder said.

"Interesting timing."

"That's what I thought. The bar might be first stop for the men coming across the border. Come across, lie low for a day to rest, move up north from there. That basement you were talking about has potential. Lilly wants to look into it."

"I want to switch shifts so I can keep an eye on her."

"Jamie asked, too."

"Keith and I already have a cover established there."

"Fine." Ryder paused. "You go to the bar. But not Keith. We have a new gang-related lead out of San Antonio that might take us to the Coyote. I want Keith to be working that angle. But if you want to spend some time looking around The Yellow Armadillo, we can set that up." He hesitated for a second. "Just don't let yourself get distracted."

"It's not like that."

"Good. That's what I wanted to hear."

Shep drove back to his apartment for some sleep after they hung up, then spent a couple of hours at the office before heading to the bar that evening. The band started playing at eight.

He went early to get a table that would give him a good view of most of the bar and the stage, and the opening to the hallway that led to the basement and the exit door to the alley. He ordered a beer and nursed it slowly as he observed the people around him and listened in on conversations.

When the bar began to fill up and he could do it without drawing attention, he headed to the back hallway. He wanted to check out the basement Lilly had discovered. Finding a way down there and figuring out Tank's identity was his mission for the evening.

The band was coming in from the back, carrying their equipment through the hallway and up to the stage.

Shep moved to the basement door, as if waiting for someone, blocked the lock with his body, and tried to pick it behind his back as people hustled around with microphone stands and extension cords, drums and whatever.

A small click told him he was getting somewhere. Once the door was open, he'd wait for a moment when the hallway was empty, then he'd quickly pull in there. Nobody paid much attention to him. The band members were focused on their equipment and hurrying with the setup, which would work in his favor.

But before he could have popped the lock, footsteps drummed behind him and the door opened, whacking him in the back.

He stepped aside. "Easy there."

The young guy who came up shot a dark look at him. He had tattoos running up both arms, his shirt covered in dust. Looked as if he'd been working hard. Doing what?

"Tank down there?" Shep improvised.

The kid had been reaching back to close the door,

but the question stopped him. He stuck his pointy chin out, trying to look tough. "Whatcha want with him?"

Shep kept his face impassive. "That's my business, ain't it? Wagner said he'd be here."

The kid shrugged then jerked his head toward the stairs. "Lock the door behind you."

Shep didn't. He wasn't about to close his only avenue of escape, not when he had no idea what he was walking into. He might need to come back up this way in a hurry.

The stairs were badly lit. He couldn't have seen down all the way anyway, since there was a turn in the staircase. He plodded down, going as if he had every right to be there. No sense in being tentative and looking as if he was sneaking around.

The basement room he reached was maybe twenty by twenty, four doors leading into other rooms, bare cement brick walls, cracked cement floor. Open boxes of booze stood everywhere. He couldn't see anyone, but he could hear people talking in one of the rooms to his left.

"Anybody who'd put a grand on that kid is an idiot. He's a greenhorn."

"He's been competing all year. Winning."

"Where? Podunk, New Mexico? He ain't never ridden in a rodeo as big as this. There're a hell of a lot more serious riders here. Kid won't stack up. You put any money on him, you'll be losin' it."

While he had the chance, Shep passed by the nearest shelf and pressed a bug on the bottom of it, out of sight. He stepped away just in time. Another skinny, tattooed guy was coming from the back room, this one bald with a row of metal in his left ear.

The kid stopped in his tracks. "Who the hell are you?"

"Howdy." Shep stepped forward, then cleared his

throat as if he was nervous. "Someone said I could find Tank down here."

At that, a mountain of a man appeared, his eyes narrowing as he looked Shep over. Okay, that had to be Tank. He looked as if he could take a guy out just by sitting on him.

He was breathing a little hard, probably from whatever they were doing in the back. His small eyes narrowed in his pockmarked face. "What the hell are you doing here?"

Shep glanced at the tattooed kid, then back to Tank. The two must have gone to the same charm school. "Can we talk someplace private?"

The mountain jerked his head at the kid, and the kid retreated into the back room he'd come from.

Tank stayed where he stood. "Talk."

Shep shifted his weight onto one foot and tried to look sheepish. Not an easy task for someone who was commando to the core. He didn't have much practice. But maybe he could pull it off in the dim light. "I'm here for the rodeo. Thing is, I really wanna win it. I'm hoping you could help me."

Tank glared. "Who the hell told you that?"

"Guy I had a beer with here yesterday. Wagner."

"Can't keep his mouth shut now? What the hell?"

"I need this, man." Shep shifted his weight again. "I'm not from around here. I don't know who to ask. If you could help..."

Tank raised an eyebrow, waited a couple of seconds. "You got money?"

Shep dug into his pocket and came up with a roll of twenties. He'd come prepared.

The man still looked more aggravated than excited with the new business. "You stay here."

He went back into the room he'd come from. A couple of minutes passed before he returned with a Ziploc bag of white pills, six of them. Probably performance-enhancing drugs. Shep wasn't about to ask questions. He needed to look as if he did this all the time.

He looked at the pills. "That'd be perfect. Just what I need."

The lab could figure out what they were. If they couldn't get Tank on smuggling, at least they could get him on the drugs. The man named his price and Shep paid it.

"Thanks." He held the bag as if the pills were made of gold at the very least, careful not to put his fingers where Tank's had been. He didn't want to damage the fingerprints. "I really appreciate this."

But Tank was already walking away from him. "It's a onetime deal. I don't know you, and you don't know me. Don't let me see you down here again."

LILLY WAS WALKING by the manager's office, on her way to the stage, psyching herself up for her performance, telling herself she could still do this, when Brian called her in.

He was sprawled in his chair behind the desk as he looked her over. "You dressed like a nun for a reason? Them cowboys like a little skin."

She wore bloodred, spiked heels, a skintight black leather skirt that barely covered her behind. It showed off the winding tattoo on her inner thigh—something she'd gotten to gain Shep's attention, back in the day, which she did, but not in a good way. He hadn't thought it'd made her a woman. He'd been angry about it.

Brian, on the other hand, seemed to appreciate the art, judging by the way his gaze lingered on the spot.

Then slowly slid higher, to the glittery shirt that was pretty much molded to her torso.

"No problem." She smiled, even if she was gritting her teeth, and undid another button on top. The lace edge of her red bra was showing now. That better be enough. She scanned his desk to see if he had any paperwork out that might give a clue to his illegal activities or a possible link to the Coyote, but all she could see were utility bills.

He kept ogling her with a lecherous grin. "A little more skin wouldn't hurt."

But breaking your face would. She kept on smiling as she shoved up the shirt enough so her belly button showed. At the same time, she scanned the windowless office and noted the file cabinets. Would Brian keep anything incriminating here? Probably not. He was slimy, but she didn't think he was stupid.

He wasn't subtle, either. "A little more?" He pushed.

"I think I'm okay. Band is waiting." She walked away before she could have clocked him.

While Brian approved of her way too much, Shep was the opposite. He thoroughly disapproved of her gig here. Thank God he wouldn't be here tonight to glower at her. As far as she knew, he was on border duty.

She ran up onstage and tore into a song, sang a couple of rock ballads to ease the crowd into the mood, took it easy with the jumping around, since she couldn't afford to pop a button. Her shirt barely concealed her bra as it was. She picked up volume and energy as she went on, and by the time the first set was finished, people were singing along with her, in a drunken-cowboy choir.

Since the lights were in her eyes, she couldn't observe the audience as well as she would have liked, except for the first two rows of tables. She would just have to use her breaks and after-hours staff time to do her spying.

By the time she was finished with the first set, she had sweat rolling down her back. The bar had plenty of air-conditioning, but it was still hot under the lights. She grabbed her bag from behind the bar and something to drink then walked back to the bathroom to throw some cold water on her face—reviving herself almost as good as coffee would have.

It'd been a long day. She'd spent the morning and afternoon working at the office before coming here.

She touched up her makeup before squeezing into a stall and switching tops, yanking on a black lace tube top, tight and strapless, she'd brought for her second set. Brian ought to be happy with that.

Except he wasn't. She ran into him on her way out.

"Overdressed again?" His sticky gaze slid down the length of her body.

She didn't want to lose the gig so, she kept a smile on. "Can't go up onstage in just a bra."

"Why not?" He stepped closer, tilted his head as his gaze settled on her breasts. "Maybe a studded leather one. I guess I could spring for the cost."

He reached out, dragged a finger up the middle of her belly, between her breasts, to her chin and lifted her head. "You give a good show. No reason why you couldn't give even better. Maybe I'll throw in a little bonus." He winked at her.

She couldn't remember the last time she wanted to deck a guy so badly. But before she could have lost her cool and her undercover position, someone grabbed her hand from behind, spun her around, and the next second she was brought up hard against Shep's wide chest.

"Babe." He flashed a sultry grin. "You were hot up there." And then he claimed her lips.

For about a half a second she tried to figure out what was going on, then gave in to the firm pressure of his mouth. *Oh, man.* So, soooo much better than what she'd imagined back in the day. *Wow.*

She couldn't not notice how perfectly they fit together, how great he smelled, how strong the arms that held her were. He was pretty damn good, playing the sexy cowboy. She so wasn't going to fall for it.

But as much as she told herself that, she was still a little dizzy by the time he let her go.

Brian cleared his throat. "Boyfriend?" He was watching them tight-lipped, his forehead pulled into a displeased frown.

Shep tipped his hat. "It's still new, but I tell you, I'm over the moon about this little lady. Luckiest day of my life was when I walked in here."

He stood a full head taller than Brian, all muscle, while the manager was made up mostly of beer weight as far as she could tell. Brian must have noted the difference between them, too, and correctly assessed his chances if they came to blows over her. He walked away with an aggravated grunt.

She pulled back enough from Shep so she could think again. "Now what?"

"Now we play out what we started." He dragged her to an empty table, yanked her down onto his lap and put a protective hand on her waist. He didn't look around, but they both knew people took notice that he'd made his claim on her.

"You're welcome," he said under his breath.

He had a smile on his face for whoever was watching, but she could feel the tension in his muscles. More disconcertingly, she could also feel the heat of his palm on the bare skin of her lower back.

"I didn't need your help," she let him know in a whisper. "Maybe I was flirting with him as part of my cover."

The fake smile slid off his face. "Don't."

"You're not the boss of me." She would have said more, but the band was back onstage waiting on her.

She began to rise, but Shep pulled her back down and kissed her again. It really was a chaste kiss, like the first, just his lips resting against hers, and the slightest pressure. But his masculine scent enveloped her, his muscles flexing under her fingers as she reached up to hold on to his arms, their bodies pressing together.

His lips were warm and firm and they…lingered. It was the lingering that did her in, the wondering whether he would go further, the tension in his body that said he wanted to. Or maybe she was reading things into a theatrical gesture.

That would be pitiful on her part. And she refused to be pitiful about Shep Lewis ever again. She pulled away and looked him in the eye. "What was that for?" she asked to clarify things. "Brian is back in his office."

"To let these other yahoos know that you're off-limits."

Right. He was acting a part. The both of them were. She had to make sure she didn't forget that. She had no intention of walking down the long road that led to heartache.

"I'm going to make sure you're safe," he promised.

"No."

"I couldn't keep you safe when I should have. I should have never let you run away."

"I would have liked to have seen you try to stop me."

"I didn't try very hard," he admitted. "I wasn't sure if the system was the best place for you."

"It wasn't."

"Had to be better than the streets."

"I made it. Chill."

"I'm going to have your back this time," he insisted stubbornly.

That protection wasn't what she wanted from him—then or now—seemed to completely escape him, she thought, frustration tightening her muscles as she walked away.

Chapter Six

Shep went to get another beer while Lilly did her rock-star act onstage, mesmerizing the audience. He stayed at the bar. It was the easiest way to be close enough to people to overhear conversations, to keep an eye on the staff and who they interacted with and how.

Shorty, the bartender, put a beer in front of him. "Weren't there two of you yesterday? Where's your buddy?"

"Twisted an ankle in training."

"Bulls are more polite in Pennsylvania, eh?" He laughed, cracking himself up.

Shep laughed with him.

An older cowboy next to him was leaning against the bar, facing the stage. He pushed up his cowboy hat with his index finger. "That's one fine filly up there."

"All mine," Shep said and puffed his chest out, acting very pleased with himself.

The cowboy grinned, patting his mustache. "If you can hang on to her."

Shep flashed him a cocky look, as if he didn't have a doubt in the world. But the truth was he didn't want to hang on to Lilly. Hanging on to her was doing things to him. Uncomfortable things.

He'd acted on the spur of the moment when he'd

kissed her, because he hadn't been sure which one of them would knock the manager's head into the wall first. Seeing the oily bastard's hands on her snapped something inside him. It was a miracle he'd been able to play it as cool as he had.

The kiss had seemed the perfect way to defuse the situation while allowing both of them to keep their covers. The second time, he did it to make sure all those horny cowhands, too, would know she was spoken for.

He hadn't meant to enjoy it.

It was wrong to enjoy it.

No way was he going to do it again. Unless he absolutely *had* to kiss her to keep their cover. But he would hate it next time. For sure.

He drew a long swallow as his new undercover girlfriend danced across the stage. No reason why Jamie would have to find out about this latest turn of events. Or Mitch Mendoza for that matter. Thank God Mitch was on an op in South America at the moment.

Shep turned his attention elsewhere and scanned the drooling men. He wasn't going to discover anything by staring at her like the rest of the idiots.

Brian was nowhere to be seen. Tank, if he was still here, was down in the basement. He would have liked the guy's full name so he could run him through the system. As it was, he'd have to scan mug shots on the computer at the office in his free time, in the hopes that he'd stumble on the guy by chance.

He drained his beer and got up, walked outside as if for a smoke, leaned against his car in the parking lot and pulled out his phone, set it to the right channel. Out here, he could hear everything the bug was transmitting from the bar's basement. Inside, it'd been too loud to monitor that, but everything got recorded, so he could go over it later tonight. Right now, all he wanted to do was check in, see if Tank was still down there.

"Is that the last crate?" somebody asked. Enough of the music upstairs filtered down to make the words difficult to make out, let alone identify the speaker.

Still, to Shep, it kind of sounded as if it might have been Tank.

"Yeah" came the response.

"You brought the empty bottles down?"

"Right here."

"All right, boys, let's fill 'em up, then."

Sounded as if they were working with some homemade booze, maybe tequila distilled on the other side of the border, smuggled up here and sold as the real deal. Whenever a genuine bottle of booze ran out, it would be refilled with the cheaper stuff, again and again. But sold at regular prices, it would increase Brian's profits twofold, at least.

Another thing Tank could be put away for, and hopefully the manager, too. That cheered Shep a little. He'd hated Brian's hands on Lilly.

He listened some more, hoping either Doug Wagner's or the Coyote's name would come up. They didn't. The good old boys in the basement only talked about booze and women. They had very limited focus as far as that went.

After a few minutes, he turned off the phone and walked inside to check on Lilly.

He wondered what her FBI colleagues would say if they could see her now. The old cowboy had been right. She was plenty hot up on that stage in that lacy black tube top and sky-high heels. She kept the crowd going.

She sang another set, freshened up, then came to

have a drink with him. Water for her. He slowly nursed another beer.

"Looks like you're having fun up there," he said.

"No point in singing to be miserable."

She had a point. "Do you have to wear so…little?"

She laughed. "Brian wants me in less."

One of these days, Brian would get what was coming to him, he thought morosely.

When she stood to go back up onstage, he figured he better not kiss her again, so he just patted her behind playfully. For appearance's sake.

Another thing he would have to learn not to enjoy, because on the first run he enjoyed it way too much, unfortunately. He wondered if he could convincingly play her boyfriend without touching her.

Not likely. No man could keep his hands off a woman like her if she belonged to him.

Halfway through the set, he got up again. This time he walked out through the back door. If the basement had any windows, he hadn't seen them from the front. He wanted to check in the back.

Two ranch hands and a tattooed young kid from the basement were leaning against the wall smoking, listening to the music filtering through the door, discussing rodeo horses. Shep stood a distance away from them, turned so he could examine the back side of the building. Old brick, no windows on the main level or the basement. The building was probably built way before there were building codes requiring outside basement exits.

He pulled the pack of smokes he kept as a prop in his shirt pocket, took a cigarette and shoved it between his lips, but didn't light it.

A couple of other places had back doors to the alley,

a pizza shop on one side, dry cleaner's on the other, a few more down the row. They all had security cameras above their doors, except for The Yellow Armadillo.

With tens of thousands of dollars' worth of liquor behind the bar, and more in the basement, their lack of concern over security was interesting. Unless they wanted no recording of who came and went through the back.

The light above the door was maybe twenty watts, not illuminating a hell of a lot. He wouldn't mind coming back here later tonight, after the bar was closed and everyone had left, to gain entry to that basement and see what Tank was hiding in those back rooms. He shifted on his feet.

The tattooed kid looked his way. "You need a light?"

Shep spit the cigarette to the ground and crushed it under his heel. "Trying to quit. Thanks anyway."

"Good luck with that," the kid said. "I try at least once a year."

The ranch hands gave him sympathetic nods.

"You here for the rodeo?" one of them asked.

"You bet. Shep," he said, introducing himself. "Down from Pennsylvania. You?"

"Brandon here might try." One of the ranch hands nodded toward the skinny, tattooed guy.

That was good. Shep needed names. "How about you two?"

"Nah, Nick has a bad back. I got a bad horse." The man gave a sour laugh.

"I hear you." Shep shook his head. "Some days I think mine is the devil's spawn."

Nick gave a rueful laugh. "I had one like that. Almost broke my neck."

Shep gestured toward the bar's back door with his head. "So this place okay? My girl is singing."

"New chick?" Brandon asked. "Best keep an eye on her. Crowd can get rowdy."

He nodded. "How about the manager? Better pay her. Last gig she had, they stiffed her more weekends than not."

"Brian's cool. He don't mind paying under the table, either. Save some on taxes, if she's interested."

The manager sounded as if he didn't mind breaking any number of laws whatsoever. Could be Tank reported to the Coyote, could be he reported to Brian. What if Brian was the direct link?

Something they had to figure out in a hurry.

THEY DID MAKE some progress with Tank. Shep put a rush order on the prints and they got the results back early the next afternoon.

"Zeb Miller, with a rap sheet as long as the Rio Grande," the lab tech said on the other end of the line and sent the file over.

Shep took it into Ryder's office.

"Wish we had time to follow him for a while, see who he meets up with." Ryder shook his head as he looked over the man's impressive list of offenses. "But we just don't. Why don't you go pick him up? Let's see if we can crack him."

They had to try—didn't really have a choice.

But Tank wasn't at the address listed as his rental and couldn't be tracked down, not even with an APB on his vehicle. Worse, that night when Shep went back to The Yellow Armadillo, Tank didn't seem to be there, either.

Maybe he had some sixth sense and got spooked.

Or maybe he was on a run across the border and he'd be back later.

Shep settled in to watch the show. Mostly he watched the audience, keeping an especially close eye on Brian, who seemed to keep to his office tonight. There was no movement in the back hallway, nobody coming and going from the basement.

Lilly put on a hell of a show, once again. And as bad as watching her dance across the stage half-naked was, the breaks were worse. He thought he'd jump out of his skin every time she sat on his lap.

LILLY CHANGED AGAIN during her last break and finished her bottle of water as she walked over to Brian's office, trying to make progress in her investigation. She flashed a smile as if his groping had already been forgotten.

"I hate to ask for favors on my first night, but..." She winced. "I could really use a dressing room. I like changing between sets. Do you think it would be possible to find me a small place that's private?"

He looked a lot less excited about her now that Shep was in the picture. He barely looked up from his paperwork. "People always used the bathroom before. That's all we got. This ain't no fancy place."

"It doesn't have to be fancy. Last place I worked at let me use a storage room. How about a quiet corner down in the basement?"

He did look up at that and shook his head. "If you want, you can change in my office."

With him right there, no doubt. "You got glass in your door," she pointed out.

"The better to keep an eye on people coming and going."

She raised a teasing eyebrow. "You don't trust your staff?"

"I don't trust anyone."

His cell phone rang and he picked it up, pointed at the door for her to close it. She did, then meandered toward the basement door, but just as she could have tried the lock, Brandon came down the hall, so she stepped away.

He flashed her an unhappy look, unlocked the door and went through. She could hear him lock it behind him.

Great.

She pulled out her cell phone to check the time. She had five more minutes before her next set. She couldn't go downstairs now. And she better clear out before Brandon came back. She didn't want him to think she was loitering for a reason and say something to Brian.

She didn't want to go sit by the bar. If she stood alone, guys hit on her. If she went to sit with Shep at his table, he'd feel the need to act like her boyfriend and she wasn't sure how much more of that she could take tonight.

She walked up front, grabbed another bottle of water, then walked outside through the front door for some fresh air. The smokers usually hung out in the back alley, so the front was nice and quiet.

The street was mostly deserted at one in the morning, the row of small shops closed, but not darkened. She glanced down the rainbow of neon lights over the entrances. She was used to big-city lights in D.C., and this was nowhere like that, yet small Texas towns did have their own charm, she thought.

Movement at the car shop on the corner caught her eye. She couldn't see at first what exactly was going on. The repair shop didn't have their lights on like the stores. It was almost time for her to go back in, but on an impulse, she stayed and waited another minute.

There was that movement again. And when she looked more carefully, she could see a man coming from the repair shop carrying a box and watched as he put it into the back of a black pickup. A passing car illuminated him for a second. *Brandon.*

She pulled into the shadows so she wouldn't be seen if he looked this way.

It was definitely him—the same height, width, the same lumbering movement. How on earth had he gotten over there?

Only one explanation came to mind. The Yellow Armadillo had a tunnel, some kind of underground connection to the car shop. They definitely needed to find a way down there.

Music filtered through the door as the band inside began to play. She hurried back in.

She didn't have a chance to catch Shep on her way to the stage. He was talking to some guys up by the bar. But as soon as her last set was done, she searched him out in the dispersing crowd so she could tell him her theory about a tunnel.

"We have to know for sure what's going on in the basement. I want to go down there. Tonight," she clarified.

They stopped next to his pickup after walking out together. "Let the team handle it," he said.

"We're here right now. The last stragglers will be gone in ten minutes. No better time than the present. There's a twenty-four-hour convenience store on the other side of the corner, past the mechanic. We could pretend to be heading there to pick up something."

He looked down the street, then back at her. "Okay." And then he reached out and wrapped his arm around her.

Oh, man, was that necessary? Him touching her unsettled her every single time. But she supposed they had to stay in character in case anyone saw them—people were still leaving the bar—so she snuggled against him. "Find out anything useful tonight?"

He shrugged. "Nothing spectacular. Got a couple of names to run through the system. If there's a tunnel, you definitely win."

Good. She liked winning. She liked the idea of him coming to see her at last as an independent, competent woman, as opposed to Miss Disaster, a total screwup.

They walked and, even as they carefully scanned the few people lurching to their cars, they pretended to be looking at each other. Not really a hardship for her. He was totally hot. He always had been.

She couldn't see any movement at the car shop now as she gave the place a quick glance. The black pickup was gone. Brandon had probably driven off with whatever he'd been carrying in that box. Considering it was past 2:00 a.m., he might not come back tonight.

That would serve their purposes just fine, she thought. It'd be easier to snoop if nobody was around.

They walked past the car shop then entered the small convenience store. Shep headed to the back. "How about some iced tea?"

But while they were picking through the cooler, Brian walked in.

He nodded at them as he went for smokes, then ended up behind them at the checkout line. He managed a leering look at her legs. "Hey."

Shep nodded at him and added a handful of condoms

to their purchases from the display before wrapping his arm around her waist. "Hey yourself."

Not too subtle, was he?

She thought about jabbing him in the ribs with her elbow as he paid then stuffed the foil packets into his back pocket, but all she could do was smile as she did her best to act her cover. She pulled him over by the magazine rack on their way out, pretending to be picking through the tabloids, so Brian would leave first. She wanted the manager gone so they could take a better look at the mechanic shop on their way back, unobserved.

His car was parked in front of the store. He got in and drove away.

They walked outside into the balmy night at last, and she looked after the car as it disappeared around the corner.

"Was that necessary?" She hissed the words under her breath. That many condoms? Really?

He flashed her an overly innocent look.

Fine. Whatever. She pushed back the aggravation and focused on the job. "I want to walk down the side street so we can check out the repair shop from the side and back. I want to get a better feel for it." A better feel for how to get in.

He looped his arm around her shoulders, keeping her close to him as they'd started out.

She would have preferred some space—her brain worked better that way—but to shake off his embrace would have meant admitting that he was affecting her. Instead, she draped her arm around his waist. Two could play this game.

The side street was badly lit and completely deserted. They kept an eye on the houses across the road while checking out the car shop from this angle. The shop didn't have a single light on in the back, either; it was completely dark. They cut through the parking lot, as if taking a shortcut to the Laundromat behind the mechanic's.

The shop's back door looked like a simple deal, with a simple lock, she saw when they got close enough. She stopped and turned into Shep, as if for a kiss, lifting her face to his. "I have a set of lock picks on me," she said as her body tingled from the contact.

"I'd feel more comfortable if I took you back to your hotel and came back here on my own."

Did he even realize that he was insulting her? "I'm an FBI agent."

His lips flattened for a second. "I know."

"I don't need your permission to do my job. And I certainly don't need your protection, although I'd be stupid not to accept backup. I'm going in."

He held her gaze, a pained look on his face. "When did you become so pushy?"

"I don't know what you're talking about."

A lone cowboy meandered down the side street. They had to wait until he passed out of sight. They kept their hands on each other, playing the part of lovers who'd stopped for a quick kiss and some sweet words.

Shep bent his head a little closer as they gazed at each other. "Why didn't you stay with music?" he asked out of the blue. "You sure know how to rock a stage."

Where had that come from? "Are you hoping I'll give up the FBI and go on tour?" A smile tugged at her lips. "You want me gone that bad?"

"You have no idea," he said with feeling.

A quick laugh escaped her. "I like the FBI. Not that I want to do it forever."

"What else?"

"I'd like to work with foster youth someday. I have some ideas about how to help kids who might be going down the wrong path." She gave a small shrug. "I have some experience there."

His face turned somber as he watched her. "Seventeen and all alone in the world. You shouldn't have run away."

"Stop saying that. I wouldn't be who I am if I hadn't." She tilted her head. "I'm good at what I do, too. You don't have to worry about me."

But he still hesitated another long minute before he said, "Okay. Let's see if there's an easy way into this place."

The cowboy had long disappeared down the street.

She moved away from Shep. "You carrying?"

He nodded.

He probably had a small weapon in his boot, since she couldn't see any bulges in his waistband behind his back.

"Me, too." She'd gotten a dainty little thing for her purse, something any woman would carry. She'd left her government-issue weapon in her hotel room. She kept her bag behind the bar while she sang, where anyone could have gone through it. If anyone snooped, she didn't want them to see anything that might give her away.

The back door was locked, but she made quick work of it.

He raised a dark eyebrow as they stepped inside. "You have a knack for this."

"A skill I had before I ever entered law enforcement, to be fair," she whispered back to him as they moved forward.

Three cars sat in the six-bay garage, no people in sight.

They moved along the wall, looking for a door that might lead down to the basement. Shep was the one to find it. Somebody had taped a piece of paper on the door that said W.C. OUT OF ORDER.

She worked the lock, again, nothing fancy. A super-security lock would have stood out, she supposed. She had it open within a minute. Instead of a bathroom, a staircase stretched down in front of them, dark and not very inviting.

He turned on the small LED light that hung from his keychain and went down first, past the rat droppings, then the mummified rat on the landing. She turned on her own keychain light and followed, closing and locking the door behind her in case they came out somewhere else. She didn't want anyone to know that somebody had been through here.

The stairs led straight down into a narrow passageway. They followed it and found nothing down there but bare brick walls, no room for anything, really.

There were a couple of turns, two branches that led off to empty storage rooms. They followed the main tunnel.

"Probably built during Prohibition," Shep said as they moved forward.

That would explain why it led to a bar.

Less than ten minutes passed before they reached another set of stairs, the tunnel still continuing beyond.

They went up, through the door at top, careful not to make any noise. The lights were off, but enough moonlight came through the windows to illuminate the place. They were in a waiting room with old plastic chairs and a scuffed reception desk.

Scribbled-over posters about the food pyramid decorated the walls. To their left a supply closet stood with its door half-open, the shelves stocked with bottles of disinfectant and boxes of bandages. They had reached some kind of a health clinic it seemed.

They hadn't passed by one when they'd walked. Which meant the place had a different storefront. It was likely an illegal clinic, the cash-only type that asked for no ID and treated gunshot wounds without questions.

"Handy for the steroid pills," Shep whispered, moving forward.

Right. He'd gotten some of those from Tank. Sounded as if Brian and his crew had a hand in a number of things. They apparently appreciated the efficiency of diversifying.

"Nature abhors a vacuum, and so do criminal organizations," she said, keeping her voice down. "Do you think Brian is stepping into the gap that was created when your team took out some of the local big dogs?"

She would have said more, but as she stepped after him, voices reached them.

They weren't alone in the building.

Chapter Seven

Shep froze and held up a hand to alert Lilly, but from the look in her eyes, she'd heard the voices, too. There were at least two people in one of the back offices.

"How long are we supposed to sit around doing nothing?" a man asked in a deep, raspy voice. "I'm losing money every damn day."

"Lie low is the word," someone else answered. "You just cool your heels until the first."

October first, Shep thought. They already knew that the Coyote had put everything on hold until then, probably to lull CBP into thinking smuggling was slowing. Then on the first, when all his minions started up business again, the sheer volume would overwhelm the border agents. In the chaos, the Coyote could slip his special cargo through without being detected.

Not if Shep and his team had anything to do with it.

"I have creditors to pay," the man with the deeper voice said.

Lilly pulled away from Shep silently and pointed toward the half-open door of the supply closet. He nodded and moved after her, careful not to make any noise. They'd be out of sight in there in case anyone came out of that office, but they could still hear the conversation.

"Tell them to wait," the other man answered.

The closet was pretty tight, shelves taking up most of the space. While Lilly was looking, trying to figure out how they could both fit, he simply pressed himself into the far corner, where he wouldn't be seen even if they left the closet door half-open. They had to do that, leave everything the same so if the men came out, they wouldn't notice anything out of place.

Lilly shot him a dubious look, then wedged herself into the remaining space, her back pressed tightly against him, the only way they'd both remain concealed.

Her soft scent in his nose was bad enough. He could have handled that, but other things… Her bottom was crushed against him, firm and round and everything he shouldn't be thinking about.

Don't move, he said in silent prayer, trying his best to focus on the men who were still talking.

"I need one shipment tonight," the deeper of the two voices was saying. "I have nothing. If I don't provide the merchandise, my buyers will go to someone else and I lose them."

"Put them off for a few days. Jonesing ain't never killed nobody."

"I've been playing that game for weeks. I need to give them something. I'm going over tonight."

"The hell you are." A chair scraped the floor, as though it were being shoved back.

"You gonna stop me?"

"If I have to."

The sounds of a scuffle filtered from the back office, then suddenly a gunshot rent the night. Then came the sound of a body hitting the floor with a dull thud.

Shep gripped his gun. He could feel Lilly tense, going for her own weapon.

"Are we gonna get in trouble for this with the boss?" a new, younger voice asked inside the office.

"You just keep your mouth shut," the deep-voiced man answered. "Dumb bastard thought he was gonna tell me what to do. Hell with that."

"What are we gonna do with him?"

"Leave him. We got a long night ahead of us. Ricky's on duty tonight at the border crossing. He won't give us no trouble."

Footsteps sounded, coming their way, boots scuffing on the tile floor. Shep held his gun ready in his right hand, grabbed Lilly's hip with the left and pulled her even closer as he flattened himself tightly against the wall so they wouldn't be discovered.

He couldn't see anything from where he was. Maybe Lilly would catch a glimpse of the men. They each held their breath as the two walked by the supply closet.

The men didn't go to the door that led down to the secret tunnel. They went to the clinic's back exit that opened to the alley.

As soon as the door closed behind the men, Lilly and Shep hurried to the back door, but they didn't open it until they heard a car start, and even then just enough to catch a glimpse of a black Chevy Blazer and its license plate.

Shep pulled out his phone and called it in. Since his pickup was at The Yellow Armadillo, a full block away, there was no way they could catch up to these two.

He turned back to Lilly, holding the line. "Did you see them?"

"The younger one was Brandon from the bar," she said as she hurried away from him, back toward the room where the men had been arguing. "The other one I haven't seen before."

Lilly Tanner. She was exactly the kind of woman that a man like him could fall in love with.

He couldn't afford to let his guard down for a minute.

TO LILLY'S RELIEF, they got back to his pickup without trouble and without running into anyone they knew from the bar.

Shep remained silent. Almost brooding, which was kind of strange, since he wasn't the brooding type. He was the type to take action if something bothered him.

They stopped by the pickup and he looked at her, his gaze searching her face. Was he still upset that she was here, that she'd been inserted into the middle of his op?

"I can just walk back to the hotel," she offered. If he needed space, she could certainly give him some—at least tonight—even if she couldn't withdraw from the op. And a brisk walk might help as she processed the latest developments.

"The hotel is on my way." And then he reached out, took her arm and backed her against the truck in one smooth move, and kissed her.

And it was *not* one of those lips-brushing-against-lips almost-kisses he'd planted on her before for show. This time he kissed her as if he meant it. With the adrenaline of tonight's work still coursing through her, she responded, her arms going around his neck as his hands grabbed for her hips.

Instant heat. Or maybe not so "instant," considering. The moment had years' worth of teenage fantasies behind it. If the sudden, overwhelming need was more than just a blast from the past, she didn't want to think about it.

His right hand slid up to her breast and cupped it.

Zing. She moaned in pleasure and he used the advantage. His tongue swept in to kiss her deeper.

Oh.

All her senses were buzzing, her body screaming that she wanted this. And maybe she somehow telepathically communicated that, because the next thing she knew he was opening the pickup's door and she was sideways on the passenger seat as he stood in front of her, her legs wrapped around his waist.

Her hands slid up his side, to his back. He had a great body, the kind that made a woman want to run her fingers all over it. Since he didn't look as if he would protest, she did. The thin shirt he wore didn't provide much impediment. She could feel every muscle, every hill and valley.

He was hard everywhere, and he ground that hardness against her, against the aching need where her thighs met. Heat rushed to that spot. Another moan escaped her throat.

Which was beyond strange because she normally wasn't the zero-to-sixty-in-three-seconds kind of girl.

But his hand on her breast was doing amazing things, his clever fingers teasing her nipple into a hard knob. She ached for him there, too. She ached for him everywhere.

In the middle of a stupid parking lot, on the front seat of a pickup. So not her. She might have been acting the tough rock chick onstage, but in the bedroom...she was more the type to turn out the light when it came to intimacy.

And none of this was real, in any case. They'd been pretending to be a couple all night, touching and kissing. Neither of them had significant others. Both could have used some release. But she couldn't be casual with

Shep. The last thing she wanted was to start falling for him again.

She didn't trust anyone with her heart, and especially not Shep Lewis, who'd already rejected her once.

"This is crazy," she mumbled against his lips. "We have to stop." Before it was too late.

He immediately pulled away and stared at her, breathing hard.

She tried to gather some shreds of sanity about her. "We should..." Should what? She couldn't finish it, because what her body and her mind wanted were two different things.

And after a long moment, he stepped away.

The shock of separation had her body protesting. She pressed her lips together so she wouldn't beg him to come back to her. She pulled her legs into the car.

His expression darkened as he watched her, his eyes narrowing with suspicion as if he was thinking maybe she'd somehow tricked him into the kiss.

"I—" She closed her mouth, not sure, again, how to proceed.

He walked around to the other side, got into the car and slammed the door behind him. "I shouldn't have. I'm sorry. It's not going to happen again, dammit."

That should have made her feel reassured. Instead, it made her feel disappointed. They drove to the hotel in the most awkward silence she could imagine.

Instead of dropping her off at the front door, he pulled into the parking lot.

"I'm coming up," he told her as he shut off the engine.

Judging by the dark clouds that sat on his face, his visit wouldn't be to finish what they'd started.

She got out, more than ready to leave him and have

some time to herself to recover. "We don't have to hash this out tonight." Or ever.

"We do. And I—" He hesitated, then pulled a folder from the backseat and came after her. "I meant to show you something."

Did his team find information he hadn't had a chance to share with her yet?

They went up in the elevator. This time it was just the two of them, nobody out this late, but he didn't say a word to her until they got up to her floor and they were inside her suite.

"Things can't go on like this," he said at last, standing inside the door. "You shouldn't be here. It's dangerous, and it's—"

"I can handle it."

"Well, maybe I can't," he snapped, holding her gaze. "I don't know what to do with this."

By *this* he meant the attraction between them, she guessed.

"We'll ignore it." She wasn't even sure if it was real. Did she really want him, *this* Shep, or was it something left over from the past?

"Because that's worked so well until now." A wry smile tilted up his lips. "The bar is a dangerous place. Brian is up to his neck in smuggling."

"It's just one last night. If we find a clue, it'd be worth anything. And you don't have to worry about me. I'm an FBI agent," she reminded him.

He shook his head. "I don't seem to be able to catch up to that."

Was that it? He came up to talk her into quitting and going home?

Anger lit a small flame inside her. He didn't think she was good enough. For the job. Or for him. She stiffened her spine. Nobody ever thought she was good enough. Not her parents, who'd sold her for drugs, not the couple who bought her then threw her away, not the system she'd ended up in.

She stepped back. "You should go. It's late."

"Are you walking away from the bar?"

"I'll do the job I came here to do, and I'll thank you for not interfering."

"Lilly—"

"Do you ever try to talk your teammates into taking it easy on their job and walking away from danger?"

His forehead drew into an annoyed frown. "No," he admitted.

"I assume you work with outside law enforcement from time to time. How about them?"

He watched her for a few long seconds. "Fine. I get your point."

"I'm not the same person I was ten years ago."

"No kidding," he said miserably.

It nearly made her smile, squashing her anger. "What bothers you more, the fact that the FBI sent someone to keep an eye on you guys, or that you're attracted to me?"

He shot her a dark look. "They're both wrong. Neither should be happening."

"Tough cookies." He used to tell her that all the time back in the day.

"The team will get the job done. You shouldn't be here." He paused. "You shouldn't look like this," he said accusingly. "And I shouldn't have kissed you. Not for show, and most definitely not for real."

She bit back a smile.

"Quit looking so damn pleased."

She let the smile bloom. "You don't get disconcerted

every day. You'll just have to forgive me if I take a moment to enjoy it."

She took her time. Then shook her head. "Listen, seven years of age difference when I was seventeen and you were twenty-four might have seemed like a lot. It's not now. I'm not in your charge or under your protection."

"You're under my protection," he said unequivocally and stood there all wide shouldered and tough looking.

He'd tried to protect her back in the day. She couldn't let him. Too many people had let her down by that point. So she'd left Shep before he could let her down, too. She'd run away.

She glanced at the folder in his hand. "What did you want to show me?"

He followed her gaze, his eyebrows furrowing as if he'd forgotten about his papers. He hesitated for a moment before holding the folder out for her. "Your case file from ten years ago. After you disappeared, I emailed the files to myself so I could work on them at home. I did my best to find you." He cleared his throat. "I realized the other day that I might still have them in that old email account. I did."

Her mouth went dry as she took the folder.

She drew a deep breath before opening it, took a look at the document on top, then paged carefully through the others. She scanned the list of foster homes, medical checkups, a list of her bad behaviors, grade cards, a report on the circumstances of how she'd come into foster care—found abandoned at a bus stop.

But what really got to her were the pictures. Her smiling at six or seven. Her looking sullen a few years later, holding a scruffy cat. Her throat tightened. She'd forgotten about the cat.

She closed the file and put it on the desk, needing a moment, then looked up into his dark eyes.

He'd given her back her missing years. Something to fill some of the empty spaces in her life. As if he'd somehow seen into her heart and knew exactly what was missing.

Maybe she could trust him just a little. She swallowed. "I appreciate it. Thanks."

He nodded and turned to leave.

"Wait." She stepped closer. She didn't want him to leave yet, but she wasn't sure what to say. "We have a complicated relationship."

He nodded, watching her face.

"I wasn't sure how it would be. I mean, us meeting again." The people you cared for, the ones who were supposed to protect you, always let you down. Or sold you for coke. "I don't do relationships." But she did want him in the here and now, this edgier Shep who sometimes looked at her as if he could devour her.

His masculine lips twisted into a wry smile. "Me, neither. I want you." He echoed her thoughts. "Pretty much all the time now. It's driving me crazy."

She took another step closer to him.

He held her gaze. "Lilly?"

She watched him and waited.

"Say no," he said as he reached out and pulled her into his strong arms.

She said nothing.

He lowered his head, fitted his lips to hers. "Tell me to get the hell out of here," he murmured.

It would have been the smart thing to do, probably. But her lips were tingling. So she pressed them a little closer to his.

He capitulated with a groan and wrapped his arms

fully around her, gathered her tightly to his chest and tasted her.

Her knees turned weak. It didn't matter. He was holding her up. All those muscles came in handy at a time like this.

He licked the seam of her lips then nibbled on the bottom lip again, scraped his teeth against it. And when she opened up for him at last, he didn't hesitate. He took all that she offered. He took thoroughly.

Since her boots had heels, he was just a few inches taller than her and they fit together perfectly. He was all hard male and she was…a puddle of need, frankly.

He eased his hands down her sides, splayed his fingers over her hips as he held her to him. The tube top left her midriff bare and he took advantage, his thumbs moving in a circular motion on her skin, sending delicious shivers across her abdomen and lower.

His hands soon moved up an inch, then another. They pushed up the lacy material in front of them as they went, baring more and more of her to his seeking fingers. His touch was so featherlight and gentle, it melted the last of her resistance. The twin assault of his tongue and those clever fingers was almost more than she could handle.

She grabbed on to his waist for support. And then somehow his shirt came untucked, and her fingers sneaked under the material, coming into contact with his warm skin. There was nothing soft about the man, she thought as her fingers wandered upward over the muscles of his abdomen, up to his wide chest and tangled in a smattering of hair, her palms covering his impressive pecs.

He shifted them slowly, her back against the door, then took his hands off her, bracing them on either side of her head as he pulled back a few inches. "Tell me to leave."

If she were half as smart as she'd thought she was, she would have. Instead, she said, "Stay."

Her tube top was history the next second, his lips back on hers as his hands cupped her breasts through the flimsy silk of her strapless bra. He trailed kisses to her ear, bit then sucked the lobe.

Then she couldn't think anymore, because one of his clever hands slipped behind her and unclasped the bra. The other tugged the silk at the front and her breasts spilled free.

He pulled his head back from her cheek and kissed a trail of heat along her jaw, then down her neck, then circled her breasts before heading to one nipple first then the other.

His mouth was moist and hot on her, and she could feel more moisture and heat gather between her legs. All her life, she kept people at arm's length, yet now she couldn't get close enough to him. Nothing would be close enough until he was inside her.

Because that was where they were heading, she realized. They weren't at the bar or in the parking lot. Nothing to stop them here from taking this all the way.

The thought scared her and excited her in equal measure.

As if reading her mind, he hooked his hands under her bottom and lifted her off her feet. When she wrapped her legs around his waist, they were lined up perfectly, if not for some inconvenient denim.

She could have sent him away and pretended, for the sake of their jobs, that she didn't want him, but it would have been a lie. He was a decadelong itch under her skin. He was her first sexual fantasy, and he was a damned good one at that. So she was going to go with the impulses that told her to rip off his shirt.

When she did, he flashed her a dark grin and carried her to the bed to lay her down on top of the covers. "Are you sure?"

"Yes." She reached for him.

"Why?" he wanted to know.

The emotions that suddenly bubbled up in her chest she couldn't admit even to herself, let alone to him. So instead, she said, "Better get it out of our system. Then we can work together without the distraction, without wondering."

Sounded better than the pathetic *Because I've been in love with you since I was seventeen.* In any case, that wasn't true. Was it?

He tossed his shirt on the floor then kicked off his boots and lay down next to her. Since she was naked to the waist, he began working on her tight denim skirt.

She reached for his rodeo belt buckle, nervous suddenly and wondering if it was even possible that this could measure up to her insanely high expectations.

"Nothing is ever as good as we anticipate it," she said out loud without meaning to.

And when he threw her a questioning look, she added in way of explanation, "It'll be better once we go for it then accept the disappointment. Then we can concentrate on the tunnel and the smuggling."

He looked at her as if she was crazy.

The belt gave at last and she tugged down his zipper. His erection sprung free, barely held by his briefs. He was *very* happy to see her, from the looks of it.

He yanked off her skirt then hooked a finger under her lacy G-string. "What the hell is this? You can't afford proper underwear?" His voice sounded a shade weaker than before.

"I get hot dancing around the stage." The less clothes the better.

"Hot," he repeated, looking dazed, his eyes fixed on those few square inches of lace. Then he gave a quick grin. "Everybody gets hot when you dance around the stage."

With that one hooked finger he drew the material down her legs then let it drop.

She lay naked before him.

He came to his feet next to the bed just long enough to shrug out of his jeans and underwear, never removing his gaze from her body. As he shook his jeans out, a handful of foil packets scattered on the bed by her feet.

"So we give in this once then forget about it?" he asked.

"Just to get it out of the way. Get the distraction over and done with," she told him. "We—"

But he bent suddenly and lay his index finger over her lips. And then, as he lay down next to her, he replaced the finger with his mouth, his finger slowly moving lower, skating across her skin to her knee, down her winding tattoo, caressing every flower and leaf then back up again to the V of her thighs. And then his long fingers parted her.

Pleasure flashed through her as he found the spot that was throbbing for him, aching with need. His mouth worked on hers while his finger worked down below. And when she was on the brink, he moved over on top and slid into her.

He didn't take it slow. He didn't move inch by tantalizing inch. He pushed forward as if he meant it and thrust into her all the way, making her moan his name as pleasure suffused her and dizzied her brain.

He filled her, stretched her, made her bones melt as he thrust in and out and picked up the rhythm. Her knees hooked around his narrow hips and she gave her body up to him completely.

He didn't take his time with this step, either. He lifted her higher and higher with ruthless efficiency, barely allowing her to catch her breath. Then her body contracted around him and she felt like a fireworks rocket, bursting into a shower of sparkles, flying.

SHEP LAY NEXT TO HER, spent and stunned, staring at the ceiling. A part of his world had shattered and he didn't know how to piece it back together, didn't know how to process what had just happened between them.

It had seemed so right, so easy. Yet now, as sanity returned, he had to seriously reevaluate his actions. He had to take responsibility for the way he'd lost control.

"I didn't come up with this in mind, I swear."

She made some sleepy sounds. "I'm not complaining."

Yet the fact remained that he *had* come up to her hotel room and made love to her. She'd been tired after work and...confused. He'd taken advantage of her. That was the way Jamie would see it. And Mitch. He winced.

He had no idea how to make this right.

"Marry me," he blurted as he looked at her and tried hard not to want her again, tried and failed. His body was stirring already. Insanity.

She turned to him, wide-eyed and a lot more awake now, as a succession of emotions crossed her face. "What?"

"Jamie and Mitch are going to kill me for this."

Her eyes narrowed. "Did you just ask me to marry you because of Jamie and Mitch?"

He looked at her miserably.

She sat up in the bed. "Get out." She bit out the words. "I want you to leave."

He sat up, too. "I should have protected you. Even from myself—"

She growled as she punched him.

Chapter Eight

Shep stood in Ryder's office and watched the interrogation through the two-way mirror, rubbing his jaw where Lilly had socked him the night before. He'd deserved it. He still felt guilty as hell for going up to her room. Shouldn't have done it. Should have never made love to her.

Last night had been an epic fail as far as getting her out of his system went. He wanted her now more than ever.

Jamie shifted next to him, his attention on the men in the other room. "The National Guard arrived at Fort Sam Houston. Supposedly for a joint exercise."

But in reality, so they'd be close enough to swoop in at the last minute if his team failed, Shep thought. He should have been thinking about that and the interrogation in the other room, but his thoughts kept skipping back to Lilly.

Jamie looked at him. "You're quiet today."

"Didn't get enough sleep last night."

Jamie raised an eyebrow.

Shep pretended to be engrossed in Mo and Ryder handling the questioning. Brandon, handcuffed to the chair, was trying to make a deal, giving testimony against his buddy.

Mo stood over him, looking damn impressive when he did his looming thing. "I don't care who did the shooting last night. We need the big boss down south. The Coyote. Who is he?"

"I don't know who he is, man. He's at the top of the totem pole. He's got powerful friends. When he don't like somebody, they're dead." The guy hunched his back. "If he even thinks I'm talking, I'll be ground to pulp, man."

Ryder and Keith had followed Brandon and his friend over to Mexico, watched the transaction. Keith had stayed to follow their Mexican link and see where that led. Ryder followed them back and had them apprehended at the border, along with their border-agent friend.

After Mo was done with the interrogation, he escorted Brandon out into the deputy sheriff's custody, and they switched to the border agent, Ricky Lowell.

"You know what happens to former law-enforcement officers in federal prison?" Mo started, not pulling any punches.

"Nothing worse than a shot in the head, which is what I'll get in some dark alley if I tell you anything." The man leaned back in his chair, all cool and playing the tough guy, the opposite of what Brandon had been.

"I heard that. The Coyote doesn't mess around. He can reach anyone anywhere."

Ricky shrugged. "I'm not going to give him a reason to want to reach me. You're wasting your time here."

Mo played things just as cool. "We put the word out that you talked. When he sends an assassin, we'll catch that guy and follow him back to the Coyote. I don't care how we catch the bastard, as long as we catch him. I doubt the death of a corrupt border agent will weigh too heavily on my conscience."

Ricky shifted in his seat. "You can't do that."

"Wanna bet?"

"You're not going to catch whoever he sends. He's got men everywhere."

"A chance I'm willing to take," Mo promised. "It'll either work or not. You're not talking, so half a chance is better than no chance."

Ricky swore. "I want a lawyer. Where the hell am I, anyway? I want to be transported out of here. You're consultants for the CBP. You don't even have jurisdiction over me."

"You'd be surprised at the kind of leeway I have." Mo shifted closer. "We need the Coyote. We need him yesterday."

"I have rights."

"Rights are flexible in cases like this. We're talking about border security. You compromise it on a daily basis from what we hear. What if some terrorists were to sneak through?"

"But they didn't—" Ricky went white, all the coolness sliding right off his face as he understood at last. He swallowed. "You can't link me to terrorism. It's not true. You can't make that up. What the hell? I want an attorney. I want to know what I'm being charged with."

"You know damn well terror suspects get none of that." Mo waited, letting the silence grow heavy. "Maybe you understand your situation better now. Why don't you take a moment to weigh your options?"

Ricky didn't need long, less than ten seconds, before he blurted out, "I don't know who he is, all right? Nobody knows. He's some bigwig over in Mexico."

"A crime boss?"

"That, but more."

Mo paused. "Politician?"

"Maybe. I don't know. All I know is he has money and power to make things happen. He leads a double life. That's why nobody can know who he really is or what his real name is."

"Who else works for him at CBP?"

His gaze shifted. "I don't know."

"The more useful you are, the better things will go for you," Mo reminded him.

"I don't know all of them," Ricky said. "I know a couple." And then, reluctantly, he named three men.

Out in the other room, Jamie moved toward the door. "I'll go pick them up."

"I'll go with you," Shep offered.

"I'll be fine. You stay and handle whatever else actionable intel Mo gets out of the bastard."

Ricky was begging on the other side of the two-way mirror as Jamie left. "You have to keep me safe."

Mo didn't look concerned. "You'll be safe in prison. You keep talking and I'll arrange for solitary confinement."

"Up north." His eyes hung on Mo. "The Coyote has men down south everywhere."

"How about Ohio?"

The man nodded.

And Mo said, "But you'll have to earn it."

Sweat beaded on Ricky's forehead. "I know a couple of mules. The regulars that always come through during my shift. They've been taking a break lately, but they'll be back soon. You can catch them in action."

"All right, we'll start with that."

Shep wrote down the names. He was about to leave

to pick them up when Ricky volunteered another bit of information.

"All smuggling is on hold until the first."

"Why is that?" Mo asked. They had their suspicions, but confirmation would have been helpful, knowing that they were on the right path.

"Don't know that." Ricky's expression switched to sly. "But there was a…request. On the first, I'm not to assign Galmer's Gulley to anyone for patrol. Like an oversight thing. You might catch someone there."

"Only at Galmer's Gulley?"

"Solitary up north?"

Mo nodded.

Rickey hesitated, but then spit it out at last. "And I'm supposed to thin the patrol schedule that day as much as I can. Approve more vacation days than usual. But put nobody at Galmer's Gulley."

Galmer's Gulley, Shep thought as he headed out to pick up the six smugglers on his list. He was smiling. They very likely had the time and place for the terrorists' transfer. Exactly the breakthrough they needed.

Confirmation would have been nice, though. And he might very well get that from one of the smugglers he was about to grab. He ran their names through the police database, printed the rap sheets, which included current employment and home addresses.

He ran into Lilly in the parking lot.

"Hey." She was just coming in, dressed like a local in blue jeans, boots, a T-shirt with a lone star over her chest and a cowboy hat shading her head. She'd assimilated pretty darn fast. She shot him a dark look.

He had no idea what to say to her. What did a man say after a night like the one they'd just spent together?

He wanted more but, of course, he couldn't very well tell her that.

She didn't wait for him to figure out a game plan. Her fine lips pressed together. "Any progress with the op?" She was all cool and professional, as if last night hadn't happened.

If she could act that way, so could he. He channeled his thoughts away from the tangled sheets. "We got the crossing point. I'm heading out to pick up some smugglers to see if they have any further details or confirmation."

Relief settled on her face. "Okay. That's good." She walked straight to his SUV instead of the stairs. "I'm going with you."

The word *no* was on his tongue. But he didn't want her to think that he couldn't handle what had happened between them the night before. So, instead, he said, "Be my guest."

And it was the last thing he said to her until they reached the first address, a chicken processing plant. Two men on his list, brothers, worked there.

He picked them up without trouble and dropped them off for holding at the Pebble Creek sheriff's office, leaving them in Bree's capable hands until they could be interrogated. He called Mo to let him know he'd have another batch waiting as soon as he was done with the border agent.

The next man on the list didn't have a permanent address, but did have half a dozen locations where he was known to hang out. The Yellow Armadillo was one of them.

"Know him?" Shep showed the printed mug shot to Lilly.

"I might have seen him at the bar." She thought for a

second. "I'm pretty sure I have. He came in after hours, the first time I was there to see Brian."

"We'll catch him at the bar later today, then." Shep moved on to the next name.

This one lived in Pebble Creek. Nothing listed for employer. He drove to the address listed, a small ranch home on the outskirts of town.

"Why are you looking for Joey?" his mother wanted to know after she'd opened the door to their knock.

"We'd like to ask for his assistance in a police matter. Is he home, ma'am?"

"He's with his friends. They volunteer cleaning up around the high school. They're good kids."

Shep drove off to look for him.

Having Lilly within reach, the light scent of her perfume lingering in the cab, a truckload of unsaid things between them, was messing with his head. He tried to push all that aside and just focus on the job.

Joey's cleaning up the road by the high school turned out to be selling weed by the high school. He took off running when he spotted Shep heading for him.

But Lilly had already gone around, stepped out from behind a pickup in the parking lot and decked the man.

"Joey Manito, you're under arrest for possession and distribution." Shep cuffed him, pulled him up and walked him to his SUV as he read him his rights.

Since there was still room in the back, he didn't take Joey to jail just yet. He drove off to the next address.

The small house, just a step up from a shack, stood deserted.

"Any other info?" Lilly asked, picking up the guy's rap sheet. She scanned the paper. There was no employment listed.

"Car?"

She nodded.

"We can call the Pebble Creek deputy sheriff and have an APB put out on the license plate," he suggested, and that was exactly what Lilly did while he drove to the next address they had.

They didn't run into any problems there. The man was so stoned he couldn't have run if he tried. He sang raunchy Mexican folk songs all the way to the Pebble Creek jail.

Shep stepped into the deputy's office while Lilly dealt with the paperwork.

"Anything on the APB?"

"I'll let you know the second I have something. Everything okay?"

"The usual nonsense." He considered Bree for a second. "If a bigwig was running all the smuggling from the other side of the border, who would be your best guess?"

She leaned back in her chair as she tapped her index finger on the desk.

"Politician? Chief of police?" he suggested.

"I don't think so. They're on the take, but not running things. What I know of the ones I'm thinking of… can't see them as a criminal mastermind. Mostly they're men who got put into positions by their wealthy fathers. They know how to take money, not make it. Top criminals are rarely politicians—too much media scrutiny. They buy politicians for their needs."

Lilly came looking for him. "Ready?"

"I'll let you know if I think of anything," Bree promised him before they left.

"She's very beautiful," Lilly remarked on their way to his car.

"She used to be Miss Texas."

"She was smiling at you." They got in.

"She's very smiley."

"Are you and her…" Lilly's face was a tight mask, without emotion.

He blinked. "Jealous?" For some reason the thought made him happy.

"Not in the least," she snapped. "She's welcome to have you."

He started the engine. "I don't think Jamie would agree with that."

She didn't say anything, but her shoulders noticeably relaxed.

Had she really been jealous? Did that mean last night hadn't been just a gigantic spur-of-the moment mistake for her? He wasn't sure what it'd been for him. He was still evaluating it.

He didn't say that, however. In fact, they didn't talk about anything personal for the rest of the day. He'd apologized for making love to her. She hadn't liked it. He'd asked her to marry him. She hadn't liked that, either.

He wanted to figure out what she wanted from him so he could avoid her decking him again.

The sixth man on their list gave them the runaround. They'd go to one address, be told he had moved. Go to the next, be told he temporarily lived someplace else. And it kept up like that. The man had disappeared.

"Could be he's been killed," Shep said as he dropped Lilly off in front of her hotel at the end of the day. No way was he going up. Ever again.

"Or got tipped off that we're rounding up smugglers," she said as she turned from him.

He didn't stay to watch her walk away. He stepped on the gas and drove off before he could do something stupid.

LILLY STOOD BY the window in her hotel room and looked out into the approaching darkness. Better than looking at the bed. Heat flooded her every time she did that.

Shep seemed determined to ignore their night together. Because he thought it was a mistake. Because he still thought of her as some young idiot under his authority. She could have screamed with frustration.

She'd sung her sets on Saturday night, and he'd shown up, supposedly to protect her, but that was all. Brian had been his slimy self, the crowd as drunk and rowdy as the night before. The band got it into their heads that they wanted to get to know her better, so she hadn't had a minute alone between sets, hadn't gotten a chance to investigate any further.

After her last set ended, Shep brought her home again, in silence, let her out in front of the hotel then drove away.

She refused to beg for his attention again. If he wanted to ignore what had happened between them, she wasn't going to bring it up if it killed her.

So she spent her Sunday with busywork, typing up a long report for her boss at the FBI and sending it off, then running personal errands all day. By the time night fell, she was tired from running around but her mind was too antsy to rest. When her phone rang, she grabbed for it, thinking it might be Shep….

She had no idea what to hope for.

She didn't want to fall in love with him.

But Jamie Cassidy's voice came through the line instead. "Hey, want to go grab something to eat? Unless you have other plans."

Right. Because her social life was so happening. Hardly. Yet, she still hesitated. She wasn't good at letting people in.

Then she drew a deep breath and plunged forward. "I'm game. But shouldn't you be on a hot date with the deputy sheriff?"

"Nothing's more important than family," he said, which made her feel good. "Anyway, it's girls' night out. Bree is taking her sister to the mall. They're getting pedicures and eyebrow shaping, whatever that means. I'd rather not know the sordid details. I have an hour before I go back on duty."

He didn't sound very threatening. And an hour seemed manageable. "Know any good pizza places?"

"Sure. But there's a chipotle *cocina* not far from the hotel that will make you glad you came to Texas. I'll pick you up."

"I'll meet you there." She always preferred to have her own ride. It was an independence thing. "Just let me know where it is."

He did. "How soon can you be ready?"

She laughed out loud. "I'm an FBI agent."

"Right. Born ready and all that."

"You bet." He was easy to talk to, she thought as she hung up.

She'd barely seen him since she'd arrived. The team was working full steam, everyone pursuing leads, the team members off gathering information and tracking down any possible connections to the Coyote. They were all running around nearly 24/7, with breaks that were few and far between.

She'd meant to catch up with Jamie, just hadn't found the right moment yet.

Family was new to her. But now that she had some, maybe she could explore the possibilities a little. Without going in too deep. She didn't fully trust the idea of one big happy family. Had never seen one truly work, up close and personal.

Her only experience was that the second she let her guard down and let people into her heart, they dumped her or hurt her. Her operating life rule had been not to trust. Part of her equated that with keeping herself safe. It was a false assumption and an unhelpful rule, however.

Past experiences created life assumptions that influenced one's attitude toward life and his or her actions, which formed their new life experiences. She'd spent enough time with the FBI shrink to know that. She had to, to pass a psych evaluation for the job.

Understanding her hang-ups, however, and shaking off old habits were two different things. But she knew what she wanted: to move forward. She wasn't about to let the past bind her forever.

So while she didn't feel a big wave of warmth and pleasure at the thought of building some kind of family link with Jamie, she made herself go. Just as she would make herself give him a chance.

She brushed her hair and changed her T-shirt. She walked down the stairs instead of taking the elevator, needing the exercise. The drive wasn't long. The *cocina* was just a few blocks from her hotel, run by a family who'd been in the area before there was Texas, according to a framed newspaper article near the front door. The place was loud but smelled amazing, and Jamie had somehow managed to find them a quiet corner where they could talk without having to shout at each other.

"Do you live around here?" she asked once she slid into the booth across the table from him.

"Renting a place in the unsavory section. The better to keep an eye on the local troublemakers." He grinned.

Their order was delivered in minutes. They were sharing a chipotle chicken-and-shrimp platter that just about covered the small table.

"I met your sister, Megan," she said, wanting to start with something positive. "She helped my brother find me. She's very nice."

"You think that because you didn't have to grow up with her," he said in a droll tone. "Once she put pink nail polish on me while I was sleeping. Sisters are the devil's instrument. Be glad you have a brother."

She couldn't help the laugh that escaped her. "When was that?" She popped a shrimp into her mouth. It tasted like heaven.

"Don't know. Tried to repress the memory as best I could. Middle school maybe."

"I'm sure you did your best to annoy her, too."

He studiously kept his gaze on the platter. "I'm not saying I never cut her hair. Or shoved the odd frog or lizard down her shirt." He flashed a nostalgic grin as he looked up.

"You have a ton of brothers. Seven?" She popped a giant shrimp into her mouth and let the flavor spread through her.

He sobered for a moment. "Six now. Billy was killed in action." He paused. "But when we were kids, the seven of them put together were less trouble than Megan."

"I missed that," she told him as an old sense of longing awakened inside her. "The family thing. I have no memories of my birth family." And although she'd met Mitch and spent an entire afternoon with him, it still felt a little strange.

"So I take it when Mitch showed up on your doorstep, you didn't recognize him?" He shook his head.

"Of course you didn't. You were a toddler when you last saw him. That had to be strange." He took a sip of his drink. "Him showing up out of the blue."

"I thought he was some scam artist. He was lucky I didn't put him on his back."

Jamie choked on his drink for a second before he finally swallowed. "I would have paid money to see that." He coughed some more. "You ever go up against Shep by any chance? And if you did, is there video footage?" He grinned.

She took a big bite of chicken so she wouldn't have to answer.

Jamie narrowed his eyes. "His jaw looked kind of purplish this morning."

Yeah. She'd seen that. She kept chewing in silence.

"If he's getting fresh with you…if you want me to beat him up, just say the word. That's what family is for."

She rolled her eyes. "There's way too much testosterone in that office. What is it with men and violence?"

He had the gall to look hurt. "What are you talking about? You're the one who socked him."

"I shouldn't have." She really regretted that. She sighed. "I ruined his life, you know. Back then."

He didn't look too concerned. "You were probably the most excitement he saw until he joined the team. It was good training."

"I was on the wild side," she admitted.

"I heard." He took a bite of his food before he asked, "So what's the first thing that you do remember?"

"Foster families. Lots of them. I got passed around. I might have acted out now and then." She took a drink as she remembered. "The adults were all right. The kids…" She shook her head. "In places it was so bad you didn't dare fall asleep. Cutting my hair off in my sleep would have been the least of it. You had to show you were the toughest. Then you got in trouble for that."

"Is that how you ended up with Shep as your parole officer?"

She nodded. "He was okay. Not that I appreciated that at the time. I just wanted to be free."

They talked some more about that, then Jamie's brothers, and Megan and her new baby.

"I'm an aunt." The thought still made her a little dazed.

Jamie watched her. "How do you feel about that?"

"Weirder than weird. I'm linked to this little kid. And I'm supposed to be someone she can look up to and depend on if needed, and all that. Scary."

"I know what you mean." He nodded. "As long as they don't ask us to change diapers, right?"

She swallowed. "That ever happens, I'm joining the navy. I'd feel more comfortable with shipping out, honestly."

Jamie looked as if he'd considered the same. But when he spoke again, it was to change the subject. "So, you and Shep?" He shook his head. "Just trying to wrap my mind around it. I feel like I should ask him about his intentions."

"Don't." She looked down at her food. "It's over. It never really was anything."

"Okay. Just want to let you know that if you need me for any reason, I'm here. I'm family. I got your back."

A different person might have taken that as a good thing, but it just brought all of Lilly's insecurities to the surface. Why the hell did everyone want to protect her?

First Shep, and now Jamie. Didn't they think she was good enough to stand on her own? She was.

She gave Jamie a flat smile and changed the subject, back to the family and all those other brothers-in-law she hadn't yet met. And by the end, she might have relaxed a little, laughing at Jamie's outrageous stories.

They stayed for an hour, then parted ways in front of the *cocina,* Jamie promising to invite her over for dinner and introduce her to his girls. Apparently, Katie, Bree's sister, lived with her.

She thought about that on her drive back, how Jamie seemed happy. That hadn't always been the case, from what she understood from the one-page summary she'd gotten on him before taking the job. He'd lost both legs, dealt with some serious PTSD in the past and heavy-duty depression. He'd been assigned to the team strictly for office duty in the beginning.

Dinner with him had been nice, but she was still antsy. So instead of heading straight to the hotel, she took a small detour to drive by The Yellow Armadillo.

Just because the bar was closed on Sundays, it didn't mean there wouldn't be anybody there. In fact, their day off might be the perfect time for Brian to run his illegal activities.

She wanted to find something, wanted progress, wanted to prove to Shep and Jamie and the rest of the team that she was good enough, that she could take care of business. That she didn't need them, didn't need anyone. Her pride didn't like that they all saw her as someone who needed to be protected.

Of course, pride was a dangerous thing. Especially when it went hand in hand with her deep-seated need to always prove herself, always stand alone, never trust a hand offered.

Pride goes before the fall. Unfortunately, she didn't remember that bit of ageless wisdom until it was too late.

Chapter Nine

The sign on the door said CLOSED, but the lights were on behind the shuttered blinds. Maybe they'd been left on for security. Most of the stores on the street were lit up. Still, on an impulse, Lilly drove around the block.

A small truck idled in the back alley, blocking her view, the empty cab facing out, the back lined up with the bar as if for loading. All right, so that could be something interesting.

She thought about calling Jamie, but he was headed to work, and dragging him back on a hunch didn't seem fair. It'd be taking him away from following other leads that might actually pan out. First she'd see if there was anything to call about. She didn't want to seem like some overeager rookie jumping the gun, trying to make something out of nothing.

She looped back to the front and parked, then got out. The parking lot was deserted, less than a dozen cars, all of which probably belonged to the people who lived in the apartments above some of the shops. None of the businesses were open this time of the night on a Sunday, no reason for anyone else to be here.

She walked up to the bar and tried to look through the gap in the blinds. But before she could have gotten a good look, the front door opened.

Brian came through, his eyes narrowing at her. "What are you doing here?"

Maybe he did have security cameras set up and they were just well hidden.

She gave an easy smile. "Oh, good. I'm glad to see you. I think I might have left my cell phone here last night. I looked everyplace else." She smiled again. "I was hoping somebody might be around to let me in to take a look?"

"Let's see where it rings." He flipped his phone open and pushed a couple of buttons. He had her number in his phone; she'd given it to him the day she was hired.

"If it starts ringing on the bottom of my purse, I'm going to feel really stupid." She reached into the purse to shuffle around and powered off her phone before it could have gone off. Then she stopped searching and turned her attention back to him. "I have no idea where I put that thing."

He waited with his phone to his ear. He wasn't leering at her or staring at her breasts, which was out of character for him. He seemed thoughtful, in fact. Maybe he didn't want to mess with Shep.

"Number unavailable," he said as he put his phone away.

"Great." She grimaced. "The battery probably ran down." She moved toward him. "It might be in the back where I was taking my breaks. Or in the bathroom where I was changing."

He didn't look happy to see her there. In fact, his fat lips had a decidedly angry tilt to them. But then he seemed to make up his mind and stepped aside with a closed look on his face. "Hurry up. We're restocking the liquor. We were just about to leave."

"Thanks." She pushed by him. "Shouldn't take more than five minutes to run through the place."

He locked the door behind them, the metallic click sending a twinge of unease up her spine. He probably just wanted to make sure nobody walked in while they were in the back.

Tank was coming from the direction of the basement. He threw Brian a questioning look. Brian shook his head.

Lilly kept smiling. "Hey, Tank. Can't believe you have to work on Sundays. That bites, man."

Tank didn't comment, just turned around and went back the same way he'd come.

She checked around the stage first, trying to steal glances at the back hallway. The basement door was open, but she couldn't see anyone coming and going.

Brian watched her wherever she went. "Doesn't look like it's here."

"God, I hope you're wrong. If it's not here, then somebody already took it. I can't afford a new phone. This was a good one. Paid for it from my last gig." She went to the ladies' room next, pushed through the swinging saloon doors in the corner by the jukeboxes.

Brian followed her. "Boyfriend of yours drove you over?"

She checked the stalls. "He's off with his buddies somewhere."

"Them rodeo cowboys never do well. Win a few purses, get hurt, get hooked on drugs, wash up in a couple of years. You could do better." He watched her. "Friendly advice."

She tried to take it lightly, even as more unease settled over her. "It's not like we're getting married. We're just having fun while we're both in town."

Since he wouldn't move, she had to brush by him to get out of the bathroom. "I'll look behind the bar. I put my bag there while I was singing."

Again, he followed, looking as if he was holding back anger. And, again, he seemed to put it away, as if coming to some sort of decision. "Want a beer? On the house."

"Sure." Whatever made him back off for a minute. He was creeping her out, frankly.

She made a show of looking behind the bar while he filled two glasses from the tap and slid one her way.

"Thanks." She gave a deep sigh, then took a gulp. "It's not here, either."

"An iPhone?"

She nodded and drank some more, playing for time. She wanted to see who else was here beyond Brian and Tank. Maybe if she hung around long enough, someone else would come from the back. She was trying to figure out how to offer to help with the stocking without sounding suspicious.

"Those are expensive. Maybe you dropped it in the basement," Brian said.

She thrilled to the suggestion. "Could be." She would have loved it if he let her go down there. She wanted to take a look at what they were really doing here this time of the night.

She drained her glass so fast it would have made a cowboy proud, then headed for the basement door.

Of course, Brian was right behind her once again. "You said you sang in San Antonio before," he was saying as he closed this door, too, behind them.

Even with the light on, the basement was poorly lit, smelling old and dank. She felt as if she was in some old castle dungeon. Goose bumps prickled on her skin.

"Which bar did you say?" he asked.

"Finnegan's." They'd set up a cover for her with the owner, should Brian call for a reference.

She reached the bottom of the stairs, and the main area of the basement opened up in front of her. The space was stacked with sealed, unmarked boxes, close to a hundred of them. When Shep had told her about his meeting down here with Tank, he said the boxes held bottles and were marked with various liquor logos. So this batch was something different.

She moved toward the boxes, making a show of scanning the floor, wishing she could find a way to look into one. She could hear Tank moving things around in one of the rooms. Then he came forward.

"You ever hang out at Finnegan's when you go up to San Antonio?" Brian asked. "Our Lilly used to be their star attraction. How about that?"

Tank watched her darkly as he shrugged. "I've been there."

"Ever see Lilly? You should have told me about her. I would have stolen her away sooner."

Tank shook his head, still watching her. "My brother ain't never heard of her, either, and he hangs out there nearly every night."

Oh, hell. She was beginning to feel as if this was some kind of a setup. She wanted to go back up, but Brian stood at the bottom of the staircase, blocking her way. God, she could have used some fresh air. The musty smell was turning her stomach.

His eyes narrowed at her. "You sure it was Finnegan's?"

"I was only there for a few weeks. Might have been Frankie's." She gave a quick laugh. "Honestly, I was drunk half the time. They gave free beer to the band, too."

Brian didn't seem to think any of that was funny. He watched her stone-faced. "Better look for that phone. I'm ready to get out of here."

Right. She moved around, scanned the ground, trying to ignore the two men and her growing sense of discomfort of being down here with them alone. Not only was she nauseous, she was beginning to feel dizzy, too.

Had to be the chipotle. If Jamie had taken her to a place that gave her food poisoning, she was going to have to revise her good opinion of him.

Tank lumbered back to his work in the room behind her.

But Brian wasn't done questioning her yet, it seemed, because next he wanted to know "When were you down here that you could have lost the phone?"

"In between sets. Just stuck my head down, really. I was looking for you for something." She covered the area, so she had to give up her pretend search. She made an unhappy face. "I don't think it's here."

"I don't think so, either. But we did find something that might belong to you." He reached into his pocket and pulled out a bug.

"What's that?" She gave a clueless look. Her head was swimming. Could food poisoning hit this fast? "That's not my earring."

The stone-faced look remained. "It's not an earring, and I think you know that."

She didn't ask what it was, just went on with the puzzled look and leaned against the wall as a sudden wave of weakness hit her.

"It's a bug," Brian told her. "We do a sweep every

Sunday. There've been only two strangers down here this week, you and your boyfriend."

"Not really my boyfriend. We're just hooking up." She tried to keep it light and did her best not to let him see that she was becoming rapidly incapacitated.

"Who do you work for?"

She gave a nervous laugh as a scared singer might. "You. For now. I mean, I like it here. But I'm not the long-term-commitment kind. If you change your mind about me, I'll just move on. There are a million small bars in the world."

"I'm going to ask you only one more time. Who do you work for, darling?"

"Are you serious? I don't know what you're talking about. I better get going. I need to find that damn phone." She turned toward the stairs.

But Brian's arms snaked out faster than she'd ever seen him move and he grabbed her arm, yanked her back. "Are you a cop? CBP? Why in hell am I paying all that money if they still send their snoops around, dammit?" He looked openly angry now, even outraged.

He yanked her toward him.

She moved in with a self-defense maneuver, too slow as the basement spun with her. But she would have been free of the bastard the next second, anyway. Except Tank appeared behind her from out of nowhere and his meaty fist came down on the top of her head.

SHE DIDN'T ANSWER her phone. Shep swore as he waited for the interrogation room to free up. He didn't like it when women did the holding-a-grudge thing. Men were so much simpler. Either they were okay with each other, or they settled their differences with their fists and then they were okay. She'd punched him. He let her. Why in hell was she still mad?

The current op was almost over. She blew back into his life for a short time, and she was about to blow back out. Good. He'd be able to focus 100 percent on the job again then. Except the thought made him miserable.

He didn't want her to disappear. At least, he wanted to keep in touch. They couldn't have a romantic relationship, but they could be…something. He needed to talk to her about that.

He shouldn't have made love to her. He knew that, dammit. He shouldn't have made the off-the-cuff marriage offer, either. Obviously, it wasn't what she wanted. A good thing, since he hadn't planned on getting married, ever.

He had no idea what had possessed him to blurt those words out like that. He needed to apologize again. He'd drive by her hotel in the morning, once he was done at the office.

Mo came out of the interrogation room with his guy and led him away. Shep went in with the next.

He clicked on the recorder, noted the man's name and specifics, the date of the interrogation, then started with the questions. "Have you ever met with the Coyote?"

"No, man," the twentysomething kid Lilly and he had picked up earlier said, looking as tired as Shep felt.

"What do you know about him?"

"He's the boss of everyone, pretty much. You cross him, you disappear." The kid made a slicing motion across his throat. "He'll ground you to dust."

"What's his real name?"

The kid just laughed. "Right, dude. He stopped by my house just to tell me that."

Shep asked another dozen questions. He received

no helpful answers, no matter how hard he leaned on the guy.

He stood to stretch his legs. He could have pushed harder, but he was pretty sure the kid was telling the truth. The interrogations were a long shot. It was unlikely that any of the men they'd rounded up had information that would lead directly to the Coyote, but he had to try anyway.

They had the date and they had the place, but what they didn't have was any confirmation and the Coyote's true identity. They couldn't afford any mistakes on this op, any crossed wires, any half-accurate intel. Being able to pick up the bastard for questioning sure would have helped.

Also, even if they caught the tangos sneaking over, who was to say more wouldn't try with the Coyote's help? The government needed that man in custody and permanently out of business.

"Do you know where Tank is?"

"I don't even know who he is."

Shep kept up with the questions, rotating the men in and out, consulting with Mo in between, until midnight, then went home to catch some sleep before his morning shift started.

On his way to the office, he drove by the hotel. Lilly wasn't in her room, didn't respond to his knocking. She still didn't pick up her phone, either. He walked through the parking garage, but he couldn't find her car.

He went to the front desk, but the guy there didn't remember seeing her going out that morning.

On a hunch, Shep drove by the bar, checked front and back, but the bar was closed and neither Lilly nor her car were there as far as he could tell.

He switched to the monitoring app on his phone and

accessed last night's recording from the bar's basement. Since the place had been closed, he didn't expect much, but he wanted to check anyway. They couldn't afford to overlook anything at this stage.

The program was set to skip silence and just go to sound. It wasn't long before Lilly's voice came through on Shep's Bluetooth.

What in hell had she been doing there, alone, without telling him?

Anger punched through him, quickly turning to worry as he heard Brian say, "It's a bug. We do a sweep every Sunday. There've only been two strangers down here this week, you and your boyfriend." Then some more conversation, her protesting her innocence, then the unmistakable sounds of a scuffle.

Then a crunch, as if someone had ground the bug into the cement floor with his heel.

He shut off the recording and called Lilly again. She didn't answer her phone. So as he drove to the office, he kept calling. Until she did pick up, finally.

"Hey, cowboy," she said, tension in her voice, and something else in the way she dragged out the word cowboy. Was she drunk?

"I was about to call you," she said in the same slow drawl.

"Where are you?"

"Out at the rodeo grounds. Listen, I need you out here for a minute."

"What are you doing there? Is everything okay?"

"Nothing to worry about. I'll explain when you get here. Sooner would be better than later. Just hop in that rickety old Mustang of yours and step on the gas. I'll be out by the bull pens."

Oh, hell. He gripped the phone. "I'll be right there. Lilly—"

She hung up before he could have asked any questions.

He drove a souped-up SUV for work and a beat-up pickup for cover. The only Mustang he'd been near lately was Doug Wagner's. Talking about that was her way of warning him there was trouble. And if she didn't simply come out with what that was, it meant she wasn't alone. There was somebody within hearing distance.

He had a good idea who. But why was she at the fairgrounds? And why did she sound drunk at seven in the morning? He didn't like any of that.

He called it in.

"I'm heading out to the rodeo grounds," he told Ryder as he turned his SUV around. "Lilly's there. There's something going on. She got busted at The Armadillo last night. I think Brian and Tank might have her."

"Need backup?"

"Don't know yet." He didn't want to call the guys off the border. He also didn't want to wake Mo unnecessarily since he'd been up all night, working. Keith was still in Mexico, following leads there. Ryder was manning the office, checking satellite images and processing last-minute intel.

"Call me if you need anything," the team leader said.

"Let me get out there and do some recon first."

He drove as fast as he could, bringing up the tourist map of the rodeo grounds on his cell phone. Within a minute, he knew exactly where the bull pens were located.

The rodeo was a weeklong event, starting that afternoon with the opening ceremonies and ending on the following Saturday with the biggest party Pebble Creek had ever seen, supposedly.

The fairgrounds, made into a rodeo arena now, were on the outskirts of town, a sprawling compound of stables and show rings. He didn't pull up into the front parking lot. He didn't pull up into the back one, either. He went to the feed store directly attached to the side of the registration building and parked there.

He checked his guns, the one he kept under his shirt stuck into his waistband at his back and the smaller one that he kept in his right boot. On second thought, he grabbed his other backup gun from the glove compartment and stuck it into his left boot before he got out. He skipped the official entrances and snuck through a hole in the chain-link fence.

Whoever had been listening in while he'd been talking to Lilly on the phone, Shep didn't want them to see him coming. He scanned the area as he walked. The goal was to see them before they saw him.

The opening ceremonies for the rodeo would start at five, after the worst of the heat was done for the day. At the moment only the work crews ambled around the place, cleaning and setting up for the crowds that would come in the evening.

Shep tried to look as if he belonged. He stayed near the perimeter as he made his way to the bull pens in the back. He was going to see what was going on, then call Ryder and report in.

THERE HAD TO BE a way out.

Shep would come for her. She hoped. He'd promised to have her back. Well, she needed that now. And she was beginning to appreciate the offer. She wouldn't have been the least upset if he rushed in to save her.

She was locked in a feed bin near the sheep pens at the fairgrounds. There weren't any cracks in the heavy plastic box, so she couldn't see anything. Lilly could hear the sheep, though, and a dog barking now and then. She breathed deeply, wrinkling her nose against the smells that surrounded her, and did her best to keep from passing out again.

Could have been worse. They could have put her in with the bulls. She was gagged with a nasty length of rag and bound hands and feet, wedged in between feed sacks. Must have been a hundred degrees. She could barely breathe.

She shifted, testing her restraints once again but, like before, they didn't give.

She couldn't remember much about getting here. She'd been fading in and out. She remembered Tank throwing a bucket of cold water into her face. He'd forced her to take that call from Shep, then let her fade out again.

How long ago was that?

Could Shep be here already?

And if he was, how would he find her?

She needed to think, but her brain was still frustratingly slow. She felt beyond tired, as if she would die if she didn't sleep a little more. She bit the inside of her cheek so the pain would jolt her back awake.

She could have kicked herself for letting Brian and Tank take her as easily as they had. She'd been so focused on Brian, she hadn't noticed Tank sneaking up behind her until it'd been too late. A rookie mistake.

She shook her head to clear the fog.

She didn't make rookie mistakes, dammit. Her stomach rolled.

And the answer hit her, ridiculously obvious in hindsight. Images flashed into her mind, Brian turning with her glass as he'd slid the beer down the bar to her.

She hadn't been feeling so out of focus because of food poisoning from the chipotle like she'd stupidly thought at the time. Brian had put something in her beer.

He had the drug ready behind the bar, slipped it into the drink with practiced ease, handed it to her without batting an eye. Had he done that to other women before? She wouldn't have been surprised.

But he'd messed with the wrong girl this time.

She pushed the gag out of her mouth as best she could and stretched her neck to rub the rag on her shoulder, trying to push it down a little so she could breathe easier. Minutes ticked by before she succeeded.

She gulped in air that smelled like sheep and manure, then refocused on freeing her hands. She didn't succeed any better this time, but when she bent to her ankles, she managed to untie the rope that bound them together, even if she broke nearly every nail in the process.

She did her best to stretch her legs and get her circulation going. Being able to move a little more freely felt nice. Okay, what else could she do?

The storage container wasn't tall enough for her to stand. She got on her knees and rammed the lid with her back. It rattled, but nothing gave. They'd probably padlocked it. She rammed it again anyway.

And then someone kicked it from the outside, hard, scaring her.

She banged with her bound fists. "Let me out of here! Let me out!"

"Shut up," Tank thundered.

The sheep bleated as something motorized started up somewhere nearby and came closer. Then the container rattled and lifted suddenly, and she fell to her side as her body shifted.

What was that? A forklift?

The feed box was definitely moving, which set her head swimming again. She nearly lost her chipotle dinner before the container was set down. And then she heard something slam with a metallic clang.

She had no idea what that was. "Tank? Don't do this!"

A different, louder motor started up next, the ground suddenly vibrating under her.

She was in the back of a truck; the stark realization hit her. They could take her anywhere, across the border even. "Tank?"

He didn't answer. Maybe he was up front, ready to drive her to wherever they planned on executing her and getting rid of her body. Her muscles clenched, cold sweat beading on her forehead despite the heat.

In case Shep was anywhere within hearing distance, she screamed his name at the top of her lungs. "Shep!"

There was nothing in this world she wanted as much as she wanted to see him again.

Chapter Ten

Three men loitered around the bull pens, talking and spitting tobacco juice in the dust now and then. No sign of Lilly anywhere, as far as Shep could tell. Then Tank and Brian lumbered forward from behind a corrugated-steel building that stood between the bull pens and the sheep, and joined the other three.

Shep pulled behind a row of portable toilets and called Ryder to give him a status update. "Yes, five men that I can see, including Tank and Brian. I think they have Lilly stashed here somewhere." He peeked out to scan the building.

"We can lock the whole place down."

Ryder scanned the sprawling area. They probably couldn't. At least not on their own. The fairgrounds were pretty big and fairly porous. The best they could do in a hurry would be to ask for help from local law enforcement and whatever security was already here for the rodeo, although the security guys were probably undertrained rent-a-cops at best. And there was no telling how many friends Brian and Tank had among them.

The bastards had to have chosen the fairgrounds for a reason. Because they were familiar here, because they had backup here, because they probably did some kind of illegal business from here.

Drugs, guns and human trafficking had all been linked to Pebble Creek in the past couple of weeks. One by one, the leaders of the local crime organization had been taken down by Shep and his team. It looked as if Brian was trying to step into the power vacuum to fill it.

Shep didn't care about any of that right now. All he wanted was to see Lilly safe.

"I don't know if we can do a full lockdown fast enough," he told Ryder.

Keith was still in Mexico. Mo and Ray were on border patrol and should probably stay there. "A couple of guys might be able to quickly run through the place and pinpoint her location, take Brian and his goons in, if it's just the five of them. We can sort them out later."

"I can be there with Jamie in twenty minutes. And I'll call Bree to send over whoever she fully trusts from her department. I'll call Grace, too. That's all I can do in a hurry."

"It'll be enough." He scanned the area and was planning the search already. "You think Grace will come?"

"It's not even a question. Of course she will. Do what you can, but try to keep a low profile until we get there. Don't engage the men. Just see if you can narrow down Lilly's location."

Okay. More than anything, he was glad for Grace. Lilly had sounded strange on the phone. As if she'd been drunk *or* hazy from blood loss—the possibility occurred to him suddenly and set his teeth on edge.

Grace Cordero was Ryder's fiancée, a tough former army medic. If Tank had hurt Lilly—which Shep didn't even want to think about—Grace would come in handy. She was as good with injuries as she was with hand-to-hand combat.

"Thanks, man."

He hung up then skirted the bull pens, ducking from cover to cover, making his way over to the corrugated-steel building. They had the sheep pens behind that, and a truck parked at the far end. Nobody sat behind the wheel for the moment, so he decided to investigate the building first. The truck didn't look as if it was going anywhere in a hurry.

He went around and kept in cover, snuck forward from the side when nobody was looking, then kept behind a row of baled hay. He slipped through the door then ducked into the shadows to his left and waited until his eyes adjusted to the semidarkness, trying to see if he was alone in there.

He couldn't see anyone. Nor could he hear any voices in here.

They had stations set up to groom the sheep, piles of feed, everything the ranchers would need to take care of and show their livestock. The piles of supplies everywhere made it difficult to scan the place fully from where he stood, so he had to go check behind stacks of feed bags and equipment.

The good news was that all the mess also provided him with cover. He moved silently and stayed low as he stole forward, little by little. Lilly could be tied up and gagged, hidden just about anywhere in here.

His phone vibrated in his pocket. A text message from Grace Cordero. I'm here. Where R U?

Corrugatd steel bldng by sheep, he texted back.

She'd come a lot faster than he'd expected. Then again, she was a veterinarian in her post-army career. Maybe she'd already been out at the fairgrounds, taking care of some sick animal. Whatever the reason for her speedy arrival, the important thing was that she was here. Shep moved forward.

Voices sounded behind him, at the entrance. He hurried to the end of a row of feed sacks and stuck his head out enough to see. Brian and Tank were coming back in.

The good news was, they might lead him to Lilly.

The bad news was, they had a couple of sheepdogs following them.

And, of course, the dogs sniffed the ground and caught his scent pretty fast. They barked as they ran straight to Shep.

They didn't attack, friendly as anything, playing greeting committee, blissfully unaware that they'd just given away his location.

Tank and Brian spread out and moved toward him. He didn't want to play hide-and-seek. He wanted Lilly. Shep drew his weapon and stepped out into the open.

He aimed at Tank while keeping an eye on Brian. "Where is she?"

Brian lifted his hands immediately and stopped next to a workstation, pulled closer to it to use it as cover if needed. Tank didn't look scared. Shep knew Tank usually carried a weapon and therefore kept his gun aimed at him rather than Brian.

"Stop where you are." He dropped the goofy Pennsylvania rodeo-cowboy act altogether and went for this commando voice and stance. "Hands in the air. On your stomach, on the ground."

But Tank just shot him a fearsome dark look and kept moving forward, his mouth set into a narrow line, anger flaring in his eyes. He reached his right hand toward his back.

Shep aimed for his shoulder.

But before he could squeeze the trigger, there was a sudden movement to his left and something punched him in the neck.

What the hell? It stung. A burning sensation began spreading down his arm.

He pulled out the dart as his gaze switched to Brian, who was holding a tranquilizer gun. He'd stopped at that workstation for a reason, Shep realized too late.

The man gave a cocky chuckle. "Just got it a few weeks ago. I thought it might be nice to have in case a bull goes crazy during training. I put too much money into some of my boys to let them get hurt."

Shep swung his weapon toward him. He meant to, in any case. His arm sagged instead, his knees buckling. That stuff worked fast. That was the point, of course, if anyone had an angry bull charging at them.

The average rodeo bull weighed close to two thousand pounds. Even as hard as Shep fought, the tranquilizer took him down in seconds.

ON HER KNEES AGAIN, Lilly kept ramming her back into the top of the storage container, still hoping to break through the heavy plastic.

At first, she could hear other cars. The truck had driven through town. But then the ride got bumpier and the sounds of the road stopped. They were on rougher ground somewhere, off-roading it.

Her entire back ached and was probably bruised, but she didn't care. She had a fair idea where they were going: somewhere isolated. And she had an ever better idea of what the men would do when they got there.

They probably thought her an undercover, overeager border agent. They needed to make her disappear. Lord knew the possibilities for that were endless in the South Texas borderlands. She knew who they were and she knew their dirty business. They simply couldn't afford to let her live.

She alternated pushing with her shoulders then lying on her back and kicking with her feet.

She had no idea how long she had before they would stop, but she meant to break free before that. Her best chance for escape was if she could either open the back door and jump from the truck without them noticing or, at least, stand ready by the door and jump on them from above as they came to get her. She'd have the element of surprise.

If she could knock them down, if she could grab a gun—

A pained groan outside her dark box interrupted that optimistic fantasy, startling her. She stilled and listened.

Nothing.

Maybe she'd only imagined it.

But just as she was about to start her efforts again, the groan repeated. This was no sheep they might have put in the back of the truck with her. The sound was decidedly human.

Friend or foe was the question. She meant to find out the answer. She banged her fist on the side of the crate. "Hey! Who is that?"

Even if it was Tank, maybe she could talk him into opening the lid for a second. If she could somehow grab his weapon…

But no response came.

She banged again. "I'm in here. Help me!"

Another minute of silence, then a rusty, croaking sound that might have been "Lilly?"

The familiar voice flooded her with relief. "Shep? I'm stuck in here. Can you help?"

"Give me a minute."

He sounded strange, slow and dazed. Was he injured? Maybe they'd beaten him before they'd tossed him in the back of the truck with her. That would explain why he hadn't responded to her banging before. Maybe he'd been beaten unconscious. "Are you okay?"

A moment of silence followed, then, "What are you doing in there?"

All the frustration inside her surged to the front. "Getting a pedicure. What do you think?"

"Okay," he said after a minute. "Move away from the lid."

She flattened herself to the bottom of the container and pulled some feed bags on top of her.

Was he going to try to shoot the padlock off? She didn't think Brian and Tank would have let him keep his weapon. They'd certainly taken everything she had.

Bang!

Then suddenly the lid popped up, and Shep was there, gripping it with one hand while holding a fire extinguisher with the other. He blinked at her slowly, looking out-of-this-world stoned, his irises wide, his movements not altogether coordinated.

"When did Brian give *you* a roofie?" She sat up, grateful to be able to breathe freely at last, every muscle in her body aching. Her clothes stuck to her with sweat, but she was uninjured, miraculously. She climbed out, with his help.

"Bull tranquilizer," he said, his eyes glazed over. "I pulled it out, so I don't think I got the full dosage."

"Thank God." The full dosage might have killed him. "Brian slipped me a roofie," she told him.

He scanned her with thunder on his face, reaching for her hands.

"Not for that purpose," she said to ease his obvious worries. "Just so they could move me around easier."

But his touch felt nice, so she didn't pull away for a few seconds.

Enough daylight filtered in through the cracks under the door, and a small hole in the roof so she could scan the back of the truck. Other than the crate, the fire extinguisher and the two of them, it was empty. "Now what?"

"Now we escape. Do you trust me?"

"Yes." She wasn't sure it was entirely smart, but she did trust him anyway. He'd come for her. He didn't leave her to her fate, he didn't abandon her—he came.

Since he was bound, hands and feet, she helped him break free, then he helped untie her wrists.

She rubbed her bruised skin before shaking off the minor injury. "Good to go."

But even as she said that, the truck began to slow, coming to a full stop after a minute. Then they heard car doors slamming and two men arguing in Spanish.

"*¡Idiota!* Why didn't you fill up the tank?"

"The boss said to hurry. Didn't want to stop before we hit the border. The next gas station is at the factory. I thought we'd make it."

The other one swore. "Now what do we do?"

"Walk?"

"To the factory? *¡Zurramato!*"

Lilly stayed still and silent as she shot a questioning look at Shep.

Dumb ass. He mouthed the translation as the conversation continued outside.

"And the ones in the back?" one of the men asked. "The boss said the Coyote would want to talk to them."

"The boss also said to shoot them if we run into any trouble."

"We could get good money for the *chica* down south."

"You want to carry her on your back?"

The other one swore. "Let's do it, then, so we can get going." He swore again, more vehemently this time. "It's still a waste just to shoot her."

"You do what you want with her first, but I'm not waiting for you. Your business if you want to die out here."

A threatening growl escaped Shep's throat as he stepped up to the truck's back door, the fire extinguisher lifted and ready. Lilly moved next to him, going down into a crouch. Whatever she had to do, she wasn't going to become entertainment for those two bastards out there.

The roofie had worn off. She was ready. They wouldn't find her quite as easy prey this time around.

Then the doors popped open, revealing two men holding guns. One gave a surprised shout, but that was that. Shep slammed the bottom of the fire extinguisher into his face, while Lilly vaulted onto the other guy, knocking him to the ground, driving her elbow into his solar plexus.

Dust flew up around them as he tried to roll her, but her self-defense skills put her on top in quick order. All good, except for the damned gun trapped between them.

The man grinned into her face. He shifted his arm just an inch or so, but that would be enough. *"Hasta la vista, puta."*

She tried to grab the gun, but just as the top of her fingers reached metal, he pulled the trigger.

She yanked her other elbow down hard at the same split second, hitting his forearm. Then she froze, waiting to see which one of them got hit.

"Lilly?" Shep was grabbing her and pulling her up.

She moved with him. That had to be a good sign,

right? She didn't feel pain, but she wouldn't necessarily. The adrenaline surge after a major injury often came with a minute of reprieve.

There was blood on her, but there was blood on the man staring up at them, too. His eyes filled with surprise before they went dull and lifeless in just seconds.

Shep shook her. "Lilly."

She rolled her shoulders. "I'm okay."

He yanked her to him and wrapped his arms around her so tightly, she could barely breathe. She let herself accept the comfort for a few seconds. Then her gaze caught on the second man over Shep's shoulder, on the ground behind him, blood pooling under his head, the dry ground drinking it in.

She pulled away.

Shep followed her gaze, his expression darkening. "Hit him too hard." He swore. "I misjudged it. Didn't know how good my muscles were working with all the drugs in my system."

The men were both dead, beyond questioning.

For the first time, she looked around and examined the landscape. They were in the middle of nowhere, nothing but desert and cacti as far as the eye could see. "I'm pretty sure we're in Mexico."

Shep nodded, gathering up the guns and giving her one of them. Then he searched the men's pockets. "Enrique Lopez and Gus Garcia." He considered the lifeless men with an aggravated look on his face. "The names say anything to you?"

She shook her head. "Brian's hired goons, no doubt. I don't remember seeing them at the bar, though. But this all ties to him. They probably worked at one of his other businesses."

Shep took a cell phone off the guy he'd taken down,

flipped it open and grimaced. "No reception whatsoever." He shoved the phone into his pocket anyway.

She bent to search her guy, found his phone, but the bullet had damaged it. It was as dead as its owner, although Lilly regretted the owner's death a lot less.

"Doesn't look like we'll be making any calls." Shep scanned the horizon. "We're going to have to walk. Let's see what we can find in the cab."

She moved up front with him, but nothing waited for them there beyond a bag of nacho chips and a few cans of beer. Not terribly helpful, since alcohol only hastened dehydration. They grabbed them anyway.

She stepped back down to the ground and walked toward the road. Standing around in this heat wasn't going to do them any favors. The sooner they got somewhere, the sooner they could get out of the sun and call the office.

She nodded toward the flat, endless dirt road, little more than tire tracks in the desert, the way home. "Back the way we've come?"

But Shep gestured in the opposite direction. "I want to check that hill first. The phone might work on top of that. Or we might see a village or this factory they talked about. Although, from the way they were talking, that might be a couple of miles from here."

"If we can make a call, we can come back here and wait in the shade of the truck until Ryder sends a chopper."

They walked side by side at a brisk pace, keeping an eye out for traffic, but the road was dead. Seemed like a seasonal dirt road, out of the way. Not impossible that it was only used by smugglers.

"This is bad," she said.

"Not too bad. We'll manage."

She shook her head. “That wasn’t what I meant. Today is September thirtieth. Looks like the National Guard will be coming in tonight. And we’re stuck in the middle of nowhere.”

“We make a good team. We’ll figure something out together,” he said with grim determination and picked up speed.

SHEP SLIPPED THE PHONE back into his pocket. Standing at the top of the hill did not, in fact, help with reception whatsoever. But they did see a lonely ranch in the distance with some goats and a horse grazing on some sparse grasses behind the fence.

“There we go,” he said and started out that way. Then he paused and looked back at Lilly. “How are you doing?”

“Fine. Better to move toward water and shade than sit here and fry to death.” Her kissable mouth was set into a determined line. She wasn’t the type to give up and roll over.

He admired that about her. She looked worse for wear, her hair and clothes a mess, yet to him, she was still the most beautiful woman in the world.

They walked side by side in the heat. His head was finally clear of the tranquilizer drug, but it left behind a pounding headache that the relentless sun wasn’t helping.

“Why didn’t you tell me you were going to the bar?” he asked. Before he’d tried the phone, they’d been talking about how she’d ended up with Brian and Tank. Anger stiffened his muscles every time he thought of those bastards. She could have been killed.

“I don’t need a babysitter.”

"It's called working with a partner. Ever heard of this new thing called a *team?*"

She shrugged. "Heard of it. Don't like it."

"Don't FBI agents work with partners? You had to have one over the years."

"I've worked alone for the last couple of months. The last partner I had… Anyway, I was dragging my feet accepting another. I volunteered for this job partially because it was a solo mission. It's easier when you only have yourself to consider."

He didn't entirely disagree with that. He'd spent most of his time with the SDDU on lone-wolf ops overseas. Yet he would have been lying if he said he hadn't come to like his current team and the way they worked together here. "What happened to your last partner?"

"She was shot to death by her boyfriend. He was drunk and jealous." She shook her head. "You go to work every day, deal with the worst kind of criminals, put your life on the line, then you go home where you should be able to relax and some scumbag puts a bullet through your head in your sleep." Her lips flattened.

That sounded rough. "Not all partnerships work."

"Yeah." She walked on. "They were poison for each other. She couldn't live with him, couldn't live without him. They tore each other down pretty badly. Maybe I should have seen it coming. I knew how it was between them."

He wasn't exactly an expert on relationships. He lived for his job for the most part, his brief hookups few and far between.

They walked in silence for a while before she added, "People who are supposed to love you and have your back will let you down. They abandon you or worse.

You don't trust anyone but yourself and you don't get hurt."

Her own life experiences bore that out, so the sentiment was difficult to argue with, but he did anyway. "Sometimes. And sometimes people who are supposed to love you do love you and have your back. There are good people. We just mostly deal with the bad in our jobs."

She blew the hair out of her face. "I think deep down I know that. But I still can't trust people. Tell me that's not stupid."

"I don't think anyone could go through what you went through and not have abandonment issues."

"I was starting to trust you. Back when. That's why I ran away. I figured I better get out of there before you punched me in the face or something and proved yourself to be a fake."

Hell. What was he supposed to say to that?

She didn't wait for him to speak. "You're not a fake."

"Thanks." The quiet declaration touched him.

They walked on, side by side, cutting through the desert together. He didn't see any vehicles around the house, or any people. Didn't look as if anybody was home.

"When I say I have your back," he said after a while, "I don't mean because I don't think you can handle things. I just mean, I want to be there for you because you're important to me."

She turned to him and stared for a long second. "I am?"

"You're the first woman I ever proposed to."

She turned away. "You didn't mean it."

Didn't he? "I had no idea what to say." He paused. "What happened between us, what we shared…I don't think it happens to people every day. I don't want it to never happen between us again. I do care about you, and I do want to protect you. Hell, I want things I haven't even dared to dream about before now. I want you to let me in."

She stared at him. "It'll take getting used to."

"We have time." Warmth spread through his chest. This was what he wanted. She was what he wanted. He'd been a fool to try to keep her at arm's length. He couldn't do that. Not when he was falling for her.

The realization made his mouth go dry.

"We have time," he said again, because he didn't think he could say what he was thinking.

"If we don't get shot in the head or die of dehydration here first," she observed wryly.

"There's always the beer." He lifted the cans.

She grinned. "Yeah, die drunk, die happy."

"Beats dying sad." He grinned back at her, relieved that the conversation was lightening up a little.

They nearly reached the corral with the lone horse when she said, "I do trust you. And I want to trust Jamie. I want to trust the rest of the team."

"They all like you." He made a face. "A little too much for my taste, actually. And they trust you, which is a miracle, considering you're an FBI outsider."

And I more than like you, he wanted to say. He wanted to tell her that their connection went beyond attraction and great sex. He wasn't sure if a relationship could ever work, but he wanted to try anyway, even if it would be long-distance and they could spend frustratingly little time together. Because he could no longer picture going back to a life devoid of Lilly.

But before he could find the words, the smile slid

off her face. She grew somber and searched his gaze as she stopped walking.

He didn't like that look. "What is it?"

She brushed her hair out of her face. "I'm not here just to observe the team."

"You're here to provide help if possible."

"That and more." She looked away.

A cold feeling sneaked up his spine. "What more?"

"I'm to make a recommendation when I get back. About whether the SDDU should be able to operate on U.S. soil."

The sense of betrayal that washed over him was staggering. He stepped back from her. "You're here to spy on us and give bureaucrats ammunition against us to shut us down?"

"It's not like that."

"Sure sounds like that from where I'm standing." He turned from her and walked away. A hard knot replaced all the warm, fuzzy feelings in his chest.

He should have known better. He'd known that his job and relationships didn't mix. What the hell had he been thinking? She'd been sent to spy on them!

Did the Colonel know about this? He couldn't have. He would have told the team.

"What we do here is important, dammit," he called back. "Maybe we're a little less politically correct than the domestic agencies. Maybe we've brought in some rougher battlefield tactics. But the enemy we fight doesn't exactly play by the rules of polite society, in case you haven't noticed."

That Lilly wouldn't understand that cut him to the quick. He turned away from her again and kept going. Maybe she wasn't who he thought she was. Maybe he'd been an utter fool about her. Sure looked like it.

He walked up to the ramshackle house. He didn't want to fight with her right now. Not here. So he called out a couple of loud hellos, but the house seemed empty. Only some mutts came running, barking their heads off. They calmed right down when he offered a handful of tortilla chips.

He tossed more onto the ground then walked up to the front door. A crumpled piece of paper was tacked to the wood, with a few lines written on it in Spanish. It was a notice to drop the feed in the barn, as whoever lived here had gotten called into work and wouldn't be home until later.

Shep knocked anyway. No response came.

"Hello?" He tried the door, found it locked, so he kicked it in.

They needed water. He already knew they wouldn't find a phone. No phone lines led to the place. Out here in the middle of nowhere, there wouldn't be any utilities.

He found some food, goat jerky and goat cheese. He took some of that, while Lilly filled up four empty soda bottles with water. He left the beer on the table for partial payment, and the pesos and dollars they'd found on the men who'd kidnapped them, then went outside to look for a saddle.

The horse was their only hope at this stage.

He found the saddle in the barn, next to the feed that had apparently been delivered already.

"We should keep going forward rather than back," he told Lilly, who came into the barn after him. "Riding through abandoned borderlands in this heat will be slow going and it'll take forever. Let's see if we can find this factory."

She held his gaze. "I'm sorry. I'm just doing my job, like everyone else."

"I don't want to fight about that right now. We can discuss it when we're home and the terrorists are in custody."

She nodded.

He headed out of the barn. "We'll keep going south. We can make a call from the factory."

"Do you think the Coyote is there?"

He shrugged. The men had talked about getting gas for the truck at the factory, and also about taking Lilly and Shep to the Coyote, but it didn't mean that the Coyote was at the factory. They might have been talking about stopping at the factory for gas on their way to the Coyote somewhere farther south.

He made sure the horse had enough to drink before he saddled the animal, not that it looked thrilled with the idea of going for a ride in this heat.

Lilly held the bridle and she patted the horse's neck to calm him. "You ride?"

"Reluctantly."

She raised an eyebrow. "Your cover was being a rodeo cowboy."

"It was the first thing we could come up with under short notice." He looked her over. "How about you?"

She gave a flat smile. "I was fostered on a horse farm for a while. I ride like the wind."

"Fine. You'll sit in front, then, and steer the beast."

She went up first, in a fluid move.

He wasn't as graceful, but he made it up behind her.

Okay, they were close. Way too close. He'd never ridden double before. The way her behind rubbed against him was pretty indecent. Even if it felt damned good. Too good. He hoped their ride would be short.

He didn't dare put his arms around her slim waist as she spurred the horse to move. He didn't want to make things worse. He was still mad at her, dammit. He didn't want to want a woman who would spy on him and his team.

But other than her being fitted tightly against him, he didn't mind the backseat. It left his hands free for his gun, in case they ran into trouble.

Which, of course, they did.

Chapter Eleven

They'd only ridden maybe a mile from the ranch when they ran into a heavily armed posse.

Lilly's best guess was that the two pickups full of men had been sent to find out what had happened to the truck that hadn't arrived on time. She and Shep were armed with handguns, while the others carried semiautomatics.

She stopped the horse as they were surrounded within seconds, all guns aimed at them. Then she raised her hands. Defeat was a foregone conclusion.

Shep swore behind her.

"Live to fight another day," she whispered as she let her weapon drop to the ground. The two of them dying in the middle of the desert would serve no purpose.

She would have dearly liked to kick Shep, maybe, but she didn't want him dead. All this time, he'd been telling her that she could trust him. So she'd trusted him enough to tell him about her job. Did he appreciate it? Hell, no. There was absolutely no rhyme or reason to him.

Even now, was he doing the sensible thing and surrendering? Of course not.

He held on to his gun as one of the men, probably the

leader, yelled at him. If he squeezed off a single shot, the next second they'd both be riddled with bullets.

"Think of the upside," she said under her breath. "I think we're about to meet the illustrious Coyote."

If these men wanted them dead, they would have shot as soon as they'd gotten within range. That they hadn't could only mean that they'd been ordered to bring Shep and Lilly in.

Shep swore again, but tossed his weapon onto the parched ground at last. "I really hope we're not going to regret this."

She had to wonder when the next second the men ran forward and pulled them from the horse, tied them up and shoved them into one of the pickups. They drove back in the direction they'd come from, their captives lying on the truck bed while the men sat on the wooden planks that rimmed the back.

Her bruised back didn't enjoy the ride. At least she wasn't gagged this time, a small mercy she was grateful for. And the men shaded them somewhat so they weren't lying in full sun, either.

Shep asked in Spanish where they were going, but they ignored him, until he insisted on an answer too loudly and one of the men kicked him in the mouth, splitting his lip.

"Quit it," she whispered. If they were to survive, they had to stick together. "This isn't going to get us anywhere."

He glared at her, probably still upset with her because she was doing her job. So unfair.

She turned her head from him and tried to see out but couldn't as she was ringed by scruffy, sweaty men. Some looked bored, staring ahead at the road. Two leered at her openly.

They didn't go far. Less than half an hour passed before they entered some kind of a factory complex and the pickup pulled into a loading bay. The first thing she saw when they dragged her out of the back of the pickup were giant reams of paper.

An impeccably dressed man stood by the sliding metal doors that led inside. He was Asian, middle-aged.

She exchanged a look with Shep.

The man's identity wasn't difficult to guess, although she hadn't met him before. But there was only one Chinese bigwig who had a paper factory on this side of the border this close to Pebble Creek: Yo Tee.

The men dragged their prisoners over to him for inspection.

"Who do you work for?" he asked with a slight accent as he looked them over.

Neither of them said a word.

"You work for border patrol, no? How much you know?"

Of course, he'd want to know that to see if his plans had been compromised.

Again, they remained silent. Lilly was scanning the place from the corner of her eye, noting avenues of escape and making an inventory of how many people they would have to deal with. She was pretty sure Shep was doing the same.

An annoyed frown flashed across Yo Tee's face. "Not answering questions very impolite." He tsked. "Take them in the back, Carlos." He turned away. "Bring them to me when they ready to talk. Sooner better than later."

By the time the men shoved them up the steps, Yo Tee had disappeared. A wide hallway lined with forklifts greeted them inside. A storage area sprawled straight ahead, but they didn't go there. They headed down a narrow hallway on their right, boots slapping on the cement floor.

Several doors lined the hallway, all of them closed. They were taken to the last one. One of the men unlocked the door and shoved them in, then the door banged shut behind them. The key turned in the lock.

Her gaze flew to the half-naked man on the floor in the far corner, all bloodied. Cuts covered his body, not a good sign for the newcomers.

He didn't look Mexican. He had fair skin and blondish hair, matted with blood.

Shep went to crouch next to him. "Hey, are you all right?"

The man moaned in response. He looked as if Yo Tee's men pulled any punches.

Shep glanced back at her and she shot him a helpless look. There was absolutely nothing they could have done to help the poor guy.

Shep must have come to the same conclusion, because he turned from the man to scan the rest of the space. "We don't have much time. They'll be coming in a minute."

"Where did they go?"

"To get their tools, probably."

She so didn't want to think about what those tools might be. Judging from the man on the ground, they would be sharp. She'd just as soon not see them up close and personal. "We need to get out."

Shep was already sitting and untying the rope from his ankles. She did the same, then helped him untie his hands and he helped with hers like before, as if this was their usual routine.

The door was locked. She tried it anyway, grabbed the knob and shook it hard. Nothing gave.

Shep nodded toward a small window high up on the wall. "How about that?"

The narrow opening had two metal bars crossing each other but no glass, probably to let some air in. It didn't look too promising as an avenue of escape. For one, the window was too high up the wall. And the bars had been built directly into the brick.

But since she had no other suggestions, she moved that way. "Let me see."

Shep stood by the wall, cupped his hands and gave her a boost. Once she was standing on his wide shoulders, she could reach the opening. Unfortunately, it seemed as narrow up close as it had looked from below.

"You're not going to fit," she said, giving him the bad news first as she rattled the bars. "But I will."

"Then you must go," he said without hesitation.

"I'll climb out through here, then come around and set you free." She rattled the bars again. They were old and no longer tight in the brick, but she couldn't rip them out bare-handed. "I need something sharp and hard."

He swayed under her for a few seconds then passed up his belt. "Use the buckle."

She attacked the mortar between the bricks with the sharp square of brass, and it did work, the dried-out material crumbling. The only question was, could she get it all done before the men came back?

She went at the task with all her strength, knowing they had minutes at best. The bottom end of the perpendicular bar came out, the rest wobbled. To free them one by one would be too much work, she realized. They weren't going to make it doing things that way.

"Loop the belt around the bar," Shep called up, apparently having come to the same realization.

She did, catching on at once what he wanted. She looped the belt then jumped to the ground from his shoulders.

They grabbed the end of the belt together and yanked hard. The bar flew out of the wall on the third try, Shep catching it with the reflexes of a superhero before it could have clattered to the ground and given them away.

Then she was on his shoulders again, pulling herself up and looking out.

She was in some kind of a ventilation shaft surrounded by four brick walls. The shaft had no exit on the bottom, but was open to the sky above.

She glanced back at Shep. "I'm going up. Try not to get into any trouble until I get back."

He looked up from weighing the iron bars, probably testing them to use as a weapon. "Be careful. Don't take unnecessary chances. Getting a call through to Ryder at the office is more important than coming back for me."

"I'm planning on doing both." And she got started right away.

She had to play with the angle to fit her shoulders through the opening. She felt his hands grabbing her feet, giving her support and pushing, helping her up and out. Then she was up all the way, outside, standing in the opening.

The drop to the ground was about fifteen feet, not a big deal, but she'd be trapped down there. The way up was a lot more difficult, at least thirty feet, and with nothing to hang on to but minuscule grooves between bricks that could crumble at any moment beneath her shoes and fingers.

And she had to rush. If the men came back, they could easily figure out where she'd gone. Them shooting up through the window would be like shooting fish in a barrel with her stuck in a tight, boxed-in space with nowhere to hide.

She brought her right foot up, wedged the sole of her shoe into the gap between two bricks and tested it, putting her weight on it little by little. It held, but she didn't shift her full weight forward; she kept some on her hands. Then came the other foot, then moving hands, never letting just one limb carry her full weight, but always two and preferably three. Up she went step by step, reach by reach.

There were other windows opening to the ventilation shaft, small like the one she'd just exited. All barred so she couldn't climb in. One she passed opened to a storage room, another to an empty office. At least there was nobody in either room, so nobody spotted her as she climbed.

Still, she barely dared breathe until she reached the roof and pulled herself up. No gunshots or shouting had come from below, so they hadn't discovered her missing yet, but that could change at any second.

She wasted no time and ran across the roof. She needed a gun, a phone and to get back to Shep before they beat him bloody.

She dashed to the edge of the roof, flattened herself and looked down at the same loading dock they'd come through. There were several trucks waiting for their loads. To grab one and drive away didn't even occur to her. She was going nowhere without Shep.

Even as she thought that, three guys came from inside and began loading one of the trucks, ending any possibility of her climbing down on this side. She pulled back and hurried to another spot, around the corner.

An abandoned courtyard stretched down below, stacked with rusty equipment. She spotted an open window directly below her. Perfect. Unless, of course, she slipped and got impaled on the machinery on the ground. Best not to think about that right now.

She pushed everything but her next move out of her mind and lowered herself next to the window. She carefully peeked in from the side. But there was nobody in there, thank God. She pulled herself over and in, dropped to the tile floor and stayed in a crouch for a second.

That had been nerve-racking. She participated in regular training sessions and worked out daily, but didn't exactly do a lot of rock climbing.

Thinking of Shep, she didn't pause for long. In a few seconds she was moving again, through the empty office, sticking her head into the hallway. There was one more door to her right, at the end of the hallway, a security door that looked as if it was made of reinforced steel.

On her other side she could see four more regular wooden doors toward the stairs. Those, too, all remained closed. She stepped out and hurried that way, glad that the doors had no glass, so even if there were people inside the offices, she wouldn't be seen. Unless, of course, they exited. But nobody did, and she made her way to the staircase safely.

But as she looked down the empty staircase, she could hear angry shouting coming from below.

They'd just figured out that she'd escaped. That should gain Shep a few minutes of a break, while the men all ran off looking for her.

She needed a gun, but for that she would have to catch one of the men. Or… She turned to the steel-reinforced door. *A top-floor office with top security. Yo Tee?*

One way to find out.

She stole back down the hallway to that last door and tried the knob. She wasn't that surprised to find that it gave under the pressure of her hand. Yo Tee wouldn't expect an attack in his own stronghold.

She shoved the door open and rushed in, counting on the element of surprise, and found herself in a small entryway with another door directly opposite her. A guy with an assault rifle guarded the space.

"Who the hell are you?" he asked in Spanish and lurched forward.

She started with a kick to the man's middle, ducked when he tried to bash her face in with the butt of the gun. "Where is the Coyote?" She turned and kicked higher, at his arm this time, but he held the weapon tightly and didn't drop it, dammit.

Instead, he pulled back to aim it at her, but she stepped right in with a hard punch to his solar plexus. Then a quick second punch to his stomach again. He bent forward at that, and she used the advantage to bring her knee up.

His nose broke with a satisfying crunch, spraying blood on her, the least of her concerns. She didn't even slow down as she grabbed his gun and whacked him in the back of the head, sending him sprawling onto the floor. She did hesitate, but only for a second, before bending and breaking his neck. She didn't want him reviving and attacking her from behind.

She kept the gun and rushed the inner door. This one was locked. But it wasn't steel. A good roundhouse kick next to the lock took care of it, and she, carried by momentum, fell through the opening.

She was in a sprawling office this time, Yo Tee coming through yet another door in the back, drying his hands. He'd probably been in his private bathroom. He froze as she pointed the rifle at him.

"Freeze."

He did. But he didn't look scared. "You think this over," he told her. "Whoever you are, I make you rich beyond your dreams. I don't think you understand who I am and what I do for the people who help me."

"Put your hands in the air."

He gave a superior smile. "You American law enforcement. You have no jurisdiction here."

She nodded at the rifle. "This gives me enough jurisdiction for the moment. Hands in the air."

He complied, keeping the smile on his face even as his gaze hardened to frozen steel.

She stepped closer and searched him, took a small pistol off him and stuck it into her waistband. "Don't move."

She sidled over to the desk and lifted the phone, dialed Jamie's cell, her gaze darting back and forth between the phone and Yo Tee.

Jamie picked up on the third ring.

"Hey, it's me."

"Where the hell are you?" he snapped when he heard her voice. "Everyone's looking for you. Is Shep with you, dammit? Are you hurt?"

She filled him in, in as few words as possible, and gave her location, requested backup, then hung up. The team would have to negotiate their next step with the Mexican government, but that was their task now. She had plenty of items on her own to-do list, the two at the top being keeping Yo Tee secured until the team got here and stopping his men from killing Shep downstairs.

She handed the phone to Yo Tee. "Call your men and tell them to bring my partner up here."

He didn't move.

"Fine, then we'll go to him." All she wanted was to hole up in some defensible position with Shep and Yo Tee until the team arrived.

"Where are the people you're planning on smuggling across the border?" she asked as she considered her options.

"I don't know what you talking about. All I know is U.S. government agent broke into my place of business held me at gunpoint. Neither of my governments be happy about that. I'm Chinese-Mexican and respected businessman in both countries."

"That'll end soon," she promised. "Where are the terrorists? Are they here? In this building?"

His lips narrowed; hate flared in his gaze.

She couldn't have cared less about his feelings. "Have they already left for Galmer's Gulley?"

He couldn't keep the surprise from his face when she mentioned the location, confirming the intel Shep's team had gathered. Good to know they were on the right track.

"I don't know what you talking about," he told her.

"Where are the chemical weapons?"

"We make paper here," he said, as cocky and superior as could be. "You crazy woman."

She wanted to shoot him.

She'd shot people before, but never without reluctance, never unless it was the last resort, in an effort to stop them from harming others. This was honestly the first time she wanted to put a bullet through an unarmed man's kneecap.

Short of doing violence, she didn't think she was

going to get him to talk, and maybe not even then. But Shep's team could handle that, she decided, when they got here. This wasn't the right time and place for an interrogation anyway, not when his men could burst through the door any second.

She scanned the room, then scanned Yo Tee. "Take off your belt."

"You want my pants off." He sounded amused now. "That against some American law. You so very politically correct all the time."

"Your belt. Now."

He shrugged and took off the belt then tossed it to her.

She walked around him, keeping the gun aimed at his head. "Hands behind your back."

He complied after a moment of hesitation. "My men kill you as soon we leave this room. You know. Why not talk reasonable?"

She bound his wrists together with the belt, kept the long end to hold him like a dog on a leash. "You'll walk in front of me. Out. Now. Move."

He did, walking to the door leisurely, then out into the entryway. He looked at the dead man lying on the floor and kicked him in the head as they walked by him, apparently dissatisfied with his service.

The hallway still stood empty. Good. She moved forward. "To the staircase."

"Your people can't come here without authorization from my government. Diplomacy takes long time. Days. You think you hold an entire factory with single gun that long?"

"I'm not the type to give up."

He took his time walking down the hallway, but they reached the stairs at last and started down. "Bravery a noble thing. Courage my people much appreciate. But a difference between bravery and stupidity."

She held the gun on him. "Let that be my worry."

"You and your friend get free leave, a car and suitcase full of money. You go wherever you want. You never have to go back across border again. You live happy long life down south on nice beach. Better than dying today, eh?"

"I'm not planning on dying."

But just as she said that, half a dozen armed men poured out into the staircase down below. From the way they all swung their rifles around to aim at her, it looked as if she might not get a choice in the matter.

She couldn't get to Shep this way. She couldn't get anywhere if she was shot. So she yanked Yo Tee back. "Come on!"

She ran back toward his office with him while the men rushed up the stairs behind them, shouting. She fixed her gaze on the office at the end of the hallway and did her level best to reach it, even with Yo Tee resisting. The steel security door would offer more protection against siege than anything else she'd seen so far in the building.

She had about a minute to reach it.

Chapter Twelve

Shep lay on the floor, all bloodied, waiting for them to be done with him, focused on protecting his body rather than trying to fight his way through a wall of armed men. Six, he could have handled. Twelve, he couldn't. And he was determined to stay alive so he could help Lilly escape from here. So for the moment, instead of fighting, he did his best to appear limp and lifeless.

They weren't here to kill him; they were just taking their anger out on him. At some point, they'd be finished.

The tactic worked. When shouting rose from somewhere deep inside the building, most of the men ran to whatever new alarm had been raised.

Only two remained, each holding their rifles on him.

He kept his eyes open only a slit, playing the part of a mortally injured man to the hilt. Not that difficult when he was in a world of hurt. He gave a weak groan and shifted, the move taking him maybe a foot closer to the bastards.

Then he drew a slow breath, filling up his lungs. And then the next second his right hand snaked out, grabbed the nearest rifle barrel even as he vaulted to his feet and shoved the man into his buddy, twisting the rifle away from him in the same movement.

The men were on the floor and Shep on them now, with ruthless efficiency. He didn't want gunshots, didn't want the others to come rushing back, so he bashed in the armed man's head first, then his buddy's as the bastard tried to roll away from him. They stayed down, the both of them.

Shep pushed to his feet, grabbed both rifles then ran through the door and followed the sounds of angry shouting all the way to a staircase. On the floor above him, he could hear men rushing up the stairs. He had a fair idea why. Since Lilly had gone to the roof and was probably on one of the top floors, it was fair to assume that she'd been spotted.

He kept close to the wall and ran up after the men. None of them were looking back down. They were all focused on something above them, pushing each other out of the way to reach the top faster. Shep pushed as hard as he could, trying to catch up without being noticed.

Gunshots were ringing out by the time he reached the first floor. He was the only person in the staircase now; the others had gotten up all the way and pushed out of sight on the third floor, the gun battle intensifying.

He ran up silently, as fast as he could, a rifle in one hand, the other slung across his shoulder. He needed to reach Lilly before it was too late.

He didn't care if she was here to assess his team. He just wanted her to stay alive.

He loved her. It became crystal clear the moment she'd disappeared through the window. He'd somehow, in the space of three days, fallen in love with Lilly. Whether or not they could ever have anything serious between them was the question.

He pushed the thought away. *Not now.*

But soon. Whatever her true purpose was for being with his team, they'd have to talk about it and sort all that out. But it wasn't going to change how he felt about her. He ran forward to save her.

He only slowed when he reached the top floor and spotted twenty or so armed men crowded at the far end in front of a steel security door, banging with their rifles, trying to break it down. They weren't making much progress. The door looked pretty heavy-duty.

He had a feeling Lilly was behind it. Smart woman. One of the reasons he'd fallen for her.

He squeezed off a round of shots at the men, then ducked behind cover as they shot back.

He didn't know how many he'd hit, but he knew that whoever was left uninjured would be coming for him. He swung both his rifles over his shoulder, ran back down the stairs and jumped through the first open door he saw on the second floor, locked the door behind him, ran to the window. Then out he went without hesitation, wanting to be out of sight by the time they broke the door down.

He needed to go up, to Lilly, but the window directly above him was closed. Smashing it in would have given away his location, so he looked to the next one, just a few feet over. The glass pane stood open a crack.

He maneuvered that way, his cowboy boots not exactly meant for climbing like this, slipping more than once. He hung on with everything he had. Failure was not an option.

When he reached the windowsill, he grabbed on tight and pulled himself up to look in. Another empty office. Maybe Yo Tee had the factory on shutdown for today, to get ready for the transfer.

He hung on with his right hand while opening the

window wider with the left. *Okay. Deep breath. Focus.* Now would not be a good time to slip.

He didn't. He pulled himself up and in.

This office was a mess, chairs turned over, the drawers on the filing cabinet hanging open. Bullet holes dotted the walls. Looked as if Yo Tee might have had a disagreement with one of his managers.

Disagreement in the ranks was rarely good for business. Or for your health, if your boss was the Coyote.

Shep moved to the door and could hear people talking at the far end of the hallway. Some of the men had run off to chase him, but others had remained at that steel door, still trying to figure out how to get in. And they'd be watching their backs this time; he wasn't going to be able to take them by surprise again.

His next move was a risky one, but he had to make it anyway.

He filled his lungs and burst out into the hall, firing at them as he went. Six men shot back at him, barricaded behind four bodies, those he'd taken out earlier.

He shot down one more before he had to pull back in.

He glanced at his left arm where a bullet had ripped through his skin. Nothing serious. The injury was nearly identical to Lilly's. They'd have matching scars to commemorate their misadventures. Provided they lived.

Five men remained at the end of the hallway, and the other ten or so who'd run downstairs to find him would be coming back now that they'd heard the gunshots. They were likely to figure out that he'd outsmarted them and doubled back somehow.

The small office he occupied was not a good defensible position, the door made of inch-wide simple wood, nothing to hide behind that would stop bullets. So out the window he went again.

Man, he hated this part.

He didn't have any phobias, but he wasn't a fan of heights. He went on regardless. The first thing he'd learned in this job was that as soon as a person let fear stop them, they were dead.

He didn't try to get into the next room or the one after that. He climbed handhold by handhold all the way to the end so he'd be outside the room with the steel door at the end of the hallway.

He looked in carefully, not wanting to get his head blown off in case Lilly took him for one of Yo Tee's men.

She was in there, armed to the teeth, crouching behind a makeshift barricade of desks and chairs, facing the door. Yo Tee sat tied to a chair with his own belt in the corner.

When Shep rapped on the glass, she swung around, her rifle aimed. Her eyes went wide when she recognized him.

"Let me in."

She hurried over. "You okay?" She looked at the blood on his arm as she opened the window.

"It's nothing. You?"

"We're trapped. But at least I called reinforcements."

Of course she did. While evading a band of armed killers and capturing one of the biggest crime bosses south of the border. She was nothing if not efficient. He grinned at her. "I decided to forgive you if you promise to get out of this mess alive."

She raised a questioning eyebrow. And when he said nothing more, she nodded. "Okay. Fine."

Being in the same room with her made him feel a hell of a lot better, but they weren't out of the woods yet. "There's a pretty big group of armed thugs in front of the door."

"How many?"

"Fifteen or so. There were about two dozen. I took a few out." He glanced at Yo Tee. "I think he shut down operations and has just enough security here with him to set up the transfer."

She shot a dark glare at the Coyote.

He knew what she was thinking. They were both well armed. Between the two of them, they could probably break out of here and get to a truck. But they couldn't risk Yo Tee getting killed. The bastard had to stay alive long enough to be interrogated.

Gunfire sounded outside.

She shot him a questioning look.

He shook his head. "Can't be the reinforcements yet." Not enough time had passed for that.

More gunfire came. And this time it was clear that the steel door was getting hit. Yo Tee's men had decided to shoot the door down to rescue him.

Shep glanced back the way he'd come, at the window.

She followed his gaze. "Can't go that way."

She was right. They couldn't go through the window, not with Yo Tee resisting.

But the door wouldn't hold long. The men outside were firing round after round into the lock. While it was a reinforced steel door, it wasn't strong enough to stand up to this kind of siege.

Shep grabbed Yo Tee, chair and all, and dragged him to the corner to the left of the door, where at least the first volley of bullets to come through couldn't hit him. He pulled a bookshelf away from the wall a little so the man wouldn't be immediately visible when his lackeys broke in.

He gagged the man just as the door gave a mighty crack.

"Get in the other corner," he ordered Lilly, a plan forming in his head.

Lilly did as he asked, wedging into the office's corner behind the door, where she wouldn't be seen when the outer steel door finally broke down.

Shep lay down in the middle of the room, pulling Lilly's makeshift barricade on top of him until he was buried under furniture. He hoped that, at least at first glance, the room would look deserted as the men pushed their way in. A moment of confusion, a second of pause was all he needed.

The steel door shook. They were ramming it, probably lined up shoulder to shoulder, hoping to snap the damaged lock. Still, the steel didn't give.

But the brick wall did, cracking and crumbling, releasing the lock.

The door banged open. The shouting stopped then restarted again as the men ran across the empty outer room into the office, jumping over the knocked-down pile of furniture on their way to the open window.

"Where are they?" more than one shouted in Spanish.

"They went down. Outside," one of the men shouted.

They'd see Yo Tee in a second, as soon as they turned. So Shep rose, kicking furniture off him, aiming at the men who had nowhere to run, no place to hide.

Lilly sprung from behind the door, slamming the wood into the faces of a handful of stragglers, knocking them back. She opened fire as the door swung open again, backing toward Shep until they were shoulder to shoulder. Neither of them removed their fingers from the trigger until there were no more enemies standing.

They were both breathing hard, both bleeding and injured when the gun smoke settled, but alive—a miracle. The carnage in the room was incredible, the bloodiest destruction that could be achieved in just a few minutes.

Yo Tee was on the ground, on his side. He'd pushed his chair over to keep down. He was staring at them wide-eyed as if they were crazy people.

Lilly went to straighten him. She pulled the gag from his mouth.

"Work for me," he said in a shaky voice. "I make you both millionaires."

"No thanks," Lilly told him.

Shep moved to make sure all the men were down for good. He didn't want to be surprised by a bullet to his back.

Satisfied that none of the men would pop up for a surprise attack, Shep moved closer to Lilly to look her over. Her clothes were ripped and she had some scrapes plus a serious flesh wound, but it didn't look as if any vital organs had been hit. She was standing up, not holding any body parts, a good sign.

"Hey." She was scanning him for injury in return. "You know where to buy a lottery ticket around here? I'm thinking this is our lucky day."

He grinned at her. He wanted to take her into his arms more than anything. But they weren't done yet.

He walked up to Yo Tee and rested the barrel of his rifle against the man's forehead. "Where are the men that you're sending over the border?"

Lilly moved to the door to watch for any possible newcomers. She had her weapon ready to greet anyone who might be ill-advised enough to come after the others.

"I don't know what you talking about," Yo Tee said, his dark eyes filled with hate.

Shep held his gaze. "If the last few minutes taught you anything, it should be that I don't play nice." He wiped his hand on his pants, leaving a crimson stain, then shrugged. "Blood never really bothered me."

Yo Tee looked away first.

"Are they coming here to be put in the back of trucks tonight?"

They could be arriving even now, in which case a reception committee would have to be set up for them. Although, if Shep's luck held, they wouldn't come until after his team had gotten here.

"There's no easy way out of this now," he warned Yo Tee. "There's only the hard way and the harder way. Trust me, if there's anything you can tell me now, it'll save you considerable grief when the rest of my team gets here. They're even worse at playing nice than I am." He paused, then he moved close enough to crowd the man. "When are your buddies arriving here?"

Yo Tee gave a superior smile. "They come and gone. You too late."

He looked cocky and pleased with himself enough to make Shep think he might not be lying.

"When?"

"The first day news came about extra attention on the border. As soon as patrols stepped up and crack-downs on smuggling started." He looked damn proud of himself, sticking his chest out. "My men got them across without trouble. They been in U.S. for weeks."

Shep grabbed him by the front of his shirt and pulled him half off the chair. "Where are they now?"

The man stared into his eyes without flinching. "They paid me. They didn't share plans with me."

Shep watched him, inclined to believe the words, yet something about the man's body language was off, something in the way his eyes darted.

He lowered his gun as he turned back to Lilly. "Better call off reinforcements. No sense in more people coming. It'd be better if we grabbed a truck and drove back across the border on our own. Nobody would even know that we've been here. Might as well avoid an international incident if we can."'

Maybe she picked up on the game he was playing, because she nodded toward Yo Tee. "What about him?"

"He has no more useful information. If his body is found with his men, local police will write it off as a battle between rival drug bosses. No sense dragging the U.S. into this."

"No! I have money—" Yo Tee protested.

Chapter Thirteen

Lilly watched as Shep shrugged at the offer of riches.

"I don't care about money. I'm here for information," he said. "You have to know more." He didn't look as if he was buying the man's I-know-nothing act.

Lilly wasn't, either. If the terrorists had crossed the border weeks ago, why the smuggling moratorium that had been strictly enforced by Yo Tee's men? That had to have cost millions, to him and his smuggling buddies. He wouldn't have done that without good reason.

She glanced down the hallway—still empty—then back to him. "So what's planned for tonight at Galmer's Gulley?"

The man pressed his narrow lips together so tightly they nearly disappeared.

Shep put the rifle barrel right between his eyes. "What are you sending across the border tonight?"

She knew him, she was in love with him, and the way he growled at the man still sent a shiver of apprehension down her spine.

Tension and the sense of impending violence filled the air, the silence broken by a single word Yo Tee squeaked out at last. "Weapons."

Lilly glanced at the hallway. He might still have men in the building, recouping and planning another attack.

But there was nobody in sight, so she looked at Yo Tee again, waiting for more. According to confirmed intel, those terrorists were going to bring chemical weapons into the U.S.

Shep glared at his captive. "Why didn't the weapons go with the men?"

"The vials weren't ready yet." Yo Tee hesitated. "They wanted a lot, and the lab messed up first batch."

"Where are the vials?"

But that was the question Yo Tee decided to make his last stand on, because he just stared straight ahead and wouldn't say a single word no matter what Shep threatened him with next.

THE MEXICAN AUTHORITIES arrived first, but they didn't enter. They simply secured the perimeter and locked down the entire factory compound, as far as Shep could tell from the window. They probably had their orders. Looked as if some kind of international deal had been made at the last second.

It wasn't long after that his team arrived on FBI choppers. Shep debriefed them and passed on the latest intel about the terrorists to the Colonel via a secure phone. Yo Tee was immediately flown out to a secure location by the FBI for further interrogation, while Shep's team searched the building for the chemical weapons.

Unfortunately, several hours of thorough work later, they still didn't have anything. Tension mounted higher and higher as they went over ground they'd already covered. By the time Shep ran into Lilly at the loading docks, he was brimming with frustration.

She was eyeing the truck they'd passed while being

marched inside when they'd first arrived, five giant rolls of paper in the back, one still on the loading dock.

She narrowed her eyes as she measured up the roll. "We know the weapons were about to be shipped to the border. This would make sense."

"They've been scanned. No traces of chemical agents," he told her. "We haven't found any traces in the whole damn factory."

But she kept looking. "Because the lab isn't here. If the vials came here in airtight containers, all they would have received here would have been extra wrapping. No contamination."

Shep pulled out his cell and called Ryder. "Do we have a plain old metal detector?"

"If we don't, we can get one. Where do you need it?"

"Loading docks." He walked around the roll still waiting to be loaded. Nothing looked disturbed, nothing betrayed that anyone had messed with the paper, no cuts, no bulges.

Lilly strode over. "Boost me up."

He did, and she moved without hesitation. They had practice at this.

She banged on the top of the giant roll, felt around. "Doesn't look like anything has been inserted through here. Maybe through the bottom." She jumped down.

Shep gave the roll a push, but it didn't budge an inch. It had to weigh a ton. "Let's try that with a forklift." There were plenty of those around.

He hopped on one and drove it over, tipped the giant roll to its side, then got out to inspect the bottom. He crouched next to Lilly, the both of them running their fingers over the ridged surface of layers and layers of paper, looking for any hidden openings.

By the time they were done, finding nothing, a Mexican army Jeep was driving up. The arriving lieutenant handed Shep a metal detector without asking any questions, then drove away.

"The collaboration is going better than expected," Lilly remarked.

Shep turned on the professional-grade instrument. "I bet it's the Colonel's doing." If there was anything the Colonel, the head of the SDDU, couldn't do, Shep hadn't seen it yet. The man was a legend in the unit.

He started scanning the roll of paper on the bottom and moved up, careful not to miss an inch. He was at the midpoint when the metal detector went off, issuing a series of loud beeps.

He put the detector down and pulled out his cell phone, called Ryder. "I think we have something."

"We'll be there in a minute."

Lilly tapped the roll as he was hanging up. "Looks like the paper was wrapped around the container in the middle. I don't think unrolling it here would be wise."

He agreed. "We'll transport everything back to the U.S."

"How about I take care of that?" She reached out a hand for the cell phone. "I'll request a reinforced truck that's built for this kind of thing. Bombproof and airtight. They'll take everything to a special lab in D.C. for containment and analysis."

Ryder was running from the back, overhearing that last bit. "That sounds like the best plan of action. How fast can they get here?"

"Couple of hours."

Shep handed her the cell phone, and she dialed while he shot Ryder a questioning look. It wasn't like their team leader to let the bureau swoop in and take over without a fight.

"We have terrorists to catch on the border." He scanned the roll of paper. "In there?"

Shep nodded. "Looks like it."

Ryder grabbed the metal detector and checked again, then jumped up to the back of the truck and scanned the rest of the rolls. Every single one of them beeped.

The rest of the team was coming from the factory by the time he came back out.

Jamie spoke first. "What do we have here?"

"Probably enough chemical weapons to take out Capitol Hill," Shep told him. "The FBI will transport them to their lab safely. We'll take the truck to our meeting with the tangos." So they wouldn't suspect that anything had gone wrong. The van had plenty of room in the back for a couple of surprises—his whole team and some serious weaponry.

Ryder gestured toward Jamie with his head. "You'll drive the truck back. The rest of us will wait here for the FBI then catch up to you with the choppers."

Jamie nodded and moved toward the forklift. "Let's get these rolls unloaded."

While he did that, Shep took the metal detector and scanned all the rolls remaining on the loading dock to make sure they hadn't missed anything. But the metal detector didn't go off again.

Jamie left with the truck, and the rest of the team went back inside the factory to finish their search of the floor and offices, hoping to find some information on the terrorists. They didn't. So they looked again. And again.

He went to the basement with Lilly.

She stopped as they reached the bottom of the stairs. "Thanks for having my back today. I mean it." She smiled. "There's something I've been thinking about. We're good together and I'm in—"

"You're in a difficult position. I know. You're supposed to evaluate us and we had this…thing," he said rapidly, afraid that she might go in another direction.

She could have been killed today. He couldn't handle the thought. He could have been killed, too. They'd make a terrible couple. Neither of them would have a worry-free moment. This was not the life he wanted for her.

"Anyway. You do the job you were sent here to do. We made a mistake. We won't make it again. It's no big deal. Just forget it, all right?"

The smile slid off her face. A stricken look came into her eyes, but she blinked it away as she turned from him, her shoulders stiff. "Forgotten already. I'll go left." She started out with hurried strides. "You go right. Call out if you find anything."

But neither of them did.

Hours passed before the FBI's special truck arrived.

Ryder let them take over at that point and ordered his team onto the choppers.

Shep ran with the others, glanced back, slowed when he saw Lilly still standing by the FBI truck, talking with the agents who'd come with it. He waited for her to turn. He wanted at least to give her a last wave.

But she didn't look his way.

"Shep?" Ryder called for him.

"Coming." He didn't know what he would say to her, even if he could run back. And he couldn't. They both had jobs to do.

He ducked his head to avoid the spinning rotors and pulled himself into the chopper, hung on as the bird lifted and banked sharply to the left.

He watched as she finally lifted her head, pausing in the conversation to look after him.

Her job with his team was done. She'd be going straight to D.C. with the truck. He wasn't going to see her again, which was for the best.

But the thought squeezed his heart, sending a pang of pain deep into his chest.

NIGHT HAD FALLEN and the borderlands were deserted, the Rio Grande a dark ribbon, snaking in the distance. Keith drove the paper-factory truck, Shep and Jamie in the back. The other three men on the team had taken the three best strategic high points around Galmer's Gulley.

When the SDDU's Texas headquarters had first been established, a dozen men had been assigned to the task. Six came to their trailer office, and another six had been sent to South America to trace why and from where the terrorists were coming.

They weren't Middle Eastern as first assumed. They were part of the South American drug cartels. They'd come in response to the U.S. shift in drug control toward stricter measures. The cartels had bought many politicians in their own countries. Those who couldn't be bought they killed. And now they decided to put U.S. lawmakers in their crosshairs, apparently.

Most likely, the attack was to be the first in a campaign of intimidation. The threat had to be tracked to the source. Except everything had turned out to be more complicated and dangerous than anticipated, so the rest of the team was still stuck in South America.

The Texas half had to handle tonight on their own. And they would, if Shep had anything to do with it. They'd been here way too long, preparing for this moment.

Small holes had been drilled into the side of the truck

and in the doors in the back so he and Jamie could see out. The team members were all in radio contact with each other.

Keith drove to the exact coordinates Yo Tee had finally given up to the FBI just half an hour ago. Nothing like leaving things to the last possible moment.

Keith pulled the truck into a spot where the elevation and some mesquite would keep it out of sight as much as possible. Someone who smuggled the kind of load he was supposed to be carrying wouldn't stay out in the open advertising it to every border agent who happened by.

Then they waited.

And waited.

Long minutes ticked by before Mo said, "Movement at the north end of the gulley," over the radio. "I see two."

"Two more a little lower," Ryder added.

"Another two on my side." That came from Ray.

Okay, all six were here now. Yo Tee had confessed to transporting six, more than the original intel had indicated, but the team could definitely handle this many.

But then Mo said, "Wait. I got more movement. Two more. I have four here altogether."

And as Shep watched the moonlit landscape, he noticed more movement. "And four more coming in the back way."

Either Yo Tee had lied or the terrorists had come in two groups and never told him about the second just to be on the safe side.

Jamie swore quietly next to him.

"Twelve. Everybody got that? Anybody seeing more?" Ryder was asking, but nobody responded. "We have a full dozen, then," he finished after a minute.

They were outnumbered two to one.

"What kind of weapons?" Shep asked. The men he was watching approached on foot and kept to the shadows and indentations of the land, making it difficult to see what they were carrying.

"Semiautomatics," Keith said from up front. Apparently, he had a better angle.

"Ah, hell," Ray swore. "One of mine has a grenade launcher. He's staying behind while the others are moving forward."

"Must be their plan B," Jamie said next to Shep.

Shep gripped his weapon tighter. A grenade launcher could take out the truck and everyone in it. Their bulletproof vests wouldn't be able to help a damn.

"Coming my way," Ray whispered.

Made sense. The guy with the grenade launcher would want the high point, too.

"Take him out quietly," Ryder ordered.

"I can see five now on my side," Shep told Jamie.

"I see three on mine. They all stopped."

"Do I get out?" Keith asked.

"Stay in the cab," Ryder told him. "Let them initiate."

The men started walking again. Three went up to the cab, five to the back. The one with the grenade launcher was climbing to Ray's high point, so that left three more out there somewhere, watching from out of sight.

Shep could hear the truck's door open, Keith's boots slapping to the ground as he got out.

He greeted them in Spanish. "Everything's okay. You take this truck, I have a ride waiting to take me back across the border." His grandfather had been Mexican. He had enough of the blood in him to pass for a Mexican driver, especially in the dark.

"Open the back first. Let's see." One of the men barked the words at him.

Shep and Jamie braced themselves for action. They had a Kevlar shield set up in front of them to duck behind, stretching the width of the truck and three feet high. As they held their weapons ready, sounds of a scuffle came over the radio.

Then Ray said, "Got him."

Okay. The grenade launcher was out of the equation.

And not a minute too soon, since the next second the lock turned and the double back doors of the van swung open to the night.

Keith was smart enough to lunge to the left, tuck and roll and disappear behind the cover of some rocks as everyone opened fire and all hell broke loose.

A bullet grazed Shep's ear. He ducked behind the barricade then up again to squeeze off another round of shots.

Two men fell. Jamie was knocked back when a bullet hit his shoulder.

Shep charged forward, vaulting over the barricade to take the heat off him.

Keith stopped shooting from the side to avoid accidentally hitting his teammates.

Three of the enemy were still standing, the rest badly injured or dead. Shep shot another one as he landed, then pivoted to the left to shoot after one who'd decided to flee.

He caught sight of Keith on the ground, holding both hands over his neck, blood gushing through his fingers.

Shep rushed toward him, firing into the night, providing him with cover. There were plenty of shots coming out of the darkness. He felt a bullet rip into his thigh just as he reached Keith, jarring him, knocking him sideways. He flattened himself to the ground next to Keith.

Then Jamie was there, laying down cover.

More shots in the distance. Probably Mo and Ray coming in. There couldn't have been more than a man or two left of the tangos, but the gunfight still went on.

Shep saw movement behind some brush, caught a glimpse of a face he didn't recognize. He shot the bastard without thinking.

And that was the last one. No more bullets came after that.

"You always want them all to yourself. One of these days you're going to have to learn how to share," Jamie groused next to him.

"Watch for more." He bit out the words as he kneeled next to Keith and grabbed his radio unit. "Man down. We need a chopper ASAP."

"Who is it?" Ryder asked.

"Keith. What's going on at your end?"

"I got one. Running up. I'll be there in a minute."

"Got two," Mo said. "How bad is Keith?"

"Pretty bad."

"Sounds like we have our twelve," Jamie remarked, but kept alert, still scanning their surroundings.

Chapter Fourteen

Lilly sat alone in her home office in D.C. as she finished her report and saved it on her laptop. She'd made her official recommendation. The SDDU's Texas team had to stay where they were. She made it clear that in her opinion, their presence was a matter of national security.

The op had been a complete success, and all the loose ends had been tied up in the two weeks since. The chemical weapons had been destroyed, the surviving terrorists interrogated.

She hadn't gone back to Pebble Creek. She had the hotel mail her things to D.C. She figured she'd caused enough grief in Shep's life already. He'd made it clear that he didn't want anything to do with her. He didn't need her hanging around with her confused and conflicted feelings. So she'd given him a clean break.

But when her phone rang, just as she shut her computer down, and his name came up on the display screen, her heart thrilled.

"I'd like to take you to dinner," he said without preamble.

His voice filled her with longing, but she tried to keep things light. "Next time I'm in town?"

"Actually, I'm in D.C. I could pick you up tonight. Or when you're free."

"Tonight is good," she said, suddenly breathless.

"Address?"

She smiled at that. "You didn't run a full background check on me? I'd have thought you would have all my personal details." His team had access to databases that were better than the FBI's.

"That would have been stalking. This is..."

Part of her hoped he would finish with *a date*.

But he said something so much better. "This is a man asking the woman he loves to have dinner with him."

Now, could anyone have said no to that? Not likely. Her heart was melting on the spot. Yet she wasn't sure what to stay in response, the words stuck inside her chest. At the end, she simply gave him her address.

"When can I pick you up?"

She ran her fingers through her hair. "Half an hour?" Best if she didn't have too much time to obsess.

"I'll be there."

She showered and dressed, brushed some makeup on with nervous fingers. She'd barely finished with her hair when the doorbell rang.

She lived in a secure condo building, so she pushed the button to let him in downstairs, then waited for him at her door.

"Hey." His voice was even better in person than over the phone.

God, she'd missed him. For the longest time, all she wanted was to be an independent woman. She wanted to be someone who could take care of herself, someone who didn't need anyone. It was a hell of a thing to realize now that she needed Shep.

She swallowed. "Hey."

He pulled a bouquet of lilies from behind his back with the hottest smile she'd ever seen.

Lilies were her favorite, her namesake flower. When she was a little girl, being named after a flower made her feel special. She liked to be associated with something beautiful when her life was anything but. She'd told him that once, long ago.

"Thank you." She took the flowers. "I can't believe you remembered."

She moved back, which turned out to be a mistake. If she'd moved forward instead, out into the hallway, ready to go, they might have made it to the restaurant.

As it was, Shep followed her in.

She pulled a vase from under the sink, filled it with water and set the flowers in it, then placed them on the kitchen table. "How's the team?"

"Good. Keith will be reinstated to full duty next week. Brian and Tank are in jail." He stood in the middle of her living room, watching her. "Nice place," he said without really looking around. He kept his eyes on her.

"I spend most of my time at work. I'm barely here," she said inanely, when all she wanted to do was scream *You said you loved me!*

"Working on anything exciting?"

Good grief, if the tension was any thicker in the room, it would have been visible.

"Can't really talk about that." She took a step toward him, but then stopped. Maybe she'd misunderstood him on the phone. Maybe she heard what she wanted to hear. "You?"

"The same." He stepped toward her and held her gaze. "I missed you. I want us to be together."

Her heart banged so hard against her rib cage she thought she was going to pass out.

"We'd make a terrible couple. We couldn't talk about anything." Stuff was just coming out of her mouth and she couldn't stop it. "Everything we do is confidential."

"We'll find something else to fill our time with."

"Why did you change your mind?"

"I went to the hospital with Keith when they took him in. A bullet just about ripped his throat out. We didn't think he was going to make it. The only thing he said was he wished he asked you out while he had the chance."

She watched him, not entirely understanding his point.

He reached out, took her hand and pulled her slowly against him. "All I could think was that if I was lying there on my deathbed, that would be my biggest regret, too. Letting you go."

He gave her time to pull away, but she had no intention of protesting. When he lowered his lips to hers, relief flooded her. At least if he kissed her, she wouldn't be able to say anything else stupid.

Nothing in this world felt half as good as being held in Shep's arms and being kissed by him.

But too soon, he pulled away. "So how is this going to work?"

"Tonight?" she asked, dazed.

He gave a wicked grin. "I'm pretty sure I can figure tonight out."

Her core temperature shot up a few degrees.

He rested his forehead against hers. "I meant the future. Together."

Right. With her in D.C. and him in Texas. "We could meet in the middle. Spend the weekends together."

"Not enough," he protested immediately. "I could leave the team."

She pulled back to stare at him. "You would?" That was mind-boggling. She considered it for a long second before she shook her head. "You already lost a job because of me. This one is right for you. It matters." She paused. "I could come to Texas."

He watched her carefully. "You're building a career here."

"Career isn't everything. There's something else I always wanted to do." She paused for a second. "I told you I've been thinking about working with kids in the system. Kids in foster care who get in trouble with the law. I'd love to put together some kind of program to turn them in another direction. If I could get government funding..."

A smile spread on his face. "You'd be perfect for the job."

His vote of confidence felt good. "I hope so. I really think there's a need." She paused. "I always thought I might be good with something like that. While I might not be good at, you know, kids in a family setting."

There. One of her deepest secrets. She'd never seen how mothering worked, not up close and personal. She didn't have those experiences. She hadn't planned on giving that a try, didn't want to mess up some poor little kid.

"I don't agree, but we'll cross that bridge when we get to it." He kissed her again. "I do like your idea of helping foster kids, though. You could start in Texas, maybe even build something that goes nationwide. You have government contacts. I have a few of my own. If we have downtime, the team and I could offer some boot-camp training. Grace Cordero, Ryder's girlfriend, is looking for ways to use her ranch. She had corporate boot camps there before. And she has animals there, too. Juvenile rehab with kids working with rescue animals is a big thing—"

She put a finger over his lips, enormously gratified how excited he was about her idea, how supportive. But for now… "We'll brainstorm in the morning. For now I just want you to kiss me."

Normally, he didn't take orders well, but at the moment he looked happy to obey.

He kissed her and then some, making her head spin. But just as she was about to drown in his touch, his familiar, masculine scent, in the feel of his mouth over hers, he pulled back again, with a pained expression on his face.

"What is it?"

He blew some air from his lungs. "Since the first time…I practically attacked you. We just fell in bed and…I wanted this to be sweet and long and more romantic. I don't want to rush it."

"You want to go to dinner?"

"No," he admitted.

"Me, neither."

His face lit up.

"You're a commando. I'm an FBI agent. We don't do slow," she reminded him. "I want fast."

"You don't always get what you want in a relationship. There's the whole compromise thing." He lifted her and walked toward the bedroom.

"How is this a compromise?"

"I wanted to take you on the carpet."

HIS BODY WAS READY, poised at her opening as she straddled him on the bed.

"I love you, too," she said.

His heart was about to burst.

She smiled. "I think we should get our own ranch."

Okay. He inched his fingers up her naked thigh.

"And I want horses. If we live in Texas, you're going to have to learn how to ride well."

She was going to discuss livestock?

He grabbed her hips and pulled her down on him, sheathed himself in her wet heat to the hilt. His eyes rolled back in his head from the pleasure.

Her breath caught and she gave a quick little moan that nearly sent him over the edge.

But then she seemed to recover. "And I think we should—"

"All right, that's it." He flipped her in a lightning-quick move so she was sprawled under him the next second.

Her eyes widened. "You're still very bossy. I have to say, you didn't mellow much with age."

He raised an eyebrow as he withdrew and then pushed in again. "You want me mellow?"

She arched her back. "On second thought, not really."

"We're doing this all the way. I want it all. There'll be no casual dating, no seeing other people. When I commit to something, it's 100 percent."

She ran her slim fingers up his chest and brushed the pads over his nipples. "I like that about you."

His entire body tightened. "Then you won't object to marrying me right away?"

"For Mitch's sake?"

"Because I love you so much I can't see straight."

"What if I wreck your life again?"

He looked deep into her eyes. "I'm pretty sure you're going to make it." He dipped his head for a kiss as he made her his.

* * * * *

A sneaky peek at next month...

INTRIGUE...

BREATHTAKING ROMANTIC SUSPENSE

My wish list for next month's titles...

In stores from 15th November 2013:

- ❑ Cold Case at Camden Crossing – Rita Herron
- & The Cradle Conspiracy – Robin Perini
- ❑ Justice is Coming – Delores Fossen
- & Yuletide Protector – Julie Miller
- ❑ Undercover Twin – Lena Diaz
- & Dirty Little Secrets – Mallory Kane

Romantic Suspense

- ❑ Colton Christmas Rescue – Beth Cornelison

Available at WHSmith, Tesco, Asda, Eason, Amazon and Apple

Just can't wait?

Visit us Online

You can buy our books online a month before they hit the shops! **www.millsandboon.co.uk**

1113/46

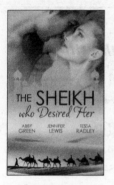

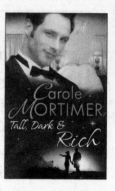